Praise for TOUCH

"An unforgettable and powerfully poignant five-star read."
— *BookViral*

"An impassioned coming-of-age story that will stir the soul."
— *Literary Titan*

"Beautifully painful and hauntingly healing."
— *NetGalley* **(five-star review)**

"Miller has gathered together a cast of unforgettable characters
and constructed one of the most powerful and chilling stories I
have ever read."
— *Readers' Favorite* **(five-star review)**

"In Miller's heart-rending tale, both Megan and Shawn are vivid,
psychologically developed characters. . .[the] plotline twists and
turns unexpectedly, making for compelling reading."
— *Kirkus Reviews*

"Megan's Voice is unpolished, genuine, and irrefutably real -
adding authenticity for readers who crave a more personal
connection. . . a beacon of light."
— *The BookLife Prize*

"Miller delicately handles the difficult topics of abuse, trauma,
and grief in a story that is, at its core, about the healing power of
compassion and love. . . the believable dialogue and
heartbreakingly relatable characters will stay with readers long
after they have finished reading."
— *The US Review of Books* **(Recommended)**

TOUCH

A Novel by Rebecca Miller

Unveiled

ISBN: 978-0-578-99523-6 (Hardcover)
ISBN: 978-0-578-86087-9 (Paperback)
ISBN: 978-0-578-86088-6 (eBook)

Library of Congress Control Number: 2021903102

Any references to historical events, real people, or real places are used fictitiously. Names, characters, and places are products of the author's imagination.

Edited by Kimberly Hunt
Original cover art by Abigail Link
Cover design by Rebecca Miller

Printed in the United States of America

First printing edition April 2021

Unveiled Publishing
Foster, RI

Why am I here? It was a question I had never wondered about. And then one day, in a totally random and senseless act—because of some reckless asshole's fuck-up—everything changed.

"We're all here for a reason," a friend's mother tried to convince me. "Things like this happen in order to help shape us into the people we're meant to be." She stroked her palm tenderly over my cheek. "Nature's chisel is chipping away at you, my dear, and she's apparently chosen you to be one of her most beautiful."

"But what if you're wrong?" I asked. To which she replied . . .

"What if I'm not?"

"The two most important days of your life are the day you are born and the day you find out why."

~Mark Twain

We all thought we knew the reason Dad decided to move.

Dad probably did, too.

Chapter 1

I don't remember the moments before I was catapulted headfirst into the shallow end of shock. But I'll never forget the look on Dad's face when he got the call, his phone dropping to the floor when he lost his grip. The chill that shuddered through me with the sound that came from him, difficult to describe—not a wail or a scream, just a noise.

Some pretty big things happened after I was blindsided by grief. For instance, everything that was once important became completely insignificant: The end-of-year school trip I'd waited months for, counting down the weeks, then the days, planning what I would wear, who I would sit with on the bus . . . What school trip? The day came and went and it never even entered my mind. The super expensive art set I begged my parents day in and day out to get me for my birthday, complete with post-it reminders strategically placed around the house. How could I care about material things when the most important person in my life no longer existed as a material being?

And my birthday? As in, the one special day of the year that took place only two weeks after the most tragic day of my life? I hated my birthday now. I never wanted to think about it again.

Everything that once grounded me ceased to exist. Like someone cut the tethers that held me in place, and I became a free-floating balloon that drifted aimlessly before landing, deflated, in some unknown place, so far off course I had no idea how to get back. The tides at my favorite beach came in and out, and back in again, and while everyone around me moved on with their lives, I remained stuck, lonely, and stumbling over every step I took, collapsing more and more inside myself, until I became unrecognizable to everyone. Including myself.

And then . . . finally . . . as the first sliver of light cracked through the darkness . . . I experienced *another massive blow.*

~

"Only about twenty more minutes," Dad said, the windshield wipers of the U-Haul squeaking intermittently back and forth, the weather the same miserable rainy it had been through the last three states.

The devastation that tore through me when he announced we were moving felt like a fist clamped down on my heart and twisted. If there was anything that came even close to the pain of losing the person closest to me, it was leaving the place that possessed every last memory I had of them. No conversation, no hint that it was even a thought, he just woke us up one morning and told us to start packing.

Two weeks. Only fourteen days—sorry, thirteen and a half—to absorb and preserve every sight, sound, and smell that reminded me. A process that scraped every nerve ending raw.

"You're going to kill your eyes." He glanced at me struggling to read in the dark cab of the truck.

"Whatever." Why care about my eyes when my spirit was already dead?

One Thousand Reasons. My friend Claire's mother, Mom's best friend, gave me the book when we left with hopes it would help me understand why things kept happening the way they did. She, somehow, still believed everything happened for a reason.

```
Our worst moments are often our
most defining.
```

A dead mother, a barely-there father, a complete lack of friends. Yeah, I could agree with that.

The heated leather under my legs did little to warm me on the chilly night, so I turned the heat up a notch.

"I saw that," Dad said with a smile in his tone, his eyes never shifting from the road.

Of course, he did. It was the same thing he said every time, right before finding some stealth way to turn it back down. He'd put in extra effort the whole trip to try to keep the mood as light as possible to make up for such a cataclysmic jolt to our lives.

"I think your brothers will have had enough of driving for a while," he commented to keep up conversation. Eighteen hundred miles alone with him while Josh and Bobby drove our two cars, and there hadn't been much. And what little there was felt forced or like meaningless small talk. But what really was there to say? *Thanks for leaving us to fend for ourselves for the past four years while you sunk yourself in work to avoid your own grief? For not noticing how much all*

3

three of us struggled too? Or how about, *thanks for finally stepping up just as I'd crawled my own way out of the abyss, only for you to throw me right back in for the sake of the one who hadn't put in any effort at all.*

The list of things I would probably never experience again continued to grow:

Waterfalls.

The ocean, burying my toes in the sand at the beach.

None of it had happened anytime recently, but it would've again eventually. At least, I'd hoped.

The art exploration program at the college. Months of just trying to get Dad to look into it and he'd finally signed me up.

"In one mile, turn right," the overly-chirpy voice of the GPS said. The road was dark, desolate. A grim sign of what was to come.

A deer flashed through the high beams of Dad's car that Josh drove up ahead. His tires screeched.

Dad slammed on the brakes. My book flew from my lap as the seatbelt bit into my chest.

Bobby, between us, missed the beat. He plowed into Josh with a bang. He fishtailed in front of us and his rear end went off the road into a ditch.

The tires of the truck hollered as Dad and I skidded. The smell of burnt rubber blitzed my nose as we slid in a straight line toward Bobby.

I dug my fingernails into the seat as Dad pumped the brakes to slow us. The holler of our tires turned to a squeal.

Oh, God, oh, God, oh, God. I squeezed my eyes shut.

4

My head whipped forward as we jarred to a stop.

A cloud of white swallowed us. As it dissipated, Bobby shone in our headlights.

Holy shit. Fifteen more feet and we would've hit him smack dab in the middle of his driver's side door.

Steam billowed from his hood.

"*Goddammit,*" Dad said, his knuckles white around the steering wheel. "Are you okay?" He looked at me.

I nodded, and he heaved open his door and lunged from the truck.

Ducking from the drizzle, he made a beeline for Bobby. He must've seen he was okay, he raised a finger to him to wait and rushed to Josh. He ripped the driver's side door open and invaded the space between Josh and the steering wheel.

Dear God, please . . .

Dad's mouth moved as if talking.

He stepped away from the car and his hands went to his hips as he inhaled a chest-expanding breath.

I let out the one I was holding and tore off my seat belt as I pulled at the hard plastic of my door handle. Bobby also got out.

Josh got out of Dad's car as we converged on him.

"What the hell was that?" Bobby's eyes bulged.

"Did you not see the deer?" Josh shouted.

"So you had to jack up on your friggin' brakes?"

Josh shook. "Are you okay?" I needed to make sure.

He sucked in a breath and nodded.

"Friggin' idiot," Bobby said.

"Seriously?" I asked him. "Were you even paying attention?" I gripped the long ends of my sleeves, shivering more from the adrenaline rush than the cold. Despite my loathing for him—as well as the fact he'd only had his license a few months—I couldn't deny that he was actually a pretty good driver. There'd been plenty of space between them. He should've had enough time to stop.

"Shut your hole, Meg. Go get back in the truck."

"Enough," Dad said, his hand pressed to his stomach in a sign of relief.

I turned to the car the boys shared. There didn't seem to be any damage to the frame, but steam still forced its way through the seams of the hood and green fluid trickled onto the ground from underneath it.

"What the hell are we gonna do now?" Bobby asked, glaring at the wrecked vehicle that would've provided him the best escape from his "intolerable" family.

Dad lifted a palm to fend him off. "Bob, just relax a minute."

"I'm sorry, Dad," Josh apologized. "I really didn't mean—"

"It was a natural response, Josh. It's not your fault."

"Like hell, it's not," Bobby said. "Thanks to him, now we're out our friggin' ride. *Idiot*."

"Robert." Dad took in a breath. "Why don't you go wait in the truck."

"Fine by me." He started walking.

"Megan, go with him," he said to me a little softer. "There's no point in you standing out here in the rain."

6

It was dark and late, and I was already glazed from the mist, if I stood there any longer, it would soak in. So I, too, turned back for the moving truck carrying our entire existence.

Bobby stole my seat, so I hoisted up and in from the driver's side and sat next to him in the middle.

"It could've been worse," I said, pulling my sweatshirt from the floor and draping it over me. "At least no one got hurt." We certainly knew something about that.

"Yeah. Good thing."

Such a jerk.

As Bobby, in his royal blue T-shirt a size too big and his dusky hair barely damp, reached for the knob for the heat, Dad, outside with Josh quivering from the cold next to him, pulled out his cell phone.

"Do you really think Dad's not gonna smell you?" I asked as I scraped my own soggy mess to the back of my head. He reeked of pot, and if Dad hadn't already, he surely would.

"Drink bleach, Meg."

"It wasn't his fault, you know." I secured my skimpy ponytail with the elastic from my wrist.

"Oh, it wasn't? It was necessary for him to almost kill his entire family over a friggin' animal? Oh, I'm sorry. What's left of his family?"

He really made my head spin. "It's called compassion," I said. "Maybe you could try having a little. Besides, it was apparently just as necessary for you to get high."

"Shut up."

7

"So, what, were you taking a hit, not paying attention?"

Bobby shook his head at the windshield with the same disgruntled squint of his eyes. "Seriously, Meg, shut the fuck up."

"I'm not gonna shut up. You ruined my life." Josh, the non-guilty party, still stood outside, drops forming on the ends of his hair.

Bobby gasped. "I ruined your life? *What* life? And get it straight. I'm not the reason we're here. We're here because Dad was sick of finding dead kids."

"Yeah, and he didn't want you being one of them. Do you not get that?"

He huffed.

Dad finished his call and walked over to the boys' car, its front wheels on the pavement, rear wheels off the road at a forty-five-degree angle. He opened the driver's side door and leaned in, his arm going directly under the seat.

He apparently didn't find what he was looking for, so he got in and reached for the glove box.

He re-emerged and started for the truck.

Dad's contentment from minutes before as we crossed the line into the county decayed, and the gauzy skin of his face showed deep lines of disgust as he pulled open the door and lifted a half-smoked joint and full baggy of marijuana into view.

Bobby's thin blue irises remained forward.

"We're not there yet, Bob." Dad was composed, but it was clear he struggled. "I meant what I said. You have seven more miles to wash yourself of this. Going from big-city commissioner to small-town chief,

I'm going from never around to always around. I assure you I am not someone you want to be stuck in the house with."

Bobby's view stayed fastened out the windshield.

"Get out of the truck," Dad said. "You wait in the rain."

Dad asked me for his jacket and stood outside with Bobby. Josh pulled Dad's car to the side of the road and waited there.

What a disaster.

We were in the middle of nowhere.

I retrieved the book from the floor where it landed, intent on finding a reason for all the massive suckage.

> Hardships develop our strengths. We
> don't truly know ourselves or our
> potential until we've been tested.

If there really was a bigger picture, I was definitely being tested.

I read a couple chapters and skipped ahead. Claire's mother dog-eared pages she highlighted passages on.

> Everybody has a battle ahead of them.
> It's easy to give up. True strength
> comes when you push forward, no matter
> the outlook.

The outlook. Right.

> The people we encounter are put in
> our path for a reason. We all have
> a unique and special purpose, each
> one of us with a gift to share.

Sure. I could share my ability to fail miserably at all things "life."

Really, I was desperate to know my purpose.

Claire's mother meant well, but there wasn't anything this book could convince me of right now. My entire world, which seemed perpetually stuck on some sort of emotional fault line, had shifted under my feet yet again.

Yellow lights flashed in the distance. The tow truck. *Thank God.*

It came from the direction we were headed. It stopped when it reached Dad's car, and the driver got out and tromped through the rain. He extended his hand to Dad. Dad greeted him with the best smile he could manage.

The driver looked between our three vehicles. He asked Dad a question, and when Dad answered, recognition lit the man's face, and he reached to shake Dad's hand again. Dad's smile was more genuine as he repeated the gesture. The two continued talking, and I rolled down my window to the cool, wet air.

"Well, it doesn't look like it's too bad, probably just a busted radiator," the man said, already saturated, his T-shirt slicked to his muscular chest. He pushed his wet hair out of his face. "I could put it on the bed, but I can probably just pull it out and tow it."

"It's not going far, just tow it," Dad said.

The man went to get his truck.

It roared forward, then sounded a warning beep as it reversed.

It was hair-raising to watch him try to maneuver on the narrow road. He nearly disabled himself in the opposite ditch trying to back up in line with the boys' awkwardly positioned car.

The people we encounter are put in
our path for a reason.

Skip, already read.

10

"I can bring it to my garage and fix it for you," the man said as he got out again. "Unless you plan on doing it yourself."

"Oh, Lord, no," Dad said. "I haven't touched a car in over two decades."

The people we encounter . . .

I couldn't concentrate.

As Bobby stood with his arms folded next to Dad in the cold rain, a boy appearing somewhere near Josh's or Bobby's age emerged from the opposite side of the flatbed. He was Bobby's height, at least, and his blond hair, not tied back in any sort of way, was more than twice as long as mine.

He didn't acknowledge anyone as he started hooking the car to the truck.

"So, are you related to Vance Brennar?" the man asked Dad. "That can't be a coincidence."

Brennar wasn't exactly the most common name.

"Yup. Vance is my brother. He's why we're here."

"No shit." The man exuded an air of acceptance. "Yeah, he's a good guy. He's got two boys, don't he?"

Dad nodded, smiling still, despite the situation *and* the elements.

The boy hooking the car up attached a cable, and then leaned into the car and altered the position of the shifter. If not for his light features, he would've blended with the night.

As the tow driver talked with Dad, the boy got behind the wheel of the truck and started it forward. In less than a minute, the car was out of the ditch and on the wet pavement.

11

The driver looked to Bobby as the boy got back out. "So, I guess you were the one driving?"

Bobby, arms hugged across his chest, rolled his eyes and looked away.

"Yeah, he was messing around, not paying attention," Dad answered for him.

"Well, boys will be boys," the man said with an affirming tilt of his head. "Isn't that right, Shawn?" he asked over his shoulder.

The boy didn't acknowledge him, just continued what he did.

"Hey, we've been there, right?" the man said to Dad, the edges of his mouth turned up. "So I assume you're taking up in the old Colonial out on Junction Road?"

Nice that he knew where we lived before we did.

Dad nodded again. "Yup. That small of a town, huh?"

"Can't get much smaller. If calm and peaceful is what you're looking for, you've found it. Just stay out of range of my garage between the hours of eight and four. It's probably the most noise you'll hear."

The boy braced the wheels, then attached two chains from the back of the tow truck to something underneath the car. He pressed a button and the car started up from the ground.

"Give me a couple days," the man said to Dad. "I'm replacing an engine right now. No more than three, though, I expect."

"No problem. Take your time. This one won't be driving for a while, anyway." Dad nodded at Bobby.

The sopping wet tow driver pulled himself up into his truck and

12

waited for the boy who I imagined by his appearance was his son.

Once finished securing the car, the boy turned for the truck. Without a single word spoken, or even a look in anyone's direction the entire time he was there, as he looped around, he glanced ever so momentarily up at me.

It was a quick glimpse, but his eyes connected directly with mine, and they were so fiercely light they startled me.

Chapter 2

When we were small, there were three things Mom and Dad told us: the world is full of bad people, so never talk to strangers; you don't want to get lost or kidnapped, so always hold hands; in an emergency, don't call us, dial 911.

As we got older, they added never walk alone, never go near vans, and if someone does grab you, yell fire, then fight like hell.

A few months ago, Dad came home from work late one night and had only one thing to say: "If a single person ever lays a goddamned finger on any one of you, you come straight to me. I don't care if they tell you not to, I don't care if they threaten you, you come to me." He then sent us all to bed.

We found out on the news the next morning that a fourteen-year-old girl was murdered and her body dumped in the tall grass behind the baseball field. Her stepfather killed her so no one would find out what he had been doing to her. Dad was there when they recovered her body.

It wasn't the first time. I think finding the nude remains of a girl so close to my age, though, raped, killed, and carelessly discarded by someone she was supposed to be able to trust, dug the hole in him deeper than any other incident. Mom was gone, and Bobby screwed off more than ever, so Dad came to a very abrupt decision to chuck a twenty-plus-year career of trying to keep other people's families safe to put a more conscious effort into his own before something else happened that would make it so he couldn't.

Josh was only a few months away from turning eighteen and argued about going, which is why I think it happened so fast.

On Sunday, March sixth, at 9:57 p.m., after thirty-one hours of driving over two days, we arrived, one less car, at the four-bedroom, three-bathroom, country-blue Colonial he purchased, sight unseen, in the place he thought would be the perfect catalyst for repair.

Jessup, Missouri.

It was the smallest of three towns that made up Jessup County.

He wanted to be closer to his brother. He said it would give us a chance to get to know our cousins. Small towns were also supposedly safer.

One positive: My room was bigger.

The whole house was bigger, as a matter of fact.

Dad had his own space in a master suite on the first floor, which, for the first time, gave us privacy on a second.

The dining room was large enough to put the leaf in the table, and there was a spot for a hutch to display Mom's china. Which meant maybe we'd actually eat together again someday.

15

The room with the rose pink walls was mine. Thin, chiffon curtains hung from the window that overlooked the backyard. It was too dark to see anything, but from what Uncle Vance said, there wasn't another house in sight.

Stay positive.

Bobby's room was next to mine.

The walls and doors were thick, so hopefully they'd dampen the obnoxious blare of his music.

~

"Hey, look at you, little chicken nugget," Uncle Vance said, jostling my head with his wide hand when he and my two cousins, Dennis and Kenny, came to greet us first thing in the morning. "Haven't you grown at all?"

I had just turned twelve the last time he saw me, so I hoped so.

"She takes after Miranda," Dad said, speaking Mom's name in my presence for the first time in probably a year.

"You're not kidding," Uncle Vance said. "I didn't think I'd see *those* eyes again." The bright green ones Mom was always complimented on. I was the only one of us who had them. "Your kids are really taking form, huh?" He hadn't seen us since the funeral.

Dennis and Kenny were always, without a doubt, Brennars. Dad showed us pictures of him and Uncle Vance as kids, and, aside from Dennis's brown eyes, he and Kenny looked just like them. Josh was the only one of the three of us who came close, with his caramel-colored hair and smoky eyes, which were darker than any of theirs. I had light hair when I was small, but I was now Mom's mini-me. So much to the point that people clung to me at her funeral in a desperate attempt to hold onto her.

Bobby was a mix. He had Dad's height and eyes, Mom's brown hair, a little lighter, and her brilliantly wide smile—when he smiled.

Deep lines radiated from Uncle Vance's eyes. "Damn, Ed, was our hair ever that thick?" He nodded at Josh's mop.

Dad chuckled. "I had hair?"

Uncle Vance was almost ten years younger than Dad, and in all my memories of him, he was merely a shorter, trimmer, lighter-haired version of Dad. Or what I remembered Dad to have looked like at his age. He still wore the same light-colored Polo shirts, tucked neatly into khaki pants, but the gap in their age was harder to detect. He neared Dad in thickness now, and though Dad always had a buzz cut to hide the thinning of his hair, Uncle Vance's was long enough to notice the lessened amount.

"What a fine-looking lad you've become," Uncle Vance said to Josh. "I hear you're quite the ladies' man."

"Ah . . ." Josh was too modest to admit it. The blush color of his cheeks answered for him.

"More like bitch magnet," Bobby said.

Ha! I had to give him that one. A "ladies' man" was an understatement, and he, for some reason, attracted the snobbiest of the snobby.

Dad gave Bobby a sharp eye.

"Hey, where's the pigtails?" Dennis, my older cousin, tugged on my hair that was barely long enough to recreate the do.

17

Dennis had just turned thirteen the last time I saw him. His ginger freckles had faded considerably, his buff, ragged hair was coarser in texture, and he was a good foot and a half taller.

He gave me a playful shove, and then reached for the football in the open box next to him and whizzed it at Bobby.

Bobby caught it and hummed it back, and raised an eyebrow as if to challenge him.

"Dude, you're on," Dennis said.

The four boys, including eleven-year-old Kenny, a miniature version of Dennis, went out to the backyard.

"So, how 'bout you, Miss Megan?" Uncle Vance said to me. "Are you still drawing? If I recall, you used to be quite the little artist."

Drawing was once my very favorite thing to do. If I wasn't eating or sleeping, I was usually sketching something. "Eh, not really."

"No?" He looked surprised. "How come?"

I shrugged. It didn't seem the right time to point out how downhill life went after Mom died. Also, that every last effort I'd made to get mine back on track was squashed with the move. The program at the college was supposed to be an attempt to reignite old interests. Or, if nothing else, find some sort of new one.

"I actually can't think of the last time I saw you drawing," Dad said with a curious tilt of his head.

Of course not. After putting the person I was aside to take over the role of the one who was suddenly no longer there, at what point did I get to press the "rewind" button and go back to who I originally was? He also didn't pay much attention. If he did, he would've noticed me,

18

just days before, sketching the willow tree at the park Mom used to sit under, reading while we played on the playground. The one she and I once carved our initials into.

"Well, then," Uncle Vance said to Dad. "Think you're ready for the slower pace? The biggest thing you'll have to worry about now is remembering to change your underwear."

"Can you make that a promise?" Dad laughed. It would be a bit of a difference from the big-city crime he was used to.

"Well, you might get a call about a loose cow or two. Old man Jefferson down the road," he threw his thumb over his shoulder, "will bug you about the Henderson's chickens crapping all over his porch. But, yeah, that'll probably be the worst of it. Not much really happens out here."

What more could in a town so small it didn't even possess a stop light?

"Go for a ride?" he suggested to Dad. "I can show you around town. It's going to be yours. Best get to know it."

Uncle Vance was once also in law enforcement. He retired several years ago when he and my aunt divorced so he could make Dennis and Kenny his top priority. Dad originally planned to retire, too, but Jessup needed a new chief, so he agreed to take the position until they could find a suitable replacement.

"You want to come, Nutty?" Dad asked me.

We'd come from a suburb just outside of Portland, Oregon. Our address had changed once before, but our farthest neighbor was never more than thirty feet away. Jessup had only eleven hundred people and three paved roads.

The tree-lined streets were a blur of brown branches through the car window.

We drove past the market, about the size of the produce sections of the ones back home.

"Is there a bookstore?" I asked. I'd stocked up, but I was a fast reader and my supply wouldn't last long.

"There isn't much," Uncle Vance said. "There's the market, a post office, Town Hall . . . an auto mechanic. Who, from what I hear, you met last night."

"What about a library?"

"There is a small, one-room library just over the line in Danielson, but it's rarely open. The library at the high school is your best bet. The school's actually probably a lot like the one you left. Being tri-town, and all. It's big, modern."

It was tri-town and in Jessup, and the one thing I wished was smaller.

Chapter 3

My eyes opened to brightness. I blinked the numbers of my clock into focus.

8:30

The pink walls confused me. And then I remembered.

Bobby's stereo blasted on.

"You gotta be kidding," Josh hollered from the opposite end of the hall.

As if we didn't already hate him enough.

Dad's knuckles fell hard on his bedroom door. "Turn it down, Bob, or you'll lose it altogether."

Again.

"What the eff?" Bobby's door swung open, bringing his favorite hip hop artist to full volume, and his footsteps thundered down the stairs.

"Get back here and turn it off. *Robert.*"

Great start to our handy-brandy new life. No different than the old one. Except we'd been completely uprooted. Yanked from perfectly good soil and heaved into a mound of sand.

I looked to the picture of Mom on my nightstand. *If you're up there, please flap your angel wings, or something, and make this all better.* Like there was actually something that could make that happen.

A second picture now sat beside hers—Claire and me, our cheeks smooshed together in our tightest "best friends" hug.

It was taken before my world was turned upside down and all the pieces shaken out.

It was hard to believe I'd once been so happy.

Claire and I were friends by proxy, pretty much, because our mothers were best friends, but we were still attached at the hip.

Were.

She sat in shock with me for a few weeks after Mom died, but as soon as hers wore off—and she still had a mom to hug before bed every night—she dropped me like a hot rock. But could I really blame her? She was popular in middle school, and the depressed, more and more reclusive friend—no matter how much her mother probably pressured her—wasn't exactly the one she wanted to hang out with.

The picture wasn't meant to serve as a reminder of a lost friendship—that wound had pretty much scabbed over—but of all my efforts to get back to the person I was when it was taken. A goal that seemed one thousand percent impossible now.

Starting a new school three quarters of the way through the year would not help.

> It's not about what you're given, but
> how you handle what you're given.

Failing. Again.

~

Dad drove us to school Thursday morning.

The mammoth size of the building was downright debilitating.

"Just take it as it comes." He guided me with his hand on my back as he walked with us through the front door of Jessup Regional. "Everything will be alright."

He moved a lot growing up, so he knew something about the distress, but his words of encouragement had yet to help. Nerves twisted my stomach in knots.

Like Uncle Vance said, the number of students wasn't much different than the school we left. With linoleum tile floors and painted cinderblock walls, though, it was only modern in his day.

The staring, the pointing, the whispering . . . *Focus. Just walk straight.* I knew what to expect—it happened after Mom—but the sad gazing was now smirking, gossipy, gawking.

Lunch was the worst—a structureless free-for-all where it was up to me to determine my fate, and the part of the day when most of the staring, pointing, and whispering occurred.

I couldn't find anywhere to sit at lunch, so I resigned to the bathroom, where I locked myself into a stall and fought with my stomach to keep it from returning the little remains of breakfast that refused to digest.

The warm drops that soaked into my pillow as I tried to fall asleep that night were as real as the pain in my chest I now knew all

23

too well.

The second day wasn't any better.

The more the walls closed in around me, the laughter that bounced off them between periods crippling my ability to think rationally, the more I shrank inside myself, wishing I could just disappear.

At lunch, an empty table in the back corner of the room provided me refuge, and I angled toward the wall and submersed myself in the pages of a thriller Josh pushed on me.

I would've continued on with *One Thousand Reasons*, but it was bad enough I read while everyone else socialized. People didn't need to see my attempt at self-help.

Thrillers weren't my usual genre, but Josh wasn't much of a reader and liked the book so much I gave it a shot.

With my elbow on the table and my head leaned into my palm, I became involved in the story more than I thought I could for where I was. I was within paragraphs of finding out who the bloody fingerprints smeared down the passenger side door of the main character's green Ford Mustang belonged to.

"This seat taken?" a male voice came from above me.

I turned my eyes up from the midnight scene to a tall boy with white skin and a tempest of tight black curls standing across from me with a tray of food.

He sat before I could answer. "So, you're Chief Brennar's daughter, huh?"

I moved to an upright position as I let the pages of my book close over my thumb.

He displayed a grin that made one eye close more than the other—as if analyzing me.

"I'm Damian. I could show you around if you like."

It was hard to hold my view of him. Nobody had ever approached me like that.

"You are just too cute. How come you're over here all by yourself?"

He kept moving into my view, trying to get me to look at him. I glanced at him for a split second and caught my reflection in his deep brown eyes and looked away. He reached across the table and picked up the long end of my pink scarf headband.

"It's cute. I like it."

He stared, holding the fringe, and pressed up against the table so close I could smell french fries on his breath.

"Nut Meg." His eyes narrowed with his nod. "It suits you."

How on earth does he know my nickname?

He dropped the end of my scarf and his hand moved more toward me, as though he went for the stud in my ear. I pulled back and did a quick scan of the room.

Bobby was at the same lunch and already on his way.

He paraded across the cafeteria with his titanium spine, the color of fervor infused in his high cheekbones as he came down the aisle between the tables.

He took hold of my arm. "Let's go." He pulled at me to stand. His tone was firm and his grip so tight I was barely able to collect my belongings. "Fucking vultures."

With my arm in his grasp and radiating an aura of red, he started

25

back to where he already basked under a rainbow of followers.

Not only was he the reason I was in this situation, nearly two thousand miles away from the only life I ever knew, I certainly didn't care to sit with him and his new crew. I jerked away and headed for the door.

"Damn, Meg." Bobby followed.

"Don't talk to me."

"Shit, who lit the fuse on *your* tampon?"

"Shut up." I exited through the open double doors, tears perched.

By the soda machine across the hall was the long-haired boy from the tow truck. He looked right at me.

I avoided him and picked up my pace before he could see me cry.

Chapter 4

Uncertainty, contempt, resentment, anxiety—things I already felt. Now I could add loneliness and desperation.

> Even in our darkest moments, we mustn't
> lose hope. Sometimes we need to get lost
> in order to truly find ourselves.

I might've had an easier time buying into the idea if I hadn't already been so lost.

I spent the better part of Saturday in my room, sorting through all my stuff. I'd yet to unpack, as unpacking would make my reality more absolute.

I sifted through the box with my drawing supplies. As huge a part of my life as drawing had once been, it was crazy to think how it had just fallen by the wayside.

I had five full sketchbooks in all.

It was humbling to look at—how far I'd come from simple line drawings to a complex use of light and shadows to create dramatic realism. And in such a short amount of time, with only the aid of internet and YouTube tutorials.

Most of my later stuff was dated. I did about two or three drawings a week—everything from people, to animals, landscapes, and 3D illusions—up until the day before Mom died. Then there was over a month and a half gap before the next one.

That's when I got into charcoal. Charcoal added a whole new level of depth. With carefully thought-out strokes of varying pressures of a charcoal crayon and just the right amount of smudging, my emotions screamed off the page.

Raw, uncensored emotions.

Though the ones post-Mom, no matter the medium, were undeniably my best work, they were hard to look at.

They came fewer and farther between, many never getting finished— I couldn't even tell what I intended some of them to be. None of them had any color.

The one of the tree was the first one I'd done in almost six months, and that was out of pure necessity. I tore it out with the intention of hanging it up, and then put the box on the shelf in my closet.

My closet. I guess that's what it was now.

~

Other than a few scratches on the bumper, the boys' car came back as if nothing happened to it. Bobby couldn't even ride in it. He didn't care, he liked taking the bus. I, however, sucked up as many rides from Josh as I could get.

28

"This wouldn't have happened if Mom was still alive," I said to him on the drive to school Monday morning. "She'd be home, so Dad wouldn't worry about Bobby so much."

"I don't think Bobby would be the way he is if Mom was still alive."

Truth. Bobby went into a tailspin after her death. We all went to therapy, but Bobby only got angrier.

The morning dragged. Two classes felt like four, and, still unable to figure out where I was going, I was late to my third.

The closer it got to lunchtime, the more difficult it was to concentrate and the sweatier my palms got.

My breaths were half of what they should've been on the walk to the cafeteria. I almost pulled my bathroom stunt again.

I entered the lunchroom, through the same double doors, and came to an abrupt stop. Exactly where I'd sat on Friday was the boy from the tow truck.

He slouched casually, as if it was where he sat every day.

The table was long and I could easily sit at the opposite end. Really, I didn't have a choice, there was nowhere else to go.

I approached slowly and was cautious as I sat. He didn't even seem to notice me.

~

"How many pairs do you have?" a girl in my history class asked, looking down at my Converse sneakers.

I was surprised by her inquiry and smiled. "Just one." The black ones I wore. "What about you?"

29

She proceeded to tell me all the colors in her collection, but then nothing more followed.

It was a two-way street, I did realize. But I didn't know what else to say.

I only left behind a few friendships I'd been struggling to breathe life back into, but Josh and Bobby left a whole ton of friends. It didn't take long for either of them to settle in. Having to fend off the girls, I imagined, made it easy for Josh. He talked about one in particular— Susan—and it quickly became nonstop. "You're gonna love her, Meg, I promise." They were words I'd never heard.

He opened the door to the bell one afternoon and there she stood.

Every feature that accented her fully-developed, five-eight frame bore the same amber tint—her barreled waves, her sparkling eyes, even the sprinkling of freckles that danced from her nose.

Freckles.

Josh liked a girl with freckles.

"I've seen you," she said to me with the most unrestricted of smiles when he introduced her. "You always look so miserable. Try to cheer up a little. It'll get better."

She was unlike any girl he'd ever dated. She didn't wear a bit of makeup, and her personality was as real as the opals that dangled from her ears.

The smile that trimmed Josh's cheeks all afternoon was one I hadn't seen in weeks.

"It could be worse, couldn't it?" Dad tried to solicit my thoughts as he scooped ice cream into bowls for the two of us.

"It could be. But it could be better." Though I'd already spent two full weekends with him for the first time in as long as I could remember. We also had another whole bathroom, an uncle, and cousins.

Where you are is exactly where
you're meant to be.

It would still take a bit more convincing.

~

Other than the style of the tables, the cafeteria at school was pretty similar to the one in my old school. There were the same greasy smells, same whiffs of too much perfume and body odor, and everyone pretty much assembled in the same types of groups. There were the athletes, the cheerleaders, the popular kids, the not-so-popular kids. In any event, everyone, for the most part, had someone.

Shawn, the boy from the tow truck, and I were the only two people who sat by ourselves.

We shared several lunches. The lunchroom was the only place I ever saw him. On the occasions he was there, he would sit in the same spot at the end of the table, and he never did anything other than nurse a bottle of soda. It was questionable as to whether he even realized I was there. He barely ever looked up from the tabletop. He never had anything with him—no books, no backpack, not even a pen or pencil. When he wasn't there, I didn't try to reclaim my spot, as it seemed I'd been the one to steal it.

The view of his eyes that first night was seared into my mind— then the day in the hall when he looked at me. I'd never seen any like them. They were so light. Intriguing. I'd peek every so often, hoping

31

for another glimpse.

After sharing the same air space for a week, I took the pretzels from my lunch bag and positioned as always to read from my book. I opened to my page, then turned my eyes to him.

With his elbows on the table and fingers laced around the bottom of his full bottle of soda, he sat so intensely in thought about something I felt safe staring.

It was the longest I'd dared to look at him. His build and carved features made me think he was a senior, somewhere near Josh's age. He was tall like Bobby but more solid, sturdier.

The features of his face were soft but etched, and his skin, fair but with enough color that it looked like it would tan rather than burn, was completely smooth.

His hair looked like it hadn't been cut in years. It descended more than a quarter of the way down his back in the natural layers it'd grown. It probably threw a lot of people. It had gorgeous highlights, though. It was at least three different shades of blond, from light, to golden, to streaks of almost brown.

I could only see a little bit of his left eye, but the lack of color made it look translucent.

Unless there was something terribly wretched about his personality, he sat alone by choice.

The cap of his soda bottle remained on and his eyes went unblinking.

Then he flinched.

It was subtle, but looking right at him, I caught it. I ripped my gaze from him and looked back down at my book.

He didn't look at me. He inhaled a deep breath and adjusted his position, and he leaned his head into his palm.

He had a prominent Adam's apple, which gave away every swallow.

After several minutes, he ran his fingers through his hair and sucked in a breath. His cheeks puffed as he let it out, and he shifted his position again and fell back into a trance.

The following day, I switched sides of the table so I could see him better.

Chapter 5

"Wow, Megan," the art teacher, Miss Devereaux, commented on my first in a series of tonal value assignments. "That is . . . amazing," she said of my painting in which the few white areas were supposed to imply a galloping horse. I was lucky to have art as an elective. There wasn't a guarantee. "It looks like you have some experience," she said. "That's a bit on the advanced side." Unfortunately, the class was on the basic side.

Painting involved a lot of the same principles as drawing, which was a main objective of the curriculum.

"Mind if I show the class?"

"Sure." It wasn't like it told my life story, or anything.

"If you look at the black and white mapping in Megan's piece—" She held my nearly completely black canvas up so everyone could see. "See how the contrast between light and dark guides your eyes?"

There were audible expressions of awe.

It was an unfamiliar feeling—I wasn't used to praise—but kind of nice.

Painting wasn't really my thing, but the black and white bit I had covered. Stencil design was supposedly up next.

Considering the genres displayed around the room, I would get bored easily.

"It's evident you're an artist," Miss Devereaux said as she handed my work back to me.

Was. All this was evidence of now was that I knew how to follow directions.

"The school's looking for a new logo. They've made a contest of it. Seeing that you have such a good understanding of the concept, as well as the skill, you should take a stab at it."

It was a compliment, but not only did I not know anything about the school, I had zero interest.

~

Each day, the lunchroom got easier. Each day, I stared at Shawn a little longer. Aside from being captivated by his unique eyes, he was the only person I could even remotely relate to because he also seemed so alone. When he wasn't there, it sliced into me. I'd try to read, but the period was longer and I became hyper-aware of my situation again.

The more I paid attention to him, the more I grasped how stunning his appearance was. His features were simply amazing.

One morning before school, I dug a sketch pad out of my closet and, stroke by stroke, during lunch, captured the most defining aspects of his face.

It was the first real drawing inspiration I'd had in eons.

He felt almost like a crush. Which was strange, because I'd had one before. At the beginning of the year, on a boy who had a cute, crooked smile you couldn't look away from and a perpetually upbeat attitude. This was different. There was no smile. Shawn looked as miserable as me.

"Girl, turn that frown upside down." Susan spotted me in the hall on my way to math. She curled her arm around me and squeezed me to her as we walked. "Hey, Mel, have you met Megan?" she asked a drop-dead-gorgeous brunette who came up beside her. "She's Josh's sister."

"I haven't," she said with a friendly smile.

"She's having a little bit of a tough time. If you see her around, try and make her feel welcome."

"No problem." The girl's long, onyx hair fell forward as she leaned into sight. "I'm going to C Wing if you're going that way."

Her gesture was genuine. "Thanks, but I'm going to G Wing." It wasn't even close.

"Alright, I'll see ya around, then."

Susan rubbed my arm. "I have a few minutes to spare, I'll walk you."

"Thanks." Her kindness was uplifting. "You really don't have to, though. I actually finally know where I'm going."

"What if I said I wanted to?" Her nose crinkled with her grin.

She pointed to people as we walked and told me who they were. "That group over there." She nodded to a bunch of goth kids. "They get a bad rap, but they're good people. Probably a hell of a lot nicer than most." She directed my attention up the hall a bit. "See that kid, there, with the blue shirt?"

I nodded.

"Be nice to him. He's super awesome and gets picked on for no good reason. He's mega intelligent and can play a seriously mean saxophone."

She rooted for the underdog, which I liked. "What about that kid Shawn, with the long hair?"

She looked at me, her eyes softening. "Someone who really looks like he could use a friend, don't ya think?" A brow peaked. "He's got some killer eyes, doesn't he?"

He sure did. "Is *he* new?" As secluded as he was, there was a chance.

"Nope. Went to elementary school together."

"Do you know anything about him?"

"His dad owns Harris Towing, but that's about it. He's really quiet."

He wasn't just quiet, he was removed. "Does anybody know why?"

She gave a nonchalant shake of her head. "He's always been that way. He just kind of blends in."

He didn't blend in. He looked like he'd stepped off the cover of a teen rock magazine.

Susan smiled. "Maybe you should say something to him."

Me? Say something? "Like what?"

She tilted her head as if the answer was obvious. "Um . . . *'hi?'*"

She laughed.

"You think?" It was such a foreign concept.

"You'd be happy if someone said it to you."

~

After school, I shut myself into my room and worked more on my sketch. I added contour lines, soft and hard edges, the contrast between light and dark in Shawn's hair.

After dinner, I worked on shading and texture to show the intensity in his expression.

I thought about what Susan said. Saying something to him would take me well outside my comfort zone. But did it really matter, seeing I was already so far out of it as it was?

~

It was a gray day. With a sky full of clouds heavy with rain, the usually bright cafeteria took on a coldness that could only be defeated by the most optimistic of minds.

Reading, with Shawn at the opposite end of the table, I teased myself with the idea of attempting interaction.

I read the same paragraph six times trying to force myself.

Each moment is an opportunity, you the creator of your own destiny. Pay attention, trust yourself, take chances.

It seemed I took something from *One Thousand Reasons* after all.

My slide as I started down the long bench was slow. The closer I got, the more erratic my heart behaved.

About three feet from him, he turned his head.

"Uh . . ." His pale eyes cut my breath short before I could get out a greeting. They were intense. I fumbled for words. "Your name's Shawn, right?"

"Yeah." His baritone voice sent a shiver through me. There was tightness to his brow, displaying curiosity.

"You pulled my brothers' car from a ditch a couple weeks ago."

"Okay." His expression didn't change.

"I'm Megan."

His gaze was stirring. If not for the outer rim of his irises that determined his eyes were blue, they looked like they would've been colorless.

My heart pounded. "Is it okay if I sit here?"

His brow became more stressed. "If you want. Nobody's paying rent for the spot."

His head still faced me, but he moved his eyes.

Reading was out. Eating didn't seem like an option either, but I needed to do something. I started to remove the contents of my lunch bag and he turned his head to face forward again. I unwrapped my sandwich, took a bite, chewed, swallowed, and then took another as though I really wanted it.

I forced another bite into my mouth and he turned his position altogether. He straddled the bench with his elbows on his knees, holding the neck of his soda, and over-expanded his lungs as he looked up to the clock.

I didn't sit directly in front of him, so I now only had a diagonal view of his profile.

I poked holes in my sandwich with my thumbs. "We have a lot of lunches together, it seems."

"Oh yeah?" He turned his head so I could no longer see any of his face.

Such a stupid move. "If you don't want me here—"

His head signaled no. "It's all right."

I forced the gummed turkey and bread down my throat. "That man you were with that night, was that your dad?" I knew he was, but for the sake of conversation . . .

"Yeah."

I didn't know what else to do but keep talking. "What grade are you in?" *Twelfth,* I anticipated.

He turned a little and his left eye came close to looking at me. "Eleventh."

Okay, maybe he'd been held back a year. *I* had, thanks to my inability to focus for so long.

"So, is your last name Harris?" Harris Towing, and all.

He sent another glimpse my way and looked up at the clock again. "Mine's Brennar."

His eyes turned back down to the bench.

So, SO stupid. "I'm sorry, I shouldn't have bothered you." I'd already died my death, there was no sense in dragging out the discomfort. I moved to stand. "I'm gonna go get a soda. Do you want one?"

He turned up the bottle in his hand.

"Want another?" I don't know why I didn't just run.

He breathed amusement and shook his head.

Tension wracked my shoulders as I headed for the door that

would provide my escape. I didn't even drink soda.

I stuck money into the machine and pressed a button. Nothing came out, so I pressed the button for the kind Shawn had.

I stood there for a good minute, depleting time.

I went back into the cafeteria and Shawn was right where I left him. He peeked past his hair at me, and then turned minutely in my direction.

I approached the table and held the soda out to him.

His brow creased. "What's that?"

"Rent."

I think he was too busy being thrown to take it, so I placed it on the table and moved a few feet back in the direction I'd come from, and sat.

I spent the remaining eight minutes kicking myself. It was the only place in the room I could sit, I was finally slightly comfortable, and I ruined it.

The bell rang and Shawn stood as I did. He scooped up the soda I bought and, not even so much as looking at me, passed through the gap between the wall and the table.

Humiliation planted me where I was until he was all the way out the door.

With a hoard of students between us, he walked down A wing toward the main office.

All of a sudden, a tall, dark-haired boy forced his way through the masses. He shoved Shawn with both hands into the concrete wall and hammered his fist into his face.

The sound was heavy. All motion slowed as a morbid gasp echoed from the crowd.

As quickly as the attack occurred, it was over. The boy turned and bulldozed his way back through.

Damian.

A teacher on hall duty fought against the rattled herd. He didn't even acknowledge Damian as he struggled to make his way to Shawn.

Shawn leaned against the wall, hand pressed to his face, obviously trying to recover.

The teacher took hold of the upper part of his arm to escort him, and Shawn reacted with an aggressive thrust of his palms into the man's chest.

Oh, shit.

Surprisingly, the man backed off. Not much, though. He spoke something to Shawn, and then stepped close to him again and positioned in a way as to block him from view.

"Keep it moving, guys," he said to the hall full of students.

It took a few seconds, but like minions, everyone started walking again. I didn't have a choice as I was pushed along with everyone else.

As I passed, I peered behind the man. Shawn's face was to the floor, eyes closed, and he wore a hard frown.

Chapter 6

What happened in the hall after lunch wasn't only unexpected, it was wrong, as Damian was never reprimanded. If he was, it wasn't very harshly, because Bobby said he saw him on the way to his last class.

I thought about Shawn all weekend. Not only did I continually replay my failed attempt to befriend him, which was a rim shot, at best, I recalled details about him I didn't realize I'd taken in—his slender fingers, the veins in the backs of his hands I'd been close enough to see.

He had ever-so-subtle lines around his mouth that gave an idea of the range of his smile, which I added to my sketch.

Each minute of the morning on Monday drove up the anticipation, and the rate of my heart increased as I closed in on the cafeteria.

I walked in to an empty table.

He wasn't there on Tuesday, either.

On Wednesday, Shawn came into the cafeteria, soda in hand, but turned back out the moment he saw me.

Rim shot apparently put it mildly.

I'd never seen him on Thursdays, so I was pretty sure we didn't share the period.

I was certain I'd displaced him, so on Friday, not even knowing if he would be there, I took extra time getting to lunch. I stopped at my locker, I went to the bathroom. I was almost a whole ten minutes late.

He was there, sitting back in his usual spot.

What happened with Damian wasn't fair. If nothing else, I wanted him to know I was on his side. Whether I spent the remainder of the period with him or not, I would at least acknowledge it.

He sat in his typical position, slouched with his elbows on the table, holding his hands around the bottom of his soda.

My feet carried me all the way down the aisle until I stood directly in front of him.

I waited, thinking he'd at least look at me. His left cheekbone was dark from where Damian hit him.

"I saw what happened last Friday," I said, his eyes focused on the tabletop in front of me.

I placed my book down and sat. "Why'd he do that?"

"Because he's an asshole."

I was a ninety-pound mouse, yet he couldn't look at me. "That's it? There's not more to it?"

"That's it."

"He didn't get in trouble, did he?"

"Nope."

"Why?"

He shrugged.

"Do you not care?" If he didn't realize I did, then he was a flake.

He lifted his eyes momentarily and looked to my right. I turned to see what got his attention. Bobby marched down the aisle toward us.

For Christ's sake. If he did it again . . .

Bobby dropped down backward on the bench and, elbow on the table, twisted to me. His eyes flitted to Shawn. "You gonna be home when Dad gets home?"

So annoyed. "Where else would I be?"

"Tell him I went out with a couple of the guys. I'll be home by ten."

He didn't really need me to do that, he was just being nosy. And now Damian was on his way. He strolled down the aisle and stood over Bobby and me, burying a glare into Shawn. By the crimson color of his cheeks, he was ready to ignite.

"You just can't fucking help yourself, can you, *thief*," he said to Shawn. "Gotta steal everything that's mine." He pushed between Bobby and me and ripped the closed soda bottle from his hands and pegged it off the wall next to us. "You stupid? Didn't get the point the other day? Don't you know when you're not wanted somewhere? Get the fuck out of here."

"Kid, who *are* you?" Bobby asked, having already determined he didn't like Damian.

"Who are *you*?"

Bobby stood. "Her fucking brother." He'd apparently decided I

45

was the issue. He got right up in his face.

Silence crashed onto the room.

Damian raised his hands and put them right on Bobby's chest. "Back the fuck up, man." He shoved him.

Bobby returned the gesture. "Go fuckin' pump your piston somewhere else, asshole."

Damian shoved Bobby harder.

Bobby grabbed him by the back of his thick, dark hair, and in one rapid curl of his arm, he slammed his face down onto the table.

Damian dropped to the floor.

"Holy shit," Shawn uttered.

Damian was flat-out unconscious on the hard linoleum.

Everyone in the cafeteria gaped.

An army of teachers barraged the room. Before I could even react, Bobby was dragged out.

Only three and a half weeks in and Dad already had to meet with the principal.

Chapter 7

Sirens. Lots of them. I wasn't there when Mom died, but it was how I imagined it. The expressions of shock on the faces of the first responders when they realized who the victim was, the panic . . . The quiver that must've been in Officer O'Fallon's voice when he called Dad to break the news. There wasn't anything that could've prepared us: a last-minute trip to the grocery store to get a forgotten dinner ingredient that she never returned home from.

With her death, Josh lost the person who went to every wrestling match and did her best to slap the basketball from his hands when Dad was too busy at work to shoot hoops with him. Bobby lost the person who endlessly tolerated his music and gave him hugs when he didn't realize he needed them. I lost the most important person in my life. Not every girl can call their mother their best friend. When I woke up in the morning, she was there. When I came home from school, she was there. She pushed through every failed ballet lesson, forever encouraging me not to be who she was, but who I wanted to be, and was the one to call it when she realized I didn't share her passion. I could tell her anything, ever, without fear of judgment, and would always get the most genuine, trustworthy advice. She lived for her family, and it reflected in the loss of her.

Dad did what he could to hold himself together for the three of us, but he eventually gave in to the trauma of losing the woman he'd loved for twenty-two and a half years. He took a sabbatical from work, had close friends care for Josh, Bobby, and me, and he used a chunk of the life insurance money to buy a bigger boat. He named it *Miranda*, after Mom, and spent the better part of a month on the ocean.

He eventually regained himself, but he was different. He smiled less, raised his voice more, and his patience level went down the tubes.

In essence, our family fell apart.

Aside from Bobby being a train wreck, I think moving was a last-ditch effort to pull us back together.

Miranda arrived in Jessup a week after we did.

The Saturday after Bobby's blitz assault on Damian, Dad made plans for us all to spend the day on the lake. Uncle Vance, Dennis, and Kenny were going, Josh invited Susan, even Bobby would be in attendance because Dad couldn't trust him home alone.

Josh poked his head into the kitchen as I loaded the morning's dishes into the dishwasher. "Meg, go look out the front window." Curiosity rumpled his brow.

I shut the dishwasher and passed him to the sheer curtains of the living room window.

"Oh. My. God." Shawn walked up our driveway.

"You should probably get out there before Bobby does." He chuckled.

Shawn's strides as he walked with his thumbs hooked in his belt loops were long, and the breeze brushing his hair from his face molded his black T-shirt to his fit chest.

I pulled at the elastic in my hair, releasing the fountain atop my head that surely made me look younger than I could afford, and jumped for the door. I shook my hair out, hoping the elastic hadn't left a crimp, and awaited his knock.

"Uh . . ." Josh watched from the window.

"What?" I looked again. Shawn was leaving. "Where's he going?"

"Like I said, you better get out there."

I heaved open the door. On the step was the book I'd brought to lunch on Friday.

Shawn was almost at the end of the driveway. "Hey." I stepped out.

He turned his head, and then came to a stop.

"Where are you going?"

He looked at me as if he didn't understand the question, and then pointed at the book at my feet. "You left that."

I motioned my hand toward the door. "Why didn't you knock?"

"Didn't think there was a reason to."

I picked up my book, which I'd apparently forgotten in the chaos of the fight.

"I would've just hung onto it, but that bookmark looked like something you might need."

I pulled out the white paper peeking from the center pages and opened the two folds. My algebra homework. "Um, *yeah*." I already did poorly in math, had he not returned it, I likely would've dropped a grade level.

"That answer's eighty-three."

I looked down to the overly erased equation and he started back toward me. "I can write out the problem if you want."

I tried to play it cool, as if my heart didn't totally flutter. "Thanks. That would be really helpful."

Josh came out and stood behind me on the step. "Hey, man." He extended his arm past me.

Shawn stepped forward and gripped his hand tight enough that the muscles of his forearm flexed. "Hey, how ya doin'?" The dark outer rims of his irises were assaulted by the light from the sun peeking over the ridge of the house, and his eyes looked almost white.

"Not too bad. You're in my gym class, aren't you?"

Shawn half nodded and looked back to me. "If you get a pencil..."

I turned to Josh, thinking he'd go in and get one.

"Hey, Bob, throw me a pencil," he called into the house.

Great.

Bobby came out as well. With his eyes on Shawn, he handed me the pencil. I took it, and he stretched his hand out. "Hey."

"Hey." Shawn grasped it, but his response wasn't as relaxed as it was with Josh.

He took the pencil from me, my paper too, and scribbled out the equation to the problem.

Had Bobby not been there, maybe he would've given an explanation as to how he did it. Instead, he wordlessly wrote out the numbers, and then handed me the pencil and paper back. He glanced up at me, and then to Josh and Bobby behind me. "I should go." He stuffed his hands into his rear pockets and started back down our circular driveway.

Gah! No! "Um, wait."

He swiveled back.

I looked quick at Josh and Bobby. "Um . . . we're going out on my dad's boat. Would you like to . . . maybe . . . come?" *Holy spontaneous!*

I turned to Bobby again, willing him to fix his expression. He likely just tried to process what was happening, but his manner wasn't very welcoming.

Shawn also appeared as though he didn't understand. With Bobby nearly glaring at him, I reached my arm back and spread my hand open in front of Bobby's face. "Ignore him."

"Dude, you totally should." Josh tried to help. "Kinda random, but hey, what the hell."

"Hey there, Shawn." Susan appeared in the open doorway, chipper as always.

Shawn's eyes batted to me and the fingers of his right hand lifted as if in appreciation. "Maybe another time. I have shit to do." Without waiting for a reply, he turned and carried on down the driveway.

"I guess you said 'hi,'" Susan said with a giggle.

51

Falling into a V in the cradle of his shoulder bones, the golden strands of his hair glimmered under the sun, and with his hands wedged into his back pockets, his veined arms dominated my attention.

I looked at Bobby. "You really do suck, you know that?"

"What did *I* do?"

"I don't know why you're letting him leave," Susan said.

Josh shoved me off the step.

"You guys have lost your minds," Bobby said, and turned back inside.

"You might not get another chance," Josh said. "He did come all the way over here."

"I asked him if he wanted to go, he said no."

"Ah, you're giving up too easy." Josh lifted a leg and kicked me out another foot.

"You got his attention, Meg, now keep it," Susan said.

"I didn't get his attention, my homework did."

He was almost at the end of the driveway.

Really, what was the worst that could happen? I broke into a jog.

"Hey," I called, my feet loud and heavy on the pavement.

I caught up with Shawn just as he made it to the road. He stopped under a patch of sun, the breeze carrying his hair in a god-like sweep.

"Um." *Words, Megan. Quickly.* I was about to lose my nerve, clammy palms and all. "I meant it when I asked if you would go with us. I know it's out of nowhere, but . . ."

He didn't say no, but his head moved. "I'm not very good around people."

"Oh, that's okay, neither am I." It just fell out of my mouth.

His opened as if he would say something. He inhaled, then looked back to the house.

The car doors started to shut and I looked to see Dad closing the front door.

"Do you really have something else to do?"

His shirt pulsed.

Josh pulled forward.

"Please come with us?"

Josh crept toward us, Susan in the passenger seat, Bobby behind her. He stopped when he reached us.

Susan leaned into view, smirking. "Anyone need a lift?"

Bobby kept his eyes to himself this time.

I looked at Shawn again and reluctantly got in.

"Sorry, Shawn, there is no way you have something better to do," Susan said with a laugh.

Shawn ducked his head to look inside, then to my surprise, made a move toward the car. He gripped the ridge of the roof with one hand and the top of the door with the other as he lowered himself in.

He pulled the door shut, his legs too long for the backseat, and expelled an unsure breath.

Susan grinned. "You'll have fun."

His arm brushed mine. Goosebumps rose all over my body.

Chapter 8

"So, how's school treating you, Shawn?" Susan held her arm around the headrest facing him on the way to the dock.

"Could be worse," he said with his eyes turned out the window.

"You have Mrs. Palmieri for English, don't you?"

"Yup."

"What do you think of her?"

"She's not bad."

"I had her last year. She screwed me over so freaking royally."

Shawn glanced at her and returned his gaze to the trees.

"I passed every test with nothing lower than a B and still got a C minus every quarter," Susan went on. "Really messed with my GPA."

"I think your grade in that class has a lot to do with your personality," Shawn said. "She probably just didn't like you."

Bobby choked on a laugh next to me.

"Seriously," Susan said. "Wait, so are you saying I'm not a likable person?" She realized what he implied.

"I don't know you."

"What'd she give you last quarter?"

"An A every quarter so far. And I don't do shit."

Josh tried to squelch a smile but didn't quite succeed, and Susan whacked him.

~

It was only about a five-minute drive to the cove where Dad's boat was docked.

Josh pulled into the gravel parking lot behind Uncle Vance. We all filed out of the two cars, Shawn keeping in the background.

Dennis nodded at him and walked over. "Hey, Shawn, what's going on?" He stretched his hand out to him.

Shawn gripped it.

"That's Dennis," I said, in case he didn't know his name.

Uncle Vance looked over and his eyes stuck on him. Then like something clicked in him, he started toward us.

"Well, hello . . . Shawn, is it?"

"Hello, Detective." Shawn extended his hand first this time.

Detective? Uncle Vance was retired, so how did he know?

Uncle Vance didn't return the gesture. It was as if he studied him. Dad came over.

"This is Shawn," I said to him, soaring over his brother. "He was the one who pulled the car from the ditch, remember?"

With a smile lighting his face, Dad leaned around Uncle Vance

55

and reached out his hand.

Shawn stepped forward and made direct eye contact as he shook it.

"Wow, that's a solid grip." The crow's feet around Dad's eyes were deep. "So, did you meet these guys at school?" He nodded at Josh, Bobby, and me.

"He's *Nutty's* friend," Bobby said.

"Well, Shawn, it's nice to meet you." Dad's smile remained as he moved through it. "Let's get this show on the road, shall we?" His enthusiasm showed in every added crease on his face.

~

It was a warm day and the thin clouds feathered across the sky eventually dissipated. We drifted along on the still water for a while as Dad let out sounds of laughter I hadn't heard from him in years.

With all of us kids clustered on the floor of the back deck, Shawn never once attempted to engage in conversation. His attention also seemed more focused on Dad and Uncle Vance. Every time I looked at him, his eyes were on them.

"Do you wish you didn't come?" I asked him.

"I've never been on a boat before."

"Never? Really?" The town possessed such an available body of water. "Not even a little one?"

He shook his head.

"So, what do you think?" It seemed the thing to ask.

"It's not bad. I guess I don't get seasick."

I laughed. "You should probably wait until there are waves to make that determination."

Dad pulled out two fishing poles, one for himself and one for Uncle Vance. "How do you all feel about taking a hike?" he asked as he handed his tackle box to Uncle Vance.

"What's that supposed to mean?" Bobby asked.

"Nothing to you. You're staying here with us and reading a book."

Bobby's mouth fell open as Dad pointed over his shoulder to a small inlet. "The rest of you take the raft and row over."

Take a hike literally meant take a hike.

"What the fuck?" Bobby said.

"*Robert.*" Dad had no tolerance for him. "Fully expect that if that word comes from your mouth one more time, you'll be hoisted up by your underwear and tossed off this boat."

It was a little embarrassing that I'd invited Shawn for a day on the boat, and now we were getting kicked off. "I'm sorry," I said to him, hoping he wasn't too put off. "This is completely unexpected."

"It's alright," he said, eyeing Dad again.

~

Aside from the life raft that came with the boat, Dad towed a six-person dinghy, and that's what he expected us to use to get to dry land.

Stepping from the last rung of the ladder to the unstable rubber raft wasn't as easy for Shawn as it was for the rest of us, he wasn't so sure about his footing, but he did it.

"Now that makes two boats," I said as he settled against the edge in the middle.

Josh rowed with one paddle and Dennis the other. We positioned alongside the woods that surrounded the cove and climbed out.

The air under the thick covering of trees was much cooler as we walked without a destination along what appeared to be an old path. Shawn kept at the rear of the group, thumbs hitched in his pockets, and was just as quiet.

"Hey, Shawn, I heard you fixed Andy Gyle's engine," Dennis said.

Shawn glanced up from his view of the ground.

"He said you did a really sweet job. Cleaned it up, and everything."

Susan turned around to him as she walked and poked her fingers into his shoulder. "C'mon, Shawn, pick your head up. Stop hiding those gorgeous eyes."

Shawn acknowledged her with a glimpse, but that was it. Susan shrugged at me with a resigned twist of her mouth.

Josh grabbed her hand and pulled her along, Susan giggling as they dropped out of sight.

Desperation grew in me. The farther we traveled, the more I worried about Shawn's lack of interaction—my inability to interact with him. I almost expected to turn around and not see him anymore.

"Hey, hold up a sec," his deep voice came from behind me.

He stopped and watched, tense, as the rest of the group continued on ahead. There was a large boulder that split the path.

"Hey, we know what you're doing up there," Dennis said, Susan's playful laugh coming from behind it.

She and Josh leapt into view and carried on down the path to the right.

Shawn expelled a breath. "Never mind." He walked again.

"Do you know where we are?" I asked.

"Yeah."

Kenny gained enough momentum that he was soon out of sight.

"*Holy*—" His voice erupted with excitement. "Hurry up, guys, you gotta see this!"

We picked up our pace as Shawn fell behind.

We came to a halt at the edge of a wide clearing, Kenny about fifty feet ahead at the rim of an open gorge.

Susan picked her legs up high as she walked, trying to clear the tall grass as Josh and Dennis swept through.

About halfway, I looked back. Shawn still stood at the edge of the woods, his shoulder turned.

"Are you coming?"

His eyes darted as he frowned. The pivoting movements of his body suggested he would leave.

"What's wrong?" *Were we not supposed to go that way?*

He started toward me. He passed, and I followed.

The air was still and a familiar sound struck my ears as we approached the top of the ravine.

Steps from the grassy edge, my eyes took in a sight I thought they never would again. A thin sheet of water cascaded over the rim of the chasm and dropped at least forty feet into a dark pool below.

It was as if I'd stepped through a portal to my childhood. Some of my greatest memories were of picnicking by and swimming at waterfalls in Colombia River Gorge. This waterfall wasn't nearly as big as those ones, but it was a waterfall still, and breathtakingly reminiscent of home.

The bow of lines in Susan's forehead couldn't have been more

59

arched. "Like, for real?" She shaded her copper eyes with her hand. "I've lived in Jessup my entire life and never knew this was here."

"Not supposed to," Shawn said. "Too many people have drowned here."

"You knew this was here?"

Shawn kicked at the ground with his eyes on the fall.

He looked over his shoulder. "Can go down over there." He pointed to a steep embankment.

Kenny didn't wait. He leapt ahead and cautiously slid his way down.

Shawn reared up the group again as we all did the same.

"Wanna go in?" Kenny asked Dennis, standing at the water's jagged edge.

"Knock yourself out."

"It's a rock quarry, so it's pretty dangerous," Shawn said. "There are spots that just drop off. Like right there." He pointed about five feet in. "It gets pretty deep in certain places."

"Never mind that it's probably freezing," Susan said.

Holding up the bottom of my pants, I slipped out of my flip-flops and took a few steps forward on the submersed rock. I stood in the cold water for a moment, looking past the abrupt drop-off feet in front of me. "Gosh, that's gotta be deep."

"It's at least twenty feet right there," Shawn said.

I tried to keep my eyes focused as I peered down but couldn't see farther than a few inches in the darkness of it.

I stepped out of the water and Shawn sat down on the ground. I sat down next to him—too close, I guess, because he shifted a good foot in the opposite direction.

"I can see why you would want to keep this place to yourself," I said. It was probably why he'd looked so disgruntled. In all actuality, he could've told us to go the other way at the split. "I'm glad you didn't."

He peeked at me, still seeming leery.

"Really." I wanted him to know the significance. "There are lots of waterfalls where I'm from. I was a little worried I'd never see one again."

He sat resting his forearms on his knees, holding his wrist.

"So where are we?" It seemed pretty secluded, yet he knew about it. We must have been near a road, something. "Do you live near here?"

He looked away.

As introverted as I usually was, I had to step up. Otherwise, we'd sit in awkward silence. "You know, I was surprised when you said you were in eleventh grade. I was sure you were in twelfth."

It was supposed to be a prompt. "How old are you?"

I got a quick glimpse of his profile. "Sixteen."

Plenty of juniors were, but again, I was surprised. "When will you be seventeen?"

"October."

October was six months away. "October what?"

"Tenth." He wanted to look at me, I could tell, he just couldn't get his eyes all the way over.

"I'll be sixteen next month. I'm supposed to be a sophomore." It

61

was better than saying I was a freshman.

There was a loud outburst from Susan. She and Josh struggled to push each other into the water. Susan won, and Josh went in.

"*Fri-i-i-i-g, it's cold!*" He did his best to tread the water while managing the temperature. "Oh, you're gonna get it!" he said to Susan convulsing with laughter.

"You got a mom?" Shawn asked, looking at them.

The question pricked like a needle. "I *did*," I said.

"Did she die?"

His manner threw me. He asked as if it was just what came next.

"Um, actually, she did."

He turned, the eye I could see catching a ray of sun, washing it out. "How?"

"She was in a car accident. Head-on collision."

"Drunk driver?"

It was always the first assumption. "Nope. A couple who was arguing about where to go for dinner."

He twisted his head to me just as I looked away. "That's pretty messed up."

"Yup. Because they couldn't agree, my mother never had dinner again." Why was this what he all of a sudden decided to talk about?

"How long ago?"

"Almost four years."

"Do you miss her?"

"Every single day." The question triggered emotion I wasn't prepared for and my eyes dampened.

"Sore subject?"

"A bit." I hated how much talk of her still affected me. I pushed my index fingers to the corners of my eyes to stop them from tearing. "How 'bout you, do you have a mom?" It seemed fair.

"Nope." He picked up a twig from between his legs and flicked it.

I wasn't as blunt as he was, so I hoped he would elaborate without me having to ask.

He looked at me when I didn't move on and shrugged. "I woke up one morning and she was gone."

"How old were you?" He seemed unaffected, so maybe it'd been a while.

"Thirteen."

Less time than my mom.

"I remember the date. February third."

"And, do you miss *her*?"

"Nope. I'm glad she's gone."

The words cut a little, considering how much I missed mine.

"My dad can take a hike too. I don't like him much, either."

Maybe if I waited.

Other than an uncomfortable silence, he had nothing else to add.

"So, tell me something I should know about you." I tried to keep him going.

I think he appreciated my change of subject, a smile flickered. "Never call me Shawny," he said without a thought. "I hate that name. I really fucking hate it." His delivery was solid.

"That's easy enough, I guess."

63

He looked over at Josh and Susan still battling each other and broke twigs between his fingers. "So, where'd you live before here?"

"Oregon. Just outside of Portland."

"Near the coast?"

"Not too far. We were about an hour away."

"That must've been cool." He cut a glance to me.

"The scenery was really nice. I'll definitely miss it."

"You ever swim in the ocean?" I got his eyes again.

"Used to. A lot." We'd once spent entire summers at the beach.

"Ever see a shark?"

"Oh yeah. Tons. My dad has always had boats. We used to go out all the time. We'd see all kinds of things."

"What about a skate?" he asked with a playful squint of his eyes, as if testing me.

I smiled at his randomness. "Yup." I anticipated his reaction. "I've actually eaten them."

"Seriously?"

"Yeah. My dad's big into fishing. I've eaten lots of things."

"Ever had lobster?"

Actually, I hadn't. "Lobster's more of an east coast thing, I think. Mostly New England."

He turned his head to face forward again. "That's where I'm going."

Wait, what? "You're moving?"

"Someday. Hopefully sooner rather than later."

A pang tore through me. My crush couldn't move. Especially not

64

for a crustacean. "Why?"

"To get the hell out of here."

Jessup *was* boring. There were lots of places he could go, though. "Do you have family there, or something?"

He breathed amusement. "That would defeat the purpose."

Family was apparently not his thing. "Have you ever been there?"

"No, but I've seen it on TV. And in pictures. The climate seems really nice, the scenery . . . Just like everything about it."

"Winters there are cold. Like, frigid."

He made a sharp turn of his head to me. "Have you been?"

"To New York." It wasn't part of New England, but close enough. "What was it like?"

Figures. Something that actually got his attention and I couldn't recall. "I don't know. I was pretty young. I just remember it being really cold."

"What'd you go for?"

"My grandmother's funeral. My dad and my uncle are from there."

"New York?"

"The Bronx."

His eyes opened wider. "Was your dad a cop there?"

"Yeah, it's where he started his career."

"He must be pretty tough, then." The eagerness in his voice dialed up.

I had to think about it. Dad, to me, was just Dad. He was pretty badass, though. Always on TV for one thing or another, giving statements or press conferences. Everyone at school knew who he was, and no one ever messed with him. Or any of us, for that matter.

I shrugged. "I guess."

"He ever shoot anyone?"

"Several people."

"What for?" His attention became straight-up focused.

"I don't know. Whatever was necessary, I guess. There was one guy who led a high-speed chase through our city that ended near an elementary school, and he got out of his car with a gun. Dad didn't feel like he had a choice."

"Any of them die?"

"That guy did. And at least one other." That I knew of. I tried *not* to know. It was part of Dad's job I pretended didn't exist.

"So, he's quick?"

Um. "I would think so." I could only assume. It seemed like something that would be a requirement of the job. I lifted a shoulder. "I don't really pay attention to that kind of—"

"Do you trust him?"

"*Trust* him? What do you mean? Why wouldn't I?" It was a weird question.

His brow twitched as if he was somehow caught off guard by his own question, and he cut his eyes away. "I don't know, I um . . . I just . . ." He tripped over his words, seeming flustered. "I guess I just watch a lot of TV. With bad cops, you know?" He shot a cautious glance at me with a deep exhale of a breath.

He turned a quick eye to me again. "So, you have enough of that history teacher yet?"

66

What? It was such a sudden, random change of subject.

Bashfulness nipped me and I looked away to hide the silly grin that lit up my face. He knew who I had for history?

Chapter 9

We were at the quarry for close to an hour.

"Bobby's gonna be pissed," Dennis said about our discovery.

"Don't tell him," Shawn said.

"It'll be kinda hard not to, considering Josh's 'drowned rat' look."

Dennis made a point. Josh didn't leave the house without putting a fair amount of effort into his appearance.

"No, seriously," Shawn said. "Could you guys, maybe, keep this place to yourselves? It's quiet here. It'd suck to ruin that."

"Of course," Susan said as if answering for all of us.

Miranda was right where we left her when we got back to the dinghy, Bobby where we left him when we re-boarded.

"What the hell happened to you?" he asked Josh.

"Dude, what are you frigging reading?" Josh's head tilted back with laughter. Bobby held a hardcover copy of *Moby Dick*. "You must have really pissed Dad off."

"Kid, shut up." Bobby stood and shoved Josh still laughing against the side railing and disappeared down into the cabin.

"See, no problem," Josh said to Shawn, unable to contain himself.

Once settled, we started back to the dock.

Josh started the grill as soon as we got home.

"Do you want to stay to eat?" I asked Shawn, him stopping short of following me into the house. "I'm sure my dad won't mind."

"Nah, I gotta get going."

"Are you sure?" I tried to talk him into it. "The grill's fast."

"Thanks." A cheek lifted. "I really gotta go." There was sincerity in his tone.

"Okay, well . . . do you want a ride?" Just about anyone there could've given him one.

"I can walk." He turned for the driveway as Dad approached the door.

"Are you leaving, Shawn?"

"Yeah, I gotta go."

"Well, it was nice meeting you." Dad reached to shake his hand again.

Shawn's grip was as strong as when I introduced them. "It was nice meeting you too, sir."

Dad went into the house and Shawn started off.

"Thanks for coming," I called after him.

He turned back as he walked, the edges of his mouth lifting in a small smile. "Thanks for inviting me."

I went inside and shut the door. Bobby passed by me and flicked

69

the back of my head. "What's *that* about?"

"Nut Meg's got a boyfriend," Josh teased.

Dad's grin was big. "When on Earth did that happen?"

~

Sunday was a day of regrets. Regretting not giving Shawn my phone number, not getting his. We had another whole day of the weekend, why didn't I ask him to come over again?

"Holy bejeezies!" Susan snuck up on me out on the deck with my sketch pad. "You did not seriously draw that." She looked over my shoulder at another sketch of Shawn I worked on. "Are you for real? I didn't even know you drew."

"Sometimes." Though my pace had picked up substantially over the past couple weeks.

"Megan, that is . . . Dear God." It was the view I got of him when we were at the quarry when he looked at me and the sun blanched out one of his eyes. "That is *crazy* good."

I'd gone soft with the pencil and he looked almost mystical.

"Can I see that?" She reached for the pad.

I let her take it, thinking she just wanted to examine it closer, but she flipped back a page.

"Oh my *God*." Her mouth dropped open, looking at the previous one of Shawn. "How are you this good?" She was in total awe. "You need to show him this."

"Um, *no*." Was she crazy? "Don't tell him, either."

"Why not? It's *amazing*."

It was embarrassing.

70

She flipped to the one before it. "Megan."

It was a self-portrait in which I had a dismal expression on my face, my eyes and lips drawn darkly with a downward smudge—like smeared makeup.

She kept turning, gaping.

As enthusiastic as she was, it made me feel naked. There was a lot of emotion wrapped up in those pages.

With each turn, it was as if she stripped another piece of clothing from me. The farther back she went, the more exposed I felt.

She gasped at a charcoal abstract that gave the impression of a person struggling to stand while surrounded by a cyclone of scribble lines. It was supposed to depict my depression and anxiety at the time.

My heart thumped in my chest, about to have an anxiety attack right then and there. I reached up and grabbed the pad back. "Okay, that's enough of that," I said through a graceless moment as I closed it and clutched it against my chest.

"What?" She expelled a breath of laughter, confusion cinching her brow.

"Sorry. It's just that nobody's ever really seen those ones." It was the truth. I actually couldn't believe she got as far as she did.

"But why? They're beautiful. You're very talented."

They were private. She could look through any one of my other sketch pads, just not that one. "Thank you." I didn't want to be rude.

"Okay, well," she said, dispirited as she started back inside. She turned back. "They're really good, Megan. You shouldn't be ashamed of them. They show who you are."

Exactly. They detailed my innermost thoughts and feelings, which I didn't have a desire to share.

I waited until she was gone before opening back to the one of Shawn I was just about finished with. I really did make him look heavenly.

The more I looked at it, the more I decided it was still missing something.

I went upstairs and dug into my box of drawing supplies in search of the colored pencils I hadn't used in almost four years, and I added the slightest bit of blue to the eye that wasn't washed out by the light.

It was barely detectable, but it was there.

For the rest of the day, I distracted myself by looking at pictures of New England on the internet. I'd learned about the thirteen original colonies in Social Studies, but that was about all I knew of the area. The rustic farmhouses, white picket fences, and quaint villages found a special spot in my heart.

~

It rained for most of the morning on Monday, which made the day feel longer.

At lunch, I watched the clock, waiting for Shawn, up to the very last minute. He was a no-show.

I went to my locker at the end of the day, and then out the front door to catch up with Josh for a ride. Shawn stood against a pillar of the bus turn around.

I approached, and he pushed off and started across the grass.

"Slow down, Daddy Long Legs." I had to overextend my legs to keep up with him. "Where are you going?"

"Did you like where we went the other day?" He barely looked at me.

"Yeah."

"Wanna go there again?"

As in, just us? I knew better than to go anywhere alone with a boy I hardly knew. While my mind told me one thing, the breeze through the leaves of the trees whispered something else. "Sure."

"How was school?" he asked with the same dull tone.

"Were you there?" He might just not have been at lunch.

He glanced back.

Moments went by with an awkward silence as we walked along the road, now in its last stages of drying from the earlier rain.

"So, how far is it?" I asked.

Shawn veered off into the woods and I nearly had to jump to keep up.

As much as the quiet bothered me, it didn't seem to concern him.

The rock where the path had split came into view. It was only a matter of minutes before we reached the clearing.

A single shaft of sunlight spotlighted the quarry, its beauty striking me even more than the first time.

We didn't go down to the bottom. I followed Shawn around to the top of the fall. He sat on the edge of the high cliff and slid down to a rock ledge several feet below.

"C'mon." He gestured for me to follow.

"Uh . . ." If I didn't land just right, I'd fall into the water.

"You can do it."

"I don't think I can." I was pretty sure. I removed my phone from my back pocket so I wouldn't sit on it, and placed it on the ground next to my backpack. I sat on the grassy lip but couldn't allow myself to drop.

With a bit of hesitation, Shawn reached his hands up.

I extended mine to his shoulders as I slid, noises of fear I wasn't proud of seeping from me. When I was within reach, he clutched my waist.

As soon as my feet were on the ground, he let go.

We were on a four-by-four section of rock shelf about thirty feet above the water of the quarry.

With my back pressed to the rock wall, Shawn faced me close to the edge. Each breath I took became shallower as I became petrified in place.

"You afraid of heights?" He could obviously tell.

"Uh, you could say that."

"Sorry." A cheek lifted with his apology. "We should probably get down, then." He reached out and grasped my hand, his long fingers wrapping around all five of my knuckles. "This really is the easiest way." He dropped backward, his grip so tight there was nowhere for me to go but with him.

Stomach-in-throat, pulse-pounding fear.

We hit the water quickly, the freezing temperature knocking the breath out of me. My hand was no longer in Shawn's as I plummeted deep into the dark water.

74

I kicked to the surface and a scream burst from me.

Shawn treaded water with a mega-huge smile. "Still afraid of heights?"

I wanted to yell at him, but I couldn't stop smiling myself. "You are *crazy*." I could hardly breathe. The coldness felt like thousands of tiny needles. "It's *freezing*."

"Makes you feel alive, doesn't it?"

"Not exactly." It had to be what it felt like to fall through ice in winter. The air was warm, but it was only early spring. The water hadn't warmed at all yet.

"Wanna do it again?"

Pure exhilaration. Before that moment, I didn't think he was capable of such positive expression.

"Uh, okay?" I think I only agreed to keep it going.

He swam past me, no way my lips weren't purple. I followed, my teeth jackhammering against each other as I pulled myself out of the water onto the rock bank.

"I don't know about you, Shawn." Shock still dictated as I stood bent with my hands to my knees trying to catch my breath.

"Well, you're not afraid of heights anymore," he said, also having to catch his. "At least not that one, right?"

It was just so unexpected. Thank God I knew how to swim.

I couldn't let it go as we trekked back up. "Just for future reference, I don't think that's a stunt you should keep up with." It really was scary.

Shawn stopped and turned back with a look more serious than I anticipated. "I've never done that to anyone before." His round eyes immobilized me. "That's my favorite place to be. I don't want you to be afraid of it."

If I understood him correctly—which I didn't think there was a way to have been confused—he said he planned on me being there with him. And everything he had just done became so incredibly, insanely awesome. I really didn't think there was a way he could've conveyed it more perfectly.

We spent the next twenty minutes or so jumping, hand-in-hand, from the thirty-something foot-high cliff into the deep, freezing water. It got only slightly easier each time, and not at all warmer.

"Want to do it by yourself?" Shawn eventually suggested.

"Uh . . ." It seemed about as much of a good idea as jumping in the first place.

"C'mon, you can handle it."

With my arms pulled to my chest for warmth, I still hesitated.

"Why don't you think you can?"

"Oh, I don't know." It kind of went against all basic instinct. It was one thing when he held my hand and I didn't have a choice, but when left on my own, it didn't make sense to create a threat to my life unnecessarily. "I guess it doesn't matter, you'll probably just push me if I don't," I said through a nervous breath.

He laughed. "Probably."

His smile flipped my stomach. I think it could've talked me into anything.

I took a deep breath, and then a step into the air.

I did it again. And again.

I didn't want to leave, but the temperature was downright painful. When it became obvious I couldn't handle it any longer, Shawn offered to walk me home.

"Only if I'm on your way," I said.

"You're on my way. Besides, you'll get lost."

We walked for at least a mile in our sopping wet clothes. There wasn't a ton of talking, but more than usual. I did most of it and felt like I rambled.

"There was this time, a couple years ago . . ." My voice shook from shivering. "Bobby got up late one night to go to the bathroom." I hoped talking about him would ease his apprehension about him. "But I guess he was sleepwalking, so instead of going into the bathroom, he went into the living room. He lifted the couch cushion—" I had to stop because I laughed so much. "Dad said he couldn't stop him. All he could do was get a bowl."

Shawn laughed under his breath and looked back to the muffled hum of an approaching vehicle. He muttered the "F" word and turned his eyes straight.

The tall, shiny, blue truck roared up on us. It slowed as it neared and drove alongside us.

His father.

He leaned into view and, grinning, nodded at me. "Hey, sweetie, you're the chief's daughter, ain't ya?"

Shawn turned on a dime and reached for the door handle. Mr. Harris stopped the truck and he got in. Shawn pulled the door shut, his eyes remaining dead ahead as Mr. Harris moved his gaze from me to him. His grin dissolved and he stared hard at Shawn.

I didn't know if I should wait, keep walking . . .

Mr. Harris turned his gaze back to me, the edges of his mouth curling up again. "Best you keep close to Daddy, little lady." His smirk slinked higher up one cheek. "Pretty little thing like you could catch a lot of eyes." He winked at me.

The suggestion in his expression froze me. Chills raced up my entire body and back down again.

There was a rumble from the exhaust and the tires screeched forward. The truck blasted off and took the left onto County Road.

It was the most unsettling interaction I'd ever had. I'd never experienced a more sinister feeling.

~

Shawn wasn't in school the following day. Nor was he the day after that.

Chapter 10

The small panes of glass in my bedroom window formed a grid, Orion's Belt dead center. The night air was soft and cool, and any other time probably would've lulled me to sleep. I'd read and spent an hour watching TV, now resorted to staring out the window. The way Shawn turned to the truck when his father noted who I was, the glare Mr. Harris dug into him. His disturbing comment to me. Shawn was now MIA. Not only was it troubling to think I was the issue, but also what Shawn may have faced in the aftermath.

~

I hunted Dennis down first thing in the morning. "Do you know where Shawn lives?" If he didn't, Uncle Vance probably did.

"Somewhere on County Road, I think. Why?"

"But you don't know where?"

"No."

"Can you ask your dad?"

He chuckled. "Um, no. Even if he knows, he wouldn't tell me."

"Why?" Considering Uncle Vance's reaction to Shawn the day we went out on the boat, there had to have been a reason.

"I'm pretty sure he wouldn't want me going anywhere near the Harris residence."

"Why?" It sounded a little severe.

"'Cause his dad's not exactly known for his upstanding behavior."

Ugh. That didn't make me feel better. "Well, how many houses are there on County Road?" It was all the more reason.

"Not a clue. Probably more than it seems, they're all so buried in the woods."

After school, I made Josh drive me up and down County Road for almost half an hour.

"Did you think of the possibility he might just be sick, or something?" he asked me.

"I really don't think so." I couldn't shake the feeling.

As long as the road was, there were only six visible houses, none with a blue pick-up or tow truck.

We drove by Harris Towing. The garage doors were open and the tow truck was there, along with Shawn's father, but there was no sign of Shawn.

"Maybe he's at the quarry," I said. "It shouldn't be that hard to find, just look for a body of water on your GPS."

"Megan, I'm not going to the quarry." Josh was done.

~

I went to the main office in the morning. "I'm wondering where Shawn

80

Harris is," I asked one of the secretaries. "He hasn't been here all week. Was he called out?" Somebody had to miss him besides me.

"I'm sorry, hon, but I can't discuss other students with you."

Of course, not. I knew that, but it was worth a try.

When I met up with Josh in the student parking lot, he handed me a torn sliver of paper.

7 County Road

"Where'd you get it?"

"Dennis got it from someone. But he also said you shouldn't go alone."

"Will you bring me?"

"Yeah, but only because I know you'll go anyway if I don't."

"Oh, thank you, thank you, thank you." Though I so totally would have.

We drove by Harris Towing first to make sure Mr. Harris was there.

We approached a mailbox with the number seven on it and Josh slowed. He came to a stop in front of a dirt driveway.

"Do you know if it's just him and his Dad?" he asked as we peered down, unable to see past a small bend.

"No. All I know is his mother doesn't live with him."

With my eyes on our destination, Josh backed up enough to be able to make the turn and started down the narrow path.

We rounded the bend and an old, beat-up trailer in a small, grassless alcove came into view.

Josh stopped but left the engine running. The door was closed

81

and there were no vehicles, no outward signs of anyone being there.

I pulled at my door handle, and Josh also got out.

"We gotta make this quick, Meg, I've got the heebie-jeebies."

Josh followed me up to the door. I pulled open the thin aluminum one and tapped out a quiet knock on the thicker one.

It was hard to hear with the engine of the car running, but no one came to open it. I knocked again, a little harder, and pressed my ear to the grungy white metal.

"C'mon, Meg, he's not here."

"Just wait a minute." I couldn't give up that easily. I stepped down to underneath the high, square window next to the stairs. "Pick me up."

"I'm not picking you up."

"Josh, pick me up," I yelled at him in a loud whisper.

He grumbled something under his breath and leaned down and wrapped his arms around my thighs. "You know this is trespassing, right?"

"This is an exception."

He lifted me and sat me on his shoulder. I grasped the thin, metal rim with the tips of my fingers and pressed my forehead to the glass. "You've got five seconds," he said.

It was hard to see. As bright as it was outside, not much light made its way in. Just below the window was the kitchen sink. There was a refrigerator, a small, round table to the right of it, a couch with a coffee table to the left. It was outdated but clean.

"Anything?"

"No." I cupped my hands around my eyes to see better and Josh dropped me.

"Let's go. We shouldn't be here."

The yard was littered with stuff—car jacks, crates of tools, what looked like an old engine.

I couldn't suppress the uneasiness churning in me as I got back into the car. My door was barely shut as Josh pulled forward to turn around.

A heavy work boot at the foot of the driveway caught my eyes as he peeled out. "Josh, stop!" The second one lay farther up. They were the ones Shawn wore when he pulled me off the ledge at the quarry.

"I'm not stopping."

"Those are Shawn's shoes." My heart plunged into my stomach. They looked like they'd been thrown.

"And?"

"That means he's in there." Or somewhere without his shoes.

"What, someone can't have more than one pair of shoes?"

For Shawn, it was unlikely. As far as I could tell, he only owned three shirts. "Josh, please go back." The sick feeling in me intensified.

"Meg, if he wanted to answer the door, he would've." We reached the top of the driveway and he turned toward home.

~

The pit in my stomach was deep. Though I didn't know Shawn all that well, I felt in my gut something was wrong.

I studied my original sketch of him. The seriousness in his expression. What once gave an aura of mystery and depth now alarmed me.

I went to the market with Dad in the morning. We passed Harris

Towing on the way. Mr. Harris was outside, leaned under the hood of an old sports car.

He was still there on our way back, so after all the groceries were put away, I slipped out.

It was about a fifteen-minute walk to County Road, and number seven wasn't that far up.

As Josh noted, I didn't know who else might live there, so I stuck by the edge of the dense trees as I crept down the long driveway. The rattle of the leaves any other time probably would've been calming, but it gave an eerie feeling I was being watched.

The bass rumble of heavy metal vibrated the air as I neared the bend.

I stopped and inhaled what was supposed to be a courage-inducing breath, then inched my head around the corner. There was Shawn. *Thank God.*

With his back to the driveway, he searched through plastic milk crates.

The music that came from inside wasn't terribly loud, but loud enough to mask the crunching dirt under my steps. He either sorted what was in the crates or looked for something. With his right arm held to his chest, he used his left hand to remove objects from one and throw them into another.

Knowing I'd startle him, I neared from the side and leaned my head forward so it would be the first thing he saw.

He spun around, wide-eyed, as he took in my sudden appearance. *"Shit."*

His right arm kept tight to his chest and there was a greenish-yellowish tinge to his left jaw.

I lifted my hand toward his face "What happ—"

He staggered backward. "Don't touch me." His jaw clenched, and the hand of the arm pinned to his chest choked the material of his shirt. "Get *out* of here." He nearly vibrated. He moved past me to the trailer and scaled the two front steps. "Get *out* of here." He fled inside and slammed the door shut.

Uh duh.

I stood there for I'm not sure how long.

~

It rained on my way home. It stormed for the rest of the day and into the night.

My stomach felt full of rocks. I was utterly baffled by Shawn's reaction to me. It made no sense whatsoever.

I'd have been awoken by a loud crack of thunder at two a.m., but I was already awake.

Chapter 11

The air was cool and the ground wet. Time escaped me, as well as distance, as I fumbled through the woods in search of the quarry.

Following the GPS map on my phone, I headed for the small body of water I figured could only be it. Even if I didn't make it there, it was something to do to clear my mind.

Thorns grabbed at my legs, mud threatened my every step, and flurries of gnats turned me into a human fly swatter.

Eventually, I ended up in the clearing.

The tall grass soaked my canvas shoes as I made my way across to the top of the waterfall.

The stream that fed the fall nearly overflowed from all the rain, bolstering the gentle spill to a rumbling gush.

I lowered to the rock lip, which was nearly dry, and dangled my legs over the side. The rain embellished spring's sweet scents and I couldn't imagine taking them in in a more beautiful place. Even the dirt smelled good.

Truly, if I couldn't have home, this certainly ran a close second. I could almost feel Mom shining down on me, saying, *see, everything will be okay.*

"Please help me with this Shawn thing," I begged her. I really didn't understand what had happened. We'd had such a good time together the day he'd brought me back there, and the day before, he acted as if I was his worst enemy. It was thoroughly confusing. As closed off as he was, all I could think was that I'd crossed some sort of boundary. Even at that, his response to me was downright rough.

The birds frolicked after the night's storm and a bullfrog croaked. I could sit there all day listening to the sounds of nature.

To my right was the ledge Shawn and I jumped from. And denim. From what appeared to be a knee.

I stood and went to the spot we'd slid down from and peered over the edge. Shawn lay curled on the small shelf, shirt off and balled under his head, sleeping. The connector of his right shoulder was nasty shades of bluish-green and yellow. "*Jeez.*" His jeans and hair were saturated and there were drops of water on his bare skin.

I slid down, having to force my fear away to allow myself to drop.

Reflecting in the sun in front of him was a razor blade.

Oh, God.

In a fetal position with his hands by his face, there were no noticeable signs of injury, and his chest rose and fell.

Careful not to fall backward off the ledge, I got down on my knees and pushed my hand over his head. "Shawn."

87

He breathed deeper.

"Shawn."

His eyes fluttered open and he sucked in a breath as though he'd been without oxygen.

He looked up at me with a scrunch of his brow, and then rushed up. He replaced his soaking wet shirt, struggling because of his arm, backed against the rock, and, brow tight, locked his sight on the open space over the quarry.

I had to make sure. I reached across him to his left wrist.

His Adam's apple jumped in his throat.

There were no new cuts but evidence of at least one previous attempt.

With his right hand gripping his shirt to hold his injured arm in place, I gently turned that wrist so I could see it. Same thing.

He stared at a point in the distance.

I brushed the razor blade off the ledge and backed up to the rock wall next to him, and hugging my knees to my chest, adopted the same view.

I searched for something to say. Dad was the Commissioner of Police for over fifteen years. It seemed something I should know how to handle.

I turned my head to him and rested my chin on my shoulder. The longer I looked at him, the more deliberate his breathing became.

His eyes glossed and lips mashed together. He grappled his opposite arm around his legs and buried his face in his knees and sucked at the air as though it would run out.

Shit.

I curled my arm around him and pulled him to me. "Okay. It's okay."

~

I sat with Shawn on the ledge for the rest of the afternoon. He never spoke a word.

I fielded several texts from Josh, within which I told him I'd found the quarry and was with Shawn.

Finally, my phone rang. I lifted it to see who was calling and Shawn lashed it out of my hand and grabbed my wrist to keep me from answering. *Whoa.* His eyes flew wide, his grip tight as he stared at my phone on the rock surface that displayed Dad's name.

Heat flashed through my cheeks as blood rushed to my face. He shook so much that the vibration went through my arm.

"I have to answer it." Surprise choked my voice. "He'll just come find me if I don't. My brother knows where I am."

His eyes were laced with terror as they bore into my phone with brutal intensity, his eyebrows scrunched together like two trains about to crash.

The ringing ended and started again. "Shawn, did you hear what I said?" I wasn't sure he did. "He'll just keep calling until I answer. I promise I won't say anything, but I need to talk to him."

Panic radiated from every line of his body.

His fingers slowly released, his breath expelling in a large rush as his hand hovered over my wrist.

I was surprised my screen didn't crack from the drop. I answered just in time before it stopped ringing again.

"You told me you were going for a walk, Megan."

"I did go for a walk. Now I'm with Shawn."

"I know that, because your brother told me."

"It's not a big deal, Dad." Maybe I should've called, but it wasn't like *nobody* knew where I was.

"It is a big deal. You left over four hours ago and you're alone with a boy I met once."

A boy he'd met once and I was sure Uncle Vance had warned him about. "I'm fine, Dad." Shawn seemed like the last person he had to worry about.

"I want you home."

It was the first time he'd ever given me such an order.

"Meg?"

"Okay." I didn't have a choice. If I didn't agree, he'd just come find me. I ended the call.

Shawn's jaw was locked tight, tension pulsing off him in kilowatt waves. "I'm in a little bit of a tough spot, here," I said, especially after what had just happened. I was pretty sure he wouldn't want me telling anyone, but his reaction to the thought I might was frightening.

His eyes glossed again and his chin quivered.

I'd dropped myself into his life with absolutely no idea of what went on. The only thing I knew for certain was that the day before I feared he might actually throw something at me to get rid of me, and now I'd sat with him for over three hours and gotten a completely different feeling from him.

I turned the ringer on my phone off—any sounds that would alert to an incoming call or text—and placed it down next to him. "My Dad is the last number that called. All you have to do is press send and you'll get the chief of police. If you don't want to talk to him, just tell him I forgot my phone and you're calling to let me know."

His neck constricted with a swallow.

"You need someone you can trust," I said. "We both do." It had been a long time since I'd let anyone in, and I had a feeling he needed someone even more than I did. "You can trust me. And you can definitely trust my dad." I didn't know why he'd asked that day, but I had an idea now. "He's one of the good guys. I promise."

His brow went tight again.

"I need to see you tomorrow. Or hear from you in some form. If I think for one second that you're not okay . . ."

Just a word, *anything*.

I had to leave before Dad called the phone I wouldn't have.

Even if I thought I could ask him to give me a boost to the top, there was no way he would've been able to with only one arm. The only way down was down.

I stood and moved to the edge. "Please don't do anything stupid," I said. "I know I don't know you that well, but I feel like I'd like to. And you made me feel like you wanted me around."

His eyes deflected.

I maintained my game face as what little fingernails I had dug into my palms, and I stepped into the air.

It was like jumping for the first time, the plunge terrifying, the

91

water numbing.

~

The walk home from the quarry sucked. I'd gone there to get away from everything that went on in my head and left with more questions and more uncertainty. I knew before I went I should talk to Dad, now I had even more reason. I'd given Shawn my word, though—something I wished all the way home I hadn't.

I didn't eat dinner, which made Dad suspicious.

"Nothing's wrong," I said from atop my comforter, trying to escape the hassling.

"Boloney, Megan. This is the second night in a row."

"I won't starve."

"I'm not worried about you starving. I'm worried about whatever it is you're not telling me."

I was surprised Josh hadn't said anything. Or maybe he had.

The sun set and I wanted nothing more than to go back to the quarry. If Shawn was even still there. The thought that maybe he'd gone home didn't ease me.

What if he was still there? When was the last time *he'd* eaten? Had I said or done anything to make him rethink whatever ill plans he may have had?

"Can I borrow your phone?" I asked Josh when he came upstairs to go to bed.

"Where's yours?"

"Shawn has it." I hoped, at least.

"You gave Shawn your phone?"

92

I didn't look for conversation. "Please just let me use yours?"

He sighed and handed it to me. "What are you getting yourself into, Meg?"

I'd never seen Shawn with a phone, so I only hoped he knew how to receive a text.

<Hey, it's Megan. Just want you to know I'm thinking about you. See you tomorrow after school.>

Chapter 12

I thought of every possible way to get out of going to school Monday. Dad was already wary, though, and I told Shawn I would see him after. I walked a line with him and didn't want to push myself on him any more than I already had.

My first three classes were a blur.

"Ms. Brennar." My math teacher said my name as if she'd already called it several times. "You'd best start paying attention, or you'll fail for sure."

I tried.

At lunch, I recalled all the times Shawn hadn't been there. How I'd been unable to figure out his schedule, it was so sporadic. I thought he was in some sort of special program, like Vo-tech, but maybe he hadn't been there at all. He'd been out of school for over a week now. What did people assume?

When the bell rang to end the day, I met up with Josh at his locker and hurried him along.

"Chill out, Meg, you're acting all crazy."

"I'm worried about him. You remember what the weather was like Saturday night. He looked like he'd slept out in it."

I'd packed my backpack with extra food and snuck one of Josh's hoodies into it.

We drove to the spot on the side of the road that led to the quarry. Josh pulled the car over and shifted into park. "I really think I should go with you," he said for the umpteenth time.

"You're not going with me. I'll be fine."

He dipped his head and held a steadfast view of me.

"No, Josh."

"Well," he gave in. "Seeing you don't have yours . . ." He handed me his phone. "All I have to say is you might want to be home before Dad gets home."

He worried, and I was grateful for that.

~

It was a dry day. The bright sun picked through the trees, splotching the ground beneath my feet as I walked.

I still didn't know how I'd approach Shawn about what I'd seen—what it seemed like he planned to do. What would I say to him? Would he talk to me? Would he talk at *all*? What if he didn't? At what point did I draw the line and involve Dad? All the sleepless hours I'd spent thinking and I didn't have a single answer for any one of these questions.

I turned a corner and the boulder that marked the halfway point came into sight. And Shawn.

He leaned against the side of the rock, the thumb of his left hand resting in his pants pocket, his right arm held loosely across his waist.

He had on a different shirt, so he must've gone home.

As I neared, he held my phone out to me. "I don't want this."

He waited for me to take it. I did, but with reluctance.

"You're wrong. I don't want you around." He pushed off the rock and moved past me to the path.

Um, what? "Shawn, wait." I followed. "What happened to you? Was it your dad?"

"Don't be thinking you know what's going on, because you don't."

"Shawn, stop." I unzipped my backpack as I rushed to catch up.

He looked back at me. "Stay away from me."

My innards turned to mush. "But what about that day you brought me back to the quarry?"

"It was stupid. I never should've done that."

"It wasn't stupid. You had fun, and so did I."

I caught up with him and took hold of his good arm. He stopped and turned around as I pulled a sketch I'd made for him from my backpack. "I drew this for you." It was of a lighthouse being swallowed by crashing waves. It easily could've been of the Pacific coast, but I'd drawn it because of what he said about New England.

Without looking at it, he took it, crumpled it, and dropped it on the ground. "Stay away from me." He started a brisker walk. "And stay away from my house. Don't you go there again. *Not ever.*"

He picked up his pace as I slowed. The chirping of the birds stopped and everything in view swirled as coldness swelled in me.

Chapter 13

It didn't fail that just as I experienced a small ray of light—the tiniest morsel of hope—I got dropkicked into another black hole of misery.

Where you are is exactly where you're meant to be.

Bull. What had I done to deserve the things that kept happening to me?

As confused and hurt as I was by Shawn, I couldn't just walk away from him and all that had happened.

The words sat in my mouth, ready to tumble out. "Shawn needs help, Dad." Four simple words that would end the anxiety, the worry, and most of all, whatever Shawn went through. At which point, I'd also be able to cut ties with him and move on, because it was evident I'd misread something. Like Shawn said, though, I didn't know what went on, and God forbid I somehow made things worse for him.

If Shawn was in school the following day, he hid well.

On Wednesday, he appeared at the soda machine in the hall, in view of where I sat, got his soda, then disappeared.

Not only had I forced him from the lunchroom, but probably the quarry, too, so if he was going to do something stupid, it most likely wouldn't be there. But I checked anyway. Both days. Because, after all, how could I not?

"C'mon, Megan, you had him on the hook, what happened?" Susan didn't know anything, just watched me mope.

"I don't know, he doesn't like me?"

"He likes you, he has to. He wouldn't have gotten in the car that day if he didn't. I think the problem is he never saw you coming. Just give him time."

Maybe that was it. Maybe he just needed to get used to the idea of me—that someone cared.

~

I tried to read through all the avoiding. It was fruitless. For two and half whole lunch periods, I didn't make it off one page.

I reminded myself of all the things that made me feel Shawn did want me around. He wouldn't have brought me back to the quarry, wouldn't have stripped me of my fear of his favorite place. That *smile*.

The more I thought about what Susan said, the more it made sense. That maybe I'd caught him off guard and now he didn't know how to handle it. Which gave me hope that maybe he didn't actually *mean* to push me away.

The people we encounter are put in our path for a reason.

If it was the case, why me? It was obvious he was suffering, but how was I supposed to know what to do?

God, Mom, I need you. It wasn't something I knew how to navigate on my own.

The one singular experience with him at the quarry motivated me not to give up. Maybe it'd taken a lot for him to get in the car the day we went out on the boat. Maybe it was my responsibility to stay close to him—keep him from bouncing back into isolation. There were plenty of occasions I could've used someone to do the same for me.

It'd been over a week, I needed to do something.

He'd been standing outside the double doors, just out of view from anywhere I could sit.

About ten minutes into lunch, I got up from the table and poked my head out into the hall.

With his once-injured right arm hung by his side, his soda dangling from his fingers, he looked at me, but nothing about him altered.

"Please don't do this," I said.

"Do what?"

"Don't stand out here."

He pushed off the concrete window sill and walked off down the hall.

"That's not what I meant."

~

Josh and I came up on Shawn walking down Center Road as we drove home.

"Do you want me to stop?" he asked.

Why bother? I'd just look like a fool again.

"Yes, no? Hurry up." We were about to pass him.

99

"Yeah, why not?" It wasn't about me.

Josh slowed and I lowered my window. "You want a lift?"

His eyes cut to me as he kept walking, and then faced forward again.

Josh crept alongside him, but he ignored us.

It's just a ride, it won't kill you. Maybe I should've said it out loud.

I put my window back up, and Josh took the cue and stepped on the gas.

I had a dream about him that night. Sitting in a dark room, only his eyes visible from light that seeped in from elsewhere. The feeling he gave off was strong, like in ones I'd had about Mom after she died. It was hard to identify—despair, desperation? Whatever it was, it was overwhelming. All it did was make me think about him more.

~

On Friday, Shawn put his money into the soda machine. He got increasingly aggressive with the button, then punched the machine so hard it was heard from inside the cafeteria. He huffed and walked out of sight. "Fuck off," he said to someone.

Damian entered.

I had a few dollars in my pocket and passed Damian on my way to the hall.

With a reddened face, Shawn's muscles pumped. He avoided looking at me as I straightened a bill against the side of the soda machine and inserted it. Once accepted, I pressed the button for the kind he drank.

Nothing came out, nor was I able to press any other buttons, so I stuck another dollar in and selected the next closest kind. That one dropped to the dispenser. I pulled it out and reached it over to Shawn.

He looked away.

I left it on the sill next to him.

I went back into the cafeteria and told the cashier at the snack stand that the machine ate a five-dollar bill on me. Without question, she gave me a five from her register.

I walked it out to the hall and placed it underneath the soda, and then went back into the cafeteria again.

Damian pounced.

"Seriously, Meg, you don't know what you're doing. That kid's the biggest loser."

I stopped and made direct eye contact with him. "You're an asshole."

"No, I'm not," he said as I walked again. "He just bugs me."

Friday was the only day Damian and I shared the period, and he followed me all the way to the table.

I didn't want him to sit with me, and Shawn didn't come in because of me, so I collected my belongings and walked back out.

"You can go sit down now," I said to Shawn as I passed, feeling less and less like I was supposed to give him time like Susan suggested, and more like an idiot who couldn't take a hint.

Chapter 14

A county fair took place over the weekend, supposedly the first of two held every year. Dad was required to attend, but only by day. Dennis, having been so many times, said the rest of us should wait until evening when the pace picked up. The only way Bobby could go was with Dad.

Josh pushed me to go. "What else are you gonna do, sit home and read?"

"I like reading." It provided a nicely controlled world that gave little chance of letting me down. Unlike an attempt at a relationship with someone who, it had become obvious, didn't want anything to do with me.

"Try living in the real world, sometimes, Meg. It's really not that bad."

"Um, yeah, I tried that. Look what good it did me."

Shawn actually started to feel like a massive mistake. I'd finally somewhat forged the pieces of my heart back together after a colossal blow, and he was crushing it all over again, one confusing stomp after another. And with seemingly no care at all.

"It's a couple hours," Josh said. "Suck it up. Maybe you'll actually have fun."

Dennis planned to meet up with a girl, so he brought his own car. Josh picked up Susan and dragged me along.

The fair was large, with rides and concession stands everywhere. There were two stages set up for bands to play later at night, and there were all kinds of shows and events scheduled to go on all weekend.

It was as if the high school was dumped onto the grounds. There were people I recognized from some of my classes, but none I felt comfortable saying hello to.

We traveled the dirt paths and grassy inlets for a bit until Dennis took off to find the girl. Josh, Susan, and I ended up at one of the concert stages. We kept near the rear of the crowd and sat among exposed tree roots as we listened to a country band play. People danced and sang and had a good time, and I sat scrunched in the cooling air watching as Josh and Susan cuddled.

Just before the show's intermission, Josh suggested we get food. "We should go now, before the stampede."

With the sun on its way down, the lights from the rides sparked a new level of energy. Susan's arm looped through Josh's as we navigated our way back to the front of the grounds where the bulk of the concession stands were.

We rounded a bend near the front entrance and my breath caught. Shawn was tucked back between the corndog and doughboy stand.

He was perched atop a picnic table up against the fence that bordered the parking lot, feet on the bench, elbows on his knees and hands clasped around a bottle of soda. His father leaned against the opposite end of the table, arms hugged across his chest, laughing along with two other men.

I kept him in sight as we continued down the dirt path that would eventually lead us past him.

His field of vision only extended to the surrounding food stands, so even in my bright pink top and a Pebbles ponytail sticking up from the top of my head, he didn't see me pass.

"Oh my God, I so want a candy apple," Susan said, and tugged Josh toward the long line.

He looked back as he was pulled away. "Meg, you want one?"

"Nah. I'll wait here." I sat at an empty picnic table at the edge of the path in Shawn's direct line of sight if he did lift his view.

His father carried on with whatever conversation kept him so entertained. Shawn didn't look at anyone or anything in particular.

A scantily-dressed girl, not much taller than myself but curvier, with a short, dark-burgundy haircut, passed in front of Shawn. With a fresh doughboy in hand, she sat on the tabletop next to him. She ripped off a piece of the fried bread and held it out to him. He didn't take it, so she popped it into her mouth. She said something to him, licked the powdered sugar from her fingers, and then took his soda and drank down nearly half of it.

She looked older, maybe in her twenties, but it was hard to tell, it could've been her excessive makeup.

I didn't want to come to begin with and was now desperate to leave. I looked back to the line for the candy apples. Josh and Susan, still arm in arm, weren't even close to the front yet. Susan, with a jubilant smile, buzzed, and with her cottony hair in a ponytail, Josh lunged at her and bit her neck, and she exploded with laughter.

I looked back to Shawn. His ice-light eyes looked directly at me.

If not for the girl next to him, I might've been able to maintain eye contact. I turned only my eyes. And then my head.

When I looked back, he also looked away.

I stared. I could almost see the girl's chest grow as she inhaled her doughboy. She wore a short jean skirt and, if closer, I probably would've known the color of her underwear.

It became clear, now, that Shawn had only been put in my path to show me just how much more miserable I could actually be.

His dad beamed, engrossed.

I prayed Susan would just forget about her stupid apple.

As much as it pained me to look, I couldn't help myself.

It was torture.

I did it to myself. *Just give up, Meg. Tell Dad your concerns and move on.*

A set of elbows landed on the tabletop next to me and a heavy sigh was bestowed upon my ear.

Damian. Again.

He straddled the bench next to me. "Seriously, Pretty in Pink, why you wasting your time on that fag?" He gushed arrogance. "He's a fucking loser. He's trailer trash."

105

"*Wow.*"

My wide-eyed response didn't seem to faze him. "At least I'm not sitting on my ass over there, ignoring you. Cute little thing like you should be having fun."

I looked to the line again. *Please, Josh, turn around.*

"You're at a fair, with all kinds of stuff to do, and you're sitting by yourself trying to get that scumbag's attention."

"You need to get a life," I said.

"C'mon. I've got a hundred bucks in my wallet. Let me show you a good time."

"Seriously. I'm not interested. Please leave."

He stared at me as if he tried to determine how to proceed.

His eyes narrowed. "That's it, isn't it? You screwed him. He got what he wanted, then bounced."

I'd never met anyone so crude. It came from his mouth with the ease of a breath.

"You did not really just say that."

He obviously wasn't going to follow my request, so I stood and started toward Josh and Susan.

He grabbed my wrist.

I yanked away before he could get a firm grasp and pushed through the crowd toward the candy apple line.

He followed right behind. "I'm sorry, I didn't mean that." He grabbed at me again, this time succeeding and pulling me to a stop.

"God, am I safe *nowhere*? Let go of me." I ripped my forearm from his clutching fingers.

Shawn walked toward us, his strides full of purpose. He came up fast.

Damian turned to him and retreated backward, throwing his arms out as if calling him on. "You fucked her, didn't ya? Had to go and ruin her."

Jaw tight, Shawn charged at him. He slung his arm back and catapulted his fist into Damian's face.

Damian's body twisted and he dropped to the ground.

A squeal burst from me as Shawn landed on top of him. *Shit, shit, shit, shit, shit!*

The two became locked together so tight there was no room for punches as they rolled across the matted grass. A crowd quickly encircled them.

Shawn, on top, lifted and started swinging.

Shielding his face with his arms, Damian rolled and got in some shots of his own.

People swarmed from all over. Nobody made any attempts to jump in or break it up, not even Dennis across the crowd from me.

Adrenaline masked any remaining signs of Shawn's shoulder injury as the two pummeled each other with frightening brutality.

"*Stop*," I kept shouting. "Both of you, *stop!*"

I was nearly knocked to the ground by Mr. Harris as he pushed through. He grabbed Damian by the back of his shirt and ripped him off Shawn. He threw him aside as though he was weightless, then turned back to Shawn on the ground and pulled him up with his concrete arms.

Mr. Harris stood between the two boys and cast a terrifying glare at

Damian. "Get outta here, *bastard!*"

"*Fuck* you!" Damian's scowl was severe, his nose dripping blood.

Mr. Harris started toward Damian, and Damian backed up.

"*Bastard,* huh?" Damian stared at the man for several tense seconds. He finally gave in and turned to walk away, but not before imparting one last dirty look.

Mr. Harris turned back to Shawn.

Shawn lunged at him, sending his palms hard into his chest. "*Ass*hole."

There was a gasp from the crowd as Mr. Harris fell steps back, but he didn't retaliate.

Shawn pushed through the tangle of onlookers. Mr. Harris stood with his hands on his hips, head hung.

He eventually followed, ending his laughter-filled night by waving off his friends who relished in an opportunity to heckle him.

Susan, without a candy apple, was first to make it to me. "Whoa."

"What was that?" Astonishment painted Josh's face.

"I've seen them fight before," Susan said. "But that was insane. They looked like they were gonna kill each other."

"Did you see the way Shawn shoved his dad?" Dennis asked.

Josh looked to me again.

I couldn't make sense of it. Nor could I handle anymore. "Can we please just go?"

~

"Just tell me Shawn won," Bobby said, bent about missing the excitement, trying to re-live it through Josh and me.

"Bob . . ." He was far too eager.

"No, seriously, just tell me he did."

Nothing made sense. Not only did Shawn fly to my rescue after putting so much effort into avoiding me, if his father was the one who hurt him, how would Shawn get away with pushing him the way he did?

It was a bizarre relationship, and the more I thought about it, the heavier I felt.

At a quarter to one in the morning, as I lay still awake in my dark room, my phone on top of my nightstand alerted me to an incoming text. The number was one I'd never seen.

`<Go to the quarry in the morning>`

I read the one line several times before responding.

Chapter 15

I half wondered if the reason Shawn wanted me to meet him at the quarry was so he could try to convince me not to say anything to anybody about whatever I'd witnessed. In any case, an unexpected thread of hope wound around me when I met him. I was going to hang onto it with everything I had, no matter how frayed it got.

Josh didn't want me to go. At least not alone. "You don't know that text came from him."

"Who else would it be from?" Though I was surprised Shawn had my number. He must've taken it from my phone when he had it the one night.

"I don't know, Damian? Shawn's dad? Two people who are making me really nervous right now."

It was something I hadn't thought of, and I didn't want to dismiss his worry, but I was sure the text was from Shawn. "He's expecting me, Josh. Not me and one of my big brothers. Everything I do pushes him further away."

"If he doesn't understand why I'm there, Meg, then he's not some-one you should be hanging out with."

I didn't disagree, but there were extenuating circumstances.

"I'll leave as soon as I know it's him."

If I didn't allow it, I'd be dealing with Dad.

~

Shawn sat in the grass near the edge of the ravine, arms hugged around his knees. When he saw us coming, he jumped to his feet. His hands went to his rear pockets as his sight landed first on Josh, and then me with a loud exhale through his nose.

"He didn't want me to come alone," I said. "He just wanted to make sure it was you." For as much as he and Damian had beaten on each other, it was hard to tell anything happened. "It's him," I said to Josh.

"I see that."

"So, you can go."

He looked at Shawn. "I just want you to know I'm not comfortable with this." He apparently spared me by not adding him to the list of people making him nervous. "I don't know what's going on, because she won't say. But we hung out that day, and you seemed pretty cool." He peered at him. "Can I trust you?"

Shawn's eyes evaded. He finally looked at him, his brow tense, and nodded.

"I don't know you," Josh said. "I need an address, a phone number . . . something." He sounded like a worried father. It could've been worse had he told him he already knew where he lived.

Shawn huffed, avoiding eye contact again.

"Is that number you texted her from a way to reach you?"

Shawn's eyes darted to him. "It's a pre-paid. There aren't a lot of minutes on it."

Josh pulled his wallet from his back pocket, drew out a twenty, and held it out to him. "Add some."

Shawn's hands remained in his pockets.

The longer Josh held the money in front of him, the tighter Shawn's expression became.

I took the bill from Josh and cued him to leave. He hesitated, but finally turned for the trees.

"I'm sorry," I said to Shawn.

"Nobody knows I have that phone. He can't call it. I don't leave it on." His words were rushed.

"It's okay. I'll make sure he doesn't call." I held the twenty out to him. "You can still add minutes, though."

He didn't even attempt to take it.

He shook his head. "I got in the car that day and I shouldn't have."

The day we went out on the boat. "But you did."

"But I shouldn't have."

"But you *did*."

He dropped his head back and sucked in a breath that seemed like it could pull a cloud from the sky.

"And I'm glad you did."

He breathed deeply enough I knew I had him on the line.

112

"I didn't want to move here because I didn't know what to expect. And I hated it when I got here. Now there's not a thing I would change. Because of you." Just like *One Thousand Reasons* said, I'd started to believe there really was a reason for it all.

Shawn tipped his head back to me. "But you don't know me."

"But I want to."

"Why? How do you know that?"

I shrugged. "Just a feeling. A really strong one."

He looked away, his jaw tight.

"For whatever reason you don't think you should've gotten in the car, you did, and there's no way of going back. Maybe we could try moving forward?"

There was movement to his eyes, but they still faced the trees that lined the clearing.

"What about over?" I motioned my arm toward the ledge. "It's your favorite spot, and thanks to you, I'm not afraid of it."

He exhaled as though he'd been holding his breath, and then removed his hands from his back pockets and clutched his arms across his chest. "Fuck it." He headed in the direction.

With his hands gripping his shoulders, his black T-shirt pulled taut and every strained muscle of his back boasted as I followed behind.

He lowered to the ground and dropped to the narrow shelf, and planted himself where he'd sat the last time.

It didn't get any easier allowing myself to fall to such a small area so high up. A lot of pebbles landed before I did.

Shawn's gaze across the open space to the thriving foliage was just as focused as before. I scrunched down next to him and made myself as small as I could in the tight space.

At least he didn't move away.

"You must've had a reason for texting me to come here."

He'd let himself be talked into sitting with me, so as punishment, he wouldn't speak. Or maybe I'd switched gears on him too much. All I had was my original thought. "I didn't say anything to anybody."

Nothing.

"I wanted to, though. Really bad."

"You *can't*."

"Tell me why."

"I can't tell you why, you just can't."

If I pushed him, I'd be left on the ledge alone. "Shawn, even if my father wasn't who he is, I'm not someone who can just turn and look the other way."

He made a sharp turn of his head to me. "I am *begging* you to turn and look the other way."

I was petrified of saying or doing something that would make him shut down again.

Just for one thing to make sense. *Anything.* "Who was that girl last night?" It seemed an easy enough question to answer.

"What gir— Why are you *doing* this?"

There was nothing in my tone that should've put him on guard. "Doing what?"

"Pumping me."

"I'm not pumping you." I felt bad he thought so. "I don't know

114

how else to interact with you other than to ask questions. I'm just trying to get to know you."

He looked away.

I leaned forward again to try to reel his eyes back. "I can't believe I'm saying this out loud, but . . . I like you." It seemed something he should've figured out by now, but maybe the other stuff he had going on blinded him. "I like you a lot." I was almost glad he didn't look at me now as heat raced across my cheeks. "That day you brought me back here, I felt like you liked me too. Everything that's happened since has been . . . ," for lack of a better word, "confusing?"

He swallowed.

Not even as much as a finger moved.

"What was that with your dad? You pushed him pretty hard."

He attempted to look at me but couldn't hold his view. "You need to back off."

How was I supposed to do that? After everything I'd seen. "I don't know if I can."

"You have to."

I apparently needed to spell it out. I reached up and, with the tips of my fingers, drew on his chin until his eyes faced me. "It's called caring," I said in a whisper.

His pupils were pinholes in the bright light. His chest rose and fell with short breaths, his mouth a small, fixed hole in his face.

I dropped my hand and he turned his head to face forward.

What was he so afraid of? Did he think I bit? Or was it the idea of letting me in?

Maybe a subject change would help. Or at least stimulate some sort of dialogue. "So, what's up with you and Damian? Why does he have it out for you so bad?"

He leaned his head back against the rock. "Because he's my brother." He covered his eyes with his arms.

What? What, what, what, what, what, what, WHAT?

He glanced at me from underneath his arms. "What's wrong, cat got your tongue?"

Something had it. "Full or half?"

"Half." His tone was resigned.

It wasn't what I expected, but it was conversation. I replayed the events of the night before. "Did your mom cheat on your dad, or something?" Mr. Harris was less than kind to Damian. Maybe he was the result of an affair.

"Nope, we have the same dad."

Wow. "Then why does your dad treat him like that?"

He shrugged. "Because he's an asshole?"

It was his answer for everything—because he's an asshole. What was so hard about looking at me? "And, so, what, Damian takes it out on you?"

He nodded and dropped his arms. "That, and I suppose he blames me for breaking up his family, seeing our dad was fooling around on his mom, then I came along."

So, Shawn was the result of an affair. It must've been one of the reasons, aside from me, that Damian called him a thief.

"Doesn't matter. Damian was just as much of a dick before we

116

found out."

"So, you haven't always known?"

"Only known a few years."

"How'd you find out?"

"Mary—" He eyed me as if I'd tricked him somehow, and he huffed. "My mom was pissed at my dad one night and trashed. She told me, then went to Damian." His posture loosened, and he started in on the scattering of twigs between his legs, breaking them. "You ever seen his house?"

"Whose, Damian's?" I shook my head.

"He ain't got nothing to complain about. His mom's really nice, his stepdad is some councilman, or something . . ."

He was apparently done and it was my turn to say something.

"Who was that girl last night?" I tried again. I could barely get him to look at me, but he'd shared his soda with her.

Now he did look at me, brow cinched. "*What girl?*"

"The one w—"

"Beth?"

If that was her name. "The one with the doughboy." There were plenty other things I could've said—big boobs, tight skirt, probably be able to see her underwear if she bent over.

"Yeah, Beth."

"Is she a friend?"

He gave an awkward, almost unsure shrug. "She's Beth."

"How do you know her?"

"She's been around awhile."

117

"In what capacity? Big sister, housemaid, secretary for the garage?"

He half glanced at me. "My dad keeps her around."

I wasn't sure what that meant. "For what?"

He looked at me with a frown for a split second, then his eyes came again. "You know, for . . ." He gestured with his head.

"For?" I didn't know. And then something in my brain sparked. "Oh." How stupid could I be? "You mean, for, like . . ." I didn't want to say the word sex.

"Yeah."

The information curdled something in me. She looked so young. And she hadn't hung with Shawn's dad at the fair, she'd hung with him. "How old is she?"

"Twenty-two."

His father had to have been close to forty. And she'd been around awhile? It made his comment to me even creepier.

"She doesn't really like him, but . . ."

"But what?"

Shawn looked at me and back to the open space above the water. "Wow."

I admit I was slow on this one. "Is she a prostitute? Does he pay her?"

Shawn breathed a laugh. "I was getting a little worried, there, for a minute."

I was so dumb. "What about you? Does she like you?" It was a scary place to venture to. I wasn't even really sure what my question was, but they were much closer in age and seemed pretty comfortable

118

with each other.

He made quick but brief eye contact. "It's not like that." He shook his head. "We get along. It's just nice to feel like somebody's got my back." *Please don't stop there. Please say more.* "You know, how she can say the same thing I do and not get cracked for it." He eyed me with a half grin. "She drives him nuts."

As odd as it was to me, it didn't come off as seeming strange to him at all. Shawn's life wasn't average, I knew that going in.

A breeze swept through, its soft murmur sedating.

"What was your mom like?" I couldn't imagine any stable mother leaving their child in such a situation.

"Terrible." He'd taken to throwing the twig bits off the ledge. "The word mother doesn't apply to her."

"Worse than your dad?" It was how he made it sound.

He stopped mid-toss of a twig, appearing as if he stared into a memory.

"Tell me about her."

He was quiet long enough I wasn't sure he would.

"My mother was a cunt." The name of all names. The "C" word. Bobby lost his phone for a week once for using that word. His head swayed. "There wasn't a day that went by I can remember that she didn't hit me . . . kick me, throw something at me." His gaze didn't extend very far as he spoke to the air. "My parents hated each other. My dad was never around. Truly, I don't know how I even came about. Not once did I ever see them sleep in the same bed together. Every single fucking day she'd tell me just how much I ruined her life."

119

His eyes were stuck.

He was stuck, as if he relived her.

He looked down at the ledge and started in again on the scattering of twigs. "Mary liked to drink. It'd be easier to excuse if she was drunk all the time, but the worst moments from her were when she was stone cold fucking sober." He glanced my way for a split second. "When I was little, she would do this thing where she'd sit there and have me stand in front of her. I'd have to stand so perfect—like I was a little soldier. She'd hold her hand out flat—like this—" He held his palm out with his fingers to the sky. "Then all of a sudden, ram it into my chest. If I budged from my position, she'd come again." He stopped to take a breath. "The woman would go all fucking day. I was all of forty fucking pounds, how was I not gonna budge?"

He stopped again.

"When you're little, you don't know that stuff is wrong," he said. "You do what your parents tell you to. You don't question them."

"It is wrong." In case he needed the reassurance.

He snuck a peek at me.

"What was your dad like then?"

"Like I said, he wasn't around. Always found other places to be. It was just me and her all the time." He looked down when he ran out of debris and swept more into reach. "She'd never leave marks on me. None that anyone would ever be able to see, at least."

"There was this one time when I was about seven that I got sick at school. Just sick. A fever. Nothing big. But they called her to come get me. I don't know if they were too vague on the phone, or what.

She took so long to get there, I was surprised she even showed up. Then I wished she hadn't. She thought I'd said something." He gazed. "She realized she could play my illness for a few days—maybe even a week or two. She beat the living friggin' daylights out of me that afternoon. I spent the next three days locked in the closet." His fingers stopped as he stared into the air again.

"Your dad didn't do anything?"

"He wasn't *home.*"

"Not for three days?"

"He wasn't *ever* home. *Never.*" It was hard to tell if he was angry at me for not understanding or his dad for not being there. "It was only when he popped in for five minutes that I was let out."

"And he was okay with it?"

He forced out a breath and his head shook, the right side of his mouth going crooked in an expression I didn't know what to make of.

After moments of silence, I figured it was the end of his story. "What did he do?" I asked in a low voice.

"Put her in the closet. He made me dinner, and then left again. Then it was up to me to decide when to let her out."

The look of question I displayed didn't need words.

"Stupid me let her out as soon as he was gone."

"Why?"

"Because she was my mother."

As awful as she was to him, there was still a bond. I wanted nothing more than to reach out and hug him. "Did it ever let up?"

He shook his head.

121

"You got older. Bigger."

"Yeah." His voice was strangled. "When I got older, she wanted to play different games." He circled his head around to face opposite me.

"She didn't." He hinted at something of a sexual nature. I took hold of his arm to turn him back, but he shirked away and squirmed. "I'm sorry." I was unable to see his face, and there was a shake to his breath when he inhaled.

As angry as I already was with what he told me, the idea of what he implied made me want to deck the woman.

"Please don't ask anymore," he said.

I dared just one more question. "How old were you?"

He took in a full breath and let it out. "Thirteen." He rested his elbow on his knee and leaned his head into his palm so I couldn't see his eyes.

I paired his birthday of October tenth with the February date he told me she left. Without forcing another question on him, I deduced that his mother had molested him, or at least tried, for, at most, four months.

"Shawn . . . how did you know how deep this quarry was? I mean, the first time you jumped from here?"

The muscles of his neck constricted.

I'd gotten a glimpse through a crack in him and it broke my heart. "How many times have you tried to kill yourself?"

I could tell by his breathing he fought not to cry. Again, I wanted to hug him, but I was afraid to touch him.

122

With his eyes facing the opposite direction, he dropped his face to his knees.

I locked my arms around my own legs, waiting. I didn't know how to proceed.

The silence weighed like an elephant.

I touched my hand to his back and he flinched.

Keeping his view far from me, he made a move to stand. "I'm gonna go." His voice was so low I barely heard him.

I stood and blocked his exit. "I don't want you to."

He stared past me to the rock wall.

Good idea or not, I reached for his hand. He jerked it away.

I reached out and took it again, holding it tighter. His jaw clenched and breaths deepened. "Please don't go."

His brow rumpled. It eased and rumpled again, a few times, as if his thoughts battled.

He turned his eyes down to me with a hard swallow. He drew in a sudden breath and leaned down and forced his lips against mine so hard I fell a step back.

He backed away and looked at me as if awaiting a reaction.

He took hold of my arm and pulled me to him, and he moved in again and his tongue pushed into my mouth. It trembled against mine, his grip on me tight.

He stepped back and viewed me again.

I was in shock. I had nothing. It was a kiss, I thought. His tongue was involved, and it had a suck sound when he pulled out of it.

He lifted the hand I still held and wove his fingers through mine.

He did the same with the other.

With his chin high, as if not to allow himself to look directly at me, he slanted his eyes down at me. "The town's having a celebration thing next weekend. They're gonna have fireworks. Do you . . . maybe . . . wanna come here and watch 'em with me?"

Yes! Yes, absolutely! Then we can practice that kiss! I think I nodded. I definitely smiled.

Chapter 16

I was going to burst from so many feelings at once. Who ever would've thought the conversation Shawn and I had would lead to him kissing me. Or at that point that *anything* would lead to him kissing me.

Whether it was the awkwardness of it, or something else, he still insisted he needed to leave. He walked me out of the woods first, though.

"So, did you . . . really draw that picture?" he asked, strolling leisurely.

I nodded, surprised he brought it up.

"Well . . . it's really good."

I didn't think he'd seen it.

He glanced at me as if to make sure I heard him. "Really."

"Thanks." He'd taken me completely off guard. Had he gone back and gotten it? I reveled in the idea that he had.

"So, drawing, is that, like, your thing?"

"Yeah. I guess." It'd been so long since I felt like it was. "I used to be really into it, but then my mom died and I just kind of lost interest." Though hearing him call it my "thing" did light me up inside.

"Well, it definitely doesn't look like something you should lose interest in." He eyed me again. "For real."

The words shot straight to my heart. I was already spinning from the kiss, now I risked floating away.

"So, do you have a 'thing'?" I asked. I expected him to say cars or mechanics of some sort.

He looked as though he gave it thought, and then shook his head. "No."

"C'mon, everybody has something."

After another moment of pause, he shrugged. "Not me."

The road came into view, and Josh's car. Shawn slowed and his posture stiffened.

"He's a friend," I said. "You don't have to worry about him, I promise."

"So, how'd you make out?" Josh asked from the driver's seat through the open passenger window, trying to be nonchalant by not looking up from the screen of his phone.

I slipped my fingers through Shawn's and turned into him with a squeezing hug. He didn't have a chance to stop me. "See you tomorrow?" I asked as I pulled away.

With hollowed cheeks, he nodded.

I got into the car, and hands in his front pockets, Shawn started across the street in the direction of County Road.

"You want a ride, Shawn?" Josh called to him.

"No." He spun back around. "Thank you."

"So, what happened?" Josh turned the key in the ignition.

"Don't call his phone. His dad doesn't know he has it."

"Did he take the money?"

"No."

"Make sure he does." He looked at me to make sure I agreed.

"Thank you." He really was the best brother a girl could ask for. "That kid has got a lot going on."

"Are you going to tell me about any of it?"

I shook my head.

"Anything Dad should know about?"

The stuff Shawn told me happened in the past, I still didn't know what went on now, so I couldn't answer for sure. Though I was pretty positive the answer would be yes.

When I only stared out the windshield, Josh shifted the car into drive.

~

Shawn sat with me at lunch. He wasn't distant, but he didn't seem to know how to interact with me. He didn't speak unless I spoke to him, and he had a hard time looking at me.

"I'm not gonna eat all this," I said as I pushed my lunch in front of him. I'd never seen him with more than just the soda.

"I'm fine."

I continued taking bites, feeling awkward with his awkwardness, and he looked at me a couple times in a fashion as though I wasn't supposed to see—as if noticing me for the first time.

When the bell rang, he stayed seated like he didn't know what to do.

I collected my belongings and stood. "Do you want to walk me to class?" I boasted a suggestive smile.

"I have to go to Guidance."

"I can walk with you . . ." I'd be late getting back to English, but it'd be worth it.

He didn't verbally answer but walked at my pace. The cafeteria was just about empty when we exited.

Shawn's long legs usually carried him farther faster, but he slowed for my much shorter ones. With his half-full soda in his right hand, and me walking on his left side, I tugged on the thumb that didn't quite make it into his back pocket with the rest of his fingers. He eased his hand out and I laced my fingers through his.

It was a loose hold. His hand nearly swallowed mine. His palm was soft, but in a hard kind of way, worked, used.

It was too short of a walk. I slowed when we came up on the door to the guidance office. He kept on. "See you tomorrow," he said as my fingers slipped from his.

The following day, I invited him over after school.

"Nah, I got a lot to do."

I wasn't sure I believed him.

At lunch on Wednesday, he held a solid view of me. Hunched with his elbows on his knees, there was nothing to his expression, just a hard stare.

"What?" I couldn't help but be self-conscious.

"I'm not gonna see you tomorrow."

We didn't share a lunch period on Thursday. "You will if you come over."

His expression didn't change.

"C'mon, it's not a big deal. It's just Josh and Bobby. Probably Susan because she comes over, like, every day."

His eyes penetrated.

Chapter 17

Handscapes. The final assessment Miss Devereaux chose to combine our previous lessons on the basics of drawing. The idea was to draw realistic hands in a fantasy "scape."

It was the first assignment I got excited about. I prided myself on my ability to draw hands and knew exactly what I wanted to do. It would wait, though—it was too private to share. I looked on my phone quickly to get an idea for an alternate for the class, and settled on one that would satisfy the assignment, while also giving the illusion of 3D.

"Wow, Megan." Miss Devereaux studied it. "That's incredible. How did you come up with that?"

The internet. I could've thought of something just as good on my own but was too caught up thinking about my original idea.

"With your permission," she said, "I'd really like to showcase your work in the art show."

She'd talked about the art show plenty. It was at the end of the year. Everyone would have something displayed, but by the sound of it, she wanted to spotlight mine. "Why me?" There were others who drew well.

"The depth and imagination in your illustrations go beyond what's typical of someone your age."

Lots of people were just as creative. Besides, she said it while looking at something based on someone else's idea. "I don't think I'm any different than anybody else."

"I beg to differ. When I assign a project, most people stumble over ideas and need a lot of direction. For you, it's effortless. You're a natural, and it shows in your work."

Again, she said it while raving about something I'd taken from the internet. Though she'd said similar things in the past.

I was a little freaked out by the idea, but the drawings I'd done for class were all pretty superficial. Nothing that gave away anything about me, so . . . "I guess."

"I'd be open to including some of your personal stuff," she said with hope. "I can only imagine what you work on in your spare time."

It went against the entire reason I agreed. "Um, I'd rather not."

"Okay." Her disappointment was evident. "If you change your mind, just let me know. If nothing else, I'd love to see some of it."

I wouldn't change my mind. Nor would she—or anybody else outside of Susan—ever see any of it.

Once I got home, I went to town on my original assignment idea. Shawn had gorgeous hands.

One drawing led to another. And another.

He never did come over.

~

"Are we still on for the fireworks tomorrow?" I asked Shawn at lunch on Friday.

He nodded. "They start at quarter past nine."

I still needed to find a way around Dad. He wanted me to actually attend the event. My hope was he'd be too distracted to notice I left. If not, Josh would be forced to supervise my "date."

"Maybe we can meet earlier," I suggested. Fireworks didn't last very long, and I could see him walking me back to the road right after. Or Dad looking for me.

"Eight thirty?"

I hoped for even earlier. "What about eight?"

"I have to work at the garage."

I didn't doubt it, but until eight? I didn't push it.

~

There were more people at the town birthday celebration than I expected. It wasn't like the fair, it was more formal.

With his hand on my shoulder, Dad walked me from cluster to cluster of folk introducing me to people, many of whom offered their name before Dad had a chance to show he'd forgotten it.

If asked a year prior if I ever expected to see him in such a scenario, I would've said never. If asked if I'd ever imagine such a wide and genuine grin on his face, I wouldn't have known how to answer, for I'd forgotten what it looked like.

132

Once finished and he was needed to fulfill demands, I slipped away.

I was surprised Shawn didn't meet me somewhere nearer so I didn't have to walk so far so close to dark.

I went to the edge of the ravine where I first viewed the quarry from. He was next to the fall on the ledge.

I wore shorts and the tall grass tickled my legs. When I approached, he stood. I lowered to the ground, and he reached up and clamped his hands around my waist as I slid.

His grip was strong. I imagined by the sting in my cheeks that I blushed. "Thanks."

We sat down together, him with his knees bent to the sky as always, I with my legs crossed.

I looked at my phone. "Eight twenty-six. I'm early."

His mouth quirked upward. "It's okay."

"So, how are you doing?" It was a question I didn't feel like I could ask at school, but here anything went.

There was the barest of movement to his head. "Good."

"Your dad was at the celebration."

"I know. He goes to everything."

With his wrists resting on his knees, I scooted closer. I reached up slowly enough he had time to stop me if he wanted to, and pulled at his pinky. I secured his hand and pushed my fingers through his just as I did when we walked to the guidance office and rested the bundle in my lap.

A peeking ray of sun lit us on its way to the horizon, turning Shawn's blond hair gold. I squeezed his hand. "I really like being with you."

His mouth contorted, and then opened as if he would say something. "Can I hold you?"

Every bit of me smiled. "Definitely."

He released his hand from mine and reached his arm around my neck. With his fingers closed into a fist, he didn't know where to place his hand. I pulled his arm tighter and eased his hand open so I could hold it again, this time with both of mine.

The embossed skin of where he'd once cut his wrist dominated my vision.

Shawn rested his head back and closed his eyes. The sun dipped out of sight and I lay my head on his shoulder.

If this was what first love felt like, I never wanted second. Being near him made my insides flutter, being held by him made my heart do flips.

The first firework shot off. It boomed high in the sky, white, with trailing ribbons of sizzling light.

The second, green and red, like Christmas.

We had an incredible view. The third banged, and blue flickered.

Shawn's eyes remained closed. I massaged his hand. "You're missing the show."

"No, I'm not."

Twenty minutes of kaleidoscopic explosions and he never once opened his eyes.

When the grand finale started, he looked down at me. Every color of the rainbow reflected in his eyes.

If only I could read his thoughts, just once.

It was the most prolonged opportunity I'd gotten to search through the windows of his soul. I couldn't make it past the guardians that were his light irises.

I willed him to kiss me. And willed him and willed and willed him. He just stared.

Maybe he willed me.

It was do or die. I moved my leg for footing and stretched up to his lips.

It was a quick kiss, my positioning wasn't good, and soft, nothing that would throw him off balance like the one he'd planted on me.

He didn't turn away, he didn't back up, he didn't react at all.

If it was going to happen, it was apparently up to me. With my left hand still holding his, I reached under his hair to the back of his neck with my right for support.

I'd never kissed anyone, never practiced in the mirror or on my hand. I captured his bottom lip between mine. He took my top, and then we did the same thing again, his eyes half-lidded.

His breath, warm and trembling, passed between my lips as his tongue entered my mouth. Tentative and testing, it found mine and lingered against it.

I pressed with mine, his pressed back, and a strange but amazing sensation erupted in me.

We were in an awkward position to begin with and our noses bumped. He tilted his head and forced his tongue harder against mine. With gentle power, pausing every so often to take a breath, his tongue masterfully ruled my mouth. It was nothing like the week before when he blitzed me. His hand in mine clutched as the other held the back of my head, and the tingling deep in my lower belly surged.

It lasted for what seemed like forever, long after the fireworks ended.

Shawn lifted out of the kiss, his hand lowering to the back of my neck, and he leaned his head against the rock.

His gaze returned.

It was dark, but the moon was bright and his eyes glowed.

What was it he searched so hard for? I was an open book. "Talk to me."

"I can't."

"You can." Maybe if he stared a little longer.

And that's what he did. His eyes were the darkest I'd seen them with his pupils so big. They were entirely less intimidating.

I drew his hand from the back of my neck and rested my cheek against his palm. "What are you thinking about?" I asked.

"I don't want to say."

"This will be a pretty dull relationship if you don't ever speak." I smiled.

He combed his fingers through my hair, his expression intense.

He leaned in and touched his lips to mine—soft, gentle—an utterly tender and sincere moment.

"When do you have to go?" he asked.

My phone next to me buzzed and Dad's name appeared on the lit screen. "Probably now." I picked it up. "Hello?" I answered in a voice as if not to wake a sleeping baby.

"I've been looking for you since the fireworks. Where are you?"

"I'm with Shawn. He knew of a place with a really good view."

"Okay. Where is this place?"

"Not too far." A bit of a lie.

"I want to know where, Meg, and I want to know now."

"Please don't worry, Dad, I'm fine."

"It's ten thirty and pitch black out. Tell me where you are so I can come get you."

"Dad, please. Can't Shawn just get me home?"

"Why do you sound funny?"

The only reason I sounded funny was because I spoke quietly. "I'm fine," I said again. "Please just let Shawn walk me home?"

His breaths were loud.

"Let me talk to Shawn."

I handed my phone over. "I'm sorry," I lipped. I didn't even know if he wanted to walk me home.

"Hello?" Shawn said.

"Young man . . . I'm relying on my daughter's good judgment of character right now as she asks for such a hard-to-fulfill request." I could hear every word. "Do you promise to get her home safely?"

"Yes, sir, I promise."

"Are you driving, walking?"

"Walking."

"Eleven thirty should be plenty of time, then, if you leave now."

It was more than enough time. The place where the town celebration

137

took place was farther from home than the quarry.

"Yes, sir, it will be."

"Okay, let me talk to my daughter again."

Shawn handed my phone back.

"Thank you, Dad."

"Eleven thirty, Megan. Not a minute past."

"Got it." I ended the call. "I'm sorry," I said to Shawn. "I never even asked you if you wanted to walk me."

"It's okay, I will." He didn't seem to mind, but it also didn't sound like it had been a thought.

He rested his head against the rock again. I think he could've looked into my eyes all night long and been content. He looked down for the slightest of seconds as he picked up my hand and rubbed his thumb over my palm. Whatever it was he found so intriguing about me, he utilized every last moment.

I was just as content with the view I had.

"We should go." I didn't need to give Dad any reason not to let it happen again.

~

We started through the dark woods and Shawn took hold of my hand, folding his fingers around mine.

"How do you know where you're going?" I asked, adjusting our hands, threading our fingers. I couldn't see a foot in front of us.

"Second nature. I do it all the time. Just be careful not to trip." His hand was strong, ready to catch me if I did.

We came up on the rock at the halfway point and my phone in my back pocket buzzed again. A text from Josh.

`<Dad's asking questions. Be prepared.>`

At the edge of the woods, just before we hit the road, Shawn stopped me. He turned into me and, holding my head firmly in place, hit me with another kiss. It was heavier, harder, filled with confidence, as if he'd done it a thousand times. Not only did he own it, I don't think I could've gotten out of it if I wanted to.

He lifted his lips away and doubled his arms around my neck. "Thank you."

~

Dad stood in the doorway, concern wrinkling his forehead as Shawn and I walked hand in hand up the driveway. I prayed he trusted me enough not to push the issue. I glanced to Shawn. "Good night." Our hands parted, and I stepped up the two stone steps and tried to walk through Dad.

He deflected me and guided me in the door. "Would you like a ride home, Shawn?" he asked.

"No, thank you, sir."

"It's almost midnight. Would you like a ride home?" He tried to steer him into saying yes.

Shawn shook his head. "No, thank you," he declined again.

"Would you like to come in?"

"Unh-unh"

Josh had said something.

"Shawn, do you want to come in?" he asked again with the same suggestion.

"No, sir."

The more Dad went on, the more scared off Shawn would get.

Dad stared at him. Shawn's eye contact was stellar.

"You're welcome to come by any time."

"Okay. Thank you, sir."

"Any time. Don't be a stranger."

Shawn nodded.

"Even come by tomorrow if you like."

He nodded again. "Night, sir." He turned and started off.

Dad shut the door and I fully expected the fifth degree. He turned to me with a full inhale and looked down his nose at me as he let it out. And then walked away.

Chapter 18

A knock on my bedroom door first thing in the morning woke me. Birds called outside my open window and bright sunlight shone through my light-colored curtains. "Wake up." Josh's voice pulled me the rest of the way from my slumber. I blinked him into view as he stood in the crack of my doorway waiting for me to come to. "Shawn's downstairs and Dad's cooking him pancakes."

"*What?*" There was no way I heard him right. "Hey," I called when he disappeared, and he came back. "What'd you say to Dad last night?"

"Sorry, Meg. I did my best. I'm not good at lying. I told him Shawn was a 'troubled youth.' Not in the sense that he's dangerous, or anything, but more the 'Megan feels the need to help him' kind of way."

It could've been worse. It was actually probably a good response. Now I would have Dad's help. He knew how to be tactful.

I was all the way to the stairs when I realized I needed to put a bra on.

Still in my pajamas and who knew what kind of bed head, I rushed down to the kitchen. Shawn sat at the small, round table, syrup-covered pancakes in front of him and fork in hand, and Dad stood at the stove, dressed as if it was a weekday, flipping more in a pan.

It wasn't even nine o'clock.

Shawn stopped chewing and looked at me. I was in clothes he was never supposed to see me in, and even with a bra on, I stood with my arms hugged across my chest.

Amusement played across Dad's face. "Go get dressed, Meg."

I dashed back upstairs. I didn't take time picking out what I put on. I ran my brush through my hair and rushed back down.

Shawn's muffled voice, followed by Dad's. Then Josh's.

They all sat around the kitchen table together, eating.

Whatever went through Josh's head, he played it off well, as if Dad cooking breakfast was a common occurrence.

"You want to think about what to have for dinner, Meg?" Dad asked me as I entered. "I'll stop at the market on the way home if need be."

"Are we not doing the cookout thing?" I got a plate from the pile on the kitchen counter. We had a cookout every Sunday afternoon with Uncle Vance and Dennis and Kenny. Dad and I also usually went to the market together.

"It'll be late, but I guess we could." He had to go back to the town thing for a second day of festivities. He stuck his last bite into his mouth and stood. "Nice talking to you, Shawn." He brought his

142

plate to the sink. "See you again?" Dad looked at him through the remaining sip of his coffee.

"Uh . . . yeah."

What the heck had happened? I stabbed a pancake on the plate in the center of the table and dropped it onto mine.

"Bye, guys," Dad said as he exited.

"Don't eat that," Shawn said in a lowered voice as I sat.

"Why, were they that bad?" I was, all of a sudden, mortified.

"I'll make you some of mine." He put his fork down, still with half a pancake left, and carried his plate to the counter.

Josh was just as enthralled.

"If you can tell me where everything is . . ." He waited for me, but then went to the refrigerator for what he knew would be in there.

"What do you need?" I got up to help, and he rattled off a list. Dad's pancakes were from a box, Shawn's were from scratch.

He turned on the gas stove as Josh, chin leaned into his palm at the table, also waited. "Make enough. I stopped eating too."

He oiled the pan, stirred the ingredients in a bowl, and the wet batter sizzled as he poured it just like the chefs on my cooking shows.

Josh lifted an eyebrow at me.

Cooking was primarily my job, so when I didn't read, I usually watched cooking shows to improve my technique, and practiced what I learned on my family that was too lazy to do anything about it.

"This is a nice kitchen," Shawn said, looking around as he waited, spatula in hand.

If he said so. It'd been remodeled, but at least twenty years ago.

He invited himself into the refrigerator again and looked at what we had.

Out came a can of whipped cream.

He flipped the pancake from the pan to a plate and, shaking the can, tipped it and swirled the creamy topping from the center to the edge.

"Do you like chocolate syrup?" he asked as he went back into the refrigerator and retrieved it from the shelf in the door. He opened it and tipped it as if he would put it on, then turned it back upright and looked at me, awaiting an answer.

"Yes. Chocolate syrup. Definitely chocolate syrup."

He drizzled it on.

He brought me the plate and switched it out with the one I had.

"Wow." It was so fancy. And delicious-looking.

"Dude, is that what mine's gonna look like?" Josh asked with hope.

I mixed syrup with the chocolate and cut off a piece as Shawn added more batter to the pan. Footsteps clicked across the living room hardwoods, Susan, I could tell from the shoes.

The pancake was Heaven. Seriously, Heaven. "This is amazing."

"Hey, hey," Susan greeted, nothing less than her usual cheerful self. "*What* is going on?"

Josh lifted his hand from the table and gestured. "Shawn's making us breakfast."

"I see that. My goodness." She sat down where Shawn had been. "Good thing I didn't eat yet." She took Josh's fork from his plate and stole a bite from mine.

I fought her off when she moved in for another. "Get out."

Shawn slid a plate to Josh, and Susan moved her focus to him. She was three bites in when he pulled his plate away. "Hey, get your own, lady."

Susan stood. "Saw the fight at the fair last weekend, Shawn," she said as she moved in his direction. "You had that twit." She opened the door to the refrigerator and bent with her rear end to the air. Her hand went in and came out holding my unopened container of strawberries I'd made sure to hide all the way in the back.

"Hey, those are mine."

"I just want three." She opened it and took what she wanted, and then stood with her back to the counter eyeing what she assumed would soon be hers.

Her pancake didn't look any different than ours, other than the stolen garnish. "New Sunday tradition started," she said as she walked back to the table with her unexpected meal.

Shawn shut the stove off and started to clean up.

"Aren't you having any?" I asked.

"Nah, your dad filled me up."

I pushed my bottom lip out in a pout. I felt bad, but at least he was full of something. Not that he was too skinny, or anything, but I'd never seen him eat.

"I did notice you have orange juice, though. Is it okay if I have some?"

"Of course." I pointed to the cupboard next to the sink. "Glasses

145

are up there."

He found one, and then went to the refrigerator. "Does it matter which kind?" There was one with pulp and one without.

"Nope." *Without, without, without.*

He pulled out the one with. My jaw went slack as I made a choking sound. A breath came from his nose as the edges of his mouth turned up. He poured it and I had to look away. I couldn't even stand the sight of the pulp on the glass.

Even with a fourth chair available, he stood against the counter. "Dude, come sit down," Josh said.

"Nah, I'm alright."

Not me, I had to turn around in my chair to see him.

"So, what brings you around so early, Shawn?" Susan asked.

Finally, the question I was dying for an answer to.

"What brings *you* around?"

"Oh, we're gonna play that game?" She smiled as she took a bite of her pancake.

"No game, just a question. It's just as early and you're here."

"Well, if you're here for the same reason I am, then I'm afraid the two of you will not be left unsupervised." Her grin was sinful.

Josh turned a scolding eye to her. "Why would you do that? There's no reason to go there."

She *didn't* need to go there. Blood rushed to my face as I turned away.

Susan laughed. "Sorry."

Really, was it Dad's invitation? Was that all he needed?

"Shawn, that was absolutely delicious," Susan said as she drove her last bite through the remaining chocolate syrup.

"Yeah, that's a secret you might've wanted to keep to yourself," Josh said. "I can only take rubber for so long."

I shot a glare at him. "My cooking's not that bad."

I cleared the dishes from the table, and Shawn moved out of my way so I could put them in the dishwasher.

"That's the one thing I wish I had," he said, drinking his orange juice as I rinsed them in the sink and stacked them neatly in.

"It is convenient." I couldn't imagine not having one. Though it would probably end up being Bobby's job. Dad sometimes made him do the dishes by hand as punishment for things.

Susan went out the back slider to the deck.

"C'mon out," Josh said to Shawn as he followed.

The three of them went outside while I cleaned up the kitchen. I could hear them talking, but not about what, and Shawn's voice plenty.

I finished and joined them. Shawn stood backed against the railing of the deck, Susan lying between Josh's legs on one of the chaises.

I sat on the opposite lounge chair, hoping Shawn would sit without me having to invite him. Our tongues had been inside each other's mouths the night before, he shouldn't feel weird about sitting next to me.

Josh leaned over Susan's shoulder with an invitation of his own. She craned her neck back and giggled her way into a long kiss.

The conversation I heard from inside no longer existed as Shawn

147

looked in the opposite direction and sipped at his orange juice.

"Hey. You." Invitation extension. "Come sit."

He turned his attention to me and pushed off the railing.

He was rigid as he lowered to the thick cushion and wouldn't look at anything even near Josh and Susan.

I pulled a piece of ice from my water and threw it at them, ricocheting it off Josh's shoulder. "Break it up, guys."

"What about concerts?" Josh jumped right back into whatever conversation he and Shawn had been in. "You ever go to any?"

"Nah, I don't really got money for that kind of stuff."

Susan snapped a shot of herself with her phone in her new sunglasses that covered half her freckled face.

"You work, don't you?"

"Yeah, I don't get paid much, though, and I'm trying to save up."

"Gotcha."

"You're a senior, right?" Shawn asked. "You going to college next year?"

"Community. I don't really know what I want to do yet."

Susan tilted her head to me. "Hey, Meg, you hear I got accepted to my top two choices?"

"Awesome." Kudos to Josh for procuring such a smart girl. One of her choices was Brown University. She'd applied late, so she would have to wait, but still.

"Now just to keep this hornball from getting me pregnant first." She laughed, but it was true. She and Josh were always upstairs in Josh's room. Like she said, it was probably where they would've been if Shawn wasn't there.

Susan aimed her phone at me and snapped a picture.

"The two of you get together," she said to Shawn and me.

"Nah." Shawn gave a weird half shake of his head and turned his eyes to the empty space between the two lounge chairs.

I leaned toward him, and she got what she could.

She kept the camera aimed, and Shawn continued to avoid her. I pressed the side of my head against his hoping he'd look at her. Just before she clicked the button, I turned and kissed his temple.

"*Aww . . .*" Susan didn't expect it. "*Oh* my goodness!" It must've been a good one.

She'd gotten two—the serious one of the kiss, and then Shawn's reaction after—a smile crooked with embarrassment.

Bobby came out in his pajama pants and a T-shirt, chomping on a bowl of cereal, and crossed between us all, warily surveying the scene.

Without a word, he circled behind Shawn and me and flicked the back of my head.

He disappeared back inside.

Josh went on about a rock band he liked. "I got tickets for a show this summer. Cost me an arm and a leg."

Shawn dug into his pocket and pulled out his MP3 player and fiddled with the buttons. "You ever hear of these guys? They're kinda similar." He reached it across and Josh took it from him.

"I haven't. Mind if I listen?"

"Go for it."

Josh put the earpieces in and pressed the play button. Shawn, elbows on his knees and able to hear the beat, tapped his right foot.

I sucked in an ice cube from my water and spit it at him, hitting his shoulder. His arm shot out and he grabbed my glass.

Freezing. Water. All over. Me. My shirt, my pants . . . Without a thought, or even looking at me, he dumped my glass. It spilled from my chest and pooled in the triangular opening of my crossed legs.

Susan broke into laughter.

Mouth agape, I pushed up off the cushion as if the water would magically dissipate. Or drain.

It seemed difficult for Susan to inhale she laughed so hard.

Shawn went on as though nothing occurred, keeping up with the song that was barely audible.

Susan got up, still laughing, and swiped at the water to get rid of it.

Josh was oblivious. "That's some good stuff. I'll have to check 'em out. Mind if I look to see what else ya got on here?"

"Be my guest."

Susan went into the house and got the hand towel from the bathroom. "Man, I wish I knew that was coming," she said as she placed it underneath me still holding myself up off the sopping cushion. "I would've recorded it." She went back and sat down again, palm to her chest with small laughs still escaping her.

It was warm out, but not that warm, and I needed to change. I moved to stand and the football careened past me into Shawn's gut.

Bobby, dressed now, stood in the doorway of the open slider. "Let's see what ya got."

Shawn replaced the breath he lost, and then stood and whizzed it back as Bobby followed him off the deck.

"Why's he always gotta be such a dickhead?" Josh asked.

I was cold and my shirt was more see-through than I was com-fortable with, but I stuck around to make sure Shawn didn't need rescuing.

The harder and faster Bobby threw the ball, the harder and faster Shawn did. Bobby didn't act like he did with Damian. He didn't like Damian, flat out. This seemed more of a test, to see if Shawn could keep up. A decision period, maybe.

"He's got some good stuff on here," Josh said from across from me, still searching through the music on Shawn's MP3 player. "Some real deep shit." He listened to bits and pieces of songs. "He's got a little bit of everything, death metal, bluegrass . . . *classical.*"

"Any country?" Susan asked with excited anticipation.

"Nah . . ." Josh continued scrolling. "Haven't found any of that yet."

"Did you guys kiss yet?" Susan asked me, an eyebrow peaked high over the rim of her sunglasses.

It was a question I wasn't prepared for. "None of your business." There was a chance I'd have answered if Josh wasn't sitting there. Though he was the brother I probably could tell.

"That's a yes," she decided with a wide smile.

"No, it's not," Josh said. "It could be an 'I'm too embarrassed to admit we haven't yet.'"

I didn't know if he really thought that or if he just tried to cover for me.

Susan pulled up the photo she took of me kissing the side of Shawn's head and pushed it in Josh's face. "It's a yes." She looked immediately back to me. "Is he a good kisser?" Her voice shrunk as if speaking secrets.

I concluded at that point that my face would be red all day.

"Leave her alone," Josh said, not lifting his eyes from the band names he explored.

"Is he?" she asked again, leaning over his leg to get closer to me.

I still didn't answer. Josh looked at me out the corner of his eye now as if questioning the excuse he'd given me.

"Okay, I'm gonna go change now."

"Seriously?" Josh asked as I stood, apparently truly believing we hadn't.

"Oh my goodness, how cute. Shawn kissing, I can't picture it." Susan was all giddy.

"Then don't," I said as I escaped inside.

I didn't like what Bobby did, but maybe he'd realize he actually liked Shawn. Or Shawn would at least meet some sort of status ranking.

I put on dry clothes and went back out. Josh had joined the football tossing and brought harmony to the two shooting it as if it were a bullet.

"For real, Meg," Susan said, fiddling with her phone. "I know you don't have a whole lot of girlfriends." She could've said none, I wouldn't have been offended. "No mom."

I got her gist. "I'll be fine, Sue."

"I'm just saying. Boys and their hormones, you've got to be careful." She looked up to me from what she did.

I didn't want to dismiss her so carelessly, she was genuinely concerned. "I know. I'll be fine." I nodded, hoping to appease her.

"Well . . . if you're ever not . . . I'm here." There was sympathy in her words.

I nodded again. "Thank you."

Shawn came up onto the deck. "Can I use your bathroom?"

I directed him to the one off the kitchen and followed him in, and I filled a glass with water from the sink for when he came out.

"Thanks," he said as he took it from me. As he drank, I handed him a framed picture of Mom I'd gotten from the living room.

"What's this?" He set his glass down and wiped his hand on his pants to make sure it wasn't wet before taking it.

"My mom." It wasn't as good as the one on my nightstand, but close enough.

He studied it without any sort of readable expression. "Wow."

Wow, what? 'Wow, she's pretty'? 'Wow, you're her twin'? 'Wow, she looks like the kindest, most spectacular person who ever walked the earth'?

"You look like her."

I took it from him and removed the back and slipped out one Dad took when they first met. She sat on the ground in front of a rose bush, her head resting on her knees as she smiled bashfully for the camera.

He looked at it with a raised eyebrow. "It looks like you with long hair."

It was easily what I would look like soon enough.

153

He examined it more intently. "She looks like she was nice." There was yearning in his tone.

"Thanks. She was."

He handed it back to me and eyed the clock as he picked up his glass of water again. "Is that the right time?" Panic rose in his voice.

"Yeah. Why?"

"Shit." The glass landed hard on the counter and he barreled past me. "Shit, shit, shit, shit, shit."

~

The pavement blurred beneath my feet as I tried to keep up.

"Shawn, stop. Please stop."

"Go home, Megan," he shouted back.

I'd started on his heels, but with a cramp in my side and much shorter legs, the distance between us greatened by the stride. I followed him down Center Road and lost sight of him when he turned down County.

He was just about at his driveway when I rounded the corner.

I'd never run so fast, nor for so long, and didn't slow down.

I made the turn down his driveway and only became cautious when I got to the bend. I poked my head around the corner before turning it. Shawn lay flat on his back on the dirt ground, knees curled, holding his face, coughing and gulping for air. His father stood above him rubbing his elbow as he adjusted his arm. "Once a week, Shawn. Once a *goddamned week*. Now *you* call him." He threw a cell phone down at him.

"Is he coming back?" Shawn choked out.

"Call him." Mr. Harris reached down for the phone, pressed some buttons, and shoved it against Shawn's ear. He no sooner took it back. "He's here," he rushed the words into the phone. "He's here." He put the phone to Shawn's ear again. "Talk to him. Quick."

Shawn rolled to his knees and, elbows on the ground, held the phone to his ear. "I'm here," he said with his forehead to the dirt.

Moments went by.

The phone dropped from his hand. "He's coming back."

"Fricking wonderful."

Mr. Harris bent down and pulled Shawn up by the back of his shirt. "Where the hell were you?"

Shawn wiped his forearm across his face and it streaked with blood.

His father escorted him inside.

Who was coming back? Who was so important he got cracked in the face by his father's elbow for being late?

I took a careful step to my right toward the woods to get closer and fingers clamped around my arm. I lost a breath as I whipped around.

Bobby.

He stopped me in my tracks. He tugged on me, and we walked discreetly back up the driveway.

Chapter 19

"You don't get even close to an opinion on this," I said to Bobby as we walked home from Shawn's house.

"Oh, I don't, do I? The kid's messed up in something bigger than you should be anywhere near."

"Well, *duh*." Just in case he thought I was unaware.

"Then what the hell are you doing, Megan?"

"Being his friend." I turned back, walking ahead of him.

"And what makes you think he wants a friend?"

"Things." I just wanted to escape him.

"What things?"

"Just things."

"Do you know what that was about?"

"No, Bob."

"Then what do you know?"

"Nothing. Not a damn thing."

"Then what *do* you know?"

I shot him a harsh glance. "Let it go."

"Let it go? Did you see the same thing I saw?" He was as frustrated with me as I was him. "Is it drugs?"

I stopped in the middle of the tree-shaded road and turned to him. "I. Don't. Know." It was the only thing going through my head, though.

"It's gotta be," Bobby said as I continued walking. "Megan, I know you like the kid, but ya gotta cut him loose."

"Why, because you said?"

"Because he's dangerous."

I stopped again. "Shawn isn't dangerous."

"Whatever Shawn is involved in is dangerous, and that makes being around him *dangerous*. Honestly, Megan, if you don't recall, this is why Dad moved us. To be away from this kind of shit."

I wouldn't allow Bobby to take charge of me. "I don't try to be your mother, Bob."

"Because you know you don't stand a chance. But now that you mention it, how do you think Mom would feel about this? You really think she would be okay with you hanging around him?"

"Yes." Mom was the warmest, most caring person I knew. She'd probably want to help just as much. "Probably actually encourage it."

"Oh, you think?"

"I do. And I wish to God she was here right now to guide me. But she's not."

"It's great and all you're such a nice person, Meg, but you need to stop. It's not gonna get you anywhere. You need to find a new boyfriend."

157

I turned and pointed a hard finger at him. "Shut up, Bobby. Leave me alone, and leave Shawn alone."

~

Josh and Susan were upstairs when we got home, unaware anything happened. I steered clear of Bobby for the rest of the afternoon. He couldn't have cared less about Shawn, only that I knew better than to have anything to do with him. He was the last person to be a snitch, so saying something to Dad was still my decision to make.

I, on the other hand, worried greatly for Shawn. I'd been within seconds of seeing him get cracked hard enough to send him to the ground by the man supposed to love and care for him, for a reason still unknown but clearly significant.

We had a cookout, as talked about. Dad handed me a cheeseburger as he laughed with Uncle Vance about a little old lady who'd told him dirty jokes all afternoon. Everyone had long finished eating when I realized I hadn't taken a bite, or even put the ketchup on.

I didn't sleep. The same questions raked through my head. Who was on the phone? Why did Shawn need to be there? Why did he need to talk to them? Why once a week?

If Bobby hadn't followed me, I would've stayed and known more.

~

Shawn strolled into the lunchroom and sat as though nothing happened. "Sorry about yesterday. I didn't pay attention to the time. I was supposed to be home."

I had to really look to see discoloration to the underneath of his nose. He knew I'd followed him, just not how far. "I saw what

158

happened," I said. I wasn't going to lie.

His breath cut short. "What do you mean?"

"I followed you down your driveway."

"You what?" His eyes rounded. "Why would you do that?" Alarm eclipsed his tone. "Are you nuts?" He pushed back up off the bench. "Are you *nuts*?"

He left me sitting there and disappeared out of the cafeteria.

I trudged through the rest of the day, sick to my stomach. Should I not have said anything? Or at least been more subtle?

When the bell rang to end school, I didn't go to my locker to switch out my books or seek Josh out for a ride. I went to the far end of A wing to the door that led out in the direction of Shawn's house. I caught up with him just as he went out it.

"Shawn, I didn't mean to make you mad." It sounded so stupid coming from my mouth. I shouldn't have been faulted for worrying about him.

He didn't stop or even slow down.

"Shawn, please stop."

He picked up his pace.

So did I. "Shawn . . . *Shawn.*"

He spiked around. "You shouldn't have followed me. You *shouldn't* have followed me." A car pulled alongside and Bobby poked his head out from the front passenger seat of the full load. "You're like a little mouse at my feet, tripping me up," Shawn said. "Stay away from me."

His words ripped the air out of my lungs. The car stopped and Bobby got out. Shawn kept on, pulling his MP3 player from his pocket

159

and placing the earbuds in. Bobby grabbed my arm.

"Let *go* of me." I tried to rip away from him.

Shawn plucked a cigarette from his back pocket and drew a lighter from his front and, acting as though nothing went on behind him, lit it and dragged off it as he walked.

I came close to using the "F" word with Bobby.

"What the hell's going on?" Josh passed on the way to the car and intervened.

My face was hot.

"Make sure she doesn't follow Shawn," Bobby said, happy to pass me off.

"Seriously, man, what is your problem with him?"

"Ask her." Bobby nodded at me, and then got back into the car that waited for him.

I wouldn't have followed Shawn, anyway. Shawn did a fine job making sure of that.

I got in the car with Josh and reluctantly told him what we'd witnessed the day before.

He sighed. "And you didn't say anything to Dad?"

I knew it was coming.

"C'mon, Megan, you know better."

"I know, but he said I can't."

"Why?"

"I don't know. He won't say."

"Is it drugs? Is he worried about getting arrested?"

"I *don't know.*" I didn't mean to come off aggravated with him, it

160

just happened.

His cheeks puffed with his breath. "Well, either say something to Dad or don't, but you really need to stay away from his house." Lines dug into his forehead. "Like, seriously. I like Shawn. He's real. Maybe just back off a little. Let him do things his way. Sue says he's opening up. She says she's never seen him like this."

Maybe he was opening up, but not anymore. He just slammed the door shut. Besides, letting him do things his own way would only keep him in whatever hell he was in longer.

~

Shawn's words burned in me. The more I thought about them—his behavior toward me—the more hurt I was. Anything and everything I'd done to that point was because I cared about him, and he'd gotten so red-hot mad at me. It was completely demeaning. Obviously, there was something terribly wrong going on in his life, but he didn't need to keep pushing away the one person trying to help him. Especially so nastily.

Eleven thirty p.m. and unable to sleep, I drew instead.

What started out as a kitten in an effort to think about something else turned into an angry tiger that oddly resembled Shawn.

A mouse at his feet. He'd taken a swipe at me, claws out.

He didn't come anywhere near the lunchroom on Tuesday, and I didn't look for him.

~

The anniversary of Mom's death loomed, and as much as I didn't want to think about it, the one person who might actually help take my

161

mind off it had moved straight over to the category of things I didn't want to think about. And I tried everything I could not to. Why put so much effort into someone who made me feel so rotten?

But he didn't always. There were instances he'd made me feel better than I ever had. And vice versa, I was pretty sure. I was also certain it wasn't his personality I was experiencing, but a manifestation of whatever he dealt with at home.

Walking away from him—which I very well should've, considering his attitude—didn't seem like a solution. Giving up on someone because a life circumstance made them "difficult" would've made me a hypocrite. It was exactly what Claire did to me, and I resented her for it.

Except I also didn't have a clue what the right thing to do was.

In art on Wednesday, Miss Devereaux gave a short lesson, which she usually did at the beginning of every class, then instructed us on what she wanted us to do. She walked around the room observing as we worked individually.

I didn't pay attention until she paused near me. Her eyes focused on another drawing of Shawn I'd started. It was my best recollection of the smile he exhibited the day at the quarry. I figured I should draw it before I forgot what it looked like. I also needed a reminder it existed.

Her eyes narrowed in assessment. "Really."

It seemed more a comment on his expression than the fact I wasn't doing what I was supposed to.

"Keep up the good work," she said with a smile, and moved on.

Yeah. It was probably safe to say at that point I'd seen something not many others had.

I didn't see Shawn at all that day. Josh said he wasn't in gym, and he didn't see him in the halls at any point.

"Did you see Shawn today?" I asked Bobby, concerned about what seemed to be yet another absence.

"Cut it out, Meg, seriously."

"I'm not going to cut it out. He's avoiding me."

"*Good*. He knows better."

It was all I could take. My disastrous mess of emotions was about to collide into a massive heap of wreckage. I went upstairs, shut myself into my room, and dropped face first onto my pillow, and tears poured out in a torrent.

Talk to Dad, Megan. Just talk to Dad. You know you should.

What if talking to Dad made things worse like Shawn was so sure it would? What if it made things worse *and* he stopped talking to me?

I'd never been so conflicted.

~

At lunch on Thursday, I sat in Shawn's spot as I usually did on that day of the week, as he wasn't supposed to be there anyway.

I didn't eat and the book I'd brought with me remained closed as I sulked.

About halfway through the period, Shawn walked through the open double doors. He came toward me with a folded piece of paper, evident he was on a mission.

I sat straight up.

He opened my book and slipped the paper between the pages,

and then held his hand on the cover, looking directly at me with a hard frown.

He turned and walked back out.

I pulled the paper out and opened the two folds.

I'm sorry

Chapter 20

Four years ago today. I didn't want to go to school. Just the mere reminder of what an awful day the date signified was bad enough, but the turmoil with Shawn had me perpetually dropping from the top of the free fall of a seemingly never-ending rollercoaster.

Dad squeezed the back of my neck in recognition of the day as I stood in front of the toaster waiting for my bagel, undoubtedly wishing for something to take his mind off it as well.

"I kinda wish it wasn't a weekday," I said, wanting to crawl back into bed and hide from the upcoming hours. Like the turn off the clock at midnight would all of a sudden make me forget.

"Yeah, me too," he said somberly as he poured his coffee. "But I've learned the only way through this day is to face it head-on."

It must've been a recent revelation. He'd taken the day off the three previous years.

"Who knows, maybe I'll be home early," he said as he walked

away with his full mug.

Most likely. I wasn't sure I'd make it through the whole day at school, either.

Shawn came to my locker before homeroom in the morning. He stood with his head against the one next to mine and watched as I removed what I needed for my first class, something akin to misery in his eyes. I thought he would say something. When I finished and replaced my lock, he turned and walked off.

I barely had any energy to begin with and could already feel the little I did have seeping out of me.

He was at lunch when I got there. He sat as always, legs spread, elbows resting on the table. Until I sat. His hands pushed up his face, his legs bounced, he couldn't look at me.

As much as it shouldn't have been the case, I didn't know where I stood, so I wasn't sure I should speak first. It didn't seem as though he would, though.

With his hands clasped in front of his mouth and focus off to my side, my voice was a notch higher than a whisper. "I was worried." It didn't seem like something I should continue to have to spell out, but apparently, I did.

I spoke up some. "I don't want to be a little mouse."

"I didn't mean it." His voice hitched.

The lines in his forehead were deep and there was a gloss to his eyes.

Damian sat down at the opposite end of the table—a first. Shawn looked away.

166

Damian stared with an amused grin.

"Do you want to go somewhere else?" I asked.

"Yeah."

He stood and waited for me to gather my belongings.

I walked alongside him, past the three tables on the way to the door, on a collision course with Bobby. If his glare had been a dagger, it would've dropped me dead.

He showed no signs of slowing. He clipped Shawn's shoulder hard and kept walking. Shawn's lungs deflated with the blow. There was a startling sound from behind us, and the woman running the snack stand gasped and reached for her walkie-talkie.

Damian lay flat on his back on the floor behind us, blood pouring from his nose. He'd apparently been on our tail and Bobby cut him off.

Everyone in the cafeteria stood.

Damian got up and lunged at Shawn. Like the paddle of a pinball machine, Bobby bounced him back.

"Fucking pussy," Damian shouted at Shawn.

The wetness in Shawn's eyes was gone, replaced by fire.

I tugged on him. Bobby had it. There was no reason to get involved.

"What, are you too afraid to fight me, kid?"

The young female health teacher pulled on his other arm. He didn't budge, so she grabbed mine and rushed me away. She then stood between the boys as if it would make a difference.

Damian continued to try to get at Shawn, but Bobby wouldn't let

167

him by.

If Shawn wanted to make a move, he'd have to go through the one-hundred-twenty-pound health teacher.

"Are you really gonna let that scumbag fuck your sister?" Damian asked Bobby, his face burnt up.

The sound of Bobby's fist hitting Damian's face was so grisly it silenced the cafeteria.

Damian must've expected it. He merely fell back a step and returned with a hit just as hard.

Shawn's fight reflexes went into full gear. The health teacher pushed on him with all her might as I forced my way back through the crowd and added one hundred more pounds to the force against him. The rippled movements of the muscles under his shirt were alarming. They felt like shifting plates of steel. "Please don't," I kept saying, even though there was no way he could hear me over all the noise.

A crowd knotted around Bobby and Damian on the floor pounding on one another. Students and teachers rushed in. The man who'd blocked Shawn from view the time Damian jumped him in the hall yanked him by his arm with more strength than the health teacher or I could ever muster and pulled him out of the cafeteria. He propelled him through the oncoming traffic, in the opposite direction of the school offices, and shoved him out an exterior door to the teacher's parking lot.

As I was knocked around by the mob, Bobby was hauled out by two very large men, his face a dangerous shade of red and kicking as if he still fought. Teachers and other staff worked to clear the area. I

168

was jammed against the concrete window sill near the soda machine. Damian shouted obscenities from inside the cafeteria, Bobby's name flying from his mouth plenty, but Shawn's mostly, and a whole lot of the "F" word in various forms.

As soon as there was an opportunity to move, I was brushed along with everyone else.

Chapter 21

Both Bobby and Damian were arrested. Dad didn't come to the school, he sent officers.

Last period was a ruckus. The fight was all anyone talked about: Bobby's punch to Damian's gut, his jab to his face, Damian's shot to Bobby's jaw, the knee Bobby took to the groin . . . I was glad I didn't see it. I was also glad Shawn wasn't involved.

Dad wanted to see me after school. Josh drove me to Town Hall where Dad's office was, and Dad brought me in and shut the door. His questions were direct. He wanted to know what happened, and only what happened. I told him Shawn had his back turned, and had Bobby not stepped in, Damian likely would've jumped him again.

He thanked me for coming, and then walked me out past the principal and a petite woman with a fancy pocketbook and curly, dark hair that matched Damian's.

Josh and I traveled down Center Road, past Junction—our road

—and then County, toward the school again. We hit the spot by the woods that led to the quarry and he stopped the car.

"Be home by dinner," he said, "or I can see a whole lot of hell being raised."

"Don't worry about me."

"Would you believe it if I said I'm not?"

I was grateful for him. Shawn needed all the friends he could get.

I wasn't even sure he would be there. It was a nice day, though, warm and bright, and not only did the fight occur, we'd left things hanging.

I finally, without a doubt, knew my way without the chance of getting lost.

The afternoon sun blazed over the clearing. Shawn wasn't on the ledge. He lay in the unkempt grass, a knee to the cloudless sky, hand resting on it with a cigarette between his fingers.

His eyes were closed and the earbuds of his MP3 player in, so he didn't see or hear me approach. I blocked the sun from him and kicked my foot into his butt.

He sprung to his elbows. "*Jesus.*" He shaded his eyes with his hand as he looked up at me and pulled his earbuds out.

"Sorry."

He sat the rest of the way up, his view turning straight.

"What are you doing?"

"Right now?" He cocked an eyebrow. "Recovering from a heart attack."

"What *were* you doing?"

171

"Just hanging." He fought with the sun to look at me.

"Is it all right if I hang with you?"

"Sure."

The music coming from his MP3 player was loud but not like the heavy stuff he'd been listening to the day I surprised him at his house.

"How's Bobby?" he asked as I lowered to the ground.

"Fine." I sat cross-legged next to him. "He got arrested."

His brow bumped up. "He did?"

"Yeah, Damian too."

"No big surprise there." His right arm rested in his lap like when it had been injured.

"He was out of control," I went on. "That kid's got some mega anger issues, huh?"

"Yeah."

"What was with that guy sending you out?"

"He's my guidance counselor."

"And?"

"He didn't want me getting arrested too?" He lay back down, easing his elbow to the ground.

"Is something wrong with your arm?"

"Yeah, he pulled me too hard."

"That's not good. Do you want me to look at it?"

His whole expression jumped. "*No*." He said it as if it was a silly question.

I wanted to kill Damian. Whatever the conversation would've been before he interfered didn't seem even close to happening now.

172

"Yeah, so I don't know what's gonna happen," I said, just trying to keep him talking. "My dad had me come to his office after school, give him my version of what happened."

"Oh yeah?" He glanced at me and took a drag off his cigarette. "Who else was there?"

"The principal. Some woman I guessed was Damian's mom."

He sighed. "Definitely not going back now."

"What do you mean?"

He heaved a breath. "Gonna get expelled."

"Why would you get expelled?"

"Principal said if I caused any more trouble with Damian, he was getting rid of me."

"*You?*" He had to have been joking. "What about Damian?"

He shrugged, his left eyebrow going high.

"That doesn't make any sense."

"Nope."

"Can you explain, because something's really messed up about that."

"The principal's a dickhead?"

Why did I need to pull every last thing out of him? "Shawn."

He shrugged again. "Damian walks on water. He gets away with everything."

"But why?"

"I don't know, his stepfather?"

The councilman. "Do you care if you get expelled?"

"Of course, I care."

"Do you really?" He didn't seem like someone who would. He didn't even carry books.

"Megan, *I* want to go to college. *I* want choices." There was intensity in his gaze. He turned his head and sucked on his cigarette. "I don't want to be stuck in this shit town for the rest of my life. I *won't* be."

He looked at me again. "I've got a good average. Probably close to a 4.0. And money saved up."

"A 4.0? Really?"

"Doesn't matter now."

"It *should*."

"Well, it doesn't."

"It's not fair. And it doesn't make sense."

"What's there to make sense of? My life is garbage."

I hijacked his cigarette on its way to his mouth. "If you keep smoking these, yeah." I'd missed something. "When did this happen?"

He curled his head back and sucked at the air with a whine. "Just one more drag."

I didn't want to sound like a mother, nor a health advisory, but it was only the second time I'd seen him smoke. "You know how bad this is for you, right?"

"I do. Expensive as shit, too."

"Then why do you do it?"

"I *had* quit. Not a single one for a whole year and a half."

I didn't want to think it, but it didn't take much to deduce. "Is it because of me?"

174

I waited for some sort of response, a cue, anything. His left arm drew up and covered his eyes.

"Do you wish you never met me?"

He shook his head and a bird dove from a tree nearby in pursuit of a bug big enough it could've passed as another bird. "It's just messing with me."

"In a good way or a bad way?" I didn't want to assume, he'd given me so many mixed signals.

He didn't answer right away. Then his head moved again. "I don't know." He looked at me from underneath his arm. "I'm scared."

"Of what?"

"Of what's ahead of me, of what's behind me."

My voice was soft. "Of what's in front of you?"

His brow pinched with his nod.

"I'm scared too."

"Of what?"

"You being scared."

He focused on me. His arm fell back over his eyes and he turned his head to face forward again.

I switched his still-lit cigarette to my left hand and reached for his fingers dangling from his head and massaged them. He turned his face into his arm more and sucked in a trembling breath.

At the risk of burning down the forest, I placed his cigarette in the grass next to me and tugged. "C'mere."

He didn't react.

"C'mere." I pulled harder, wanting to hug him. He ripped his hand out of my grasp.

Butterflies communed in the grass, almost as if to take the edge off.

Shawn rushed up to a sitting position. Knees high, with his injured arm guarded in the crevice of his waist, he pushed his left palm over his eyes to dry them and, face out of view, produced another cigarette and lit it.

This was his hide-out, and I'd forced myself on him. Whether he regretted it or not, though, he'd shared it with me, and that meant something.

He took several drags from his cigarette before it became something just to hold. One of the butterflies that darted off with his sudden movement returned and fluttered by my hand.

"I don't know how to do this stuff, Meg."

Boyfriend/girlfriend stuff, or be cared about?

"I was mad. I didn't mean the stuff I said."

"I was worried," I said again. "That's something that happens when you care about someone."

His hand lifted to his face and made a subtle movement as though he pushed away more tears.

With everything he had going on, whatever it was, if he wouldn't let me help him, I'd at least make sure he knew I was there for him. I scooted over and leaned on my arm for a view of his face. He tried to turn away. The white of the eye I could see was pink.

"This mouse isn't going anywhere. So stop trying to get rid of me, okay?"

Chapter 22

Time dissolved. Shawn and I lay in the grass at the quarry, facing each other, him with his hand on my waist, I pushing mine through his soft, long locks. For the first time, the silence was easy. He closed his eyes and became so relaxed he drifted off to sleep. His arm twitched, and it startled him awake.

"Sorry." His mouth twisted with embarrassment.

"It's okay." I smiled. He could've slept for as long as he liked, he looked so tranquil.

It seemed the perfect opportunity to bring up the significance of the day, but it had taken so much to turn the mood, and it was one I didn't want to take a chance ruining.

Shawn gazed as if in a daze.

I wanted to kiss again.

If I'd been right the night of the fireworks, that he waited for me to do it, or maybe he just had a hard time initiating it, then it was up to me.

I pushed my fingers through his hair, this time to the back of his head, and held my hand there as I leaned in. With his mouth ajar, I gently kissed his bottom lip. He didn't react or partake in any way. When I pulled away his gaze remained.

"How was that?"

"Perfect."

Utter perfection, he was—the curve of his full lips, the arc of his high jaw, eyes as clear as the water in the Caribbean Ocean, and a physique to die for. He was the most beautiful being I'd ever seen.

I ran my fingers through his hair one more time and dragged them down the warm skin of his neck to his injured shoulder. He didn't jump or flinch, he merely moved his hand up from my waist and drew mine away.

"Was it still hurting from before?" I asked. His previous injury was pretty awful-looking.

"It always hurts."

It was as if he was high, like I'd seen Bobby so many times. He wasn't, though, just that uninhibited. The complete opposite of when I'd first gotten there.

My phone buzzed on the ground between us and Shawn's fingers gripped my waist. "I don't want you to go."

It was a text from Josh. <Dad's gonna be late, so you've got extra time. Let me know you're ok>

Another came in as I read. <Dad wants to talk to Shawn>

<I'm ok. Why does he want to talk to Shawn?>

<Didn't say>

I placed my phone back down. "We're good," I said, and resumed my position.

Shawn's gaze was more lucid, as if he thought. He leaned his head in like he would kiss me, but drew back. Then he went for it. His lips met mine and his tongue pushed into my mouth. I teased him with a quick taste of what he searched for, grazing mine against his. I did it again and laughed. He laughed too. "Stop."

Why me? How was I the one lucky enough to be inhaling his breath into my lungs? He had a difficult time making the move, but once he did, he was golden. The feeling he sparked in me was the same as our kiss during the fireworks, like a charge in my core. Over and over, his tongue brushed mine, so gently I chased after it to make sure it was still there. And then it waited against mine, as if it too could fall asleep there.

He drew away and lifted his arm, careful not to injure it more than it already was, and touched my face, his fingers, like fine paintbrushes stroking my cheek, more delicate than necessary. "Can I hold you?"

"Of course." It was a question I couldn't imagine ever saying no to.

"Turn around."

I did, and he curled into me, fitting his body to mine. He pushed his left arm under my neck and rested his bad right one, hand in a fist, diagonally across my chest, and clutched me.

I placed my hand over his. His grip, which wasn't that tight, slowly loosened, and his arm twitched again, a couple times. I would've liked to fall asleep too, but if I did, we'd be there until morning.

What had started out as a day I wished I could erase from the calendar turned out to be a pivotal one in so many ways. I couldn't help but wonder if Mom actually did have something to do with it.

When the sun was between the two pines at the far side of the quarry, illuminating the thick tangles of vines, I added pressure to Shawn's hand. He sucked in a heaping breath and his muscles stretched awake.

"I have to go," I said as he came to.

"Please, no."

"If I don't, this will never happen again."

His hold of my hand as we walked through the woods wasn't loose and casual. The scoop of his fingers pushed all the way to mine in a tight embrace.

"I have to work in the morning," he said when the pavement of Center Road was in view, and turned into me. "I might be able to come over after." I barely smiled and his mouth consumed mine.

The more we kissed, the more comfortable we both became. Shawn stood solidly over me, holding my waist, and took charge.

He broke away from my lips. "God, you make me feel so good." He said it as if frustrated, and a giggle bubbled out of me.

He took hold of my head and did it again.

"*God.*"

Chapter 23

"Get yourself something to eat and go to bed," Dad said to Bobby as they trudged through the door at almost a quarter to ten. He dropped his soft-sided briefcase in his chair. "That was not how I planned to spend my Friday night." Especially not that one. He rubbed his eyes under the glasses he rarely wore. "Did anyone tell Shawn I wanted to see him?"

If it was important, he would've had him come to his office. "No, but he might come over tomorrow," I said. "Is it bad?"

"No, Megan, it's not bad. There are just a few things I want to get to the bottom of."

Like why he's got a 4.0 average and possibly getting expelled?

He went into the kitchen, and I followed Bobby upstairs.

With a plate of microwaved chicken Parm from the night before, he tried to kick his door shut on me. "What did *I* do?" I walked in anyway.

"Oh nothing, Nutty Nut Meg. Nutter Butter. Meg-a-roo." He spun and dropped onto his bed, somehow keeping his food on his plate. The whole left side of his face was one big black and blue. "I only got arrested because of you."

For real? He blamed me? "How was that my fault? You didn't have to do what you did."

"Yeah . . ." He aimed the remote controller for his TV, turning it on, and flipped through the channels. He found what he wanted to watch and took a bite of his late dinner as if I wasn't there. "I really hope whoever I marry doesn't want kids," he said. "Because I'm pretty sure my testicles are messed up for life."

My intention when I came up was to express my gratitude. "Thank you."

"Mm-hmm."

~

In the morning, I went for a walk by Harris Towing. Not to check up on Shawn, but to see him work. The garage doors were open. He was there, and I stayed out of sight. Mr. Harris talked with a customer while Shawn did something with a car up on a lift.

Each turn of the wrench in his hand made the muscles of his arm flex. The harder he worked, the more I savored the view.

Mr. Harris finished with the customer and went on with his own work, and the volume of the music that came from inside went up. The clinking and clanging of metal tools being shuffled and dropped, power ones zinging and zanging, and swear words being slung around were surely the reason he warned Dad to steer clear if looking for

182

peace.

Shawn stopped and his arm dropped. The wrench in his hand fell to the concrete under his feet, and he stretched his head back as he massaged his shoulder.

He disappeared inside, and I made my exit.

~

The doorbell rang just after two o'clock.

Instead of inviting Shawn in, I went out. I closed the door behind me, pushed up on my toes, and kissed him.

I smiled.

He scooped me up and tightened his arms around me, expelling a soft sigh. "Just what I needed." His face buried into my neck and he inhaled long, deep breaths.

Holding his hand, I brought him inside and led him through the house with a destination of the deck.

We passed Bobby at the refrigerator and Shawn halted. He pulled his hand from mine and shoved it into his pocket. "Hey, man. Thanks for yesterday."

Bobby stared.

The silence was charged.

Shawn nodded. "Thank you," he said again, and passed me out the door.

I got the brunt of Bobby's glare and gave it right back.

Shawn was tired. He moved slowly, his eyelids were heavy. He sat on the chaise Josh and Susan occupied the last time he was there. "Sun feels good." He reached for his shoulder like he did at the garage.

"Maybe you should try some ice." I went back into the house and got the ice pack Dad got for Bobby when he blew his knee out playing basketball.

He draped it over his shoulder. Leaving one foot on the deck, he lifted the other to the cushion and lay back. He struggled to keep his eyes open.

"You didn't have to come over," I said. He looked like he wanted to go to bed.

"I wanted to," he nearly cut me off.

He was out within the minute.

I went back into the house and shut the slider so no one would bother him. Good thing, too. Susan came back after having lunch with her mother, and Dennis came over shortly after.

"What's he doing?" Susan asked.

"Megan has a boyfriend who falls asleep on her," Bobby scoffed.

"He's tired from working and his shoulder hurts."

"Oh, his shoulder hurts?" Bobby asked. "How 'bout my *face*?"

Dad came home from his fishing trip with Uncle Vance as it approached dinner time. I was quiet as I went out onto the deck. I leaned above Shawn and rubbed my hand over his opposite shoulder.

He lurched up and flew back to the bend of the long chair so fast it nearly tipped over with the violent shift of his weight, and he threw up a sharp elbow as if ready to physically defend himself.

Uh. . . A half-full glass of water teetered on the table next to him and fell, the clatter making both of us jump.

Whoa. I had no idea what had happened.

184

Neither did he, apparently. Confusion clenched his brow.

"I'm sorry," I said, his posture loosening. "I just figured—"

A dark spot grew in the crotch of his pants.

Oh, God. The water hadn't spilled anywhere near him.

He followed my eyes down. He ripped his gaze back up to me, humiliation washing over his face as he moved his hands to cover it.

Oh, shit balls, this isn't happening. It's fine. Stay calm, don't panic. My mind raced in search of a quick fix.

I bumbled to pick up the fallen glass. "Don't worry about the water," I said, trying to pretend I thought it was that. "I'll get you some more. And a towel."

Ugh. The water wasn't even his.

There was no way he believed I really thought that—aside from my verbal blunder, I'd watched it happen—but a slight look of relief came over him, probably just thankful I didn't call him on it.

I scurried inside, soaking up every second of my escape as I refilled the glass, utterly embarrassed for him.

I took a deep breath in an effort to cool the heat of my cheeks, and then schooled my expression before going back out.

Though the strain in Shawn's face had lessened, he was still visibly fazed as he sat bent at the edge of the chair, his left hand in a fist, his right nonchalantly pulling at the bottom of his shirt to hide the stain in his pants.

Dad followed me out.

"Hey, Shawn," he greeted him as I handed Shawn the towel.

Shawn glanced uneasily up at him.

185

"I accidentally spilled water on him," I said, setting the new glass down.

"Some hospitality," Dad said to Shawn with a joking smile as Shawn pushed the towel to the wet spot. "Did Megan tell you I wanted to talk to you?"

What sucky timing. "I didn't get a chance," I said.

Shawn stopped blotting and looked up at him.

"I had a long day yesterday," Dad said. "And only partially due to the incident between my son and that Damian Donovan boy."

Shawn's eyes flitted to me.

"It was brought to my attention that you're in a little bit of trouble at school."

Shawn looked away like he had done something wrong.

"The principal's actually looking to expel you."

He waited, probably expecting Shawn to say something.

"Well, I had some interesting conversations," he said. "Your guidance counselor spent over two hours in my office yesterday."

Shawn turned his eyes back to him.

"I then spoke with several of your other teachers. Not one of them could give a reason why that should happen."

Shawn seemed too leery to turn his whole head.

"They're all very upset about it, actually, and as long as it's okay with you, I've agreed to look into the situation."

Puzzlement rumpled Shawn's forehead.

"What's happening isn't right, Shawn," Dad said. "I don't know why it is, but I'd like to find out."

186

"Okay." Shawn sounded skeptical, and he still wouldn't fully look at him.

"Okay." Dad nodded. "You sticking around for dinner?"

"Uh." Shawn looked between Dad and me and at the towel on his lap that covered what Dad thought was water.

Dad's mouth turned up in a smile. "They'll dry. You're welcome if you like." He went back inside.

"I can find you another pair of pants," I said to Shawn in a lowered voice, hoping he would stay.

He dipped his head with an embarrassed shift of his eyes. "Thanks."

~

Wet jeans, no matter the cause, were never comfortable, so Josh easily lent Shawn a pair of sweatpants.

"So, I hear you're a good cook," Dad said to Shawn, pulling a box of frozen burgers from the freezer.

"I'm not too bad, I guess."

"I was going to have Megan whip up some macaroni salad. Do you think you want to try your hand at it?"

"I guess."

Dad opened the refrigerator. "Take a look. See if there's anything in there you want to use."

Stealth. And he had authority Shawn couldn't ignore.

Shawn leaned down and looked in. "Is there anything you don't like?" he asked.

"If it's in there, I like it."

Shawn moved things around, pulling out the mayonnaise first.

187

"So, I hear you have close to a 4.0 average."

"Do I? I was pretty sure."

It still shocked me.

"You know, that's not easy," Dad said. "Your guidance counselor says you're a math wiz."

"Yeah, I like math." He removed the sweet pickles.

"Math is Megan's worst subject," Dad said with a little laugh as he separated the burgers and got them ready for the grill.

"Yeah, I've noticed."

Milk?

"I also hear you're a big Shakespeare fan. That's a little unusual."

Shakespeare? Ick! I filled a pot with water and put it on the stove to heat.

"It's a lost art," Shawn said.

"You could say that again."

Susan came in from the living room and saw what Shawn was doing. "Yeah, baby! Step aside, Big Ed, he's got this one."

Dad smiled. "Like kids these days don't understand Shakespeare, I don't imagine I'll ever understand texting lingo. What's your favorite of his works?"

"*Romeo and Juliet*, by far. Read it six times."

Six times?

Shawn shut the refrigerator. "Do you have a spice cabinet?"

Dad directed him to the one between the refrigerator and the stove. "'But soft, what light through yonder window breaks?" Dad recited. "It is the east, and Juliet is the sun—'"

188

"'Arise, fair sun,'" Shawn cut him off, "'and kill the envious moon, who is already sick and pale with grief that thou, her maid, art far more fair than she.'"

That, without a doubt, impressed Dad. I had read it and was supposed to know what it meant, but didn't.

Susan narrowed her eyes at him. "Yeah, so that's why Mrs. Palmieri likes you."

"Can I use these?" he asked about an unopened jar of roasted red peppers.

"Absolutely," Susan said before Dad had a chance to answer.

"As long as you leave enough for my burger," Dad said.

The idea brought a smile to Shawn's face. "And mine," he said, looking at the jar.

"So, where'd you learn to cook?" Dad asked.

"Boredom. Lots of experimentation."

"You do most of the cooking at home?"

Tread carefully, Dad. Things can go south really quickly.

"For myself. My dad and I kinda just do our own things."

"Is there anything I can do?" I asked, trying to reroute the conversation from anything that might put Shawn on guard.

He held a container of minced onion. "Do you have a fresh one?"

"Megan, you want to grab one," Dad said, directing me to the bag of onions on the opposite side of the stove.

"Want to cut it up?" Shawn asked me.

Of course, he would give me the job that would make my eyes tear.

189

Uncle Vance appeared through the doorway next to the table. "Well, what's going on in here?" His voice boomed. He eyed Shawn, and then quickly moved his attention to the food on the countertop. We were apparently having our full-family cookout a day early.

"Big Ed's taking a seat to a real master," Susan said, chewing her gum from her viewing spot at the table.

Shawn stood idle, cautiously following Uncle Vance with his eyes.

"A *real* master, huh?" Uncle Vance gripped Shawn's arm with one hand and patted him on the back with the other, and kept moving. It was a much friendlier welcoming than he'd given him the day at the dock.

Shawn got back to what he did, and Uncle Vance carried on with Dad.

I hoped Shawn wasn't too overwhelmed. The kitchen, which started out with him, Dad, and me, filled to nearly capacity when Josh and Dennis joined Susan at the table, and Kenny galloped in. The noise was almost too much for me.

"Elbows or bowties?" I gave him a choice of pasta as I peeled the onion under running water.

"Which do you usually have?"

"Elbows."

"Bowties, then."

I put the pasta on to cook and chopped the onion. He stood next to me and sliced the roasted peppers. "This is nice, huh?" I said, hoping to get a hint of how he felt.

"Yeah, it's cool." He seemed fairly comfortable.

Maybe if we had more days like that, where he was able to get to know Dad better, he'd gain some trust in him.

"How many burgers, Shawn?" Dad asked.

"Um . . . can I have two?"

"Certainly can. How do you like 'em?"

"Medium, please."

Bobby passed behind us and jabbed his fingers into Shawn's bad shoulder, on purpose or not, and leaned toward his ear. "Way to take over my family, kid." He kept walking and went outside.

Seriously?

Shawn stopped and displayed the same demeanor as when Uncle Vance came in.

Dad turned around. "He didn't just say what I think he did, did he?"

"He did," I said.

Dad whacked Uncle Vance's arm. "Did you hear that, Van? He likes us. He *actually* likes us." His smile was big.

It wasn't so much that he liked us. Bobby was like a dog. He was the alpha male. We were part of his pack and belonged to him.

~

Shawn's pasta salad blew us all away. There was sugar in it, vinegar, olives, onions, peppers, even milk. I didn't think Bobby would eat it. He did but didn't offer any compliments.

Dad and Uncle Vance quizzed him with math problems to determine the speed at which he could think.

"Unbelievable." He had Uncle Vance's attention.

191

"Name the oceans in alphabetical order," Dad said.

I couldn't even name all the oceans. He did, and the questions kept coming.

"What are the seven countries that begin with 'I'?" Dad asked.

"There are eight," Shawn said through a mouthful of his fully-topped burger. He waited until he finished chewing. "Iceland, India, Indonesia, Iran, Iraq, Ireland, Israel, and Italy."

"Kid, do you have, like, a photogenic memory, or something?" Bobby asked.

"Photographic," Josh corrected him.

"It's not like I have anything else to do," Shawn said.

Dad shook his head. "I'm walking you in myself Monday morning, Shawn." He wiped his mouth with his napkin. "It just doesn't make sense."

~

Shawn eventually said he needed to go.

I got his pants from the dryer, and he quietly changed back into them.

"Thank you for dinner, sir," he said to Dad. "I enjoyed it."

"Thanks for cooking half of it," Dad reciprocated. "I meant what I said. The principal was pretty heated, so meet me at the front entrance of the school Monday morning. I'll make sure you don't have a problem getting in."

Shawn nodded. "Thank you."

"I'm going to get to the bottom of this. The one thing your teachers did say was that they have a hard time getting you to do homework. If we're going to make this happen, you need to work on that." Dad opened the door for him, and Shawn stepped out. "Make sure you do all your work. Show up to class on time."

"Okay."

Dad looked to me. "Is that it? You're not going to say goodbye?"

"Uh." I looked past him to Shawn. "Bye?"

Dad turned his eyes up. "Get out there." He waved me on with a smile.

I passed him out the door, and he shut it behind me.

Shawn was as awkward as I was. What kind of goodbye were we supposed to give each other knowing Dad was just on the other side of the door, with the window right next to us?

"So, how was it?" I asked. "Were you totally overwhelmed?"

"A little. But it wasn't too bad. Your brother hates me."

"He doesn't hate you. He wouldn't have done what he did yesterday if he did." He didn't hate him like he hated Damian, at least. It was a different kind of dislike. He'd have been fine with him if he wasn't attached to me.

He swung his arms over and hooked his fingers to mine.

"So, *Romeo and Juliet*, huh?" I simply couldn't picture it.

He shrugged. "Do you not like it?" His eyes squinched as if disappointed.

"I don't know, maybe if I understood it."

"It's not that hard if you pay attention."

I paid attention, and it was still hard.

"It's a good story, ya know?"

Possibly. I'd probably never know.

He glanced to the road. "Just don't ever do what they did, okay?"

"What do you mean?"

"Just don't."

"I don't get it."

"You know how it ends, right?"

It was about the only thing I did know. "Yeah, they killed them-selves." Unnecessarily. Romeo thought Juliet was dead, so he took his own life. When Juliet realized it, she took hers.

"You know. Just don't ever do it."

"Okay." It was an odd request.

He looked to the road again and gave a gentle swing to our hands. "See you Monday, I guess?"

"Not tomorrow? I'll be around." When wasn't I?

He shook his head. "I don't think Sundays are gonna work out. It's not a good day."

After what happened the week before . . .

He leaned in and pecked my lips. I wasn't ready for his haste and rushed after his. I got him with a quick kiss, but that was all. He glanced at the window behind me and a grin flashed on his cheeks. "This is weird."

"I know."

A car drove by, taking his attention. "I have to go."

It didn't seem I'd be able to stall him any longer. "Well, I guess I'll see you Monday."

His fingers tugged at mine, and he looked at the window and stole another kiss. "See you Monday."

Chapter 24

Dad had gone up against some pretty influential people in his time. Taking on a high school principal shouldn't have been that hard. There were only two weeks left of school. If he couldn't talk the man into letting Shawn come back, even if only for the remainder of the year, then the principal was downright spiteful. Or there was something Shawn didn't tell us—which it didn't sound like there was.

I rode with Dad on the way in.

At seven thirty in the morning, Shawn stood against a pillar of the bus turn around waiting. "See ya, Meg," Dad said, hinting I wasn't welcome to tag along.

"Good luck," I said as I got out of the car.

"I don't need luck, I need facts. This whole thing stinks of fish."

Dad scooted me along as he walked Shawn into the building, and the two hooked a left toward the office.

I didn't know what to expect and waited at my locker after first period.

Then again after second.

Four minutes before the end of lunch, Shawn came into the cafeteria, books and a piece of paper and pen in hand.

He exhaled a full breath as he sat.

"So, what happened?" I asked.

"Your Dad's pretty hardcore."

"Why, what'd he do?"

"Um, I'm not expelled." He sounded surprised.

"So, what happened?" I was eager to know the conversation.

"I'm not totally sure. I know the superintendent was involved. I wasn't in there, but I heard your dad talking to him through the door. Said he wouldn't wait for a meeting, a conference call would have to do. He really went to bat for me. He was in there for almost two hours. Got pretty loud a couple times."

I was happy to hear. And glad Shawn did. "So, how come you're late to lunch?"

"My English teacher was talking to me."

"What's this?" I swatted the written-on paper on top of his two books.

"Notes for a history test I have Wednesday."

He was doing the work like Dad told him to.

"Which brings me to the downside. Your dad walked me to every one of my classes before he left and told my teachers I agreed to do all my work."

Eek. Holding him to it.

"You should've seen the principal, Meg. He was shaking in his friggin' shoes. I think he actually shit himself."

I knew the business side of Dad, so I could imagine. "So, did my dad say why he was trying to expel you in the first place and not Damian?"

He shook his head. "I don't think he will."

"Why?"

"I got the impression, from what I heard, it was because I was too much of a trigger for Damian, so he was just trying to get rid of me. I don't think your dad will want to bring attention to how ass-backward the system is."

"I still don't understand. Why you, not Damian?"

"Because his stepdad's a councilman. It would look bad."

Ass-backward was right.

"Yeah, so, um, guess what else."

"What?"

"Damian's not graduating."

"Nuh-uh!" It was logical, but that would definitely look bad.

"No, shit, huh? And he's not coming back to this school. Ever. He did get expelled."

"*No way.*"

"Kid's gonna be out for blood now."

His parents, probably, too.

It was a feat he probably didn't think was possible.

It was weird to see him with books. He slid a pre-cal one off the top and opened the history one underneath it. "A downfall to go with the downside. I have a paper on socialism due Friday."

"Yick." I rolled my tongue out. "When was it assigned?"

"A month ago."

"Sucks to be you," I said with a teasing grin. "Better get moving."

"I think I'll stay after today and use the computer lab. You don't mind, do you?"

"You can come over if you want. Use my computer."

"Nah, I don't see myself concentrating much. Besides, I should probably get a feel for it. I think I'm gonna be there a lot."

~

Shawn stayed after school that afternoon, and the two following days.

He sought me out at my locker first thing Thursday morning. "Meg, I don't know what to do. This thing's never gonna get finished. I don't type fast enough." Panic quickened his words.

"How much do you have left?"

"A lot. I have all the information, but I still need to type it all up. It's due tomorrow."

"Well, I can help if you want." Socialism wasn't exactly a subject of interest, but if all I had to do was type . . .

"Will you? It would really help."

He met me at my locker again at the end of the day. "Can you hurry?" He was overly anxious.

He walked at a faster pace than usual, making it difficult to keep up. As we neared the computer lab, the teacher overseeing the room came out and appeared as though he was locking the door.

"Hey, wait up," Shawn called. "I need to get in there. I have a paper to finish."

"Sorry, Harris," the stiffly-suited man said as we approached. "I checked your search history. If that's what you're going to use this lab for, forget it." He removed the key and twisted the knob to make sure it was locked. "It's a little troubling, actually, and I'm wondering now if Principal Jacques was right about his initial expulsion." He stuffed his keys into his pocket and passed us down the hall.

Shawn stared in a daze at where the man had stood.

"Wow, that was harsh," I said, unable to imagine anything bad enough to warrant a response like that. "What'd you search?"

His head jerked as if not expecting my voice. "Nothing." Creases lined his forehead. "Can we just do it at your house?"

~

Susan was a much faster typist than I and volunteered for the job. Shawn had printed out and highlighted everything he wanted to touch on, and the two of them sat at the dining room table with my laptop, and Shawn recited what he wanted her to write.

"We'd probably be done by now if you could stay focused," Susan said to him after nearly two hours. He'd tell her what to write, she'd type it, and he'd drift off somewhere and have to remember where he was. He was like that since the computer lab. I was dying to know what he searched. If he didn't own a computer, he probably didn't know they kept track of history.

"*Duuude.* I'm giving up on you soon." Susan surely wouldn't offer her help again.

Shawn snapped back to attention. "We're almost done, I promise."

"That's what you said a half hour ago."

"I swear. Just a little bit more."

All in all, it took them just under three hours.

Shawn read the pages over and over, making sure they were right. Once satisfied, I showed him how to print them. He stapled them together, I gave him a folder, and he left.

"He didn't even say thank you," Susan said.

"Don't take it personally," I told her. "I think he has other things on his mind."

Chapter 25

Only six minutes left to lunch, where was he? He had to be in school, his paper was due.

The bell rang, and I slogged back to class.

When school ended, I sought out Shawn's history teacher. "Did Shawn turn in his paper today?" I asked the pleasant-looking, middle-aged woman in a knee-length skirt and matching suit jacket.

"Shawn wasn't in class today," she said with a mild-mannered tilt of her head.

How was he not in class? He had worked so hard. "He did his paper," I said. "I know because he finished it at my house yesterday. He put a lot of work into it."

"Okay, dear, I'll take that into consideration. Thank you."

~

It was a dreary day. The air was thick and the mist licked at me as I ran.

He wasn't at the quarry.

I wasn't supposed to go to his house, but I didn't have a choice. I raced.

I turned down his driveway, less than cautious. I rounded the bend and the sight of the blue Chevy tailgate sent me leaping into the woods. The dim sound of his father's voice froze me.

Another voice.

I took careful steps in the thick brush, mindful of my bright white top. I slipped it off, exposing the less noticeable brown tank top beneath it.

The trailer came into view and I stopped. Shawn's father stood in the driveway, cell phone to his right ear, left hand to his hip, while a second, thin, red-headed man sat atop the steps at the door.

Mr. Harris paced as he listened.

He ended his call and forced a breath.

"What'd he say?" the red-headed man asked.

"We're good. That sufficed. But it can't happen again."

"Well, obviously," the red-headed man said in a mocking tone.

"Shit ain't in my control, Jack."

"Well, thank God we had a 'Plan B.'"

"Yeah." Mr. Harris lit a cigarette. "You need to watch what you put in that kid," he said on the smoky exhale. "He ain't a horse."

"He's not a horse, but he sure is turning into the Incredible Hulk. I don't know how much longer we'll be able to take him."

"I know," Mr. Harris said as he took another drag. "Not that I don't love my kid, or anything, but if I lose him, I'm as good as in the ground. It's hard enough making sure he don't take off, I sure as hell don't need him overdosing on some shit you put in him."

"He's fine, John," the man said in an aggravated tone. "I just checked on him. He's alert and firing off swears and insults as always." He stood, taking a beer from the step with him and sipping from it. "I'm gonna take off. Let me know when that shit comes in. So I know where we stand." He placed the beer back down and, in a collared shirt tucked into nice, light-colored pants, walked to the car parked next to the blue truck. I snapped a photo with my phone as best as I could.

Mr. Harris dropped his cigarette on the ground, stepped on it, and went inside.

I sat on the damp ground under the thick covering of trees with my chin on my knees for nearly an hour, staring at the aluminum-sided trailer. Mr. Harris's voice penetrated the thin walls: "Shut the hell up, Shawn!" "Keep it up and my foot's gonna come through your teeth!" "Kid, I am gonna pound you!"

The numbers 911 sat on my phone, waiting for me to muster the courage to press the send button.

For Christ's sake, Megan, it's one button. It was what I'd always been taught to do, why was it so damned hard?

I cleared it and keyed in Dad's number.

You can't. Shawn's voice from when I told him how badly I wanted to tell someone ran through my head.

God, this sucks. I cleared that, too, and dialed Bobby.

Shawn trusts you.

Every thought I could possibly have fought one another as Bobby's

203

number, too, just sat on my phone.

Mr. Harris came out again, his hair slicked back as if wet from a shower, and lit another cigarette as he walked toward his truck. The engine roared to a start, and he turned around in the small dirt clearing and drove up the driveway.

As soon as the rumbling sound was gone, I pushed up off the wet leaves and darted for the door. I ripped open the screen and my hand slipped around the knob as I tried to open the thicker one. "*Shawn!*" I rapped on the heavy metal. "*Shawn!*"

I gave up on the door and dumped two of the tool-filled crates and stacked them in front of the window Josh lifted me to the first time we came looking for him. I pushed on the screen, ready to bust it in if necessary. With some hard persuasion, it lifted. "*Shawn!*"

"Megan?" His voice was smothered.

I lifted my leg to the window, nearly doing a split as I contorted myself through the small opening and over the kitchen sink.

What was neat and clean the last time I looked in was now a trashed mess. Items that looked like they belonged on the kitchen table were scattered about the room, the chairs arranged haphazardly, the TV in the living room pushed off the stand and on its side on the floor.

In the grim space I wasn't supposed to be in, I froze. "Shawn."

"Megan, is that you?" His voice sounded funny.

My heart pounded. "Where are you?" I took steps toward a dark hallway at the back corner of the living room. There were no windows, I couldn't see a thing. I felt for a light switch, flipping one on, and a dim light shone on dark, paneled walls.

Straight ahead at the far end of the narrow hall was a door held closed by a thick yellow bungee cord pulled taut from the knob to the one diagonal with it. Goosebumps raised on my arms.

I moved past a cove with a washing machine and dryer, and then a bathroom. "Shawn?" The wood at the bottom of the door straight ahead was splintered.

I pulled with all of my weight to loosen the tension on the bungee cord, it snapping back when the hook was off the opposite knob.

I eased the door open to darkness. About a quarter of the way, it stopped, and a leg lifted out of the way. I pushed it farther until it hit the second one.

Shawn lay on the floor, feet facing the door. He looked like he'd been through a war. His shirt was torn, the knees of his jeans were ripped and covered in dirt. "Holy . . ."

"Hey, beautiful, what are you doing here?" His arms were strewn by his sides, and he didn't make any attempt to move. Whatever the red-headed man had given him hadn't worn off yet.

I stood over him, straddling him, and reached for his arms. "C'mon, stand up." I tugged. They were lifeless. I could barely hold them up.

"Hey, you're not supposed to be here," he said with slowed speech, his eyes glazed.

"You're right," I said. "Guess you're gonna have to get up and show me the way out." I pulled on him again. He wasn't getting up for anything.

"Are you an angel? Am I dead?"

"Not quite." Though I did like the reference. What the hell did the man give him?

"Please don't leave me." He sounded relaxed, happy. Not afraid.

"Not a chance." I cupped his face in my hands. "You need to get up."

"'For thou art as glorious to this night, being over my head, as is a winged messenger of heaven.'"

Whoa boy.

His eyelids fluttered and I patted his cheek. "Shawn, you need to get up. *Please*," I pleaded with him.

"Why?" There was nothing to his voice.

"Because I said so, that's why." I felt like I talked to a little kid.

"Listen, Megan." He stopped to take a breath. "I'm gonna leave soon. Disappear. Okay?"

"Okay." *Whatever.* "Now you listen. You need to get up."

His eyes closed and his head fell to the side. "Shawn. Hey." I pinched him, I jostled him, I massaged the palm of his hand. I felt for his pulse in his neck. It was strong.

I weighed my options. If I stayed and his father came home, there'd be a whole lot of trouble for both of us.

I couldn't leave him.

I could call for a rescue, but who knew the consequences to that. And did he really need one?

Bobby would probably know what to do. But then I'd never hear the end of it.

Over and over again, I brushed my fingers through his hair with

206

Dad's number on speed dial in the event Mr. Harris came home.

At least twenty minutes went by.

The weight this kid put on me.

But it was weight I chose.

The burdens we accept when we choose to care. It was one thing *One Thousand Reasons* definitely got right.

"Shawn." I didn't like that he slept.

"Mmm."

"You're making me nervous, you need to wake up. If I get too worried, I'm calling 911."

His head moved and he swallowed. "Megan?" It was as if he was surprised to hear my voice, and his eyes pried open. "Shit. What are you doing here?" His left arm pulled in and his body moved in a slow, snaking motion. "Get out of here, Megan, why are you here?"

I pushed my hand up his forehead, opening his eyes more and forcing him to look at me. "I'm here because you didn't come to school today. Your paper was due."

His head moved on the floor. "Go away, oh my *God*, go away, you can't be here."

"You have to get up, I'm not leaving you here."

He lifted his head a little and tried to focus his eyes out the door. "Who's here?"

"It's just us."

He dropped his head back down. He inhaled and his lungs filled like balloons.

"C'mon." I pulled on his left arm as I stood.

207

He made no effort, only groaned. "Oh, I'm gonna throw up."

"Shawn, please. Get. Up." I tried to lift him from under his shoulders and he let out a bawl. He gripped his right shoulder and his breathing quickened.

Enough was enough. I picked up my phone and dialed the nine, and Shawn ripped it from my hand. "Get that thing out of here." He whizzed it into the dark, pegging it off a wall.

A sound from the living room. The door. Shit! I scurried to find my phone. There had been no rumble of a truck engine.

"Jesus, John." *A female's voice.* "Friggin' mess. Asshole."

Shawn moaned with his hand clamped to his shoulder.

"Dude." The voice neared. "Your dad called. Said Jackson lit you up again." *Kind-sounding, pleasant.*

A face didn't appear. Instead, sounds came from the kitchen. An ice tray banging on the counter, glasses clinking together, the sink turning on.

Footsteps coming down the hall again. Shit, no place to go.

Beth, the burgundy-haired girl. Shorter than short shorts and fitted tank-top that flaunted her abounding cleavage and holding a large Ziploc bag full of ice and a glass of water.

"I heard you gave 'em a run for their money," she said as she placed them on the floor and leaned down over Shawn. She drew his hand from his shoulder and he shouted in agony. She touched it lightly with her fingertips and felt around as he breathed short, fast breaths. "I don't know, buddy, I think it's out again."

Shawn grabbed at it again, and she lifted his hand and placed the bag of ice underneath it. "What do you want me to do?" She stood bent over him with her hands to her knees.

"Make her go," he said through his labored breaths.

"Make who go?" Beth lifted her head and her eyes searched. I was in a corner of the room without light. "*Oh, snap.*" She looked directly at me. She jumped up and flipped a switch on the wall, turning on a lamp on a single nightstand. Her face brightened as our space did. "Shawn, you got a girl in your room?" She beamed a smile. "Way to go, buddy!" She bent down and slapped his thigh in praise. Her eyes bugged. "She wasn't here, was she?"

Shawn's head shook on the floor. "Get her out of here."

"C'mon, honey." She moved toward me and reached her arm out as if to help me up. "This isn't a good place for you."

I shook my head. "I'm not going anywhere. Not without him." I clutched my phone.

Beth's eyes wilted with sympathy. "Oh, hon, I'm here to take care of him. I'm gonna make sure he's okay. I promise you, I've seen him a lot worse than this."

Was that supposed to make me feel better? "What are they doing to him? Are they experimenting with drugs on him, or something?"

"Shut up, Beth," Shawn warned. "Get the *fuck* out of my house, Megan." He writhed as tears stung my eyes.

Beth reached for me again. "C'mon. He doesn't mean it. He's just had a bad day."

A bad day? She said it as if he'd failed a test or spilled his soda on himself, or something.

My forearm somehow ended up in her grasp, and she guided me up and led me out of the small room. She pushed me along into the living room and held her hand out to me. "I'm sorry, but I have to." She wanted my phone.

She was out of her tree. "I'm not giving you my phone."

"Hon, he can't take any chances."

"With *what*?" Somebody would give me answers.

She seemed like a compassionate person. If not, she would've wrestled it from me. "Look, I think it's cute he has a girlfriend, *you're* cute, but this isn't for you. I'm not quite sure why you're here right now, but if you care about him, you'll forget this ever happened."

It was almost laughable. "And how do I do that?"

Her head moved in toward me. "I don't care how you do it, you just do it."

If ever it was my moment to take a stand, now was it. "My father's the chief of police."

She appeared unfazed. Then she looked away, her eyes enlarging. She looked back to me. "Holy shit."

She took hold of my arm and pulled me out the door, off the landing, down the two steps, and to the middle of the dirt clearing. "I don't know how the hell this happened, but you need to get out of here." She shoved me toward the driveway. She turned for the trailer again, but then turned back. "That kid in there is like my little brother. You do anything to screw this up . . ." Her face shriveled and her eyes dropped tears.

"Screw *what* up?" Maybe if somebody would tell me something.

"The less you know, the better, okay? All you need to know is that he knows he needs to get out, and he's working on it. He has this covered. Don't mess this up. Do *not* mess this up." She charged at me and I ducked as if she would hit me. She tore my phone from my hand. "Oh my God," she said, her hands going to her head as she tramped back toward the trailer.

Oh, like hell she is. She wasn't getting my phone. I needed it more now than ever. I stormed after her like she was Bobby any one of the given times he'd antagonized me in the same fashion. "I don't think so. That's *mine*." I grabbed the back of her shirt, just as much on a mission as she was.

She turned around, and in a startlingly strong one-arm push, she knocked me off my feet, and I landed hard on my butt on the ground. "Try it again, little girl, and you'll have more than just a sore ass."

My pulse beat in my throat as she stared at me through a flinty gaze.

My shock quickly turned to blazing hot fury. It was clear, though, by her strength, as well as her intensity, that I didn't stand a chance. Defeated, I could do nothing but scowl at her.

She turned around and stomped up the steps. "You have *got* to be kidding me," she said as she went back inside. "Un-fucking-believable."

Bitch.

~

Shawn threw up. A lot. The door was wide open and I heard every last gag and hurl from the woods that bordered his driveway. His scream when Beth popped his shoulder back into place was shrill.

211

"The chief's daughter, Shawn? What are you thinking?" She yelled at him to no end. "It's stupid! How could you be so stupid?"

"I know it's stupid, *shut up!*"

"I pray for your hormones to kick in, and when they finally do, you get stupid. Just like every other guy, *stupid.*"

"*Shut. Up.*"

There was about an hour of quiet.

I stood and walked back to the trailer. Shawn sat on the couch, legs open and head back, with the bag of ice on his shoulder. Beth stood bent over the peninsula of the kitchen counter, fiddling with my phone.

I stepped up the two steps. Shawn's head lifted, and he looked at me through the screen, surprise rounding his eyes.

"I need my phone back," I said.

Beth jumped. She looked at me, and then to Shawn. "See, what'd I tell you? *Stu.pid.*"

I kept my eyes on Shawn. "I'm not leaving here without it."

He looked at Beth. "Give her phone back."

She pushed up off the counter. "Kid, you are friggin' whipped."

"It's my only line to you," I said to Shawn. "I'll sleep in your woods if I don't get it back."

"Give it back, Beth."

She shook her head at the air and continued to press buttons on it as she walked to the door. "You need to add some new games on here." She opened the screen and handed it to me.

The screen slammed shut and she walked back to the counter.

212

I pulled it open and went in directly to Shawn. I leaned down to him and pushed my arm underneath his neck and hugged him tighter than I thought possible. "You're not stupid," I said into his ear. He was in trouble, and he was in a relationship with the chief's daughter. Deliberately or unintentionally, it was the smartest thing he could've done.

Chapter 26

The knot in my stomach rounded loop over loop. Shawn was in grave danger—as if I didn't already know—and a second person now told me I wasn't supposed to say anything. Beth, I wasn't so sure I could count as a reliable person, though. Josh seemed like more of an adult than she did.

I didn't eat, I didn't sleep. My phone lay on my pillow next to my head all night. I didn't text him, but I was surprised I didn't get one from him. I'd like to have thought the words I left him with had an impact. Maybe Beth's stirred more.

"How come you didn't go last night?" Susan asked me about the art show when she came over in the morning. I'd forgotten all about it. "You had some pretty killer work on display."

Whatever. I couldn't think about it. Not with everything else I had going on.

In the afternoon, I went with her and Josh to the market while

Susan shopped for her mother. Partially for something to do, but mostly because we'd pass Harris Towing on the way. The garage doors were open, but there was no one in sight.

"You should try this," Susan said, holding a package of light purple eye shadow to my face while Josh ordered a sandwich from the deli counter.

It was a color suited more for her auburn tones.

There weren't any books, and I'd already read through all the greeting cards when Dad and I shopped, but still picked one up.

> *During the journey of our lives, we occasionally meet someone who is exceptional and unforgettable. You are that special person who will always be remembered fondly by everyone who knows you.*

Fitting. Except it was from the farewell section.

The bell on the door jingled, alerting that a customer came in. "Hey, Charlie," a loud voice blared across the store to the stout old owner serving Josh.

"Hey, John. Hey, Shawn."

My muscles clenched.

I stood on my toes to see over the rack. The top of their heads moved toward the deli counter.

"Oh, hey, Shawn," Josh said, starting back toward Susan and me. Susan plunged a loaf of bread into her basket.

"Any corned beef this week?" Mr. Harris asked.

"As a matter of fact, there is. A Rueben?"

215

"You got it."

"And for you, Shawn?"

His answer was too quiet for me to hear. At least he was alive. And being fed.

"You hurt your arm again?" the owner asked.

"He's got a weak shoulder," Mr. Harris said. "It doesn't take much."

Asshole. I was pretty sure he was the reason his arm was like that.

"You don't have him working today, do you?" the owner asked Mr. Harris.

"Hey, when you're busy, you're busy."

"Oh, jeez, John, you can't be that busy. Give the poor kid a break. He's right-handed, for Pete's sake."

"Ah, he ain't workin'," he said. "He's just hanging with me so I can keep an eye on him. He's been pulling his disappearing act again."

That answered that. Wouldn't see him until Monday, *if.*

Susan scraped together the rest of what was on her list—eggs, milk, a box of some sort of granola cereal—and emptied the contents of her basket onto the tiny counter at the register.

"Be right there, Sue," the owner called across the store.

"No problem, Charlie, take your time."

Mr. Harris came up in line behind us and stiffened when he saw me. Shawn followed, his right hand pulling at the neck of his shirt to hold his arm up, his sandwich cradled in his left, and a fresh new bottle of soda dangling from between his fingers.

Mr. Harris turned his eyes down to me, and then looked at Susan. "Hey, how's your mom's new alternator doing?"

216

Susan nodded. "Pretty good, I guess. She hasn't had any problems."

Being in such close proximity to the man gave me the creeps. His gray T-shirt, tight to his rigid chest, was wet with sweat, and the smell, combined with his body odor, burnt my nose. I glanced up at him, and he closed in even more, reaching past me and placing his wrapped sandwich on the counter behind Susan's stuff. I couldn't see Shawn behind him. I couldn't see beyond him, period.

Josh, with a handful of items for himself, appeared and forced his way between us. "Pardon me." He looked directly at Mr. Harris, and then pushed the sandwich out of the way and dropped his own stuff down.

Josh knew what happened the day Mr. Harris plucked Shawn off the road when he saw the two of us walking together. Whether the man tried to intimidate me or not, he did, and I was thankful for Josh's fearlessness.

Mr. Harris reached behind him for Shawn's sandwich and tossed it on the counter with everything else. "Ring it all together, Charlie, I'll take care of it."

"Well, that's mighty nice of you, John. Are you sure?"

"Yeah, I've got this."

Josh's brow bent with skepticism.

"Go get yourself a candy bar, sweetheart," he said to me.

Did he hope to buy us off?

"Go ahead, now."

"It's a free candy bar, Meg," Josh said. "Go get one."

I went over to the candy rack and retrieved a Hershey bar. My eyes stayed fixed on Josh as I walked back.

The owner totaled everything on the counter, ringing it all out at just over fifty-six dollars, and Mr. Harris opened a wallet full of bills. I held my breath as he stretched three twenties past Josh.

As soon as a bag was filled, I took it and pushed through the door. I walked right into the small, dark-haired woman that was at Dad's office the day of the fight.

Way too small of a town. Damian was right behind her.

"Oh, look, Damian," the woman said. "It's not just John, it's a whole gang of troublemakers."

"Not in here, guys," the market owner said. "He's on his way out, Gina. Just give him a minute."

"I don't have time for this." The weary woman grazed by. Damian followed, and as the woman—his mother, I still guessed—disappeared down the bread aisle, Damian stopped at Mr. Harris and Shawn.

"Did you hear what I said, Damian?" the store owner asked, reaching for the phone. "Not in here. That applies to you too."

Damian looked back and forth between the two, and his view landed on Shawn, hard and threatening.

"Take it outside, boys," the owner said. "I'll call the police, I will."

Please do. Then Dad would hear about it.

Shawn's gaze remained neutral.

Mr. Harris looked back to the owner. "Oh, and I forgot, a pack of smokes."

"Split them up, John." He retrieved the cigarettes, starting to dial.

218

"I got in trouble the last time I split them up."

The owner sighed. Mr. Harris pulled more money from his wallet and exchanged it for a package of Marlboros.

"Shawn, you're better than this," the owner said. "You're all paid up, you've got your soda, just walk out."

He couldn't just walk out, he'd get jumped.

Damian's mother passed to the next aisle, a package of hotdog buns in hand.

"Seriously?" Susan said. It was ridiculous. Both their parents were there, and the only one who tried to intervene was a spectacled old man who couldn't do anything about it.

Damian's muscles pumped even though Mr. Harris stood right there.

"Uh, excuse me, Mrs. Donovan," Susan called through the store.

"Gina," the owner pleaded with the phone to his ear.

Shawn did absolutely nothing to provoke him.

Josh wasn't like Bobby. He would get involved if he had to, but only if he had to.

Mrs. Donovan appeared from the snack aisle. "Damian, c'mon, don't do this to me." She took hold of his arm and pulled on him.

"When you're least expecting it, Harris," Damian said to Shawn. "When you are least fucking expecting it."

Mrs. Donovan pulled him in one direction, and Mr. Harris pushed Shawn in the other, out the door.

"You have a nice day, now, you hear?" Mr. Harris said to me with a smile, plucking a cigarette from his fresh pack.

"Never mind," the owner said to the person on the other end of the phone.

Shawn kept his eyes off me as he hoisted himself up into the passenger seat of his dad's truck. With a gassed-up start of the engine, the two were off.

"That was effed up," Susan said as we got in her car. "And what was with him buying my groceries?"

More effed up was my knowledge that Mr. Harris had once fornicated with Mrs. Donovan, and that was how Damian came about.

The slight bit of hope I had disintegrated. Had the call to the police gone through, Dad would've heard about it, and it likely would've prompted him to check on Shawn more. It also might've provided me an opening to let him in without breaking Shawn's trust.

Chapter 27

The weight Shawn's situation continued to pile on me—though it was weight I took on voluntarily—was immense. Considering he didn't want me to involve other people, I'd have thought he would've kept in better contact. He did, after all, know that was why I needed my phone back.

On Sunday morning, I still hadn't heard from him. I finally broke down and texted him.

<I'm trying to stay away but haven't heard from you. Please let me know you're ok.>

It was well after lunchtime when my phone buzzed with an incoming text.

<Not gonna be around for a few days>

Not going to be around? <Where are you going? When will you be back?> *Would* he be back?

<Don't know>

<What about school?> We only had a week left and Dad just ensured he wouldn't be expelled. <Will you have your phone?>

I lost count of the number of times I texted him over the next several days. Mr. Harris went about business as usual, at his garage every time I forced Josh to drive by. The red-headed man was even there once, killing my suspicion that Shawn was with him for some reason.

The only thing I had left was the man he was forced to speak with the Sunday he was late getting home—if it was a different man. I hadn't seen him on a Sunday since, and it was Sunday when he texted me. If it was drugs, which I was almost positive now, it was, maybe he was on some sort of run.

On Wednesday, as I walked from second period to third, my phone—snug in my back pocket—vibrated. I stopped in the middle of the hall, forcing the droves of students to move around me as I checked it.

<I'm back>

Thank freaking God. <Are you ok?>

<Yeah>

<Meet at the quarry after school?>

<Tired. Gonna crash>

<You can crash with at the quarry.>

<Too tired. Passing out and sleeping til tomorrow>

Ugh . . . I was glad to finally have heard from him, but I was just as anxious. I needed to see him. Hold him, feel him. Count his fingers and toes to make sure they were all there.

~

222

Shawn didn't meet me at my locker before homeroom. He didn't seek me out between periods or leave class during lunch to show his face.

<Did you have gym yet?> I texted Josh. It was fifty-fifty as to whether he would get the message.

<Shawn was not there> He guessed my reason for asking.

What the hell?

I scrolled down to Shawn's number in my contact list. <How come you're not at school?>

The bell to end the day had just rung when I got a response. <Didn't feel like it>

Didn't feel like it? There was one day left. He'd worked so hard on his paper. <I need to see you.>

I exchanged my books at my locker and met Josh at the car. <Be at the entrance to the quarry in twenty or I'm coming to get you.>

Josh went to get gas first, in the opposite direction, giving Shawn plenty of time to get there, even if he didn't see the text right away.

"Hurry up, Josh, please." Every minute felt like an eternity.

Relief washed over me when we pulled to the side of the road and Shawn came into view. He stood in the woods just out of sight of cars, hands stuffed in his back pockets.

I got out and Josh drove off.

Shawn merely glanced at me as I approached and started walking in the direction of the quarry.

Whoa, wait a minute. After all the worrying I'd done? I choked back the irritation that thickened my throat, wanting answers more than confrontation.

"Hey." I quickened my pace to catch up with him. I grabbed hold of his arm to slow him and he yanked away, throwing distance between us as he whipped around to me.

"What?" He stood rigid, almost as if startled, his eyes quickly going in search of anything that wasn't me.

He'd said he was okay. Physically, he looked okay—from what I could see—but the energy he gave off left a different impression. "What's wrong?"

"Nothing." His eyes continued to wander, then met mine for an instant, as if to see if I bought the lie. With a breath of frustration, he started walking again, this time slower.

His posture relaxed, but with his hands remaining in his pockets, he left no opportunity for me to even try to hold his hand.

I was pretty positive he wouldn't tell me where he'd been, so I just bypassed the fact that he was MIA for three days. "I talked to your history teacher," I said, dancing around it with what seemed like safe enough conversation. "She was nice. Sounded like she might accept your paper late."

"Yeah, I'm over it."

Over it? "You worked so hard on it, though."

"Big deal. She'll probably pass me anyway. She always does."

Did he not recall I'd witnessed how enthusiastic he'd been? It was so frustrating when he was in a mood like this. I didn't know if I should push him or back off. *Why* was he in this mood? Was it everything Beth said to him? I was sure there was more than what I heard. "Well . . . if you want to give it to me, I can turn it in for you."

He'd missed a whole week, I couldn't imagine he'd go for the last day.

"Megan, just forget it. It's stupid."

Seriously? After all Dad had done? Heat pushed at my eyes. I came to a stop, aggravation bubbling up in me like lava. "You're 'over it.'" He stopped, too, and turned around to me as I fell hard onto the eggshells I walked on. "'It's stupid.'" God, I hated that word now. "I really don't get you, Shawn. You got a second chance and you're just throwing it away like it's nothing." It was maddening.

He just stared at me.

"Say something. Please. Because I'd really like to understand."

"I don't want to go to the quarry."

My heart did some funny flip thing in my chest. "Why?"

"You saw me, I'm fine. I'm gonna go."

"To where?" He couldn't escape that easily. "To that trailer, to your dark room with no windows?" I wanted to shake him.

His face was without expression. "I'm tired, Megan."

God! Shawn! "You don't think I'm tired?" How could he not realize? "I barely slept while you were gone." Besides, he'd slept in the grass before. He made it sound like he didn't even want me to walk with him. "You told me you planned to disappear." If he even remembered. "For all I knew, you had." I couldn't corral my emotions and had to look away so he wouldn't see the gloss to my eyes.

Then again, maybe it wouldn't be so bad if he did. I looked back. "I missed you. I thought I might never see you again."

He looked past me and swallowed.

225

"Is it the stuff Beth said?" It had to be. Or maybe he didn't like that I'd seen him in the state I had.

His eyes flitted down to me. "No."

"Then what? Why are you being like this?"

"I'm tired, I told you."

This wasn't tired, this was something else entirely. He was lethargic, but in more of a depressed kind of way. "Did something happen while you were gone?"

He looked away and a shine built on his eyes.

"What? Where were you?" It was worth a shot.

His jaw flexed as his eyes filled.

I reached up and drew on his cheek to turn his eyes back. "You can talk to me." Maybe if I said it enough, something inside him would give.

He refused to look at me, the tears perched on his lids about to spill over. "Megan, I can't—" They did. "I can't do this right now." He made a move to leave.

I reached my arm out, blocking him. With hopes of reminding him of something he enjoyed, I grasped the back of his neck, and I stretched up and kissed his lips. He winced, and then shoved me away and gasped as if he tried to breathe out a bad taste. "Oh, God." He gagged as if he would throw up. He nearly knocked me over as he barreled past me and booked it back down the path.

What the . . . "Shawn!"

Honestly?

Every emotion I had plunged into a pit of hurt and confusion.

226

Chapter 28

The last day of school was my birthday. Susan sang to me over the loud-speaker during morning announcements. So. Freaking. Embarrassing. Apparently, she hadn't gotten the memo about how much I hated the day. Either that, or she decided to take my emotional growth into her own hands. In any case, I could've gone without the extra attention. People were already riled up, but that made my entire homeroom burst into laughter.

So. Unnecessary.

Shawn skipped, as I expected he would. No call, no text.

Dad said he needed to work late. He walked through the door about an hour and a half after his usual time, toting two large paper bags that seeped the amazing aroma of Chinese food. There were no Chinese restaurants around, so he'd traveled far.

The all-paramount "sweet sixteen." As usual, I would've been perfectly fine if the day went unacknowledged. Now I had even more reason. There was nothing sweet about it.

"What, you don't like Chinese anymore?" Dad asked, pulling the Styrofoam containers from the bags in his own subtle attempt to work my birthday back into rotation.

"I love Chinese."

"Yeah, I can hear the enthusiasm." He looked at me. "What's up, kiddo? I figured this would be a nice, low-key way to celebrate one of the best days of *my* life."

It was sweet, and I appreciated the attempt. "It's not that." As in Mom. My expression contorted.

"Then what? Is it Shawn? I did notice he's not here."

I didn't have to say anything, my face did all the talking.

"You did invite him over, didn't you?"

I shook my head. "He doesn't even know it's my birthday."

"Why is that?" He opened the containers to check their contents. I wished, now, that Mom *was* the reason. He looked at me when I didn't say anything. "Did something happen between the two of you, or is this something else?" I was sure, by now, he had a list of thoughts as to what the something else could be. Josh and Bobby got themselves plates and moved around us to get their dinner.

I couldn't do it anymore. "It's something else." The weight had become too much to bear.

Dad looked at me again and his eyes stuck on me. "Should I not be putting food on a plate for myself right now?"

Josh eyed me as he scooped lo mien. Dad's even tone had me, hook, line, and sinker. "Probably not."

228

He gave me a once over, then straightened and looked to Josh and Bobby. "Okay, boys, you're on your own." He placed his hand on my back and led me upstairs to my room.

I stepped in ahead of him, and he eased the door shut behind us. I sat on my bed, and so did he.

I didn't know where to start. There were so many things I knew full well I should've already told him. Maybe the beginning was the best place.

I took a breath and words were supposed to come out. I tried again, but the same thing happened, and he blurred in front of me.

"It's okay, Meg, take your time."

I *had* taken my time. I had taken too *much* time. I wiped my eyes. Dad's presence was open and caring.

"How about starting with why Shawn missed the whole last week of school," he said.

"You know?"

A breath came through his nose as a smile flickered. "Of course, I know. Do you really think the principal would let an opportunity to rub that in my face pass?"

"Why didn't you say anything?"

He shrugged. "I haven't seen him."

Still, he hadn't said anything to me. "I don't get it. He was so excited. He did that paper, and everything."

"Well . . . sometimes when you have substantial things going on in your personal life, it detracts from everything else." I guess that's what the word "troubled" told him.

"I don't know what's going on." I made sure he knew. "I really don't. I've tried and tried, but he won't tell me."

"Well, there must be things that have concerned you, or I don't think you'd be talking to me right now."

"Lots. But I think you're gonna be really mad at me."

"If you really, truly care about him, Megan, then you'll remind yourself that it's not about you."

It was true. I couldn't hold back. Shawn needed help.

I took another deep breath, and this time the words came. I told Dad about my impression of Shawn before we met, our outing to the quarry the day he kicked us off the boat, the time I found him asleep on the ledge with the razor blade. Every word I spoke led to another and I told him things I never thought I would. He wavered when I told him about the day Shawn ran from our house and I came within seconds of seeing his Dad drop him to the ground. His eyes closed and he tried to breathe away my stupidity.

I told him the things Shawn confided in me about his mother.

I told him everything.

"Remember the day he was here and helped to make the pasta salad?"

He nodded.

"He fell asleep out on the deck. You came home, so I figured I should wake him up. I barely even touched him and he flew up, and he peed his pants."

Dad frowned. "That's why his pants were wet?"

"I said I spilled water on him because everyone would obviously

230

notice."

"Well, for people with a deep history of abuse, that's not so uncommon. Especially sexual abuse."

"But could sexual abuse from three years ago still do that?"

"There's no saying. There could be repercussions from that for the rest of his life."

What about all of a sudden being repulsed by a kiss from your girlfriend?

His eyes shut again as I told him about how I'd stalked Shawn's trailer the day his paper was due—being in such close proximity to his father and the other man, climbing in the window, finding him the way I did. Beth.

I told him how I'd hugged him and told him he wasn't stupid.

"He texted me on Sunday and said he wouldn't be around for a few days. And then he texted me on Wednesday to let me know he was back. But that was it, and he's been really weird since. You need to get him out of that house, Dad. Whatever's going on, I think it's just getting worse."

Dad inhaled a deep breath through his nose. "Okay, Megan, I'm not debating anything you're saying, or saying that any of it's not true, there is obviously something very wrong going on. But the law states that you can not just go and take someone out of their home. There needs to be an investigation, evidence, all of the same stuff that would apply in any other instance."

"But there *is* evidence. *Me*. Things I saw, things I heard, my experiences with him."

231

Dad looked me squarely in my eyes. "You're fifteen, Megan—"

"Sixteen."

"Sixteen. You don't have any physical evidence, and there is no one to verify your accounts. From the sounds of it, Shawn wouldn't even."

"I have a photo." I'd forgotten about it. I scrolled through my phone. "This is the red-headed man." It showed both him and his car. "I think his name is Jackson." Beth had said it.

He viewed it. "It would've been better if you recorded the conversation, but it's something. It shows who he's acquainted with. If it's not already public knowledge."

What the hell? "So, what do we do?"

Dad's lips pursed. "I get to work."

"Can you be inconspicuous? I don't know what Shawn will do if he suspects you know something. Or his father."

"I know how to be discreet, Megan. I've known for a while that there was a problem, and his father has a long history with the law."

"What do *I* do?"

"Same thing you have been. Continue to affirm for him that he's not alone, be a hand he can hold. I don't want you going near his house, though. Not even close. If you're worried something's wrong, you tell me. I also don't think you should be with him unless he's here or you're with Josh or Bobby."

"But—" How would I do that?

"He knows he's welcome here, Meg. I think he would understand, and I wouldn't be doing my job as a parent if I said otherwise."

232

I would try, but I couldn't promise. "Is there any chance Shawn will get in trouble for anything?" If he was involved in something illegal, charges could be brought against him.

"He's a minor, and it doesn't sound like he's a willing participant, so I doubt it."

He exhausted a breath and reached his hand to my cheek. "I'm glad you told me. You did the right thing. I do wish you hadn't waited so long, and there were events that should've sent you running to me, but ultimately, you're here in front of me now. It's always better late than never."

As long as it wasn't *too* late. Building a case could take months. Or longer.

"Now, do you think you can eat? It is a very special day for *me,* and I did drive a long way for our favorite food." His expression lightened.

"I can try." After all that, I wasn't very hungry. I couldn't remember the last time I had been.

I followed him back downstairs, and we each got a plate from the cupboard.

Bobby patted me on my back as I scooped General Tso's chicken. "Happy Birthday, Sis. Who bought you the 'big girl' pants?"

I could've punched him. I was glad Dad was involved, but I'd betrayed a confidence.

Chapter 29

I hadn't heard from Shawn since he had the ill reaction to my kiss, nor did I try to contact him. Like Dad said, it wasn't about me, but that was one instance that was difficult to get past. I figured I'd gotten too close and he tried to push me away, but why would he have nearly vomited when I kissed him? He'd kissed me so many times without issue, why now?

There was a chance I'd caught him off guard and it triggered memories of Mary. Just the thought made me want to vomit, myself. More likely, though, he'd probably had some sort of experience with drugs again and still felt the effects of them. Which was just as disturbing.

Then again, maybe I put too much thought into it. Maybe he was just sick. It's what I tried to force myself to believe. It was the only thing that made me feel better, and it would've lent to his presence and his claim he was tired.

In any case, I wished I hadn't gotten mad at him. It was exactly what I tried so hard not to do. And, of course, now I didn't know how to fix it. I could be patient with hopes he would come around, but patience, where he was concerned, didn't ever seem like an option. Especially now that Dad imposed restrictions.

I was relieved I'd talked to Dad, but the chains clinched around my chest didn't feel any looser.

Saturday, just before dinner time, the doorbell rang. I pulled the door open to Shawn on the step.

A-freaking-men. I took what felt like my first breath in days.

He stood with his thumbs hooked in his belt loops, brow pleated, bouncing on his toes. His mouth moved as if he would speak, but words didn't come.

He backed up as I stepped out. "What's wrong?" He shook.

"I can't lose you, Megan, I can't."

All the while, I thought I'd annoyed him with all my check-ups. Two days of not hearing from me, and he apparently panicked. I wove my arms through his and clamped them around his waist. "You will *never* lose me."

He clutched me, his left arm stronger than his right, and his lips fell to the top of my head.

I circled my hand over his back.

"Is that Shawn?" Dad asked from his chair in the living room, surely having heard every word. He got up and came to the door, and Shawn backed out of our embrace.

"Hello, sir."

235

"Good to see ya, kid." Lines dug into Dad's cheeks. "Sticking around for a little? Dinner's almost ready."

"Uh . . . no, I need to get home."

"Well, that was a short visit."

"I needed to tell Megan something. I gotta go."

"Well, uh, I was hoping to catch up with you. I got a call from Principal Jacques—"

"I'm sorry," Shawn cut him off. "It was out of my control. I had to go to Kentucky with one of my Dad's friends to help transport a car. There was no way out of it."

A car? He said it so fluidly.

"Does that kind of stuff happen often? I mean, will it be a common occurrence once the school year starts again?" Dad gave no indication he didn't believe him.

"Nah, he planned the trip before all that happened. I didn't realize it. I really am sorry. I do appreciate everything you did. Next year'll be different, I swear."

There was a chance he told the truth. But he hadn't told me that. He hadn't told me anything. And he hadn't acted like someone who'd just gotten back from delivering a car.

"Alright, well . . ." Dad's head tilted. "Are you sure you don't want to stay for dinner? There's a pot roast in the oven Megan put together."

"I really can't," he said, glancing at me.

Dad's light expression remained. "Well, why don't you at least say happy birthday to her."

236

Color rose in Shawn's face. He caught himself mid "F" word as he looked to me. "I'm sorry."

"It was yesterday. It's okay."

"How 'bout dinner tomorrow?" Dad said.

"Monday?" Shawn asked me. He knew I knew Sundays weren't good.

I smiled. "Sure. But you don't have to wait until dinner time to come over."

"See you Monday," Dad said, and went back inside.

"I really gotta go," Shawn said to me.

My smile this time was forced.

He seized me in his arms. "You'll text me, right?"

I laughed through a breath. "You'll respond, right?"

Chapter 30

At a quarter to four, I had yet to hear from Shawn. He hadn't texted me since he left my doorstep two days prior, nor did he return a single one of mine. Now, not only did I expect him, Dad did too.

<Where are you? Why aren't you answering?> There was a chance he was at the garage. <Are you still coming?>

Just before Dad was due home, he texted me back.

<Can't come. Sick>

<Sick how?> A cold, the flu?

<Throwing up. Talk to you tomorrow>

What was I supposed to do with that? There was the possibility he told the truth, but how was I to know? It wasn't exactly the season to be sick. <Can you call me?> Maybe if I heard his voice.

<Throwing up>

Ugh . . .

"Do you believe him?" Dad asked me when he got home.

"Did you believe him when he said he had to deliver a car?"
He'd been so convincing.

"Well, wait 'til tomorrow. See what happens."

~

A struggling sun greeted me when I woke up. I reached for my phone on my nightstand, not expecting a text, but discouraged when there wasn't one.

I had two choices. Wait the day away at the mercy of Shawn's poor response practice, or call Dad.

I dialed Dad's number but got his voicemail.

I texted Shawn and told him if he didn't get back to me, to expect to see me, and I called Dad again. He still didn't answer, so I left a message.

I waited almost half an hour. Finally, I called the secretary at Dad's office.

"He's in a meeting with the town manager, hon."

"Can you have him call me as soon as he's out?"

"Sure thing."

Thirty more minutes passed. The more time went by, the more anxious I got.

It would be disobeying Dad's direct order, but I needed to go check on him.

Knowing they'd probably try to stop me, I left the house without telling Josh or Bobby where I went.

A light sprinkle from a passing cloud dampened me as I walked.

Mr. Harris was likely at work, but I still kept near the edge of the woods as I traveled down Shawn's driveway. There was no big blue truck, nor tow truck, and it appeared as though the front door was open.

I waited, listening. There wasn't even sound from the television.

Tense, I set across the dirt clearing and up the two steps. My heart did double-time as I cautiously cupped my hands to my eyes and peered through the screen. Shawn lay on the couch, facing the back wall, a pillow under his head and a blanket covering him from his toes to his shoulders.

"Shawn."

Not even a twitch.

"Shawn."

His head jerked.

I pulled open the screen and went in. I sat on the edge of the couch and touched my hand to his forehead. He groaned and his eyes blinked open. "Hey, you're not looking so hot." His face was without color.

"I don't feel good," he muttered.

"I can see that." It was no lie.

He turned his position and lifted higher on the pillow. "Can you get me a glass of water?"

I left him and went into the next room. When I returned, he maneuvered his position again to drink. The water rippled in the glass when he took it.

He drank almost all of it in one long chug.

"How long have you been like this?"

He dropped his head back. "Since Saturday night."

I combed my fingers through his hair. "Why don't you come home with me?" I didn't want him to be alone, and I also couldn't imagine him getting well in such a stagnant environment. "You can sleep in my bed, nobody will bother you."

"I'll be fine." His eyes closed again.

"I'm not leaving you like this."

"Megan, I'm sick. Everyone gets sick."

"You're burning up."

"Yup, that's what sick people do." He pulled the blanket higher to cover his shoulder.

It wasn't even eleven yet. I couldn't spend the whole day worrying about him. I left him again and went down the dark hall to his bedroom. I felt for the switch on the wall and flipped it on. There was a bureau to my right. I pulled the drawers open.

In the third one down was a zip-up sweatshirt. It neared eighty degrees, but he was cold, so I grabbed it.

"C'mon." I helped him to sit up. "I'll call Josh and he can pick us up."

"He can't come here."

"It'll be for two seconds." I slipped the sweatshirt onto his left arm. He leaned forward so I could get it around his back, but he couldn't move his right arm to get that one in.

"Again?" It had been okay when he came over on Saturday. His whole body was tense. I pulled the sweatshirt off and started with his right arm this time so he wouldn't have to move it. I zipped it up and dialed Josh.

241

Shawn couldn't keep his eyes open. Josh arrived and he barely acknowledged the sound of his car outside.

"Hey." Josh shook his shoulder. "You gonna stand, or what?" He just about had to carry him out.

He sat him in his front passenger seat and belted him in. "I don't know, Meg, do you think we should bring him to the hospital?"

It didn't sound like a bad idea.

"No hospital," Shawn mumbled.

Josh lifted out of the car and shut the door. "He doesn't look good, Meg."

"I know. I'll call Dad when we get home."

I was surprised Shawn didn't protest more than he did. He was probably too weak.

Josh turned out of the driveway toward home. We turned onto Center Road from County and a cherry-red sports car passed us.

Josh's eyes went to the rearview mirror.

"What?"

"That was Damian." He watched the car.

It wasn't only Damian. There were at least three other people with him. And he was turning around. "He's not alone," I said.

"I saw that." Josh pressed on the gas. "I can't take all of them, Meg. Call Dad." He pushed buttons on his own phone as I dialed. "Center Road," he spoke into it. "About to get into a brawl."

Damian's engine screamed.

Panic dropped on me as I waited for Dad to pick up. "Go, Josh."

"I *am* going."

We were so close to home.

Damian closed in on us. He moved to the opposite side of the road and pulled alongside us. Josh accelerated. So did Damian, and he turned his wheel. "He's gonna drive into us," Josh said as I listened to the ring of Dad's phone.

"He won't mess up that car," Shawn said, limp.

Damian cut his wheel harder and Josh reacted. Had there been a ditch, we would've been in it. Damian took over the road, not allowing Josh room to recover, and Josh slammed on his brakes to avoid hitting a tree. "*Shit, fuck, fuck, shit!*"

I was shrieking when Dad's voicemail picked up, and I rushed a plea for help into the phone. "Maybe he's just trying to scare us. Maybe he'll go away."

"Yeah, he looks like he's gonna go away," Josh said sarcastically.

Damian got out of his souped-up Mustang and walked around the front of it to our car. "Let's go, Harris, c'mon." He called him on with his hands.

Josh got out, cautious of the car full of delinquents. "Don't do this, man, just get out here. The cops are on their way."

Damian's eyes remained on Shawn. "Let's go, Shawny boy!" He slapped his palms on our hood.

Josh's arm flew out toward our passenger seat. "Kid, can't you see there's something wrong with him?"

"I am gonna kick that kid's teeth in," Shawn muttered, his hands resting loosely in the pockets of his sweatshirt.

"Not today, you're not," I said.

243

Drops of rain spattered on the windshield. One by one, Damian's crew got out of the Mustang.

"You have got to be fucking kidding me," Josh said. "You call that fucking fair?"

Josh pushed at one that came at him. Then another unleashed.

"I don't see this going well," Shawn said. His seatbelt released and he reached for the door handle.

"Shawn, *don't*." I gripped the arm of his sweatshirt from the back seat. He pulled out of my grasp.

Damian went back to his car and opened the passenger side door. He leaned in and reappeared with a metal baseball bat. He walked toward Shawn, circling it in front of him.

"Shawn, get in the car," Josh yelled at him, fending off the other three boys.

"Shawn, get in the car!" I hollered. I dialed 911, and then dropped my phone on the floor and lurched out of the car. "*Shawn!*" His hands remained tucked in his pockets as Damian approached him.

Damian drew back the bat as if he would hit a ball. Shawn turned his head, his eyes connecting with mine in a soft gaze. "*Shawn!*" Damian swung. The bat made contact with Shawn's forehead. His head whipped back and he spilled to the ground.

The sky opened up and gave way to an onslaught of pelting rain. Josh went ballistic and fought with everything he had.

I careened over the hood of the car past the brawl and dropped to the ground. Shawn was unconscious, hands still in his pockets. The bat hit so hard it split his skin, and the rain created a bloody wash underneath his head. I rushed the zipper of his sweatshirt down and tore it off. Damian stood with his bat as if he'd just finished a hard day's work.

"*Get out of here!*" I shouted at him. I wadded an arm of the sweatshirt and pushed it to Shawn's head, and then pressed my fingers to his neck to feel for a pulse. My own pulse pounded and it was hard to feel anything with the rain.

I cloaked him with my body and was pretty sure I felt something. "Don't do it," I said to him. He'd done it on purpose. I pressed my cheek to his. "So help me, God, Shawn Harris . . ."

A hand jerked my shoulder.

Bobby. "What the fuck happened?" he asked.

Damian and his crew were gone. "*Josh?*" He lay on the ground, face turned from the rain that washed blood from him as well.

"Megan, what happened?" Bobby asked again with haste. He was who Josh must've called.

"*Damian.*" Sobs burst from me.

"Chill, I'm calling 911." He took his phone out of his pocket as he dashed for the car.

"He's not alone, Bob." Josh spoke as best he could.

"Which way did he go?"

Josh must've pointed, and Bobby backed up and screeched off.

The blood from Shawn's head wouldn't stop. "Why would you do that, Shawn, *why?*" My tears got lost with the rain. I held my cheek to his again, praying it wasn't the last time I'd ever feel him.

245

The single red light Dad placed on the roof of his car in emergencies shone in the distance.

Dad descended on us, skidding to a stop, and he bolted out of the car. "*Joshua?*"

Josh lifted his arm, signaling he was okay.

"Megan, don't move him," he instructed me, and got down on his knees. Holding Shawn's head with one hand, he drew my wrist back with the other to see underneath the sweatshirt. "What'd he hit him with?"

"A *bat.*"

He felt for a pulse.

"Bobby and I both called 911," I said.

"I heard the rescue get dispatched. We've just gotta hold tight."

"Bobby went after them, Dad," Josh called.

"What kind of car, Meg?" he asked as he stood and went back to his.

"A red Mustang."

"I need a redirect," he said into his radio, and told the officers who they looked for. He gave them Bobby's description as well. "I want my son found and detained until those boys are in custody."

The sirens from the rescue blared. It came up on us as fast as Dad and stopped diagonally across the road.

Two paramedics jumped out.

A brace was placed on Shawn's neck to secure it, and a bandage was taped to the injury on his head. He was strapped onto a stretcher and loaded into the truck. I tried to get in with him.

246

"Megan, no." Dad held me back. "We can follow in the car."

I watched until the doors were closed.

Josh sat in the front seat of Dad's car, bloodied and bruised, but for the most part, okay. As the rescue started off, Dad placed a call to Harris Towing. He called twice more in route to the hospital and finally left a message. He then sought out alternate numbers for Mr. Harris. He left a message on his home phone, as well as his cell.

~

It took a full half an hour to get to the hospital. Shawn was unloaded, and moans and groans droned from him as he was wheeled in. Dad's fingers folded around my arm to ensure I didn't follow while he made sure Josh was attended to. Once he was, we gave chase.

"Stay here," Dad said to me as he joined the barrage of nurses that had converged on him.

The only thing separating me from them was a thin fabric curtain. The noises that came from Shawn got progressively louder as they took his blood pressure and checked all his vital signs.

There was a long groan of pain. "No," he grumbled in protest. He said it again with more force, and the sounds he made were as if he struggled. "*No . . . No . . .*" All I could see were his feet at the end of the stretcher, and they moved as if he tried to get them free of the straps that held them down.

Every last one of my nerves pinged off one another, wishing I could rush in to help him. A nurse came out and used a telephone across the hall. She spoke quickly, and then hung up and went back in.

The commotion behind the curtain escalated. Shawn struggled

even more, and there became a growl to his voice.

Then he didn't struggle at all. The beeping from the monitors decreased and the chaos returned to order.

A doctor passed me, and then another. There were now more people in the curtained-off area than seemed possible. There was a lot of talking, nothing I could make out, and no noise from Shawn at all.

A nurse came out, closing the last bit of curtain I could see through, and went to the phone. She made a call, hung up, and dialed again. "She'll be down," she called across as she hung up the second time. "She said to take him to CT first."

I strained to hear. The talking didn't cease but was more hushed. Dad's voice was intermingled.

The curtain whipped open and the stretcher started out. With the plastic collar still around his neck, Shawn was covered from feet to chin with a thin white blanket.

He appeared asleep as they wheeled him past me, a bloodied gauze taped to the injury on his head.

A doctor followed as the other hung back and talked with Dad, Shawn's shoes and sopping wet clothes in a pile on the floor next to them.

Dad's eyes were closed with his fingers sprawled across his face.

A nurse alerted them to my presence, and Dad, his own clothes slicked to him from the rain, looked at me as if he forgot I was there. He excused himself from the doctor.

"Megan, hon, you're going to have to go wait with your brother."

"Why, what's going on?" He guided me with his hand on my

248

back. He dialed his cell phone and put it to his ear as we turned the corner to where Josh was.

"Hey, Linda, it's Ed. I need an APB out on John Harris, ay-sap. He's probably trying to get out of the area, but check at his garage and address anyway, and consider him armed and dangerous."

A brick dropped into my stomach.

Dad listened to the woman on the other end.

"I'll call you back in a few. Just get that APB out." He ended the call.

"Dad, what's going on?"

He guided me to a small waiting area. "Hang here for a minute." He went to the nurses' station at the corner.

Something had happened. He knew something.

He waved at me to come along. We followed a nurse to another curtained-off area where Josh lay flat on a gurney holding an ice pack to the left side of his face.

"How ya doing, buddy?" Dad asked.

"I've seen better days. How's Shawn?"

"He's seen better days too." Dad lifted Josh's wrist to see under the ice pack. His eye was swollen shut. "Your sister's here. She's going to wait with you."

"They find Bobby yet?"

"Yup. Damian and his bunch too. Luckily, we found them before Bobby did."

"They smelled like alcohol," Josh said.

"Yeah, they'd been drinking."

249

"What's going to happen to him?"

"You let me worry about that." Dad looked at his watch. "I'm going to be here for a while. I'll probably have Bobby come and pick you guys up."

"I don't want to go," I said.

"Megan, you can't stay here."

"I can't go."

"Don't fight me on this, Meg. I've got to get back to Shawn." He started off. "I'll come get you when your brother gets here."

"Dad!" *What the hell?* "*Dad!*"

Chapter 31

Josh hobbled into the house and dropped onto the couch. Susan stormed through the door minutes after we got home.

"Are you effing kidding me?" she said when she saw Josh. "That kid has got it coming."

"You better believe it, he does," Bobby said.

Dennis wasn't far behind her. "Anything on Shawn?" he asked me as I stood bent over the kitchen counter with my head in my hands.

I signaled no.

"He'll be all right, Meg."

I wasn't so sure. Dennis didn't see how hard he got hit. There was also whatever else went on.

It rained all afternoon and evening. The water that spilled over the edge of the gutters hammered the deck, and the backyard pooled. I called Dad numerous times, but with no answer.

The hollowness in me only continued to deepen as Shawn's words from Saturday ached through me. *I can't lose you.* Here I was, with the feeling I was losing him.

At seven thirty, the house phone rang.

Bobby in Dad's chair answered it. "He's right here," he said, and handed the phone to Josh.

Josh went through the whole how he was feeling bit, because Dad must've asked. "Yeah, I took some," he said. "I will. How's Shawn?"

Dad's response was long.

"Yup." Josh handed the phone to me.

"Meg, I know you're worried, but you can't keep calling me. I have a lot going on."

I had a lot going on too. "Is Shawn okay?" He had to answer me at least that. He hadn't answered a single one of my questions yet.

"He is okay," he said in a calmed manner. "He's got a pretty bad concussion, but he's awake and responding accordingly."

Thank freaking God. "Can you tell them to look at his arm while he's there?"

"They're looking at everything."

"And he really was sick."

"I know." His tone took a grave turn.

Something occurred behind the curtain that morning that made it obvious they needed to go after Mr. Harris. Something obvious to them but not me. "Dad, what happened this morning? Why'd you send out the APB?"

"I can't talk right now, Megan. We'll talk when I get home, okay?"

When would that even be? "Please don't leave him, Dad." I

252

couldn't imagine how scared Shawn must've been.

"I'm not going to leave him."

A voice in the background took his attention.

"Megan, I need to go."

~

Evening turned to night, and the agonizing minutes that ticked by ushered in a new day. Bobby fell asleep in Dad's chair watching TV, and Susan got Josh a cold ice pack before kissing him goodnight.

"Let me know if you hear anything," she said to me in a lowered voice as I sat curled at the end of the same couch Josh lay on.

Dennis put on a late-night talk show and got comfortable on the loveseat.

I must have dozed off. I woke up at a quarter to two in the morning. Everyone was asleep. The TV still blared audience laughter, and there was still no Dad.

~

My eyes fluttered open as Josh dragged me off the couch by my arm.

Daylight cut through the fog of my brain as Dad, Bobby, and Dennis carried Shawn, passed out, through the open front door.

In gray, loosely-fitted, cotton pajama pants and a white T-shirt, his arm in a sling, he was dead to the world as they struggled to get him to the couch.

"Somebody go grab some pillows," Dad directed as he positioned him on his left side.

Bobby scaled the stairs.

The top half of Shawn's forehead was deep shades of purple and blue. Just below his hairline in the middle, beneath a piece of thick transparent tape, was a row of stitches.

Bobby returned with two pillows. Dad put one under his head, and the other he gently placed between his knees. He then covered him with the blanket from the back of the couch.

"All right, phones, guys." He held his hand out to us as Uncle Vance came through the open front door. "C'mon, pronto. No calls, no texts, and there'll be no computer access until we figure things out."

Figure things out?

Bobby reached into his pocket as Josh handed him his, and Uncle Vance took Dennis's.

"Now everybody needs to go upstairs," Dad said.

No explanation, nothing.

"C'mon, guys, just do it." Dad looked ready to drop. "It's been a long night, and I need to talk to Uncle Vance."

I followed the boys up the stairs. Josh took a right toward his bedroom, Dennis following, and Bobby went into his. I started toward mine, but then turned back to the stairs and peeked down.

Dad talked quietly, using his hands to gesture as he recounted to Uncle Vance what had happened. He gently brushed the hair from the back of Shawn's neck, revealing a dark black and blue mark. He reached up to the back of Uncle Vance's neck and motioned what someone must have done. He then moved his hands toward his own inner thighs and did the same.

"The bruising's so deep and so dark," he said in a voice I could barely hear.

Uncle Vance breathed disgust. "Is it a one-time thing, or ongoing?"

"Ongoing."

"Not John, though," Uncle Vance said about Shawn's father. "He doesn't fit the bill."

"Not sure. Shawn's not talking. But he's leading me to believe it's on a large scale."

"Beautiful."

"Yeah, cows, huh? Chickens?" Dad said sarcastically. "We're just plain stupid thinking this shit isn't everywhere."

Uncle Vance sighed.

"I'm going to call Dana and see if I can get her over here first thing. I'm not equipped in the least to deal with something like this."

What on Earth were they talking about? And who was Dana?

"Yeah, that's probably a good idea." Uncle Vance looked past Dad to Shawn. "I have to be honest with you, Eddy, I'm not quite sure why he's even here."

"Because I had to make a decision."

Uncle Vance shook his head. "I'm not so sure you made the right one."

"You didn't see him, Van. He was out of control. He was out of his mind with fear. He literally clung to me. There was no way I could leave him."

"Right, he clung to you because, if this is what you're implying, then he's a target."

Dad rested his elbow on his opposite arm and rubbed his fingers over his forehead. "I understand that."

"Damn, Ed, should he even be out of the hospital?"

"My decision was supported."

"What about Child Welfare? Did you involve them? It's not like you can just take a kid from the hospital and harbor him in your home."

"Van, I haven't gotten that far yet, it was the immediacy of the situation."

"In the immediacy of the situation, you still need to involve Child Welfare."

"I involved the judge. He signed over temporary custody to me."

Uncle Vance balked. "Oh. Okay, then."

"He's a sixteen-year-old boy, Van, the same age as your oldest son, who I'm pretty sure you wouldn't want anyone turning their back on. He needs help, and I'm in a position to give it to him."

Uncle Vance's head showed continued disapproval. "It's your choice, Ed, I'm not telling you what to do, but you're putting your family in jeopardy."

"You're right, it is my choice. Thanks for your input, but moving forward, I'd appreciate it if you kept it to yourself."

Uncle Vance sighed. "All right." He turned for the stairs, and I ducked back behind the wall. "Dennis, let's go."

Dennis came out of Josh's room and passed me down the stairs.

"I need you back here at eight," Dad said.

"Yup."

Dennis followed Uncle Vance out the door, and Dad walked out of sight.

What had happened to him? What kind of target was he? What jeopardy?

Dad's voice came from the kitchen as if he spoke to someone. I moved down to the middle of the stairs and strained to hear.

"You name it, Dana. I don't even know where to start. They said he was sodomized so badly they don't know how he doesn't have colon damage."

Sodomized? I probably wasn't supposed to know what that meant but was pretty sure I did. Dad's voice dulled as the word reverberated in my head. Any thought I tried to have derailed. The information was un-processable.

"He was pretty classic. He was down for the count when we brought him in, but as soon as they started removing his clothes, he livened. They needed to sedate him." He paused as Dana must've asked questions. "For physical, lots of severe bruising, torn ligaments. I really don't care to get into the rest, it's pretty graphic . . . Hey, this is your arena, not mine . . . He had a fever of over a hundred and four, so they pumped him full of fluids, started him on antibiotics . . . Shawn Harris. The doctor you want to consult with is Doctor Maria Vasquez . . . Do me a favor and get on it as soon as you can, I need you here . . . A hundred and two point eight when we left . . . I know. One minute, he was hooked up to all sorts of monitors and IVs, the next, he was in my car. I got a very eerie feeling from him, though, and needed to get him out of there . . . Thanks, I appreciate it. I'll also need your help with Social Services. I woke the judge at one in the morning, and he signed him over to me temporarily. I need you to make sure he doesn't leave my custody. He's a target, and he's suicidal."

I knew Shawn was suicidal, and Uncle Vance had just said he was a target. The combination of the two words made me aware of every heartbeat.

Dad appeared and, phone to his ear, looked up through the rungs of the railing at me. "Thanks, Dana, I'll see you in a few hours." With his eyes on me, he pressed the button to end the call. "If I wanted you to hear it, Megan, I wouldn't have sent you upstairs."

I moved my hand off the railing, it shaking from a combination of the long day and the information overload, and sat. Dad started up. "Sodomized. Does that mean, like, when a guy—"

Dad shook his head. "It wasn't meant for you to hear."

"Does it?"

He cupped my face in his hands. "This day's not going to end, is it?" He pulled me up by my arm and led me back up the stairs.

"Who's Dana?"

"She's a psychiatrist who works for the county. She specializes in these types of cases." He brought me into my bedroom and sat me on my bed.

"I should've said something sooner." My eyes blurred more and more until I blinked away the tears. "He just kept convincing me not to."

Dad sat down next to me and pulled me to him in a tight hug. "I try and try and can think I did my best, and then something like this happens to make me realize I'll never really be able to fully protect

258

you guys."

"I was so close, *so* close to calling you the day I took that picture."

Dad pushed on my forehead, forcing me to look up at him. "That man is now in custody. You did the right thing."

My emotions peaked. "Not right enough." I sobbed into his shoulder.

Dad held me, rubbing my arm until I calmed down. "How long has it been going on?" I asked.

"A long time," he said as if I didn't have control over it anyway. "Think of it this way, Nut Meg, you kept him alive. I honestly don't think he would've had the will to keep going, otherwise."

"I don't think so, either."

He squeezed me and kissed my forehead. "We'll get him through this, you and me, we've gotta work as a team, okay?"

I nodded against his tear-soaked shoulder. "What happens now?"

"Not quite sure. We're still trying to figure that out."

"Did he know he was coming here?"

"I don't know. They gave him a hefty dose of some sleep medicine. He woke up a little bit when they were getting him dressed, but he was pretty out of it."

"Why *is* he here?"

A smile tugged at his cheeks. "Oh, are you complaining?" His smile faded. "Because of the way Shawn acted and things he said, I didn't trust his safety with anyone else."

"That's a little scary."

"Yes, it is." But I could detect no fear in his eyes.

259

"So, what Uncle Vance said—"

"Megan." Dad held my face again, shaking his head.

"Is Shawn's arm broken?"

"No," he said with a slow blink. "He has a separated shoulder. It'll be fine with rest and possibly some physical therapy."

I took a lung-filling breath, my body and mind both jarred.

"Try to get some sleep, hon." Dad pulled my head to him and kissed my temple. "I'm going to try to do the same. That medicine is going to wear off, and I imagine we'll need full team effort when it does."

Chapter 32

The creak of the stairs was the only sound that filled the house as I tiptoed down after tossing and turning for over an hour. Dad slept in his easy chair next to the couch, and Shawn still lay passed out from the sedative he'd been given, the lack of stress in the muscles of his face providing a believable appearance of peace.

I continued on through the kitchen and out the slider to the deck. I sat there and watched the sun rise higher in the sky with dawn's slow promise of warmth, reviewing every moment I'd ever been with Shawn—the times he shirked away from me, his skittishness, his moods. The kiss that nearly made him vomit. What happened to him in those three days? Three. Whole. Days.

At least an hour went by. Dad poked his head out the door, startling me. "I've got a fresh pot of coffee in here, do you want some?" He was dressed as if going to work.

"No, thanks."

He left the door open as he made himself a cup.

"Are you going there?" I asked him.

"Where, hon?" He stepped out, sipping.

"The trailer?"

"Yup, as soon as your uncle gets here. Why?"

"Just wondering." Shawn would never go back there. Not ever. Did he realize that yet? If not, what would it be like the moment he did?

Josh passed by the open slider and coffee sloshed into a mug.

"How you feeling?" Dad asked in to him.

"Like I got the shit beat out of me." He appeared in the doorway with both hands wrapped around his cup. "Where are you going?"

"To the Harris residence."

"Did they find that dickwad yet?"

Dad shook his head and Josh made a sharp turn of his. Shawn stood dazed in the threshold between the living room and the dining room.

Dad stepped in past Josh and set his coffee down. "How ya doing there, buddy?" He walked over to him and took hold of his shaking left arm to support him. "You really shouldn't be standing." The injury to his head, alone, was bad enough. "Why don't we go back to the couch."

"Can I take a shower?" His voice shivered.

He didn't look as much dazed as he did rattled. "Absolutely," Dad said. "Do you think you can manage it?"

"Yes."

He must've really needed one for those to be the first words out of his mouth.

"Okay, it's a plan. But let's take your temperature first. Make sure it hasn't gone back up."

Shawn walked slowly and held to the countertop between the refrigerator and stove while Dad dug for the thermometer in the drawer next to the sink. "Josh, go get him something to wear for when he comes out. Something similar to what he has on." He found it and slipped it into Shawn's mouth.

A beep signaled it was done, and Dad pulled it out. "One hundred and two point two. Good." He rinsed it under the water of the sink. "I need to leave for a little while," he said. "My brother is on his way over. He won't let anybody in, and there'll also be an officer outside."

Shawn's bloated eyes gazed at Dad's chest.

"There's a woman by the name of Dana Pulaski who will be here around ten. She's a psychiatrist who works for the county." His voice lowered for my potentially eavesdropping ears. "You've got some really tough emotions you're dealing with right now, and you shouldn't be taking them on alone. There's probably no better person for you to talk to than Dana."

I couldn't picture Shawn talking to anyone, but at least the woman would be there if he decided to. She had a thousand times more credentials than I.

Josh returned with a pile of clothes and a towel.

"I'll have you use the bathroom in my room," Dad said. "It's a little bit more private."

"Will you stay outside the door?" Shawn's entire body trembled.

Dad's expression dulled, realizing he probably hadn't heard a word he said. "Sure."

~

I stayed out on the deck, trapped by my thoughts. Uncle Vance had long gotten there, and Dad had yet to leave.

He called into the bathroom several times to make sure Shawn was alright, regretting his decision to let him take a shower for the simple fact he had such a bad concussion.

"Shawn, you need to be done," he said through the door. It'd been over half an hour. "Shawn, do you hear me?" He spoke loudly enough I could hear him all the way out on the deck. "Answer me, or I'll need to come in."

Shawn must've, because Dad's voice lowered.

After another fifteen minutes or so, Dad came out. "I'm taking off," he said.

I nodded.

"I'll try not to be long, but I have no idea how this day will go."

I looked at him this time as I nodded again.

Bobby graced the lower level earlier than usual and scored from the still-hot pot of coffee.

"Shawn see you yet?" I asked. He had on only the boxers he wore to bed.

"No, why?"

"You should probably get dressed."

"Why?"

264

"Just do it." Any sort of male nudity didn't seem like a good idea.

Josh's voice carried from the living room. Uncle Vance's too, as if a conversation took place, but nothing I could make out.

Bobby put clothes on and returned to the kitchen table with one of his music magazines. He was on his second bowl of cereal when Josh came out to the deck.

"You possibly wanna come inside?"

I wasn't so sure I was ready. I'd yet to get a handle on my emotions, and not only was I uncomfortable, I didn't know what I would say to him.

"Megan, the kid took a bat to the head because of you."

He took a bat to the head with hopes of ending his life. Josh hadn't heard the stuff I did, so had no idea what really went on.

"He knows you're out here."

He eventually took the hint and went back inside.

Shawn could've told me. Did I not make him feel as if he could've told me? Did he worry what I would think? Or that I would leave? Or was it just that he worried I would tell Dad? Which I would have, and his suffering would've ended months ago.

A sound behind me turned my head.

Shawn. Shit.

He stood barefoot outside the open slider in a pair of Bobby's pajama pants and one of his faded, gray Abercrombie T-shirts, his face flushed, his wet hair soaking his shirt.

I would've turned my eyes away if I could've. Instead, I moved my feet to the floor and stood. "Your head looks pretty bad." I stepped to him and lifted my hand to the dark row of stitches. "Why did you

265

do that?"

Catatonic. It was the only way to describe him.

"You could've told me," I said, pulling together all my uneasiness and doing my best to transform it into courage. "You're my best friend, Shawn, you said you were sick." If he didn't know I knew, he did now, and a sheen came over his eyes. They widened to accommodate the tears filling them, and his chest rose and fell more rapidly. I couldn't keep my own eyes from tearing. "Yesterday was *Hell*. You could've died." He *wanted* to.

Shawn's tears splashed off the plank floor of the deck. "I wish I did."

"God, Shawn, *no*." Did he not know how much I cared about him? How could he not? "I don't think you have any idea what I went through yesterday, thinking I was never going to see you again."

"What you went through?" His voice cracked. His brow tensed and color rose in his cheeks. "What *you* went through?"

Fuck, it came out wrong. "Shawn, I didn't mean it like that. It's just that the only thing that's ever sparked so much emotion in me was my mom's—"

"What part do you want to know?" He cut me off before I could recover from my verbal screw-up. It was hard to make him out through his trembling breaths. "That five days ago, my father stripped me naked, bent me over the back of the couch, and held me down so a two-hundred-fifty-pound man could slam his dick up my ass? All while his wife recorded it?"

Oh. My. God.

266

"Aw, shit." The feet from the kitchen chair slid across the tile floor, and Bobby appeared in the doorway behind him.

"That it hurt so bad I passed out?"

Josh, too, appeared, and then Uncle Vance. "Shawn." Uncle Vance tried to intervene.

"Or how 'bout that my dad made a whole two grand off me that night?"

"Shawn."

"Maybe you should know how much that actually happens, seeing he isn't the only one who sells me." He could barely catch his breath as his eyes, wider than I'd ever seen, continued to drop tears. "Sometimes, if I fight, they drug me so I can't do anything about it."

"Shawn, that's enough." Uncle Vance took hold of his arm and Shawn ripped away with a chilling vociferation. The little bit of color in his face dropped and he breathed as if he hyperventilated.

I pulled him to me and locked my arms around him. "Don't touch him," I said. "Everybody go away." He tried to grip the back of my shirt but didn't have control of his fingers.

My family just stood there, Josh and Bobby both wide-eyed.

"Go. Away," I lipped.

Shawn's face fell, and he wailed into the top of my head. I squeezed him as tightly as I could. When I didn't think I could squeeze anymore, I squeezed tighter.

He was finally able to get a grip on my shirt, and I pulled his head to my shoulder, his wet face burying into my hair.

Uncle Vance loomed in the doorway and made a dramatic motion of his arm into the kitchen. "He needs to be inside," he said inaudibly.

My foundation had quaked off balance, but I couldn't let it show. Shawn needed me more now than ever. I clamped my arm around his neck. "We need to go in," I whispered into his ear.

With his face planted in the nook of my neck, he took some quick, hard breaths.

He backed away. Still shaking, his eyes aimed down as he pushed his palm over them to dry them.

"C'mon." I took his hand and led him in.

It was a slow walk through the kitchen to the opposite entryway and to Dad's first-floor bedroom. It was the most privacy he would have because of the bathroom.

"Is this okay?" I pulled the door closed behind us. The bed was made since Dad hadn't slept in it, and the curtains still drawn. I let go of his hand and stepped to the miniature refrigerator by Dad's bed. A full supply of water.

Shawn stood quavering in the middle of the room, his legs looking ready to buckle. I took his hand again. "You should probably lie down." I guided him the rest of the way to the bed.

He pushed his palm to the mattress and eased himself down, but kept going to the floor. With a view of the door, he lay on the oriental rug and curled into a ball.

God, can this get any worse?

He at least needed a pillow. I took one from underneath Dad's spread, and he lifted his head.

I got a second to place between his legs like Dad had the night before. "Is this okay?" I asked as I slipped my hand between his knees. He provided space, and then set his leg back down on the fluff separator.

I couldn't imagine not staying with him. I made sure there was a bottle of water within reach and wedged myself between him and the bed. I fought with his hair for pillow space, and with a view of the badly bruised back of his neck, I held him as Mom used to hold me when I was little and had a bad dream.

Chapter 33

Shawn was nearly seventeen years old. He was muscular and strong. How could that stuff happen to him? And how for so long and nobody know about it?

Dana, the woman Dad spoke with on the phone, came at ten as Dad said she would.

She and Uncle Vance went back and forth briefly, and there was a tap on Dad's bedroom door. "Shawn, may I come in?" Her voice was as small as her knock.

Shawn tensed, and my grip on him tightened. "Is it okay if she comes in?"

I lifted up on my elbow, having to make the decision. "You can come in," I said.

The door opened to a tiny sparrow of a woman. She entered, shut the door behind her, came over, and squatted in front of us. "Hello, Shawn. My name is Dana. Did Chief Brennar tell you I would be coming?"

I nodded when he didn't answer.

She looked at me with an expression as soft as the sunlight filtering through the curtains. "Megan, would you mind leaving Shawn and me alone for a little bit?"

I wasn't comfortable with the idea. He already shook again.

"It's okay, he'll be fine," she said.

He was far from fine. I pressed my lips to his temple. "I won't be far."

Dana retrieved the remaining two pillows from the bed as I stood. She placed one of them where I had been and held onto the other as she watched me leave. "Thank you, Megan. We'll call if we need you," she said as I closed the door behind me.

~

The sun was bright and the air outside hot, but we all remained in the security of the house.

"Megan, the stuff they're talking about in there is private," Uncle Vance said when he caught me with my ear to the solid wood door.

It would be true if something was actually said. Besides, I didn't try to hear the conversation, I only wanted to make sure everything was okay. It'd been over an hour, and Dana's voice was the only one I heard.

Uncle Vance's cell phone rang, and he walked away as he answered it. "Yup . . . Yup . . . I'll let her know." He hung up and came back and knocked on Dad's door. "Dana."

Dana poked her head out.

"Ed needs you over at the Harris residence."

271

That couldn't be good.

"Okay, give me a few minutes."

She came out after about five. "I'm going to leave the door open," she said quietly to Uncle Vance. "He shouldn't be alone. But I also don't think you should be in there."

The reason was obvious after Shawn's reaction to him earlier. "What about me?" I asked.

"I hate to say it, hon, but while we evaluate the situation, with the state that he's in, I don't think it's a good idea."

The state he was in? As in, terrified? It was all the more reason I should be with him.

"She was in there all morning," Uncle Vance said. "It didn't seem to be a problem."

"Well, I'll leave it up to you," Dana said to him. "Just know the risks. He's extremely traumatized, which can lead to unpredictable behavior."

"Go ahead, Megan," Uncle Vance said. "But, if for any reason I say you need to come out, you need to do it."

I nodded.

"Keep an eye on him," Dana said to him as I went back in. "Keep your distance, but pass by the door frequently so he knows you're here. So he knows he's safe."

Shawn lay on the floor where he'd been, clutching the fourth pillow.

I faced him this time, my head on my arm as I combed my fingers through his hair, his eyes desolate as tears drained from them.

~

"Megan, out." Dad's voice crashed onto my ears, awakening me.

I pushed up off the floor to see him walking toward Shawn and me carrying a red and black backpack.

"Go," he said to me, and set the backpack down. Using the bed for support, he lowered to the floor as Shawn moved to an upright position. He was none too gentle as he forced his arms around him and enveloped him. "I'm gonna break his neck, Shawn." Uncle Vance pulled me from the room and shut the door. "I'm gonna find him, and I'm gonna *fucking* kill him." His voice was muffled, but I still heard him—we all did—and Shawn's let loose in loud and unsettling crying.

Josh took hold of me, and my own tears soaked the front of his shirt. I'd never heard Dad like that. The conviction in his tone was frightening.

~

Not only did I now think of all the times I was ever with Shawn, the things he said or did, and how I could've interpreted them, but all the occasions I could've involved Dad. Something had happened in the few hours he'd been at Shawn's house to turn him from a law-supporting man of over twenty years to someone ready to commit murder.

The numbers of the digital clock on the DVR were only a few away from what they were when Dad called from the hospital the night before, and Uncle Vance had long left. I hadn't eaten a single thing in double that time, and my stomach had yet to tell me it was hungry.

I put the TV on and went to the guide, but that's as far as I made it. My mind wouldn't let go.

273

Dad's bedroom door opened and Dad came out. He closed the door behind him and went into the kitchen.

Uncle Vance simultaneously pulled into the driveway. He came in carrying a stack of file folders and also went into the kitchen.

"What's going on," I asked, following.

"Go back into the living room, Meg," Dad said.

"But what if I can help?"

"You can't help. This isn't something you can be involved in."

Unfortunately, I was already involved. Did he not realize that? Besides, what had happened to our "teammate" status?

Uncle Vance riffled through one of his file folders. He pulled out a piece of paper and turned it to me.

"Did you not hear what I just said?" Dad asked him.

"She's close to him, Ed. She may have answers we need."

Dad's hands pushed to his face. He was tired and stressed.

"Beth?" Uncle Vance asked me, holding a black and white photocopy of her face with ruled lines behind her head and the name "Elizabeth Jennings" scrolled across the top.

I nodded.

He placed the piece of paper face-down on the counter and picked up another one. Though it was a black and white copy, it was easy to tell the lightness of the woman's eyes. "What about this woman?" It was the same ruled background, and across the top read *Mary-Jo Harris*. "Have you ever met her?"

Shawn had called his mother Mary. The resemblance was uncanny. He looked more like her than he did his father. "No, but Shawn told me about her. The stuff she used to do to him."

"Who's that, his mother?" Dad asked, not having a view of what I looked at.

"John's sister," Uncle Vance said.

"No." He had to have been wrong. Unless they were both named Mary. "Who's his mother?"

Uncle Vance fished another paper from the folder and handed it to Dad.

"*Excuse* me?" Dad's eyes opened wide. "You mean, the woman who sat in my office and pleaded with me to have Shawn removed from Jessup Regional, then told me where I could go when I didn't?"

"That's the one," Uncle Vance said. "Came about the information when checking to make sure John was really Shawn's father."

I took the paper from him. It was a copy of Shawn's birth certificate. In the spot next to "mother", the name Gina Donovan. As in Damian's mother. "*What?*" I read it again, trying to make sense of it. It meant Shawn and Damian were full-blooded brothers. "Shawn referred to his mother as Mary," I said. "A woman named Mary physically and sexually abused him."

"Had to have been Mary-Jo," Uncle Vance said. "She used to live with them. John and Mary-Jo aren't originally from Jessup. Or Gina, so it's probably why people didn't know."

The information made me sick to my stomach.

"Let's do this," Uncle Vance said, and picked up the file folders.

He and Dad headed for the bedroom.

"What are you doing?" I asked. "What else do you have in there?"

275

The stack was thick.

"They're John Harris's known associates," Dad said. "Shawn will hopefully be able to identify the ones we need to jump on first."

"Do you need to do it now?" I stepped between them and the door.

"We've already lost a lot of time, Meg. Shawn knows this is happening."

"Don't show him the picture of Mary-Jo."

"Why?" Uncle Vance asked.

"Her face isn't one he needs to see right now."

Chapter 34

Though the burden of Shawn's situation was less on my shoulders, I now knew just how damaged and emotionally fragile he was. I'd experienced trauma in my own life, but even at my worst, I knew there was a body of people who loved and would care for me no matter what. Aside from us, who Shawn really didn't know all that well, he had no one.

The sky darkened, and it was almost midnight before Dad and Uncle Vance resurfaced. Uncle Vance left, and Dad went into the kitchen again.

"How'd it go?" I asked.

"As good as could be expected," he said, slapping the pieces of a turkey sandwich together. "Didn't say all too much. Had to go on physiological cues more than anything." I was surprised he told me even that much. It was probably because he was so tired. "Why don't you get to bed, Meg."

"And what are you going to do?"

"Pass out from exhaustion?" he said through a mouthful of his skimpy dinner as he walked back to his bedroom.

"Do you think you should try to get Shawn to eat something?"

"No point."

~

Thunder cracked, jolting me awake.

9:36

I dressed and went downstairs. Dad sat on the couch, feet crossed on the coffee table, his laptop on his lap, and some sort of English muffin sandwich in his hand as he chewed.

"Good morning, sunshine."

Thunder boomed again. "Is it?" I didn't want to get excited.

"Breakfast is in the kitchen."

"Did Shawn eat?"

"Dana's working on it."

A plate of ham, egg, and cheese sandwiches sat on the counter next to the stove. I squeezed an ample amount of ketchup onto one and went back into the living room.

"How are you doing?" I asked Dad.

"Peachy." He was sarcastically upbeat.

"Did he sleep?"

"Not sure. *I* did."

I sat hunched over the kitchen table with my chin on my arms, watching the lightning that lit up the sky for most of the morning.

Afternoon was just as quiet. Josh and Bobby stayed in their

rooms mostly, and Shawn never came out of Dad's. Dana left just after three. Dad checked on Shawn several times, and the third time, he didn't come back out.

Bobby spent the evening on the couch in a daze. I passed by him at one point, and he gave me an indistinguishable look.

"Not a word, Bob," I said in anticipation.

"Did I say anything, Meg? Did I say a fucking thing?"

Josh made grilled cheese for dinner. I stacked four on a plate and tapped out a quiet knock on Dad's door. He opened it with a finger to his lips.

"I think he's sleeping."

"Where is he?" Neither he nor his nest of pillows was anywhere in sight.

He pointed to the other side of the bed as he took the plate from me. There was about two feet of space between the bed and the wall. "What's he doing over there?"

"Hiding would be my guess."

Numerous pill bottles sat atop Dad's nightstand, along with the thermometer, and on the floor was a clear plastic bag with items that looked like they were from the hospital.

"Thank you," Dad said for his dinner. He collected all the medications and handed them to me. "Do me a favor and put these in the back of the silverware drawer in the kitchen." As in, hide them. "I'm going to try to get some z's too."

~

Dana came again in the morning, and Dad delegated from home once

279

more. Dana left Dad's bedroom door open, and Dad sat in the same spot on the couch, where Shawn would be able to see him if he needed to.

Dana said he was in shock. It took all day, but she was finally able to get him to eat something. Not much—a couple slices of cheese and some deli meat—but more than he had, and he spoke. Clear, intelligible words about how scared he was.

Dad became more and more conscious of my eager ears, and anything and everything surrounding the case was discussed in utter privacy. If on the phone, he'd make sure he was somewhere I couldn't hear, and any discussion between him and Dana or Uncle Vance was hushed.

Shawn now took every extra bit of Dad's attention. And I didn't mind one bit.

"You guys are going to Uncle Vance's today," he said on day number four. "Dana wants to try to get Shawn out of my room."

"So, why do we need to leave?" Bobby asked. It was hard to know if he was dense or selfish. I was sure it didn't help that Shawn knew we all knew what happened to him.

Dad gave him an eye. "Because it would just help, Bob. Never mind that I'm sure the three of you could all do with a little bit of time away from all this."

We were there all day and came home just before dinner time.

"Act normal and do what you would usually do," Uncle Vance said as we got out of the car.

The living room curtains were drawn, the front door locked and deadbolted. Dad opened it, and we walked in past Shawn sitting on the couch, head back with the arm not in a sling covering his eyes.

Dana, teetering on the edge of the couch next to him, smiled at us as we entered.

Bobby took Uncle Vance's instruction literally and picked up the controller for his video game and sat in Dad's chair.

"Meg, want to make dinner?" Dad asked as I walked toward the kitchen.

It was a given, which was why I headed in the direction. "Sure. Got any suggestions?"

"Something easy."

"Pasta, or hot dogs and beans?" Act as if nothing happened, I imagined, was the goal. Dana leaned over to Shawn and spoke something to him.

"Hot dogs," he lipped, still shielding himself from view.

Josh and Bobby ate at the kitchen table. Dad scarfed down a hot dog at the counter as he put two together for Shawn.

"Do you want beans, Shawn?" I asked, looking out from the kitchen.

His head moved as if to say no. It seemed to take a lot for him just to stay where he was. Dana still sat by his side coaching him.

Dad brought him his plate and placed it on the coffee table in front of him, and then came back into the kitchen.

Leaned forward with his eyes on his food, Shawn picked one up and took a bite. He held it in his hand for a little while, and then took another.

281

Josh finished and went upstairs, and Bobby put his plate in the sink and took a third hot dog back to Dad's chair, and resumed his game. The more nonchalant we acted, the more Shawn's pace picked up.

"Are you sure you don't want beans?" I asked from the kitchen, unsure of where to place myself. "I made way too many."

"I'll take some beans," he said in a low tone with his eyes focused on the coffee table.

I brought him a bowl. He took it from me, not even attempting to make eye contact, and I sat at the opposite end of the couch where I would normally sit if we ate without Dad.

Dana eventually worked herself out of the equation and left.

~

A loud crash woke me first thing in the morning. Bobby burst out of his bedroom, his feet hard and fast on the stairs, and commotion downstairs ensued. I rushed out of bed and, on Josh's heels, flew down the stairs.

"Robert, get out. *Get out.*" Dad was on the floor in his bedroom with Shawn in a standard police hold, knee on his back, securing the arm not in a sling behind him. Shawn, in a frenzy, struggled to get free. "I don't want to hold you like this, Shawn, you need to calm down. You're safe here. Nobody's coming into this house."

"*No, he'll be looking for me. Let me go.*" His blood pumped, his face redder than I'd ever seen. I don't know how Dad held him with the amount of desperation charging him. "*Oh, God, get off of me. He's coming.*" His arm broke free and Dad scooped it back up.

"Shawn, please relax," Dad pleaded with him. Shawn's ferocity was terrifying.

"Dad, you're hurting him," Josh said. Shawn now all-out cried.

"I'm not hurting him, Joshua. I promise you I'm not hurting him." It was chilling to watch. "If you don't calm down, Shawn, I'll be forced to call Dana, and she'll take measures you don't want her to."

Saying that didn't help. Shawn fought more and his voice became shrill.

"Jesus. *Dad*." Bobby couldn't take it.

Sunday.

"Dad, he's wheezing," Josh said.

"I need you guys to get out of here," Dad said. "Someone take my phone and call Dana."

"Dad, it's because it's Sunday." I fumbled through the mess of his tipped-over nightstand and fished it from beneath the broken lamp. "Remember, the person he always had to check in with?"

"Call Dana, Megan."

"I don't know how to use your phone." I couldn't even unlock the keypad to get to his contact list.

He recited his numerical password, my hands shaking as I keyed it in, and instructed me on how to find her number. "Press send and put the phone to my ear," he said. "Shawn, you're going to hurt yourself." I didn't know how he would hear her over him. "Yup." Dana must've heard what took place and spoke first. "It's not gonna happen . . . It was my natural response. It's what I'm trained to do. I can't change positions now . . . He's strong and has an overload of adrenaline

283

coursing through him, and I'm already winded. It's not gonna happen. Just get here." He lifted his ear away from the phone.

"Dad—"

"Joshua, *get out of this room*. Take Megan with you."

Bobby backed out as Josh pulled me by my arm.

Shawn just kept on. "*Let me go. He's gonna come.*"

"I'm going to move your arm, Shawn," Dad said. "And then I'm going to pull you up, and we're going to sit together, okay?"

Dad took a couple deep breaths, and then tried to alter Shawn's position. The moment he moved Shawn's arm to his side, he tried to use it to push himself up to get away. Dad weighted him down again. "What will help you right now, Shawn?"

"*For you to let me GO.*"

"I can't do that. Right now, the safest place for you is in this house. If there's somewhere else you think would be better, just say the word."

"*Away.*" He sobbed.

"A place, Shawn. You're not just going away."

Oh, God. Away could've meant dead.

He cried just as loudly but his struggling lessened.

Dad made another attempt. He slowly unbent Shawn's arm from his back and placed it by his side. "Nobody will hurt you, Shawn. I promise. I won't let it happen." He lifted his knee from his back, simultaneously doing a quick scoop maneuver, and landed with his back against the side of his bed, with Shawn between his legs. He quickly reached across him and secured his free arm, and he pinned

284

his legs with his own. With his head tucked behind Shawn's shoulder, he held him in position.

Shawn gave in and no longer fought. His face was red and wet as he cried. Dad spoke calmly to him. Whatever he said, he chanted it.

By the time Dana arrived, the noises Shawn made had lulled to quiet spurts of despair. She came in carrying a black leather bag, went into Dad's room, and shut the door.

Chapter 35

The incident in Dad's bedroom was intense and frightening, and I worried it would make Dad send Shawn away.

"I'm not going to send him away, Megan. I don't know what our long-term plan is yet, but I know what I signed on for, and that was no different than what he displayed at the hospital." He did send us all to Uncle Vance's again, though.

A little after lunchtime, the phone rang.

"That was your father," Uncle Vance said when he hung up. "He wants the three of you to stay the night."

"Why?" I asked. "Did something happen?"

"He just doesn't see a reason for you guys to be around all this right now."

"Did Shawn say something?" He very well could have. Like I already figured, it couldn't be easy for him feeling like he had an audience.

"No, Megan. It's just not a healthy situation for you to be in."

"Not healthy?" Was he kidding? "Who said?"

"Your father, Dana. And I can't say I don't agree."

"Seriously?" Nobody seemed to think anything of it when Dad ditched us for a month after Mom died. Did they forget what we'd already been through? We could handle it. I could, at least.

"It's one night, Meg."

Sure. Until it became two, then three.

I couldn't sleep. Even though I knew Shawn was perfectly safe, I still worried. As unpredictable as Dana said he might be—and we'd now witnessed—I prayed she wouldn't say something to make Dad change his mind. I was sure it was her suggestion that we not come home.

As eager as I was, Uncle Vance again waited until it was closer to dinner time the following day to bring us home.

"Hey, guys," Dad greeted us as if only a few hours had passed.

The scene was much the same as before.

Shawn didn't hide his eyes this time, only rested his head against his hand with his view faced away.

Bobby resumed his position in Dad's recliner, just happy to be home, I was sure, and turned on his game.

"Why don't you go take a shower before dinner," Dad said to Josh, giving him something to do, and followed Uncle Vance into the kitchen.

They spoke for a few minutes, and once Uncle Vance left, I took the opportunity to thank Dad for not making us stay longer.

"Well, hon, I admit it was a tough decision." He pulled me to him in a hug. "Dana's concerned it's not the best environment for you guys right now." He rubbed my back. "But, unfortunately, I think we can all agree that 'best' doesn't always exist."

It sure didn't.

"It's going to be tough." He pushed his hand over my head, forcing me to look up at him. "But we've been through a lot, and I think we can handle it."

I nodded. "We can do tough." Lord knew we could.

"You know, Dana made other good points," he said, his hands landing heavy on my shoulders. "I let too much responsibility fall on you after your mother died." He pushed a palm to his chest as if it hurt. "It wasn't fair, Megan. It shouldn't have happened, and I am so very sorry."

By the sound of it, he'd gotten a lecture. I knew he was sorry. Not only by how pained he looked, I was certain he didn't even realize it happened. As bad as I felt about his regret, it was still gratifying to hear him say it.

"Listen, Megan, it can't happen again. We're really winging it right now. You need to promise me that you'll tell me if I put too much on you."

I nodded.

"I'm serious. This is your life. I don't want to get to the end of mine, only to look back and say, 'Damn, I got it wrong.'"

"I will."

"Promise."

I nodded, his heartfelt sincerity tugging at tears.

"I love you, Meg." He curled an arm around me and pulled me to him again. "In case I don't say it enough."

"You do." It was one area he never failed in. "I love you too."

I needed to end it before there was a deluge. I squeezed him, and then released myself from the embrace and went to the sink to wash my hands to start dinner.

"I'll do it tonight, Meg," Dad said as he opened the refrigerator.

"You don't have to." Nobody expected him to be Superman.

"I want to." He pulled out a bowl of homemade dough he'd apparently already made. "Believe it or not, once upon a time, I loved to cook."

I couldn't imagine it. I hoped Dana hadn't been too hard on him.

Josh hung upstairs while I occupied myself with a book.

Bobby played a couple rounds of his game, then retrieved the second controller and tossed it at Shawn. "Play with me, kid."

He was either desperate or, more likely, told to do it.

Shawn hesitated but picked it up and pressed the button to add himself as a second player.

He played a round, and then lay down and played another.

During round five, Shawn dethroned Bobby, beating his highest score. Bobby swore pretty fiercely and had to keep himself from throwing the controller. Shawn didn't react, and even went on playing with him.

Dad made pizza for dinner. Josh came into the living room with two plates, each with two slices, and handed one to Shawn. "It's sausage and pepperoni. There's plain cheese if you want that instead."

Shawn took the plate from him, and we all ate in the living room around the TV. Josh put on a racy comedy and took over the love seat, while Bobby sprawled out on the floor, and laughter billowed throughout the house.

Arms crossed, Dad covered his eyes with his hand as he shook his head in disapproval of a vulgar scene, and a bend in Shawn's left cheek hinted at a smile.

The movie ended, and Josh and Bobby both disappeared upstairs. I carried the five plates to the kitchen and loaded them into the dishwasher. Dad cooked, so I cleaned.

Dad's voice came from the living room as if he talked to Shawn. Shawn spoke too.

Whatever they talked about, Shawn got progressively louder.

A loud crack and breaking glass made me drop the plate in my hand. "I'm not going," Shawn shouted.

Dad's bedroom door slammed shut as I rushed back into the room.

Dad sat in his chair, legs crossed, elbow on the arm, leaning his forehead into his palm. Still on all four legs, the coffee table was split down the middle, the glasses from dinner, some that were empty, some not, tipped over and/or in pieces on the floor.

"What the hell was that?" Bobby asked from the stairs with Josh behind him.

Dad huffed. "Exactly what I expected." He knelt on the floor and picked up pieces of glass. "Go back upstairs, boys."

"I got it, Dad." I got down with him.

"Don't cut yourself."

"What happened?"

"I told him he has a doctor's appointment in the morning." He pushed up off his knee.

"That's it? He broke the table because of a doctor's appointment?" He must've kicked it.

"It's understandable, considering what it will entail."

I took into mind the nature of his injuries. He didn't need to go just to get his stitches out.

Dad went to his bedroom door. "Shawn, I'm opening the door. I don't want it closed." He didn't wait. He turned the knob and pushed it open to the dark room. "You can stay in here, but the door needs to be open."

Shawn gave some sort of heated response.

"Alright. Okay." Dad backed out of the doorway. He eyed me. "Hang there for a minute while I let Dana know what's going on," he said quietly, probably because after what happened the morning before and the worry Shawn might be a flight risk.

Dad went into the kitchen and I cleaned up the broken glass and spilled liquid.

I put the glass pieces in a pile on the split table and moved toward Dad's door. Shawn sat on the floor against the side of the bed, his leg viewable in the light cast from the living room.

"Go away," he said.

"But, can I just talk to you?"

"I'm sorry for breaking your family's table, now leave me alone."

"Nobody cares about the table," I said, and stepped in. I gauged his approachability. His left arm rested on his knee.

I lowered to the floor a few feet away from him. "What we do care about is that you get well."

The discontent in his expression as he stared straight ahead was deadly.

"Nobody wants you to have to go through this," I said. "Nobody. Especially anything that might make you uncomfortable. But they need to make sure you're okay."

"I'm okay, *I'm okay.*"

The wetness of his eyes contradicted his tone. "Please just let them make sure?"

"Megan, they strapped me down, they cut off my clothes." Panic elevated in his voice. "They did so much stuff to me." Tears dropped from his eyes as his voice cut out.

"But they did it to help you, not hurt you."

Dad appeared at the edge of the doorway, his hands in his pockets as he leaned in. "They strapped you down for the ride to the hospital. It's what EMTs do to every patient they transport. Had you not been strapped down and resisted the way you did, then they would've restrained you in order to be able to treat you." He nodded. "I would've done it myself if they hadn't. There was something clearly wrong with you, and I care about you. Everything that happened that day was because people cared about you. Every person who laid their hands on you that day was someone who cared about you."

"But I said no. I said no over and over and over."

"I know." Dad's lips pursed. "I'll make a deal with you. Anything you say no to tomorrow won't happen."

Shawn's welling eyes held on him.

"However. I don't know how this stuff works. If you say no to something, it may extend your recovery process and the number of times we need to go back."

Shawn dropped his head against the bed and inhaled deepened breaths. "Will it be the same doctor?" He looked at Dad again.

"It will be the same doctor. Unless you don't want it to be."

"I want it to be."

I was in awe of Dad's composure, as well as his patience and compassion.

Chapter 36

Dad and Shawn had already left for the hospital when I woke up, and they were gone for most of the day.

I started out reading and somehow ended up on a nature channel watching a program about hummingbirds.

They were fascinating little creatures. Pretty, too, with such vibrant colors.

Despite their small size, they were one of the most aggressive species of birds, attacking other birds even as large as hawks that infringed on their territory.

They were the only bird species that could fly backward, and the only living thing that could stop dead in its tracks from full speed.

As prevalent as they were in Oregon, and probably Missouri too, I'd never actually seen one in person.

A ruby-throated hummingbird, weighing only three grams, could travel up to five hundred miles without stopping. *Impressive.*

Despite having gone through an entire bird drawing phase, I'd also never drawn one.

Before the hour was over, I had my sketchpad on my lap.

With a robust chest and a wingspan that stretched from one side of the vertical page to the other, I drew a ruby-throated male. Because males were the more colorful ones, of course.

I made him emerald green—like Mom's eyes. Deep and enchanting.

It felt nice. To be doing something random and lighthearted. I couldn't remember the last time I had.

I was upstairs in my room putting finishing touches on it when Dad and Shawn came home. I closed the pad, and as I rolled over to get off my bed, my door pushed open.

What the . . . For a split second, I thought Shawn was Bobby. He was all decked out from head to toe in his clothes, his long hair pulled back and hidden underneath one of Bobby's Dolphin hats he had on backward, positioned as not to irritate the injury on his forehead, but also to hide his tucked-up hair. It was the first time he'd been on the second level, let alone in my room.

With lines radiating from his eyes, he pressed his palms to my mattress and got right in my face.

It was his first smile in weeks. "So, I guess it went well?" I wasn't so sure I'd see positive expression from him again. "What's that I smell?" His breath was telling. "Is that ice cream?"

He licked his lips. "Can you tell what flavor?"

"I don't want to tell what flavor. Who said you could get ice cream?"

"Your dad said you'd be mad. Don't worry, though, I got you this."
He pulled a lollipop from his pocket.

I laughed. "They gave you a lollipop?"

His ponytail fell free as he lifted the hat off his head, and he held
back the loose fly-aways of hair at his forehead. "Pretty good, huh?"

There was still a bit of bruising, but the stitches were out and the
split in his skin sealed. "Nice." He didn't have the sling on and was
using his arm. "What about your shoulder?" I asked as he stood back
up.

"I don't have to wear the sling as long as it doesn't hurt, but they
want me to do physical therapy to build up the muscle."

"Makes sense." That's where my questions ended. There wasn't
anything else I expected him to tell me about.

He backed away from my bed and his expression dropped. "You
know they did blood tests when I was first brought in?"

"Okay." My face flushed.

"Do you know what they tested for?"

"No." I could guess. HIV, AIDS, other sexually transmitted
diseases.

"Everything."

I nodded, my cheeks heating as I anticipated the worst.

"Would you believe it if I said I'm clean?"

I repeated it in my head. "As in, you're negative? For everything?"

A smile exploded onto his face.

"Whaaa . . ."

"Can you friggin' believe it?"

I stood and wound my arms around his neck.

"Negative for everything except drugs. But they knew I didn't do them myself."

I gave a sympathetic twist of my mouth.

"I still can't believe it." He shook his head. "I'd pretty much accepted I probably had every disease in the book. They said I have to be tested again in six months, but so far, so good, right?"

I gave a sharp nod, experiencing the twinge in my nose that usually preceded the tears.

"Hey, guess what?"

"What?" I wiped the moisture from my eyes.

"I have asthma."

It explained the wheezing.

He breathed amusement. "If that's the worst they could tell me, I think I'm doin' all right." His grin was so big it created dimples under his eyes. "I'm gonna go change." He left me and trotted down the stairs.

I followed. As he shut himself into Dad's room, I sought out Dad. I went into the kitchen and he greeted me with the same smile I did him. I walked into him, and he folded his arms around me. "He did great," he said, his hand rubbing over my back.

"Thank you, Dad. I don't think he could've done it without you."

"Or you." He took a step back so I could see the encouragement in his expression. "You make a pretty good partner, Nutty."

Where you are is exactly where you're meant to be.

I'd finally started to believe it was true.

~

297

We ate dinner in the dining room. Shawn wasn't any more interactive than he'd been, but his bright, alert eyes suggested he still reeled from the information he'd gotten.

His hair remained pulled back in the elastic, drawing serious attention to his angled features, and I had to force myself not to stare. He looked like a different person.

"So, Shawn and I talked," Dad said when we were finished as I brought my plate to the kitchen. "He agrees we need to come up with better sleeping arrangements while we try to figure everything out." Shawn's eyes went low. "We went over some options, and the reasons why they might or might not work, and if it's all right with you, Josh, he'll try camping out with you in your room."

Josh looked to Shawn. "Yeah, man, of course," he said with an upbeat tone.

"What, am I chopped liver?" Bobby said, joking.

Shawn flitted a glance at him.

"I think if Shawn had his way, he'd be by himself," Dad said.

"What about a bed?" Josh asked. "Is another one gonna fit in my room?"

"That's something else we need to figure out. We also talked about his need to sleep in a bed, and he'll try."

I didn't know for certain what his problem with beds was, maybe that bad things happened to him in them.

"Obviously, we'll need to switch around your room. We'll also need to go over some ground rules as to what will be considered appropriate and what won't be." That could've meant things like

298

keeping distance, not dressing in front of him.

Josh looked at Shawn again and nodded. "Okay."

"You guys can have your phones back, but it's of the utmost importance that no one, and I mean *no* one, knows he is here."

"What about Sue?" Josh asked. "What do I do about her?" She'd tried to come over the day after everything happened, but Uncle Vance sent her away.

"I've spoken with Susan *and* her mother. They both know. But that is as far as it goes." He glanced to me in the doorway. "I can not stress the importance to the three of you that no one else finds out." He stood from the table and retrieved a file folder from the hutch, and removed a piece of paper. "These are the names of the three officers who will be keeping watch on this house, along with their badge numbers. When I or Uncle Vance isn't here, one of these three officers will be outside the house. One of these will be on the refrigerator and the other taped up on the front door."

"When are you going back to work?" Josh asked. It'd been six days.

"That's still undetermined." He looked down the table. "How ya doing, Shawn?"

With his view still low, he nodded.

"Anything else you can think of I need to add?"

He shook his head.

Dad turned his eyes to Josh and Bobby. "Okay, disperse."

They both got up and brought their plates into the kitchen. I approached Shawn and leaned into him, and circled my hand over his back.

"My brother still has one of the boys' old beds," Dad said. "He'll bring it over in the morning. He's also going through Dennis's clothes. He seems the closest to your size."

With his hands in fists, Shawn's thumbs rubbed uneasily over his index fingers.

Dad ducked his head for a view of his face. "Why don't you bring your plate to the sink, Shawn, and go take a breather."

Shawn stood, ignoring me against him, and took his plate with him into the kitchen.

Chapter 37

Dad called Josh, Bobby, and me into the living room first thing in the morning while Shawn showered. "While we have a few minutes," he said, standing in the doorway of his bedroom.

"You mean more like forty-five?" Bobby said, searching for marshmallows in his bowl of cereal.

"Shut up, Bobby." I glared at him. If what happened to Shawn happened to him, he'd take long showers too.

"Now that Shawn's more with it, there are some things we need to go over for his stay. First off—"

"First off," Bobby interrupted again. "How long is his stay gonna be?"

"Quit it, Bob." If I was closer, I would've slapped him.

"Quit it is right," Dad said. "Be a little bit more sensitive to the situation. Unless you're behind a closed door where there's no chance of being seen," he carried on, "the two of you boys need to be fully

301

clothed at all times. No hanging out in your boxers, no showering and coming out of the bathroom in a towel—"

"Shouldn't that go for Megan too?" Bobby flicked a piece of his cereal at me, hitting me square in the cheek. I wiped the streak of milk away.

"For now, don't physically touch him. If you're sitting on the same couch, don't even as much as brush arms with him. Watch what you say and do around him. Be careful what you put on the television—"

"*Jesus.*" It was too much for Bobby.

"What were the things we needed to go over about him staying in my room?" Josh asked.

"All of the above, plus. You'll need to come up with a morning and nighttime routine, probably all the way down to the way you get in and out of bed. At least for now, so there's nothing unexpected."

"Why didn't you just put Bobby and me together and give him one of our rooms?" he asked.

Bobby shot a look at him.

"It was a thought, but it's best he not be alone. We'll see what happens down the road."

"Great," Bobby muttered.

"So, does that mean he is staying with us?" I asked.

"We're still not sure what's happening, Meg. Everything's still very much up in the air right now."

"I hope he goes somewhere else," Bobby said. "This stuff is ridiculous."

Dad lifted a brow at him. "It wouldn't be ridiculous if it was you."

"It wouldn't *be* me."

"It wouldn't have been Shawn either, but with a gun to your head, you tend to let things happen you wouldn't ordinarily." He said it so casually, and Bobby's gaze stuck on him. "And by the way, Bob, you're not chopped liver. In terms of who he would feel safer with, you were it." It was as if Dad's eyes were magnetized, Bobby couldn't look away. "Aside from being as terrified as he is, he is embarrassed. Try your best to be considerate of that."

Bobby was successfully lowered a notch. "I haven't done anything," he said with his tail between his legs.

"He hasn't." I actually stuck up for him.

"Make sure it stays that way."

~

Shawn sat at the kitchen table eating a bagel Dad forced on him, wearing jeans like he wore the day Damian sealed his fate and Bobby's brown "Slim Shady" shirt, the water that drained from his hair dripping onto the table.

"Can I brush it?" I asked, picking up the wet ends on his back. It didn't look as though he'd even attempted to.

"Whatever," he said.

I got a brush, and elastic too.

I pulled the bristles through his hair, barely able to make it two inches without getting caught up. "Sorry, I'm not trying to hurt you," I said. "Have you ever tried conditioner?"

He just continued chewing.

"You have the most gorgeous hair," I said once through all the

303

tangles and successfully able to pull the brush through. "Such beautiful highlights."

"I should shave it off."

"No, definitely not." Though it would probably best suit the situation. "It's way too nice."

I pulled it all to the back of his head and secured it with the elastic in a tight, low ponytail.

I sat in the chair next to him and observed my work. "You look *so* good like that."

Shawn took in the last bite of his bagel. He stood and, looking directly at me, pulled the elastic from his hair, and then turned and walked out of the room.

Dad, at the counter buttering his own bagel, didn't look surprised. "What did I do?" I asked.

"Unfortunately, Meg, there are things you also need to refrain from doing. Like telling him he looks good. He's heard it a lot. He doesn't want to look good."

Wow, how could I not have figured that one out? "Is that why his hair is long?"

"Possibly. Dana did suggest it. I think it's more the lack of effort."

"He looks good no matter what, though."

"That's the problem. He's a very attractive young man."

"So, I shouldn't say anything about his eyes?"

Dad breathed a laugh. "Absolutely not. Not ever."

~

Uncle Vance came over just after noon with the bed. Dennis followed him through the door, and Shawn got up off the couch and shut himself into Dad's room.

Dennis, holding an over-stuffed garbage bag, looked between us all. "I brought him some clothes. What should I do with them?"

"Thank you, Dennis," Dad said. "Just go ahead and leave the bag."

"I tried to find things I thought he might like," he said as he set it down. "Like, be his style. But if not, let me know. I have a lot of stuff."

"I'm sure he'll appreciate it," Dad said with gratitude.

He and Uncle Vance, with help from Dad and Josh, brought in the pieces of Dennis's old bed. "Want me to help set it up?" Dennis asked once everything was upstairs in Josh's room.

"I'm actually going to have Shawn do it." Dad turned him down.

"He doesn't have to. I can do it."

"I have a reason," Dad said. "But thank you."

~

Shawn stood against the wall in Josh's room with his hands in his pockets as Dad and Josh moved furniture. They decided where the bed would go, and also the bureau Uncle Vance still needed to bring, and Dad got tools.

"Let's do this," he said, and handed Shawn a wrench.

Josh held pieces together, and Dad handed Shawn the bolts he needed to secure them.

Josh's bed and his were set against opposite walls, Shawn's closest to the outside window, but in view of the door.

Dad didn't usually come upstairs when we went to bed, but he made sure Shawn was comfortable with the plan they'd made, and comfortable with Josh. He told Bobby and me to carry through with our regular nightly routine while he talked the two of them through theirs.

The hall light was left on and Josh's door stayed open a crack.

~

My eyes opened at nine a.m. to bright sun and the aroma of bacon and eggs.

Plates clanked and silverware rustled as I came down the stairs.

"Morning, Nutty." Dad scooped scrambled eggs onto a plate from a pan on the stove. "Grab some breakfast while it's hot."

My entire family, plus Shawn, was already up and eating. Josh and Shawn sat at the kitchen table, Bobby on the couch in the living room.

Dad fished bacon from a paper towel-covered plate in the center of the table and stood against the counter as he shoveled his food into his mouth. "I've got some stuff I need to do, so Uncle Vance is on his way over." He wore a button-down shirt, dressier than his normal work attire.

As I made myself a plate, he finished and added a suit jacket— the one he usually wore when he went on television.

The doorbell rang and he let Uncle Vance in.

I followed him out to the living room. "Dad, is there something new?"

"No, sweetheart, just need to stay on top of things. Go on and go eat."

I turned back for the kitchen.

"I'll put a car outside in case someone sees me and decides to make a move." He spoke quietly to Uncle Vance.

Whatever went on, I was the only one paying attention. "Pass the ketchup, Meg," Josh said as Shawn added two more strips of bacon to his empty plate.

I wanted to ask how the night went. All seemed well. If not, both boys put on a good show.

Uncle Vance sat at the dining room table with his glasses on, sifting through case notes while the boys convened around the TV playing a video game.

"Kid, you need to stop frigging doing that." Bobby couldn't handle that Shawn killed him once again.

At ten o'clock, Shawn put his controller down and went upstairs and shut himself into Josh's room, and Dad's voice seeped through the crack underneath the door.

"Shawn's watching Dad on TV right now," I said to Josh on the couch with his laptop.

"Yeah, he's giving a news conference. Dad told him he could watch if he wanted to."

"Why aren't we?" It was kind of a big deal. "Pause your game," I said to Bobby as I picked up the television remote and switched the channel.

Dad stood at a podium in a small room, surrounded by news cameras.

"If you have any information on the whereabouts of either of these men, contact your local authorities immediately." He held two photos, one of Shawn's dad, the other of a man I'd never seen.

"Are there any new leads?" a voice from the crowd asked as if already aware of the manhunt.

"We're working off several."

Questions came from all over the room. "Have any new charges been added?"

"Not as of yet."

"I don't think you're supposed to be watching that," Uncle Vance said from behind me.

"Shawn is."

"That's because it's about him."

"Have other victims come forward or been identified?" a dark-haired woman with bright red lipstick asked.

"Not in this case."

The questions all collided with one another. "Is the victim in this case seeking therapy?" "Where is the victim? Is he or she in protective custody?"

Where is the victim? Had an adult seriously just asked that?

"There's been word the victim is male."

"Oh my God, what is *wrong* with people?" How could they be so stupid?

"Yeah, Shawn probably shouldn't be watching, either," Uncle Vance said.

Dad didn't answer anything more. He held the photographs up again as the questions continued to fly at him. "If you have any information on the whereabouts of either of these men, contact your local authorities right away," he repeated. He then handed the conference over to a man standing behind him and disappeared through a door to the left of the podium.

Shawn locked himself in Josh's room. I was on my third attempt to get him to open the door when Dad came home and took my place.

Chapter 38

Shawn still didn't know Mary-Jo wasn't his mother. I wanted to be able to give him the good news, but it would be bittersweet, as I would then have to give him the information as to who really was.

"That will be jarring, Meg," Dad said. "Let me get Dana's take on it first."

Dana agreed it was information Shawn needed to know but didn't know when it would be best to tell him. Gina hadn't made any effort to contact him since being made aware of the situation, which may have made the news even harder to take. Finding out Mary-Jo wasn't his mother, though, might've made him feel a whole lot better about three-quarters of his life.

Because of the chance of him taking the Gina part poorly, Dana decided not to wait until he was on an upward swing to tell him, only to knock him back down.

She was encouraged by the fact that Shawn opened up to me

about Mary. It took a bit of persuading on my part, but in an effort to remind him of the connection he'd made with me, she agreed to let me be the one to tell him.

She came over, and Dad stood in the door of the kitchen as she and I sat with Shawn at the table.

There was stress in Shawn's brow as to why I was present.

"Shawn, we have some information to share with you," Dana said. "Information which doesn't pertain to the case."

Shawn's eyes shifted back and forth between Dana and me.

I lifted the folded, black and white photo of Mary-Jo from my lap and Shawn's view held on me. I opened it and put it on the table in front of him.

He looked down at it and stiffened. His jaw tightened and legs bounced. "Is she dead?"

"She's not dead," Dana said, and Shawn looked up from the picture.

With black ink from a Sharpie marker, I wrote across her face:

NOT YOUR MOTHER

His legs nearly vibrated. He looked at me and Dana, and then back down.

"She's not your mother," I said in a quiet voice, in case my message didn't convey properly.

His eyes twitched to me and went back to the picture of the light-haired woman. "Who is she?"

"Your aunt," Dad said from behind me. "Your father's sister."

Mouth ajar, his eyes went unblinking as he looked at the woman

311

who, if not for his masculine features, he would've been a spitting image of. Aside from their light eyes, they even shared the same triple-toned hair.

Shawn lifted his eyes to Dana. "Who *is* my mother?"

Dana's mouth firmed into a hard line. "Gina Donovan."

It didn't seem like he processed the name right away.

His brow tightened and loosened with thought several times.

He pushed away from the table and stood, and started slowly toward the bathroom. Mid kitchen, he broke into a run.

He barely made it to the toilet and lost the contents of his stomach.

~

Shawn spent the rest of the afternoon on the couch staring into the air, absorbing the idea that his life had been a lie. That the woman who'd given birth to him lived the high life just a few miles down the road, while the woman who'd claimed to be his mother spent nearly his entire life torturing him. It couldn't have helped to realize that Damian, who'd given him so much grief for so long, who just a week and a half earlier, struck him with a bat so hard he could've taken his life, was his real brother—his one hundred percent, full-blooded brother.

I couldn't begin to imagine what he went through. There wasn't a single thing to say that would've made him feel better.

Though he didn't eat, Dad forced him to sit at the table for dinner.

"Thinking about getting out of Dodge for a few days," Dad said mid-meal. "What do you guys think about taking a trip somewhere?"

"You mean, like a vacation?" Josh asked.

"Yeah, something like that." It was so spur of the moment. "I think

312

we could all use a little break."

"Where to?" Bobby asked. Other than the actual move, we hadn't taken a trip anywhere since before Mom died.

"Anywhere that's not here."

"When?" I was a little concerned about how he planned to be in two places at once, with such a major investigation going on.

"As soon as possible. Once we're done eating, you all go upstairs and get some stuff together."

When we were finished with dinner, Dad provided Shawn with a large duffle bag. He stuffed it full with everything Dennis gave him.

Chapter 39

Dad meant business when he said we'd hightail it out of town for a little while. Uncle Vance and the boys were at our house at seven o'clock in the morning with an eight-passenger van.

"Hey, man," Dennis said to Shawn when he came in, reaching his fist out to him to bump knuckles.

Shawn didn't have a choice, he couldn't go off and hide somewhere, we were all about to be squished together in the van. He reluctantly lifted his hand and made a fist.

Dad didn't tell us where we were going. There was a lot of laughing in the tight quarters, and plenty of fighting. Shawn sat with the backpack Dad retrieved from the trailer on his lap with his view out the window for most of the ride.

With only one side-of-the-road bathroom break, we made it to our destination five hours after leaving home. We spilled out of the van to a view of a lake so serene the water appeared as a flawless sheet of glass.

Camouflaged in a forest of tall pines were two small cabins, separated by a single dock, each of the two-bedroom abodes fully stocked with all the amenities of home.

I was captivated. It was remarkably similar to a place we'd gone the summer before Mom died. Dad had had a rough couple months at work, so Mom surprised him with the trip. It was one of our best and most memorable vacations because Mom put so much effort into it that Dad forced himself to relax—something we'd grown so unaccustomed to.

"Nice job, Dad," I said, truly appreciating the thought behind it.

He winked. "Thank your mother for the stepping stones."

As critical a reason for the getaway, with Mom's influence, I was pretty sure anything was possible.

We spent the first hour unloading and unpacking.

"This is cool, huh?" I said to Shawn in the living room of the cabin Dad chose as ours, not letting on to the personal significance as I pulled items from my bag.

"It's nice." He appeared lost in thought as he sorted through the stuff in his. I wanted to tell him how much Mom would've loved it there, but "mothers" didn't seem an appropriate topic.

He turned to me an instant later. "Do you think he'll let me stay?"

"With us, you mean? At our house?"

I assumed by his gaze. I couldn't answer for sure. I didn't know anything that went on. "I don't know." I really hoped so. "Whatever happens, though, just know that he cares so much about you, and anything he does is with your best interests at heart." I

315

prayed he did know that.

His expression didn't change. Then he stepped over to me and doubled his arms around my neck. "I'm so glad you made me meet you."

I clasped my arms around him. Everything really did happen for a reason. I finally understood that.

The moment didn't last. He let up and turned back to his bag.

I unpacked mine, while he merely took inventory of what was in his.

As the other four boys scouted the area, Shawn kept close to Dad and Uncle Vance. Whatever was in his backpack was important enough to carry around with him.

Evening approached, and a tackle football game started. Shawn exited the commotion and walked to the end of the dock.

"Mind handling dinner?" Dad asked Uncle Vance, leaving the fire he'd built, and he grabbed two fishing poles and joined him.

The two stood staring out at the sun as it gave in to the inevitable draw of the horizon for several minutes, and then boarded the canoe tied up next to them.

Dad gave Shawn a lesson in rowing, and as they got farther out into the water, I found myself at the end of the same dock.

Dad showed Shawn how to cast out his line, and both whipped through the air.

A hand landed softly on my shoulder. "How ya holdin' up, kiddo?" Uncle Vance looked out in the same direction.

"Okay, I guess. I just don't get it."

316

"It's a rough road to reality, isn't it?" He knew where my mind was.

I looked up to him with hopes of a better answer, and he hooked his arm around my neck. "There's nothing to get, Meg. That's all there is to it. There's nothing to get." He sounded so resigned. "We live in a world full of sick people, and now we just know one of them. Shawn simply got dealt a really bad hand from the parent deck."

"Not just the parent deck, the life deck." No matter how rough the circumstances of my own life were, they didn't even compare to his.

"Whatever the cards may be, Meg, I don't think we're ever really meant to understand the tapestry of life." He stared out over the water for a moment, then turned to me. "But I sure do think it's good he has someone like you around. There's a saying that a friend is someone who walks in when the rest of the world walks out. Not many people would volunteer to step into *his* mess." He inhaled a breath of the crisp air. "I have to tell you, young lady, you're growing into quite the young woman, and I sure am proud of you." He nodded. "And I know your father is too."

"Thanks, Uncle Van."

"It just stinks when you have to grow up too fast." He sighed.

"Nah, it doesn't bother me yet. Maybe when I'm old like you." I joked.

"Yeah, you just wait 'til you're old like me," he said with a laugh. He turned me away from the end of the dock and walked me back.

~

317

When the afternoon light started to die, as Uncle Vance cooked dinner, I pulled out my sketchpad and drew the vivid orange sunset that lit up the sky. It was one of the most beautiful I'd ever seen.

I used every warm-colored pencil I had.

Dad and Shawn fished until dusk. They returned just after we'd finished eating, Shawn ahead of Dad as they walked up the dock.

"Mind if we borrow the fire?" Dad asked.

Shawn, with his backpack over his shoulder, looked exhausted.

Dennis and Kenny followed us into our cabin, and we started a game of cards while Dad showed Shawn how to gut and cook a fish.

Dad prepared a whole meal, with corn on the cob and potatoes baked over the fire, and the two of them ate what they caught.

Shawn eventually came inside, and Uncle Vance passed his cards off. "Here, we're playing blackjack. Take over my hand."

Shawn looked more like he wanted to go to bed, but he took the cards from him.

When blackjack ended, as Dad and Uncle Vance enjoyed quality time by the fire, Bobby talked Josh, Dennis, and Shawn into a game of poker.

The more I didn't understand how to play, the more aggravated Bobby got, so Shawn sat next to me and tried to help.

It just wasn't my game, so I bowed out, and Shawn slid his chair back to where it had been.

"Kid, you did not just do that," Bobby said when Shawn won another round.

"I did."

Josh laughed. "Bro, you are gettin' schooled."

It'd been years since I saw Dad with a beer in his hand. His face glowed by the fire as he laughed with Uncle Vance, their voices progressively louder.

One by one, the boys threw in their hands. Dennis and Kenny went to their own cabin, and Josh, Bobby, and I argued about who would get which bed.

Shawn pulled a blanket from one and brought it to the couch, then sat back at the table with the deck of cards.

"Want me to stay up with you?" I asked.

"If you want."

I curled up on the couch with the blanket and watched TV while Shawn played Solitaire. I must've fallen asleep because I woke to Dad's voice.

"There isn't a single soul who knows where we are." He leaned on his elbows at the table next to Shawn, who stared straight ahead. "You can not stay up all night."

"Yes, I can. I do it all the time." He sat rigid.

"But you don't need to now. I'm here, my brother's here. We're both armed."

"I'll stay up with him," I said, giving myself away. "We can watch movies, or something."

"That doesn't help him, Megan."

There wasn't much that would. He was hundreds of miles away from home in a completely new situation within days of being placed in a new situation. "Just tonight. And then maybe we'll all be more

319

used to it tomorrow."

Dad sighed, and then dropped into a chair.

Even with caffeinated soda, I barely made it through the first movie. As heavy as my eyelids were, Shawn's showed no signs of closing.

I eventually fell asleep again and awoke at three a.m. with the urge to go to the bathroom. I didn't recall seeing more than five minutes of the second movie, and something completely different was now on. Dad sat at the far end of the couch, snoring, and Shawn in the middle with his head back, eyes closed, and breathing as if deep in sleep.

~

Dad had events planned for each day. If Shawn didn't want to participate, he could hang back with either him or Uncle Vance, because the escape was as much for us as it was for him.

On day number two, we drove another whole hour away to an amusement park. Because of his concussion, Shawn wouldn't be able to go on most of the rides, but Dad still hoped the atmosphere would be uplifting.

While Dad stayed with Shawn in the van, trying to talk him into it, Uncle Vance brought the rest of us in and released us.

Josh dragged me onto roller coaster after roller coaster while Bobby busted into me over and over on the bumper boats.

"They're in the park," Uncle Vance said to me when we crossed paths at the flume.

I really didn't expect it.

He was slow to warm up and looked over his shoulder a bit, but eventually put his focus into shooting water cannons at the people on the pirate ship river ride. The more he soaked unsuspecting patrons, the more his smile grew.

He itched to try a roller coaster, watching intently as they raced along their tracks. Had Dad not been there to stop him, I was certain Josh would've had a new partner.

By the end of the day, there was a smile stuck permanently on his face.

It was his second Sunday with us, and we successfully made it through without incident.

On day three, Dad left Uncle Vance with us all at a nearby arcade, and he and Shawn went elsewhere. Uncle Vance wouldn't tell us where, and neither Dad nor Shawn offered the information when they returned. They disappeared two more times over the next three days.

On the seventh and final day of our trip, we visited a wildlife sanctuary. It was similar to a zoo, but the animals were in a more natural habitat setting. It wasn't that big of a deal for any of us, but other than on television, Shawn had never seen animals like that before. He had a child-like wonder about him and wanted to go through a second time once we were done. It seemed his favorite part of the trip, trumping even the amusement park.

Chapter 40

Dad went back to work the Monday after we returned from our trip.

"Uncle Vance is on his way over," he said as he poured coffee from the pot into a travel mug. "I'll call throughout the day to make sure everything's okay, but if there's a problem," he lifted his eyes to Shawn, "you can call me too."

"You can't call the house phone," Shawn said. "We were gone for a week. Someone could've come in and bugged it."

He sounded like he'd seen too many movies.

Dad gave a slow blink as he stirred creamer into his coffee, and nodded. "There's a security company coming Wednesday to install an alarm. I'll see if I can get someone out here to check the phones as well."

I wasn't sure if he took him seriously, or if he was just appeasing him.

"You don't know, the whole house could be bugged." Shawn's

speech was accelerated.

"We'll check," Dad said just as calmly. "In the meantime, my brother will be here, and I'll be just a phone call away. On his cell."

As much as Shawn tried to hide his apprehension, his entire aura shouted unease.

"Dad, is it okay if Sue starts coming over again?" Josh asked as he came into the room.

Dad looked to Shawn.

"She doesn't know the real reason you're here," Josh said to him.

"Oh yeah?" Shawn said. "She hasn't seen those press conferences or watched the news? Everybody knows now." He turned and walked out of the kitchen.

"Let's wait on that a little while," Dad said to Josh. "If you want to go over there, I don't have a problem with that."

"Do you really think his dad's capable of bugging the phones?" Bobby asked.

Dad's lips pressed together through an exhale. "Let's talk when I get home, guys, okay?"

Finally. He probably realized he couldn't avoid it anymore.

~

After the sketch of the hummingbird I did, my passion for drawing that Shawn re-sparked in me took hold, and I drew, now, almost as much as I read. It was something I didn't think would ever happen again but was utterly grateful for. With only a few necessary implements and my imagination, there were no limits as to what I could create. I'd captured several of the picturesque views at the lake while we were there. My current work in progress: the buck from the family of deer that grazed nearby early one morning.

Dad called Uncle Vance's cell phone several times throughout the day as he said he would, speaking to Shawn on only one of those occasions. A bunch of yups and mm-hmms later, Shawn handed the phone back to Uncle Vance and retreated to the pages of one of Bobby's music magazines.

"Does he talk to you?" Josh asked me in the kitchen, making himself a sandwich.

"*No.*" The amount of emphasis on the word when it blurted from my mouth surprised me. Other than the day he got the good news about his blood tests, and the fleeting moment he thanked me in the cabin, there was little evidence of the relationship we'd worked so hard to build. I seemed now to be no more than the youngest of three siblings who lived in the house he hid out in.

"Chicken Francaise for dinner, or Marsala," I asked him about an hour before Dad was expected home. He was a quarter of the way through a stack of Bobby's back issues.

"Don't matter." He didn't even lift his eyes.

The entire house was infused with the sweet, robust smell of Marsala when Dad came in. I sent Uncle Vance off with a full Tupperware container, and we sat down for dinner.

"How was work?" I asked Dad as he scooped a heaping helping of my creation.

"Busy. I couldn't see my desk beneath all the papers on it. How's Sue?" he asked Josh.

"Good. She wants me to ask you if we can go to the fair in Montgomery City tomorrow."

"A little too far."

"Dad, I'll be eighteen in two weeks."

"Then, in two weeks, you can go."

Josh sank into his chair with a sigh.

"This is delicious, Meg," Dad said.

"Thank you."

"Careful, you'll give her a big head," Bobby said with a mouthful.

Dad twisted his eyes to him. "Really, Bob?"

Shawn scarfed his food down. When there was nothing left on his plate, he pushed his chair from the table and got up, and he left the dining room and went upstairs.

"What's up with him?" Josh asked. "He's being all weird today."

Dad cleared his throat. "I spoke with him this afternoon about the need for me to fill you all in on some of the details of what's going on. That's him choosing not to be here when I do it."

Bobby looked tentatively to him.

"Bob, do you remember what you asked me this morning?" Dad's voice was gentle.

Bobby gave a quick nod. "How bad is it?"

"Welp, we're really not sure." He pushed his plate out of the way and folded his arms on the table. "Do I think John Harris is capable of bugging a house? Maybe, maybe not. But John Harris doesn't appear to be the primary threat. The things he did to Shawn were wrong on every level, and he will go to prison for a very long time once he's

325

found. But my understanding is that he's running just as scared right now."

"From who?" I asked. "The other guy whose picture you held up on TV?"

"Nope." His head moved. "That's just someone I had a good, clear image of committing an act against Shawn. That man is under a rock somewhere trying to stay out of jail."

An image. So there were pictures. Or more.

"Then from who?" Josh asked.

"We don't know, because Shawn won't say."

"Why not?" I asked. "If he tells you who, then you can go and arrest them."

"Unfortunately, Megan, what Shawn's the victim of is an actual business in which people make lots of money. Like drugs. It's called human trafficking. And those on top are dangerous people who stand to lose a lot."

"Or sex trafficking," Josh said.

Dad's lips pressed together as if wishing he didn't use the word.

I'd heard of both but never paid attention to what they meant.

"So, he's truly in serious danger," Bobby said.

"We're not sure. We don't know where the top of this is or how deep it goes. From what we're gathering, what his father was doing was child's play in comparison. No pun intended."

My dinner threatened to come back up.

"Like, does he talk to you?" Josh asked. "Does he tell you this stuff?"

Dad's eyes fell shut with a slow shake of his head. "This is what an entire team of people—Dana, another psychiatrist, the doctors—are coming up with."

"So, what's your role?" Bobby asked. "I mean, other than catch the bad guys? You spend an awful lot of time with him." There was a hint of resentment in that last part.

Dad gave a sincere purse of his lips. "What do you think my role is?"

"Make him feel safe."

Dad nodded.

So did Bobby. "I think you're doing a good job."

The crow's feet around Dad's eyes deepened. "Thanks."

"I still don't understand why he can't just tell you," I said.

"It's not that easy, Meg. People hide, they change their names. As soon as they get wind we're looking for them, they could come after him. If there's more than one person, when one goes down, others might do what they have to to ensure it doesn't happen to them."

"But they can't if they don't know where he is," Josh said.

Dad sighed. "We can't say for certain they don't."

Josh dropped his head back.

"We're walking a very thin line right now. So, Josh, please, I would really appreciate it if you didn't go to Montgomery City, no matter your age."

Josh nodded with a view of the ceiling.

"I'm trying to solicit help from the FBI, but it's difficult with the little we have to go on. Sal, back home, you remember Sal." Sal was someone who worked for his old department. We'd met him a couple times at holiday functions. "He's helping out, searching the internet to see if we can pin someone to him that way."

"So, there's a chance Shawn's—"

Dad nodded before Josh finished.

"I don't get it," I said. "What does the internet have to do with anything?"

"Porn—"

"There's a chance Shawn's being exploited on the web." Dad cut Josh off.

Not soon enough, though. Josh's word, or the start of the word, punched me in the gut. *That's* what Shawn searched for on the computer at school. He looked for himself.

"Shouldn't he be in some sort of protective custody?" Bobby asked.

Dad could be considered protective custody on some level, I guess, but to us, he was just Dad.

"Right now, we're it," Dad said. "That may change depending on what comes to light. I'm between a rock and a hard place, though, because I fear for his mental stability if he goes elsewhere."

The thought wrecked me. There was a twinge in my nose and I swallowed against the ball in my throat.

"I still don't get how this stuff happens to guys," Bobby said. "I thought only girls were trafficked."

"Believe it or not, it's very common. Which is something we're trying to get Shawn to understand. According to Dana—though statistics don't show it because it's so under-reported—up to fifty percent of trafficking victims are male." He exhaled a hard breath. "Which presents our biggest hurdle. Ideally, Shawn would be in a targeted mental health facility somewhere, receiving intense, daily therapy for everything he's been through. More specifically, in this circumstance, an anonymous place that offers security against potential threats. But because trafficking is so widely *thought* to be a female-centered problem, resources for male victims are nearly nonexistent. The few such places that do exist for males in his specific situation are already at capacity."

How was it possible? *Any* of it?

"Do what you need to for him," Josh said. "Don't worry about us."

Dad's mouth puckered as Bobby looked to me with acceptance lightening his expression. Dad nodded. "I just want you all to understand that even in the moments he seems fine, he's far from it. The stuff that happened to him will be with him for the rest of his life. There will be high moments, low moments, setbacks, instances of lash-outs . . ." He looked to Bobby.

Bobby nodded as if to say it wouldn't be a problem.

"I need to hear it from you, Bob. He's not explosive, but my understanding from what the school says is that he can be reactive and just as volatile. I need to know that if, for some reason, his fist comes flying your way, you're not going to react as you usually would."

"Give me some credit, Dad."

"I am."

It just got worse and worse. With my elbows on the table, tears leaked from behind my hands. Shawn was such a beautiful, caring soul, how could this be his life?

"Do you guys have any questions?" Dad asked.

"Now that he's upstairs, what happens if he doesn't come back down?" Josh asked. "How do I go to bed?"

"Just as we talked about. He knows that at ten o'clock you're coming in. If he's not comfortable with that, he'll either let us know, or he'll come out."

A lull seemingly signified the end of the conversation.

"This is less than ideal," Dad said. "He needs far more than what I, or any of us, can give him. But unfortunately, there is no other solution right now. The three of you can come to me at any point," he made sure to say. "No question or concern is too big or small."

Silence ensued, and then came the sound of chair legs pushing away from the table, and dishes clinked as they were placed in the sink.

Dad's hand pushed over my shoulder.

"I don't know what to do, Dad. I want to help him, but I don't know how."

He leaned down over the table next to me and rubbed my back. "Just be you, Megan. It's already helped him tremendously."

Be 'me.' I didn't know who I was before, I certainly didn't know now.

Chapter 41

I wanted nothing more than to be whoever it was Shawn needed me to be, but the more I knew, the less capable—and more awkward—I felt. Nor did I know what exactly I'd done to that point that, according to Dad, had been so affecting. Especially now that Shawn barely acknowledged me.

Dad stayed home on Wednesday so the house alarm could be installed, and Shawn waited upstairs when the man from the security company was supposed to come.

The door to Josh's room was open. Shawn sat at the end of his bed, his backpack open at his feet with a ratty, brown stuffed bear in his hands.

He caught sight of me and his eyebrow twitched with surprise.

"Sorry, didn't mean to sneak up on you," I said.

He looked at the bear he clutched.

"Does he have a name?" I asked.

He shook his head.

"How long have you had him?"

"Since second grade." He manipulated it in his hands. "Santa visited school." He resigned to tell me the story. "Everybody sat on his lap and told him what they wanted. I don't remember what I said. I just remember going back to class and them calling me back down. He gave me this. Said his elves made him special for me."

"He looks like he's seen a lot of love." He was pretty scruffy. Even in the second grade, people saw a need, and it went unfulfilled.

He nodded an almost embarrassed kind of nod. "Silly, huh?"

"Not at all." I wasn't so sure I should admit how many stuffed animals I still had in my closet. I went in and sat down with him. I squeezed the belly of the mangy thing, able to see him as an eight-year-old clinging to it at night. And a ten-year-old, and a twelve-year-old . . . "I do think if you've had him this long, he should have a name, though."

A breath came through his nose.

"So, what else do you have in that bag?" I asked.

"Just stuff." He shoved the bear back in and zipped it up.

Just stuff? He didn't carry it around the way he did for a bear. "Do you think you'll feel better once they put this alarm in?"

He shrugged, looking like he didn't hold out much hope.

~

Shawn didn't feel better, so Dad followed through and hired a private contractor to inspect the house and telephone lines for evidence of

332

bugs and/or wiretapping.

"Are we good now?" he asked Shawn when the man came up empty.

Short of building a fortress around us, I don't think anything would've made him feel truly safe.

~

Requiring Shawn to sit with us through meals, I thought, was one of Dad's best ideas. Sometimes he ate, sometimes he didn't, but he was there, a real person surrounded by other people coming together largely in support of him. He wasn't expected to talk or interact, but sometimes he did.

"Dude, you should probably get that checked out," Josh said to Bobby, busting on him for snoring so loud the night before that he could hear him from his room.

"You should get your face checked out," Bobby said.

A smile lifted Shawn's cheeks as he munched on a dinner roll. "Megan snores."

"No, I don't!"

"Yeah, ya do. I went to the bathroom one night and had to go look because I didn't believe it was you."

"Ahaha," Bobby laughed.

"That is so not true. I do not snore!"

"You snore sometimes," Josh said, amused.

How embarrassing! "Does Shawn snore?"

"No." He shook his head, and then looked away as if thinking about it. "No."

It was just as Dad said it would be. Some days were better than others. Shawn was much more comfortable with just the four of us. If Uncle Vance came over with the boys, even though we'd spent the week at the lake together, he'd usually retreat upstairs.

Dad finally gave Josh permission to have Susan over. He didn't ask Shawn, and Shawn got about a five-minute warning before she walked through the door.

"Hey, loser," she said to him, pushing her fist into the meat of his arm. "What the hell, you don't want to see me? I've missed you."

Shawn couldn't look her in her eyes, but he stayed put.

"Hey, Megan." She stepped over and curled her arms around me. "How have you been?" Her bushy hair smelled like peaches.

"Good." It was nice to finally see a female again, other than Dana.

Her hand went into the tote bag over her shoulder and came out clutching the sequel to the chick lit I'd just finished. "No suh!" I couldn't take it from her fast enough.

Her hand dove in again and she turned to Shawn. "Just in case you're starting to forget what it looks like." She handed him a framed, five-by-seven picture of the quarry taken on a bright, sunny day.

Shawn's mouth contorted as he viewed it.

His eyes, completely translucent from the angle I stood at, lifted and met hers. "Thank you." It was thoughtful, and Shawn's response was genuine.

Had I not had the awful experience of him crumpling the sketch of the lighthouse, maybe I would've thought to draw it for him.

~

Looking out the closed windows that sealed in the central air, one would have no idea how oppressive summer in Missouri was. Temperatures soared over a hundred and the dank, humid air made it difficult to breathe, so being cooped up didn't bother me as long as I had something to read or proper drawing supplies. Shawn, however, was used to life outdoors.

Dad slowly scaled back on the number of times he called during the day, and Uncle Vance gradually spent less time at our house.

Twice, I overheard Shawn ask Dad if there was anything new on his father. "Has he tried to call you yet?"

"I promise you that if he tries to call me, you'll be the first to know," Dad said to him with the utmost care.

"Why would he ask that?" I asked Dad.

"Because he's worried about him and hopes he'll reach out for help."

"He's seriously worried about him? After everything he did to him?"

Dad shrugged. "He's his father." His lips mashed together in an expression of wishing he had a better answer.

~

Josh's eighteenth birthday fell on a Monday. Past plans of extravagance were put aside, and instead, Dad put the leaf in the dining room table, and our family gathered at our house.

"Adult" wasn't a word that seemed to apply to someone still in their teens, but according to the law, that's what Josh now was.

The night was drawn out with a three-course meal, sparkling

cider—wine for the adults—and a peanut butter ice cream cake Susan made.

Shawn was quiet but observant, and wasn't at all stealth when he reached past the sparkling cider for the wine while Josh opened his gifts, and poured himself a glass.

Dad cued Uncle Vance, who was closer, and Uncle Vance reached over and took it from him.

Dad had supplied me with a photo album, and I'd filled the pages with pictures of Josh through the years, from the day he was born to a month prior, to include Susan. "I freaking love it," he said. "Thank you, Megan." He leaned over to me next to him and pulled me to him in a one-armed hug.

The festivities wrapped up just after midnight.

Susan said goodnight to everyone and sprung a hug on Shawn. "You'll have to let me know what kind of ice cream you like before October," she said into his ear.

He sucked in a breath and tears dampened his eyes.

It stung to see her have such an effect on him a second time.

Chapter 42

I'd checked every room in the house. Shawn was nowhere.

"He was still sleeping when I got up." Josh panicked with me.

"When did you get up?"

"About an hour and a half ago."

Bobby fumbled down the stairs. "What the hell's going on?"

My heart raced. I couldn't find his shoes. "Call Dad." I pulled my Chucks on. "I'm checking the quarry."

It was so humid out and I ran so fast I choked on the air.

I tore through the woods and across the clearing to the edge of the ravine.

Thank you, Christ. Shawn was on the ledge.

I dropped to my knees, my chest heaving with gasps.

Holding a lit cigarette, Shawn watched me as I sucked at the air.

`<He's here>`, I texted Josh once I recovered from the run, and started over.

He was soaked from head to toe, his backpack on the ledge next to him. "Are you trying to give me a heart attack?" I asked down to him.

"I'm not trying to do anything," he said with his attention focused straight ahead, and lifted his cigarette to his mouth.

He moved his backpack out of the way as I slid down.

Just be you.

"Are we that bad?" I asked, joking.

"It has nothing to do with you."

"I mean you feeling like you needed to leave."

"I wasn't going anywhere, I just needed to get out of the house."

His hair dripped as if he'd just gotten out of the water. "My family is very worried about you right now."

"Sorry."

"Are you?" He didn't sound like he cared very much.

His gaze stayed straight as the ashes on his cigarette grew. "Why do you think Gina would do that?"

His mom. The real one. So, that's where his mind was.

I assumed he meant leave him with his dad.

There was no answer that would make him feel better. "I don't know, but it sure is her loss."

"Why would Mary do that stuff to me? Why would she *tell* me she was my mom?"

"Because she was a sick, sick woman."

Maybe it was the way we'd celebrated Josh the night before. He'd never experienced any of that kind of stuff. Who knew what his birthdays were like.

His cigarette smoked itself.

"Not one single thing that ever hinted she was my mom. No extra glances in my direction, no unexplained smiles, comments."

I didn't want to make excuses for Gina, but he needed to hear something. "Maybe you didn't notice because you weren't looking."

He turned his eyes to me. "She's not here now . . ."

I wanted so badly to take away his pain. I wanted to go down the street and pound on Gina Donovan's door, shout at her what a terrible woman she was, and slap sense into her. It wouldn't do Shawn any good, though. She'd abandoned him and left him with a monster. She wasn't worth a millisecond of the thought he put into her. I reached up and smoothed away the tear that traced his nose. "She doesn't deserve you."

~

Dad recognized Shawn's need to stretch his legs, so outings were planned. Carefully and meticulously.

Shawn probably would've been content just going to the quarry, but Dad wanted to expand his horizons. Our first venture was a family hiking trip down a portion of the Ozark Trail, where a raging river that was host to several small waterfalls put him in his glory.

"This is freaking awesome." A gigantic smile stretched across his face as he handed his backpack to Dad and, as incognito as he was the day he had his doctor's appointment, jumped in and cooled off beneath one of them.

Bobby, Dennis, and Kenny followed, and before I could get my shoes off, Josh pulled me in.

Laughter and goofing off filled the twenty minutes that the rushing, frigid water cleansed half a day's worth of sweat away.

"We should take a trip back home sometime and show Shawn Colombia River Gorge," Dad said as we started our hike back up.

Oh my God, yes. "You would die," I said to Shawn. "There are waterfalls ten times the size of the one at the quarry."

We stopped at a small ice cream stand on the way home. I re-twisted Shawn's ponytail into a bun, he put the hat back on, and replaced the sunglasses he'd worn most of the day, and we sat at picnic tables beneath weeping willows in the back of the building as we savored our cold treat.

"You gonna finish that?" Shawn asked me about my two scoops of cookie dough, and dug out a spoonful before I answered.

I battled his spoon as he dove in again, and he got up and straddled me. Using his left arm to pin both of mine, he took another heaping bite, and then smeared some on my nose before I could get free of him.

He picked on me along with the other boys, and laughed from the front seat on the way home when Josh and Bobby stunk me out in the back with farts.

Slowly and surely, his better moods became more consistent.

I captured every version of his smile in my sketch pad. I had no idea there could be so many.

He read every music magazine Dad brought home for him within a day, and he had gone through Bobby's entire three-year stock of back issues.

"If you could play an instrument, what would it be?" Dad asked him at dinner one night.

"I think I'd like the drums." He'd started randomly tapping out beats on his knees—even my knees, sometimes, if I was close enough and he wanted to add toms.

"Then let's do it. Bob's mentioned a guitar a few times, let's go the gamut. It'll give you guys something a little more constructive to do during the day than play video games."

"Hell *yeah!*" Bobby was in.

"Seriously?" Shawn's eyes brightened.

The two sat side by side on the couch, Bobby with his laptop, Shawn with Josh's, and given a budget, picked out what they wanted.

The guitar was hard for Bobby to learn, but it wasn't long before Shawn tore up the basement with ten-minute-long solos that sounded as if he'd practiced for years. It was as if I could hear his soul come through each beat.

Mine came through in the form of graphite in a sketch of a human heart pumping out musical notes.

I even drew a guitar for Bobby.

~

As I loaded the dishwasher after dinner one night during Shawn's sixth week with us, Dad pulled open one of the kitchen drawers and removed a sealed envelope. Shawn brought the last of the dirty dishes in from the dining room and Dad handed it to him. "You'll probably want to go somewhere private to read this."

Shawn's eyes rounded. "What is it?"

341

"A letter from your brother."

Shawn stared, lips parted, and then took it and disappeared upstairs.

"You saw Damian?" I asked Dad. Damian was in juvenile detention for his violent act against Shawn.

"Several times," Dad said. "I'm actually the one who suggested he write the letter."

"Why have you been going to see him? Is he part of the investigation?"

"No, Meg, he's Shawn's brother, and he's a troubled teenage boy. They have more of a connection than they knew, and if we can get them communicating, there stands a chance of saving two lives rather than just one."

"But what if Shawn doesn't want that?" Damian was such a negative person in his life.

"Shawn can't know what he wants until he has all the information."

"What information? Damian's a jerk."

"Megan, you need to remember we don't know any more about Damian's life than anyone knew about Shawn's. We have no idea what he might have been going through at home to cause him to act out the way he did."

"Does he know?" I meant everything that had happened to Shawn. Dad nodded.

"And?" I wanted to know his response. He was such an a-hole to him.

"He's getting help. I think he still has a little farther down to go, but he's working through things."

"Things like smashing his brother's head with a baseball bat because he was jealous of him, and then finding out he could've been the one on the receiving end of two-hundred-and-fifty-pound men?"

"Megan, please tone it down a notch. I know you're passionate about this and it's hard for you to understand, but life is a series of causes and effects. Like Bobby starting his downward spiral when your mother died. Let's leave it to the two of them to hash out. If all goes well, Shawn gains a brother. If not, at least he'll know where all the animosity came from."

"Do you know what the letter says?"

"I do."

"And it doesn't say anything bad?"

"If it said anything unfavorable, I wouldn't have passed it along."

"What about Gina?" Shawn was hurt by her, but I was angry. "She completely ditched him."

"She knows there's an open line of communication." He sighed. "But I don't hold out much hope for her."

Tears snuck up on me anticipating Shawn's anguish. "You're not going to tell him that, are you?"

"I'm not going to bring her up again unless he does."

~

Shawn never acknowledged the letter with me, and if he was affected by it, it didn't show.

Chapter 43

The hummingbird: a bird of joy that symbolized great courage, determination, flexibility, adaptability, and endurance. Among other things.

I researched them more after I found myself continually gawking at my drawing. I'd pulled the shading off so well you could almost feel the iridescence.

They were described as "impossibly strong and fast."

For such a little guy—which you couldn't really tell from the page—mine had quite a powerful and commanding presence.

He demanded a background.

Not flowers full of nectar—fire.

The contrast between the green and orange was bold. Like he was. Brazen and fearless.

"Do you know a hummingbird egg is smaller than a jelly bean?" I educated everyone at dinner.

"Is that right?" Dad glanced up from cutting his meat.

"Random," Bobby said.

"Yup. A baby hummingbird fits on a penny."

Bobby looked at me with a confused shake of his head, questioning the topic.

The more I learned about them, the more my fascination grew. If something so tiny could be so strong and fierce, how could I have any excuse not to be?

Everything I'd heard and read said that if you hung a hummingbird feeder, they would likely come.

Red attracted them.

I found a pretty easy version of one to make online but needed Dad to order the supplies. I could've just had him buy one, but with all the time on my hands, I wanted to make one. I was too impatient to wait, so in the interim, I took another idea from the internet and cut a wedge out of a disposable red cup. I filled it to the opening with the appropriate sugar water mixture and hung it from one of the plant hangers on the deck.

"What is that?" Shawn asked, stopping and looking out the slider as he passed by.

"It's a hummingbird feeder."

His brow lifted. "That's pretty ghetto."

"It's only while I wait for stuff to make a better one."

"I think you could've done better than that." He went to the cupboard by the stove and pulled out one of the several jars of roasted red peppers we now had. He emptied the contents into a plastic container. "Go get me a drill," he said as he washed out the jar.

345

I went to the basement and found one of Dad's.

He drilled holes into the red lid. He tied string to hang it from underneath the lip of it, filled it with the water from my cup, and hung it. "How's that?"

"*So* much better." I loved it. And loved that *he'd* made it.

"So, what's up with the hummingbirds?"

"I don't know, they're just really interesting." I told him some of the things I'd learned. "Do you know that they have the fastest metabolism of any living thing and need to eat up to three times their weight a day, or they could die overnight?"

"I didn't."

I showed him my drawing.

"Wow." He ran his fingers over it as if he expected to feel a texture.

"The average ruby-throated hummingbird," —which that was— "weighs three grams. That's two less than a nickel. It would take a hundred and fifty of them to equal a pound."

"I think I'm going to have to call you the bird lady now," he said as he continued to examine it. "How'd you do that?" he asked about the iridescent effect, lifting the paper to look at it from a different angle.

"They're just really inspiring, don't you think?" Maybe they would boost his optimism as well. "Have you ever seen one? A humming-bird?"

"Once." He was entranced.

"When?" It meant I had a chance. "Where were you?"

"Last year, maybe? At the quarry."

346

"What did it look like?"

"A bug. I thought it was at first, but then it hovered in front of me. Stood completely still in mid-air. Looked straight at me."

So cool. I told him all the different things they symbolized. "Their wings, in motion, move in a figure eight pattern," I added. "Like an infinity symbol."

"So, what's that mean for me, that I'm infinitely doomed?"

I sighed. Of all the things I'd listed. "Can you think positively for two seconds, please?" He'd said it jokingly, but still.

Chapter 44

I stared out the glass of the slider for an embarrassing amount of time over the next several days waiting for any and all hummingbirds in the area to discover they had a new food source. Nothing.

"Maybe it's my feeder," Shawn said, acknowledging my disappointment as he stood next to me.

"Your feeder's fine." I actually liked it enough that I no longer wanted to make my own.

"There probably just aren't any around here."

"You saw one."

"Yeah, *once*."

I sighed.

"Well, looks like no joy or hope for you."

Again, he said it jokingly, but it was a bummer. I really did want to see one.

~

If ever there was such a thing as PMS for boys, Bobby had it, and it was his time of the month. We weren't even safe looking at him without it rubbing him the wrong way.

"Is there anything anyone wants from the market?" Dad asked as he and I were ready to walk out the door.

"Yeah, a new sister who doesn't ruin all my friggin' laundry."

I'd accidentally left a tube of lip gloss in one of my shorts pockets, and he'd been going on about it all morning. "Do your own laundry," I hollered at him for the bazillionth time.

"Alright, you two." We were probably half the reason Dad wanted to go shopping when he did.

It was nice to get out for a little while, and we took our time. When we finished at the market, we stopped by the post office.

Josh helped carry in the groceries when we got home, and Shawn helped to put them away.

"You're cool," I said to Bobby at the kitchen table practicing chords on his guitar. "Feel free to get off your butt and help any time."

"Shut your face."

The entire atmosphere was charged because of him. Shawn was rigid, Josh wouldn't look at him. "Why don't you take a breather, Bob," Dad said. "Go take a walk, or something. Bounce the basketball off the side of the house."

I tripped over a bag of groceries on the floor and bumped into the table, sending his glass of water into his lap. He flew out of his chair and lunged at me.

Shawn, only inches from me, threw his arm around my neck and

349

jerked me behind him.

Bobby halted.

Dad jumped between the two boys, eyes on Shawn.

Shawn surely didn't realize the strength he imposed on me, his stance as if ready to physically fend Bobby off.

"Shawn." I pushed up off his hips to ease the pressure on my neck.

Bobby leaned around Dad, stunned by what he'd sparked. "Shawn, I'm not gonna hurt her." He all of a sudden changed his tune. "I promise, I'm not gonna hurt her."

Shawn eased the tension in his arm and I slid out of his grasp. Eyes wide, he looked between the three of us as if trying to figure out what happened. "I'm sorry." He pushed past Dad and Bobby and disappeared.

~

The more time went by, the less anxiety Shawn exhibited, but Dad remained just as vigilant in his search for John Harris and anyone else who took part in or had knowledge of the crimes against him.

At the end of the sixth week, with still no viable leads, he scheduled another press conference. I watched in private on the countertop TV in the kitchen.

"Why such an intense manhunt?" one reporter asked. "These types of crimes happen every day in every corner of the world, the country, even the state."

"We have reason to believe this extends beyond just a few individuals to maybe a ring or trafficking boss."

"Where are you getting your information," another voice asked.

"The original victim, or have more come forward?"

Dad's eyes panned the roomful of cameras. "Nobody has given us this information. Let's just call it a hunch."

"So, you're wasting taxpayer's money on a hunch?"

Dad wasn't fazed. "No, sir. As a father, myself, with one of the highest ranking positions in law enforcement for almost two decades, I'm going on a gut feeling and protecting your family and mi—"

A thumb came from behind me and pounded the power button on the TV. "Shut that shit off." Shawn wasn't watching and apparently didn't want me to either.

He didn't talk to me, and other than the one night after dinner, Dad didn't tell us anything, so how else was I supposed to know what went on? He got a bottle of water from the refrigerator, and as soon as he was gone, I turned it back on.

"The number of sexually exploited children in the United States rises exponentially each year. It truly saddens me that an issue such as this would be regarded as a waste of taxpayer's money."

Shawn stepped back into the room and ripped the television cord right out of the back of the TV, and he whisked it, clearing items on the opposite counter. "That's my fucking life all over the news, not yours."

Fuck.

~

Even though Shawn didn't watch the press conference, it put him in a mood for the rest of the day and most of the next. Dad never disclosed who the victim in the case was, but Jessup was a small town, and everybody knew who John Harris was and that he had a teenage son.

351

Chapter 45

The heat outside was more bearable when the air wasn't saturated with water, and I took those opportunities to read or draw out on the deck or on a towel in the grass under the sun.

"Come in here, Meg," Dad called to me from the kitchen as I sketched one of the daisies that popped up along the back of the house.

I stepped inside in my bathing suit top and a shorter-than-needed-to-be pair of cut-offs.

"I think it's time you start paying attention to what you wear."

"Why, it's just my bathing suit." If there was water around, I wouldn't even have had the shorts on.

"Because I'm not comfortable with Shawn seeing you half naked."

"Do you think it bothers him?" I guess there were plenty reasons it would.

"Not why I'm saying it." He cocked an eyebrow, suggesting Shawn might actually like it.

I laughed. "Believe me, Dad, Shawn doesn't think about that stuff." In hindsight, it was amazing we'd ever even kissed.

"Maybe not usually, but five minutes ago, he did."

What? How did he know that? "Did something happen?"

Dad's expression pinched. "Please just go put some clothes on."

Did he see him looking at me, something more, what? "Where is he?"

"Don't worry about where he is, just do as I ask."

Nuh-uh!

~

The sun shot like an arrow through my window as I lay in bed for nearly an hour thinking about what Dad said the day before about wearing more clothes. Other than kissing, and for a brief time loving it, Shawn never gave any other sort of indication he was physically interested in me. And I could understand why.

I wasn't even sure what our true relationship was.

My door was shut as I took my pajama top off and searched through my underwear drawer for a bra. Footsteps came up the stairs fast and down my end of the hall. I reached for my shirt on my bed and the knob turned and Shawn pushed open my door.

His eyes sprawled.

With my bare back to him, I held my shirt to my chest, fairly certain he hadn't seen anything.

I turned my eyes from him for only a moment and he disappeared.

Giving up on the bra, I threw my shirt back on and went after him. "Shawn." I rushed to the opposite end of the hall.

He stood behind the door of the room he shared with Josh in his typical nervous stance, hands in his back pockets, rocking against the wall with a view of the ceiling. "I'm sorry, I'm sorry, I'm sorry."

"It's okay." He appeared embarrassed enough for both of us.

He still didn't look at me.

I reached behind him and eased his hands from his pockets and ushered them to my waist. It wasn't anywhere they hadn't been.

I held mine over his.

It was a "take it as it comes" moment. I pulled the bottom of my shirt up, removing the cloth barrier.

His warm hands sent a shiver through me.

He drew in a heaping breath.

"Is this okay?" I wasn't sure what my intentions even were.

He nodded against the wall, his inhales deep and exhales shaky.

I let him get used to the idea of where his hands were, then drew on them a little. "You can if you want."

I wasn't the kind of girl to typically encourage a guy to feel them up, but this was different. If I didn't, Shawn—nor I—would probably ever experience it. There wasn't much to me, which made me that much more self-conscious.

His hands didn't move. And then they did. Tentatively, towards a destination I wasn't sure I was prepared for.

Every bit of my skin reacted to his warm palms moving up my sides.

He stopped mid-torso and, head still against the wall, peeked down with an awkward turn of his eyes.

354

He tipped his head forward for a better view.

I lost my nerve and kept mine focused on his chest. If he moved his hands in even a little, the tips of his fingers would brush my breasts.

They acknowledged where they were with a twitch, and he gasped. He shifted his position as he dropped his hands from me and slung his head back to the wall. He stiffened and tugged at the bottom of his shirt.

I panicked. "I'm sorry." I left him standing there and rushed out.

I hid in my room for the rest of the day.

Chapter 46

I didn't know how I'd look at Shawn after our encounter in Josh's room. I thought for sure I did something wrong. What on Earth possessed me to think he would be okay with touching me like that? It was awful, I felt like I'd violated him.

I had to come out of my room sometime, and dinner wouldn't cook itself.

Shawn sat on the couch with a foot on the coffee table Dad glued back together, flipping through a magazine. He looked up at me as I walked down the stairs. I was the one unable to hold eye contact this time as he watched me walk into the kitchen, where I hid until dinner time when Dad came home.

"So, how was everyone's day?" Dad asked, cutting into his pork chop.

Josh and Bobby both said, "Good."

"Megan?"

I shrugged. "Okay, I guess."

He looked to Shawn.

"Joyous." He stabbed a piece of meat. "Full of hope."

Excusez-moi? I totally expected him to say horrible. Had I *not* done something wrong?

"Saw a hummingbird," he said.

"You *did?*" All awkwardness momentarily got pushed aside as the words burst from my mouth.

He looked at me. "I tried to tell you, but . . ."

My whole body heated as my cheeks surely brightened. It must've been why he came into my room the way he had.

~

It took me a little while to pull myself together the following day, but once I did, it went on as usual. Shawn made no mention of the occurrence the morning before and acted as if it didn't happen.

I wanted to ask him about the hummingbird, but it would bring up a topic I desperately tried to avoid.

He spent the morning on the couch watching movies while Josh and Susan fought with Bobby about turning down his music.

Just before noon, Shawn turned off the TV and sat up. With his feet on the floor and elbows on his knees as Bobby's hip hop drowned out all sound, he leaned his head into his hands.

"Want some earplugs?" I asked.

"I can't hear. I need to be able to hear." He lifted his head and his hands shook.

"I'll go talk to him." Bobby would have no choice but to listen, it

357

was no longer about winning a battle with a sibling, it was about safety.

Bobby's bedroom door was open—so Josh would be able to hear him that much more—even though Josh and Susan weren't in the house anymore—and he was on his bed playing one of his hand-held video games with headphones on, not even listing to the music he blared.

I pushed the power button on his stereo, and he looked up from the small screen in his hand. "Yeah, I don't think so," he said, pulling his headphones off.

"You're not the only one in this house. Have some respect."

"I'll have some respect tomorrow." He aimed his stereo remote and turned it back on.

I turned it off again. "Go tell that to Shawn, who's shaking out of his skin because he can't hear anything going on around him."

Bobby rolled his eyes. He didn't turn the music back on, though.

Shawn stirred for another hour or so, unable to calm down. He looked out the curtains, he peered through the blinds on the slider. I rubbed his back as he bent with his elbows to the kitchen table taking deep breaths.

I never realized noise was a factor. When I thought about it, he didn't shower unless Dad was home, he didn't play the drums unless Dad was home.

"Hey, sorry, man, I didn't realize," Bobby said when he passed to the refrigerator. It was something, at least. It was the second time his actions set Shawn off.

~

358

Dad rushed through the front door. "Joshua, Robert . . ." He passed me on the couch and went into the kitchen. He pulled open the slider to the deck where Josh still hung with Susan. "Both of you, inside, now."

They came in, and Dad slid the door shut behind them and locked it. "Go check every door and window and make sure they're locked," he said to Josh.

"What's going on?"

"Just do it."

Bobby came downstairs.

Dad met Shawn halfway and directed him back up.

When they were out of sight, Bobby went three-quarters of the way back up and listened.

All was quiet for a moment, and then there was a loud noise—as if a piece of furniture knocked against a wall. A strange sound came from Dad, and it was as if he physically struggled.

Bobby bolted the rest of the way up the stairs as I lunged from the couch.

Shawn fought with Dad to get out of the room. Dad wouldn't let him by.

Shawn backed away from him, eyes wide, and the color drained from his face.

He swayed, and Dad jumped to catch him as he went down.

He lowered to the floor with him, where Shawn fell into a puddle.

"Out, guys. I need you to get out."

Bobby backed out of the room.

"Megan, please."

Shawn inhaled as if his heart had been restarted, and a loud, bawling cry erupted from his lungs. He turned his face to the floor, every one of his breaths drawn to a gasping point.

I backed out into Josh.

"Is your inhaler in your pocket?" Dad asked, cautiously patting Shawn's pants, feeling for it.

Shawn's fingers clawed into the rug. *"Leave me alone."*

Dad drew back. He waited while Shawn cried, and then leaned over his ear. "We're here." His hand weighed down on his head. "Take as long as you need." He stood and came out, pulling the door shut some, and motioned for us all to go downstairs.

"What happened?" I asked once we were all back down in the living room.

"We found Shawn's father."

Chills swept over me.

"About twenty miles outside of town, hands tied behind his back with a bullet in the back of his head."

Oh, dear God.

Susan's hands drew to her mouth, Josh's to his head.

"The asshole deserved it," Bobby said.

"Maybe so," Dad said. "But Shawn's not ever to hear those words, do you understand?" He turned to Susan. "I need you to call your mother, have her come get you. This situation just intensified ten times over, I can't be worrying about an extra person right now."

Susan's cheeks were the rosiest I'd ever seen. "Sure." She turned to Josh. "Make sure you call me, okay?" Her eyes were wide and full of worry.

Dad pulled his cell phone from his pants pocket. "I'm going to make some calls. I don't want you guys outside until we figure stuff out." He went back upstairs.

Josh, Bobby, and I sat in the living room, looking back and forth between one another in silence, listening to Dad as he paced the upstairs hallway. His first phone call was to Dana, telling her she was needed at our house. He then called the alarm company. "I need cameras, and I need them yesterday." He now knew the threat was real, and cost didn't seem to be a factor. We had brought Shawn into our house—and our lives—now we were a part of his.

When the appointment was scheduled, he hung up and dialed an old contact at a K-9 company that specialized in training dogs for law enforcement.

Beyond Shawn's initial ten-minute loss of control, all upstairs was quiet. Then the sound of glass shattering set off a long and loud destruction spree. He yelled and shouted, and we could hear, quite clearly, objects hitting walls.

Josh stared straight ahead, not seeming to care that his room was being destroyed.

I could only take it for so long. While Dad arranged for the utmost protection possible, I went back up. Dad couldn't stop me as I barreled past him and went into Josh's room and enveloped Shawn in the tightest hug I could.

"I did this," he cried. "I knew this was gonna happen. I never should have come here. I never should have left." His face, red and streaked with tears, was a clear definition of agony. "He's dead. He's dead and it's my fault."

"It's not your fault. This is not your fault." I couldn't have held him tighter.

A set of arms encompassed us. *Bobby's.*

It was truly unexpected. Not even after Mom died did he offer such solidarity.

Before long, Josh was upstairs as well, all of us huddling in support.

~

Dana arrived within the hour, and a pair of FBI agents was at our house by dinner time. Shawn got very little time to grieve. Dad handed over the evidence he had, and we were all sent to our rooms while Shawn was grilled.

"I told you, I don't know anything." He gagged on a myriad of emotions.

Dana's small voice spoke gentle words I was unable to hear.

"Do you realize you're putting this family in jeopardy every moment you conceal this person's identity?" An agent pushed him.

"Okay, enough is enough." Dad put a stop to their questioning.

It wasn't fair. Shawn's worst fear was materializing in front of him, and he didn't have room to breathe, let alone think.

362

Chapter 47

After Shawn's father was found, our house went into full lockdown. The doors and windows went back to being locked at all times, and no one was allowed outside. Within days, we were the proud owners of two very large, very trained German Shepherds. They were let loose at our front door, and they tore through the house sniffing out their new surroundings.

The man who brought them spent the day teaching us their commands, all German, and wouldn't leave until Shawn reluctantly came downstairs and interacted with them.

Samson, the male, was a little over two, and Maxi, the female, only a year. She took to Shawn right away. He wouldn't have been able to ignore her if he wanted to. She jumped on him, licked him.

"Tell her *nein* for no," the instructor said.

"Nein," Shawn said.

"Like you mean it."

"*Nein.*"

"Now give her a treat."

Shawn tossed one into her mouth, and, tail wagging, she gobbled it up.

"Tell her sitz, for sit."

"Sitz." Again, there wasn't a lot of conviction in his tone. She sat, though, and Shawn gave her another treat.

By the end of the night, Maxi had gotten a whole lot of treats and hadn't been told no or sit at all. She slept next to Shawn's bed and didn't leave his side to even go to the bathroom in the morning.

Samson was more of a wanderer, mingling among everybody, not attaching himself to any particular individual. Both dogs barked fiercely whenever anyone pulled into the driveway or knocked on the door, but calmed when told to. It was as if they knew why they were there and what their job was, but they fit in just as if they were pets.

We were only allowed to go outside if the dogs were out with us, and we had to send them out for at least ten minutes before we could follow.

"Why does she do that?" Shawn couldn't handle Maxi's pleading eyes on the opposite side of the slider.

"Because she can't stand to be away from you."

He opened the door and let her back in.

"You're a bad dog owner, you know." He gave in more often than not.

"Yeah, let me see you do better."

He didn't care much for her name, so he usually shortened it to Max.

Though Dad had already purchased cellular service for Shawn's phone, we all had to get rid of the phones we had, and he got us all new ones with new numbers that couldn't be traced, and we were required to carry them at all times. He programmed them with the necessary emergency numbers, and even went as far as to make sure the volume of their keypads was set to silent, ensuring if ever any of us were abducted, a call for help would hopefully go undetected.

~

"The agents who were here last week are coming back," Dad told Shawn in the kitchen after dinner one night after I'd just stepped out. "I need to warn you, it will probably be intense."

"Why, what are they gonna do?"

"They've got some pictures they want you to look at."

"Of what?" Dread shrouded his tone. "Of me?"

"I don't think you'll be in any of them."

"Why do I have to look at them?"

"Because they want to see if you can identify any of the people who violated you."

"I already told them I couldn't. Why don't they believe me?"

Dad's breath was audible from the living room. "Please believe me, Shawn, I don't want you to have to go through this any more than you do."

"Then why do I have to? I want this over. *I just want it to be over.*" Maxi was at his heels as he stomped out and charged upstairs.

Josh, Bobby, and I were sent to Uncle Vance's this time. We were there for the better part of the day. When we got home, the agents were gone, and Shawn was upstairs with the bedroom door shut.

He didn't come out at all the following day, and the agents came again the next.

Shawn was the same after both visits. He didn't eat, sleep, or talk to anyone.

Though Dad was happy to finally have the FBI's help, it did neither Shawn nor the investigation any good. Shawn still claimed he couldn't identify anyone, and his mood deteriorated.

"Did he talk to you today?" I asked Dana from where I sat at the top of the stairs waiting when she came out of Josh's room.

She shook her head, and then sat down next to me and hugged her arm around me. "Understand, Megan, that he's dealing with a lot of things right now."

"I do. I just don't get why he came off so much more fine when all of this stuff was actually going on." It was just images now rather than the actual people and events. "Why is he so depressed now when he seemed okay then?"

"Do you know what PTSD is?" she asked me.

"Post-traumatic something?" I was pretty sure.

"It's Post-traumatic Stress Disorder. Shawn was perfectly able to function in the heat of the moment. He actually excels in it." She nodded. "He was so preoccupied with trying to keep one step ahead of the game that he never really had a chance to process anything. Now with so much free 'down time,' it's all kind of caving in on him."

"He was doing so well, though." I thought. Two months of working

366

his way up, and now he was in this horrible place.

"He was." She pressed out a smile. "He put in a valiant effort, but now that's he's being faced with it all again, it's bringing all the feelings and emotions again, and he's crashing."

Shawn monopolized my sketch pad.

The drawings I did of him, now, bled pain. He was in a worse place than I ever was. Or could even imagine. It was hard to believe a single human being could endure so much suffering.

Early one morning as I absorbed the hot sun on the deck, I wrote about what they say about the eyes being the windows to the soul.

. . . His are crystal. So light they're almost white. Shooting straight to my core, unintentionally drawing me in as I slowly become privy to his dark and lonely existence—a cruel and perverse reality etched solely by paternal betrayal. As I passively invade his distant and unimaginable world, he teeters on a brink so close to acceptance that he's nearly impenetrable. He's my shriveling rose, struggling not to bend under the weight of the mud.

~

"I'm sorry, but you'll have to work with what you have," Dad told one of the agents the next time they called. "He's not holding up, and I can't jeopardize his mental stability any more than we already have."

Not even Maxi could elicit a response from him. She'd lie at the end of his bed and wait for him to make a move, which didn't

367

happen often.

"If he doesn't start eating, he'll need to be hospitalized." Dana worried.

"I don't like the idea," Dad said. "But I don't know how else to help him at this point."

I couldn't fathom it, and it wasn't what Shawn would want. Determined, I went up to Josh's room, where, as far as I could tell, he was asleep. Maxi jumped to attention when I entered.

"C'mon, Maxi, off the bed. Platz." I commanded her to get down.

Shawn opened his eyes.

I stood next to his bed and took hold of his wrists. "Get up." I pulled on him.

He didn't make any effort.

"*Shawn*," I yelled at him. "*Get. Up.*"

He brought himself to a sitting position on the edge of the bed, and I got clothes from his bureau. "You need to take a shower." I couldn't remember the last time he had.

A tear streaked his cheek. I ignored it and, sneaking a pair of underwear between the shirt and pants, placed the pile on his lap and crouched down in front of him. "Go take a shower, it will make you feel better." I was almost certain. His eyes lifted, his gaze meeting mine, and I nodded. "Okay? Please?"

I went to my room at the other end of the hall and waited a good ten minutes. The water never turned on.

I went back into Josh's room and he was right where I'd left him.

"Shawn." I forced my fingers under his armpits to pull him up. He jerked away and grabbed my wrists.

My hands closed into fists in his grip as his chest pumped. "I'm sorry. They're going to put you in the hospital, though, where a whole ton of people will touch you in all kinds of ways."

His forehead strained and throat pulsed with constrictions.

"You need to move, Shawn. You need to get up. Please, just try to take a shower." Maybe it would motivate him to eat something.

The lines in his forehead were deep, like a hundred-year-old tree.

I needed to get drastic. I had to pull out all the stops. Pushing all uneasiness aside, I went to my room and got my sketch pad.

I squatted down next to him with my back against his bed, my pad on my lap where he could see it, and opened to a drawing of our two hands conjoined. It was the original idea I got from the handscapes project Miss Devereaux assigned. His hand and arm, drawn with charcoal, was encompassed by a tangle of scribble lines. Mine, once encircled by the same mesh of chaos and disorder, depicted now by only a faded scattering, was an array of warm colors.

"This is you," I pointed at the turbulence-ridden hand. "And this is me." He probably wouldn't notice I'd colored two of his fingers.

"Why are you showing me that?" His voice broke as if he would cry. "Do you think I like being like that?"

"I'm showing you because . . ." I flipped through the earlier drawings that were a display of black and white that showed the darkness I'd been stuck in. "I want you to see what you did for me." He didn't only add color back to my drawings, he added it back to my life.

369

Please, God, don't let this be in vain. I'd never shown anyone those drawings. "You're getting stuck thinking about the things that happened to you, but . . ." I flipped through my most recent stuff. All the vibrancy. "Look what happened to me." I looked up to him. "Because of *you*."

I just kept talking. "I know you probably see yourself a certain way." Who wouldn't with the stuff that happened. "But . . ." I turned to the first sketch I'd done of him smiling. The one from the day at the quarry. "I see you completely differently."

I pushed through the pages to the one I did the day he found out his blood test results. The one with the smile that created the dimples under his eyes. Did he even know they existed?

I had to be careful what he saw as I flipped. I went through each one of him smiling, hoping he'd see the theme.

It was hard to know what he thought. I hoped he wasn't mad at me for drawing him. "I was stuck too, Shawn. Just like you. But you un-stuck me."

God, give me something, please!

"Think about the hummingbird." I went to the one I drew. I was reaching, but as much as I wanted to see one and hadn't, he did—twice. "You're the one seeing them, not me." Even if it was complete BS, it sounded good, as the things they symbolized fit. "You're *not* doomed." He surely really thought it. "You have *incredible* strength." Like nothing I knew. "*Infinite* strength."

As frustrated as I was not to get any sort of response, at least he didn't argue any of my points. "You are too important a person to this

370

world, Shawn, to make it through everything you have, only to curl up in a ball on a bed in my brother's room and starve to death."

Short of dancing and singing, which would've sent anyone running from a room, I didn't know what else to do. I tore the hummingbird from the pad and set it on his bed next to him. "I want you to have this." *Please don't crumple it.* It was one of my very favorite drawings. "You are so much stronger than you think. Please snap out of this?"

Eye contact would've been nice, but at least he appeared more coherent than when I first went in. "Take a shower," I said. "When you're finished, come downstairs and I'll make you something to eat." I left him again.

After many minutes, the bathroom door shut and the shower water turned on.

~

Dad looked up from his laptop as Shawn came downstairs. "Good afternoon, Shawn." Awe lit his face.

I directed him to the kitchen.

We must've caught Bobby's eye outside on the deck practicing his guitar. When we entered, he reached for his shirt at the end of the chaise and put it back on.

Shawn sat at the table as I looked through the fridge at my options. "I can make you a turkey sandwich. Can do turkey, lettuce, tomato—"

"Eggs." His voice was muffled with his face buried in his arms.

I brought him a glass of orange juice. I nudged my fingers into his shoulder and he showed his eyes. "Drink this," I said as if he didn't have a choice.

His hand wrapped around the glass, and he tipped it into his mouth and chugged.

"Do you want anything else? Toast, an English muf—"

"No."

Okay, then. He would get a lot of eggs. I cracked seven into a bowl and whisked them.

"You know the FBI talked to my mom?" He lifted his face and looked ahead with a blank stare.

I didn't know. Thinking about Gina wasn't what was immobilizing him, but she was apparently still bogging him down. She'd still made no effort to contact him. I put the bowl of eggs down. "You have a family right here, Shawn. I hope you know we would do anything for you."

He dropped his face to his arms again.

I couldn't stand to see him that way. How would the tiny shards he was broken into ever be put back together again? I went over to the table and pulled out the chair next to him, and sat and lowered my head to him. "I know we're not your real family, but we care about you like you're ours."

His arms closed in to hide all bits of his face. It seemed as much as we could tell him Gina didn't matter, she did to him.

Despite any ill reaction he might have, I tugged at his arms. "Look at me, Shawn, seriously."

He showed his eyes again, this time bearing irritation.

"*I* care," I said. "That boy out there . . ." I pointed out the slider at Bobby. "*He* cares. He cares more than I've ever seen him care about anything. My dad, Josh, Sue . . . my uncle, they *all* care. Blood doesn't always make family. Unconditional love and support do. Which is what you have here. We won't ever let you down, I promise."

His head started back down, and I grabbed his cheeks and made him look directly at me. "You need to eat. A lot, okay?"

Dad came into the kitchen, envelope in hand. "I don't know if it's a good idea to give you this right now, not knowing what it says, but it seems to me someone else wants in on the family bit." He dropped the letter from Damian on the table in front of him.

Who cared what it said, maybe it would move his mind off the visuals the FBI agents seared into it. His eyes fixed on the letters across the front of it that spelled out his name in sloppy handwriting.

"Megan's right, though, you need to eat, and I want to see you eat a lot. That's gotta happen before you disappear with this."

Whether it was what I said or having Damian's letter to look forward to—if a letter from Damian was something to look forward to—Shawn perked up. He ate all seven eggs I scrambled him, and an English muffin Dad toasted and put on his plate, minus two bites he gave Maxi sitting eagerly by his side waiting for him to drop something.

Dad wouldn't let him go back upstairs for fear of losing him again, so he read the letter in the dining room.

Uncle Vance and the boys came over in the meantime.

Dennis, football in hand, led the way to the backyard, Kenny and Bobby following.

What started as a friendly toss between the three of them quickly

373

turned into a game of "Monkey in the Middle," with my eleven-year-old cousin stuck without the ball.

Josh joined and, in an effort to help Kenny, started a game of tackle, with the dogs trying to steal the ball.

The dining room chair sounded across the floor. Shawn appeared and veered toward the living room. Dad moved into his path and redirected him to the kitchen table, where he'd have to deal with everyone passing by, and he placed Josh's laptop and a magazine in front of him.

"Hey, Shawn," Dennis said when he came in. "I have that new war game. Wanna go try it out?"

Shawn looked down at the envelope in his hand. He removed the letter and read it again.

Josh came in and sought Dad out. "Is it okay if Sue comes over?"

"I'm not so sure it would be a good idea." He eyed Shawn in the kitchen, bringing attention to the fact that he was up.

"Shawn usually responds well to Sue, she'd probably help."

I hated hearing that. Mostly because it was true.

Dad looked like he considered the idea. "Alright, I guess. But if anything happens to make me change my mind, you need to respect my decision to send her home."

"Awesome, Dad, thanks." Josh left to call her.

"Yeah, Dad, awesome. Thanks."

"What's the problem?" he asked. "I thought you liked Sue."

"I do. I just don't like that she has such a positive impact on *my* boyfriend. If that's even what I can call him anymore. It's selfish, I

374

know. Forget I said anything."

Dad's exhale was hard. "It is selfish, coming from you." He placed his hand on my back and guided me to the couch. "Is that really how you feel?" he asked, sitting down in his chair.

"More and more every time she's here."

"NutMeg, everyone plays a role."

"And I'm just that. NutMeg. The little girl who just is."

"You're not a little girl, Megan, and you've played probably the biggest role in all of this. I know there are times when you probably feel like you're not needed, or Shawn may act strange toward you, but he's here because of you. He's *safe* because of you."

"He's here because of Damian."

"He didn't commit suicide, Megan. How often do you think he thought about it before you came along? Or tried? I do believe we've had this conversation."

"I know." I did. Hence why I said I knew I was being selfish. "It's just that Susan's going to come in here and give him a big ol' hug, and he'll be okay with it, when this morning he reacted so poorly to me touching him, I thought he might actually hurt me."

"That may happen, and if it does, you need to remind yourself that there's a big difference between this morning and this afternoon. This morning, he was shut in his bedroom hiding away from everyone, probably lost in his mind somewhere. This afternoon, he's present, both mentally and physically. Because of you."

I wanted to be okay with it, I did. I liked Susan. A lot. I just wanted her role too. Greedy. Totally greedy.

Dad gave in and let Shawn watch TV with me in the living room. By the time Susan got there, he was asleep on the couch.

Maxi's bark was as ferocious as Samson's when she knocked on the door.

Dad opened it, and Shawn turned his face into the leather as she entered.

"Hey, hey." She looked to anyone who might respond.

Shawn turned the rest of his body so he was completely face-down in avoidance, and Josh scooped her up.

Dad and Uncle Vance cooked chicken on the grill for dinner. Shawn couldn't—and *wouldn't*—go outside, so Dad left the slider open and set the patio table, as well as the kitchen one.

"Why don't you and Josh sit outside," he said to Susan when she pulled out a chair at the kitchen table.

Susan's brow crinkled with confusion as she pushed the chair back in.

Shawn was present, but that was about it. He ate less than half of his dinner—though he did drink a lot of water—and tried to go back into the living room.

"You need to eat more than that, Shawn," Dad said when he was halfway out of his seat.

He huffed and sat back down.

Menstrual cramps ripped through my gut. Dennis and Bobby told jokes back and forth and Susan's laugh was loud, only enhancing the pain.

"Can I be excused?" I asked out the door with my arms clutched

376

around my abdomen.

Dad eyed me as if he didn't believe me.

"Really, Dad, I don't feel good."

"Alright, then."

I stood under the hot spraying water of the shower for a while, trying to make the ache go away at least a little. I took some Ibuprofen, and then lay down on my bed.

I missed the entire rest of the night and drifted off as I read.

Chapter 48

A loud outburst sent me flying out of my bed at two a.m.

I rushed to the other end of the brightly lit hall and poked my head in the crack of Josh's bedroom door.

Josh, sitting straight up in his bed, put his finger to his lips to shush me. "I think he's still asleep."

Shawn tossed and turned, obvious he was having a nightmare. "Shouldn't we wake him up?"

Josh shrugged.

With Shawn facing the opposite direction, I leaned over him to see if he was really still asleep. His eyes were closed.

"Shawn." I touched his shoulder. It was tense and stiff.

I couldn't believe he didn't wake up. He'd typically jump awake if touched. "Shawn." I rubbed his arm.

"It's just how he sleeps," Josh said, and lay back down.

"All the time?"

"Yup. All the time."

The more I rubbed, the more the tension eased, until his shoulder fell to a more relaxed position.

With Shawn settled, Josh fell back to sleep.

I gave it less than half a thought and got into bed with Shawn.

With him dressed in his clothes from the day before, I got underneath the covers and cuddled into him.

I lay my arm over him, assuring that if he woke to the feeling of someone else in the bed, he would see my hand.

My cramps hadn't let up much, making it hard to fall back to sleep. Shawn was still, for the most part, until he turned underneath my arm and, facing me, started moaning.

"Hey," I whispered, rubbing his arm again.

The noises he made became louder and more distressed.

"Shawn, wake up." I shook him.

His eyes popped open.

"Hi."

His brow tightened. "What are you doing here?"

"You were having bad dreams."

His expression didn't loosen. Fearing I'd done wrong, I shut my eyes as if going back to sleep.

His lips pressed to my forehead. "Thank you."

I opened my eyes again. His face was devoid of stress.

He now looked as awake as me.

I pushed my fingers through his hair, and he lifted his hand and rubbed his thumb back and forth over my cheek. "How come you left dinner?"

He'd probably regret asking, but it was nice to know he cared. "Cramps. I got my period."

"Do you still have 'em?"

"Yeah. I feel a little better." Josh showed no signs of being awake.

His hand moved off my face and swept down my side, and he massaged my waist with gentle pressure.

I turned onto my back so his hand placement would be more accurate.

He slipped it underneath my shirt. "How's that?"

The heat from his palm as he pressed it to my stomach provided instant relief. "It feels really good." He pushed it soothingly back and forth.

Not only did it feel good, he was under my shirt. An indication that maybe I really didn't do anything wrong the day I encouraged him to touch me.

Shawn moved his leg over mine and butted his forehead up against my temple. His hand eventually slowed, then stopped as if he fell back to sleep.

My eyelids just started to get heavy when Shawn's hand under my shirt moved again. He fit himself snugly to me and rubbed my stomach with the same motion.

"Megan." Josh's voice boomed. Shawn's arm sucked back to him. "Get out of Shawn's bed and go back to your room." He'd never sounded sterner.

I slid out from under the covers and scurried back down the hall.

Chapter 49

My eyes were barely open when Josh came into my room and scolded me for the occurrence in his room during the night.

"I didn't do anything," I said. "He was having bad dreams. I wanted to make them stop."

"You got into bed with him."

He made it sound like something it totally was not. "It wasn't like that."

"Maybe not for you, but you don't know it wasn't for him."

"It *wasn't*." I was pretty positive. Even if it was, Josh was no one to talk. I knew full well all the stuff he did with girls.

"His hand was moving, what was he doing?"

"Rubbing my stomach. I had cramps."

"You need to have a conversation with someone other than your dolls before you go doing stuff like that, Megan."

My dolls? Really? "It wasn't *like* that," I said again.

"You have no idea what was going through his head. Stuff happens to guys when they sleep, we can't control it. It's like getting goosebumps. Even if it wasn't like that, there are plenty other reasons you shouldn't have done it."

"Like what? He likes cuddling, and it helped."

"Megan, the kid leaves his clothes on at night. He tightens his belt *notches* before getting into bed. He has nightmares about the things that happened to him. He shuts down and doesn't talk to anybody. He can't handle any of that kind of stuff right now."

"He can handle cuddling." We'd done it before. I was pretty sure he needed it, and it wasn't like he'd pull out a stuffed bear in front of Josh.

"I'm just saying. Nobody knows what goes on in Shawn's head except for Shawn. A lot of stuff happened to him. I can guarantee you he doesn't think like you and me."

"You don't need to tell me that." It was my biggest stressor, not knowing how to interact with him. There was a lot I *had* done wrong over the course of the past few weeks. Maybe I shouldn't have gotten into his bed without him knowing, but cuddling with me had always had a calming effect on him, I took my chances. And he thanked me. It was the one time I didn't feel like I'd done anything wrong.

"Think you know all you want, Megan, but tread carefully. Shawn probably doesn't even know what he's feeling half the time, I don't know how you can."

I didn't disagree, I just didn't like the way he came at me.

~

382

There were only a couple weeks left of summer vacation, and as excited as Shawn had been about not getting expelled, he wouldn't be able to go back to school.

"You'll graduate," Dad said to him. "It just won't be the way we thought."

But he still moped. He was bored to begin with, and with both Bobby and me returning, he would be even more bored.

"We'll eventually get a handle on this," Dad said to him. "Then you'll know what a normal life is."

~

For the first time in Jessup County history, the high school was provided with a police detail. All doors in and out were locked at all times, and every person entering had to pass by an armed officer. It was for every student's safety, but I think mostly for Dad's two children still in the school.

Shawn was never publicly named as the victim of the crimes talked about on the news, but everybody knew his father, and now that Shawn wasn't in school, the rumors were cemented. People talked and stared more than when I first got there.

A lot of people asked how he was—people who maybe should've asked *him* when he sat alone at the lunch table for three years.

"I haven't seen him," was the only thing I could safely say.

One sophomore gave me a letter to give to him.

"I don't know where he is," I told the gangly boy with dark glasses.

"Maybe your dad does?"

I took it. It wasn't like the letters from Damian, though. As much as I trusted the boy's sincerity that it didn't say anything hateful, I still needed to make sure. I went into the girls' bathroom and peeled open the seal.

Dear Shawn,

My name is Luke. I'm a tenth grader at Jessup Regional. We've never met, but I know who you are. At the beginning of my freshman year, one of my teachers kept me after school. He told me I was his favorite student and put his hands on me in ways he shouldn't have. He said he could tell I liked it. Then he kept me after school once a week for the rest of the year. I think I might be gay, but I'm not sure. I dreaded coming to school and still do. I don't know what to do. I'm afraid to tell my parents and don't know who else to talk to. Any advice would help. My number and e-mail address are on the back.

Sincerely,
Lucas D

P.S. I'm really sorry for everything you've been going through. You've given me a lot of courage. Before now, I've never spoken any of these words to anyone.

My heart ached for this boy. He needed help, but not from Shawn. I didn't even want to give him the letter. I didn't want him knowing people had put the pieces together. He probably already did, but he didn't need anything solidifying it. It was a tough call because maybe he also wouldn't feel so alone.

384

I gave the letter to Dad instead. He would know how to reach out to Luke, and also whether or not to approach Shawn with it, and how.

Chapter 50

Going back to school was more challenging than I thought it would be. No matter how much I tried to cover for Shawn, the questions didn't stop: Did you know it was happening? What was it like being his girlfriend? Did you guys ever . . . you know . . . do stuff?

The one that got me the most was, did he ever try to rape you?

People were morons.

They didn't question Bobby. If they did, he just told them to get out of his face.

The weekend provided a reprieve, but not enough of one. "Please let me stay home," I pleaded with Dad on Monday morning. "It's just one day."

"Alright, but we can't make a habit of this."

"I won't, I promise."

Dad drove Bobby to school, as was the new routine. No more taking the bus or hitching a ride from friends.

Josh got up before Shawn, and I made the two of us breakfast. Rain poured down outside, and the sky was dark.

"You are the omelet queen," Josh said, almost finished before I even sat down. "I think you should make me another one."

"Can I eat mine first?"

"You should just give me that one and make another for yourself."

"That's kinda rude," I said as I folded the egg over top itself.

"I feel it's gonna be a rude kind of day."

"Go hang with your girlfriend, then. She'll whip you back into shape."

"I think I just might. Give us a change of scenery. Seeing you're home, and all."

Even with an officer outside, Dad didn't want Shawn ever to be alone, so Josh had been trapped. "Make sure Shawn's okay with it." Shawn would surely feel safer with Josh than me.

"Yeeeah . . ." He dragged out the word. "I have a feeling he'll be okay with it." Susan had been at our house all week, and by the sound of it, someone had gotten on someone's nerves.

If Josh wanted another omelet, he'd have to make it himself. I sat down with the one I made myself as he called Susan to give her the good news.

"Hey, Red, I'm a free man. What do you wanna do today?"

Susan's *woohoo* was loud.

Josh cleaned up the kitchen, and I followed him upstairs to his room to get himself clothes.

"Hey, you awake?" Josh asked Shawn flat on his stomach with

his arms by his sides.

"Trying not to be," he mumbled.

"Megan's staying home today, so I'm out."

"Thank friggin' God."

As Josh rummaged through his drawers, I lifted my leg and kicked at the side of Shawn's butt that was under the covers. "Rise and shine, time to get up."

He pulled his blanket over his head.

I leaned over him and, with my palms, bounced on his back, forcing air through his larynx.

"I'm gonna kick your ass, Megan."

"So, is it a good trade?" Josh laughed.

"C'mon, get up, I'll make you breakfast."

"I'm not getting up, I'm sleeping."

"I don't know, man, her omelets might actually be worth it," Josh said. He pulled pants from his hamper and added them to the pile in his hand, and went into the bathroom to get dressed.

"C'mon, wake up." Shawn was usually an early riser but was sleeping later and later.

"Call me if you need me," Josh said when he finished in the bathroom, and left.

Shawn was a lump, so I let him be and went back downstairs. I had only a few pages left in the book I was reading, but I also hadn't had control over the TV in as long as I could remember.

I flipped through the guide, checking a couple of my cooking shows, and spotted a movie I would've been harassed for watching if the boys were around. It was on one of the women's networks, so was sure to have all the love and sap they would never tolerate.

It wasn't long before I was engrossed. There was about half an hour left when Shawn, arms hugged across his chest, staggered down the stairs.

"So, I recall you saying something about breakfast?"

"Oh no. You snooze, you lose, buddy. That offer's long off the table."

"Fine, I guess there's no reason to be up, then." He turned and started back up the stairs.

The heat of the scene in the movie dialed up.

"Seriously?" He turned back, surprised I didn't try to stop him.

I wanted to get through the rest of the movie. "You can go back to bed. Come back in twenty minutes."

He sighed in defeat and came back down.

"Can we turn on the heat?" he asked. It was unusually cold. He lifted the thin blanket that covered me and slid under.

I flipped the channel from the half-naked bodies on the screen. "*Jeez.* Comfortable?" He coiled forcefully into me.

With my arm on his side, I searched through the channels and stopped on another, cleaner movie—one I'd already seen and sappier than the last.

"What are you watching?" he asked with a tone of scrutiny after listening for a few minutes. He raised his hand in front of my face to block my view. I pushed it away, but he did it again and again.

"Did you come down here just to annoy me?"

"Payback's a bitch."

I held his arm down.

"Cuddle with me."

"Aren't I?" I had about an eighth of the couch compared to him. I altered my position a little and he pulled my hand to his side again and circled it as if he wanted me to rub him.

I did, using my whole palm, pushing it up and down his back, and then switched to just my fingertips.

The movie wasn't nearly as good as the one I turned it from.

I must've stopped because Shawn wiggled to make my hand move again.

I blindly dragged my fingers.

He pulled my hand underneath his shirt.

Whoa. Shocked.

I did just as I had been, basking in the feel of his smooth skin. He squirmed with the tickling sensation and jumped when I hit a certain spot on his waist. Eyes closed, he smiled.

There was no way for him to get closer, but he tried, pushing tightly to me.

I swirled my finger over the same spot on his waist, watching him try not to laugh.

"Stop," he said when he couldn't take it any longer.

I loved the lines his smirk created, they were so rarely seen.

I moved my fingers up and down his side. He turned onto his back more, and they dipped into the ridges of his abdomen as I pulled them lightly across.

I never expected to feel any of these parts of him. I knew he was toned, it was easy to tell by his structure, and I'd also seen him the day I found him on the ledge, but feeling him was a whole other thing. I could identify almost every muscle.

He apparently changed his mind, because he turned into me again and pulled my hand back to his side.

Tread carefully, Josh's voice went through my head. "I don't know what to do," I said. At least if I did something wrong, he would know I didn't mean it.

I progressed up his back. The higher I went, the more his shirt lifted.

Scars. Lots of them.

A cluster of small, circle-ish ones peeked from the elastic of his underwear. There were a couple more dotted up his side, and one that looked like a tear across his skin showing from under his arm.

With his face buried in my shoulder, he pushed into me again. His private area felt different.

Uh. It felt really different.

I continued to skim my fingers and it moved. Pulsed.

Holy shit.

Air came through his nose and his entire body clenched. He gripped my waist and pushed as far from me as he could on the narrow couch. Eyes closed, he breathed in short breaths.

He turned off the couch and stood, and, walking with an awkward bend, rushed upstairs, and the bathroom door shut.

I knew the word erection. I was almost positive that was what happened. I really didn't know if it could've been more awkward. He stiffened like the day in his room. Maybe that was what had happened. He seemed completely unprepared for it.

The shower water turned on. He didn't take showers when Dad wasn't home.

We'd be alone together all day. How would we move past it? If he even came back down.

I shut the TV off and went up to get dressed. The shower was still on when I came back out of my room, so I had more time to digest what happened.

We hadn't kissed in months. I wasn't even sure what the nature of our relationship really was. There was a chance the kissing we'd done wasn't even real. It wasn't like he'd ever experienced the right forms of affection. It could've just been experimentation. Did what just happened happen because I made him comfortable, or did he actually have those kinds of feelings for me? Did *he* even know? Maybe it was great it happened. Maybe it wasn't. Maybe it made him feel gross and he was turned off by it. There were different reasons as to why he could be in the shower.

What would usually be considered a decent-sized house shrunk considerably when I thought of my options for when Shawn came out. I really didn't know what I'd say to him. Or how I'd look at him.

One of my cooking shows would be on in few minutes. I'd seen a preview for it, so I scoured the kitchen for the necessary ingredients.

I washed bowls.

I cracked eggs and beat them.

I measured milk, cheese, and bread crumbs, taking my time so I'd still have something to do when and if Shawn came back down.

Jean pant legs swishing behind me. Crap.

His wet hair dripped as he passed me to the refrigerator.

I couldn't detect even a hint of the earthy scent of the body wash he usually used.

He pulled out the orange juice and poured a glass.

I kept my eyes focused on the stretched cotton of where his fist pushed into the pocket of his hooded sweatshirt as he gulped it. "Don't you look all nice and cozy."

"What are you doing?" he asked as he tipped the glass to his mouth again.

"Preparing dinner."

"Now?" It wasn't even lunchtime.

"I know, but this was on."

"You couldn't record it?" He knew I was avoiding him. I never prepared dinner that early. He poured more, then walked by me again, headed for the living room.

"Shawn?"

He turned back.

"Are you okay?"

His eyes rounded, as if startled by the question. "I'm fine."

"Did I do something wrong?" I needed to know.

He gave a jerky shake of his head.

I waited to see if he'd waver. His eyes were stuck.

"Good." I forced a smile, praying he told the truth. "You'd tell me if I did, right?" Hopefully, he didn't feel like *he* had.

He nodded with the same rough movement.

"Want me to come back when I'm finished? We can watch something together?"

"Okay."

"I'll just finish this," I said, now wishing I hadn't started it.

He nodded again, then carried on into the living room.

I didn't need the man on the television to tell me how to make meatballs. I dumped all the ingredients into one bowl and sunk my hands into the raw meat to mix it. Shawn put the television on, and Maxi curled up on the couch next to him.

The power on the TV cut out.

The power in the whole house was out.

There were no longer raindrops hitting the deck, so that wasn't the reason.

There was commotion from the living room, as if Shawn or Maxi got up, and Maxi barked. She continued to bark, and I poked my head around the wall to see why.

Through the translucent layer of the curtains were the lights atop a police car.

Shawn opened the door to the officer as I pulled the raw meat from my hands.

Maxi's bark was fierce. I looked again before going to the sink. Shawn held her by her collar as she tried to get at whoever was on the steps. "*Nein. Sitz.*" He ordered her to stop and sit.

She did but sustained a nervous whine.

I turned the sink on and washed my hands, and Maxi barked again, this time with a sound deep from within her. She carried on like I'd never heard her.

Samson barked ferociously from outside and dug at the slider to get in.

I grabbed the towel next to the sink and went to see what had happened. Maxi stood on the couch on her hind legs clawing at the window.

Shawn was nowhere.

The dogs' frenzied behavior shot panic through me. I pulled back the curtain. The police car was gone and Shawn wasn't anywhere in sight.

Maxi jumped down and paced, barking with an angry growl.

It was the officer watching our house, it had to have been. The power went out, so he secured Shawn. But what about me? Wouldn't he have taken me too?

I opened the front door and Maxi shot off.

It felt as if all the blood in my body dropped out.

I raced upstairs for my cell phone and dialed Dad. He didn't answer. I flew back down, dialing Uncle Vance, and heaved open the backslider. Samson bolted through the house and out.

My speech when Uncle Vance picked up was hurried as I explained what happened. "You need to find my dad."

"Megan, calm down. Let me get in touch with the officer that was outside."

I hung up with him and Dad called within the minute. "Meg,

which way did the car go?" The immediacy in his tone was alarming, as if he didn't have knowledge of Shawn's departure.

"I don't know." My heart was in my stomach. "They must have gone right. The dogs went right."

"How long ago?"

"Three minutes. Maybe four."

"Does Shawn have his phone with him?"

He'd just taken a shower and probably put a lot of effort into coming off as cool and collected as he was. His phone wouldn't have been on his mind. I raced upstairs to Josh's room, where it sat on top of his bureau. "*No.*" I came unglued.

"Megan, I'm two minutes away, at most. I'm sending someone to get you. Hang up the phone and call every number on the list on the fridge."

I did as he said. It was no sooner than I hung up that I dialed again. The first call was to an unknown man, then the FBI. The phone hadn't even begun to ring on the other end when the call went out over Dad's scanner. He moved quicker than quick.

Chapter 51

It'd been almost fifteen minutes since Shawn disappeared out the door. I did as Dad told me and called every number on the emergency call list on the refrigerator. I'd never felt so helpless or panicked in my life. I couldn't stay in the house and wait. I needed to look for Shawn in every place I knew to.

"*Shawn*." My breath couldn't keep up with the rate of my heart as I ran.

I went to his house first. The property was still strewn with police tape and there were boards on the windows to keep trespassers out. The door was locked. I pounded on it with all my strength. "*Shawn*."

I went to the quarry. He wasn't at the top, on the ledge, or by the water's edge.

"*Shawn*." I scoured the woods.

He wasn't at the rock at the halfway point.

"*Maxi, Samson*."

I still didn't know the town that well, so there were only a couple places I knew to look. I ran the couple miles to where Dad had his boat docked.

The area was desolate and steam rose off the water under the dreary sky. The dock was wet and slippery as I raced down it.

I boarded *Miranda*. *"Shawn."* I kicked at the locked cabin door.

I prayed he would somehow be able to get away from whoever took him and get to one of these places.

I spent just as much time calling for the dogs. I knew if I could find them, they would be able to lead me to him. Maxi, for sure, wouldn't give up, and whether or not they would be able to keep up with the car that took him, they would most likely be able to follow his scent.

Every time I stopped, if even for a moment, my fear took over and pushed me on.

~

The sirens that blared through Jessup all day gradually lessened. I had no idea how much time had passed as I walked, crying—phoneless— along a dirt road I'd never been on. I didn't know where I was or how to get home, but that didn't matter. I had no intentions of going home. Not until I found Shawn.

A car raced toward me. It screeched to a stop and Bobby flew out of the driver's side of Uncle Vance's Chevy Caprice. He ran to me and threw his arms around me and lifted me from the ground. He held me so tight I could barely breathe.

"Shawn's gone," I cried into his shoulder.

"Where have you been?" His heart hammered against my chest. "Everyone's looking for you."

Standing in the middle of the road, he held me as I cried.

"We're gonna find him," he said.

"No, we're not." Reality had set in. The whole reason Shawn had been under lockdown in our house for so long was because there were people out there with the clear intention *and* ability of making him disappear.

After thanking God several times that I was safe, Bobby set me back down. He walked me back to the car, dialing his phone. "I found her," he said to whoever was on the other end. "She's okay."

I sat crying in the passenger seat staring out the window as he drove, still trying to think of where else we could look.

When we pulled up to the house, there were more cars than I could count. Lights remained flashing on some, while others still had their engines running.

Bobby stopped the car and got out, but I didn't. I wasn't finished looking.

Dad must've seen us pull up. He raced out of the house, flung open my door, and yanked me out. "Where the hell have you been?" He was frantic. "I told you I was sending someone for you. I thought I lost you too."

I fell apart all over again. His comment confirmed for me that they hadn't found him. I wouldn't walk into the house and see Shawn sitting on the couch. I clung to Dad's neck, and he picked me up like I was a little girl and carried me inside.

He begged me to stop crying, as I only worsened the already heightened atmosphere. As Dad let go of me, Josh stepped in.

"Thank God," he said as he took hold of me.

Our house buzzed with people. There were officers in uniform, there were plain-clothed detectives. Susan's mother was even there. She'd grown up in Jessup and listed all the places she could think of that may not have already been checked. Calls came in over the radios from towns away. Shawn had been missing since a quarter to eleven in the morning. It was now four o'clock.

There were people from the alarm company there, along with the FBI. As I was able to calm down some, I absorbed more of what went on. Whoever had taken him spent a good deal of time planning it out. The storm earlier in the morning provided them their opportunity. The officer who was supposed to be outside our house responded to a false report of an accident down the road. He was the only one in the area, and there were claimed to be injuries, so he went. That's when the power to the house, as well as the alarm and cameras, was cut. As the officer was rendered unconscious and secured in his trunk, a second person in a separate car made a move on the house.

"Megan, did you notice *anything* about the car? Anything at all?" Dad questioned me for the numerous time. "Was it one of ours?"

"I didn't know I was supposed to." I broke down again.

Dad wrapped his arm around my head in a tight hug. "It's okay, baby."

There were at least six different people who had me repeat exactly what happened in the small amount of time it took for Shawn to walk out the door with the unknown man.

Night approached. Soon the sky was pitch black, with still no sign of him.

My eyes somehow found a way to continue to produce more and more tears.

As the buzz slowly died down and the crowd of officials that lingered got smaller, I approached Dad with a desperate question. I tried to contain myself long enough to understand.

"Dad, when Shawn opened the door, Maxi was right there next to him. She knew something was wrong. She could've torn the guy to shreds. Why didn't he let her?" I needed an answer. "He told her to *sit,* Dad." I was unable to keep control and cried. "He walked out and shut the door behind him. Why did he do that?"

My continuous outpour of emotion was something Dad couldn't keep up with and his eyes welled again. "Megan, you should've been at school."

That was my answer.

I turned to Josh behind me.

"I never should have left." He shook his head. "This wouldn't have happened. He wouldn't have walked out the door if I was here."

"You don't know that," Susan said from next to him.

Josh made a sharp turn to her. "Yes, I do. He left so nothing would happen to Megan." He turned back to me. "You should've been in school and I never should have left." He was angry and yelling, I think mostly at himself. "I knew where Dad's gun was, and Shawn *knew* I knew. He never would've left if I was here."

Susan walked away to find comfort in her mother's arms.

I couldn't think about what Josh said. Not then.

The last stragglers left around midnight. Dad's radio remained on and he couldn't let go of his phone. He sat alone in his chair in the living room while the rest of my family sat quietly around the dining room table.

Dad sat hunched with his palms pressed to his eyes as I knelt at his feet. "He was cold, Dad. He wasn't even wearing shoes."

Dad lowered his hands from his eyes and looked down at me. He almost said something but refrained.

"Megan, did you ever see what was in Shawn's backpack?"

"Just a stuffed bear."

He sat with his elbow on the arm of the chair rubbing his eye in what appeared to be another moment of hesitation. "Megan, when I brought that backpack home, there was a gun in it. A nine millimeter, semi-automatic, fully loaded, with two full clips to go with it."

Wha . . .

"Along with the bear, almost thirty-five hundred dollars he'd saved up, his phone, and some other items."

Chairs moved across the dining room floor as the boys got up and migrated into the living room.

"He said the gun was to protect himself. That he was waiting for the right moment to take off. I took it from him, obviously, but I took him to a shooting range and let him practice. A couple times." A smirk flashed on his face. "He knew what he was doing, Meg. He was a natural. A perfect shot." He forced a teary-eyed smile. "We practiced self-defense. He knows protective moves now." It must've been when we went to the lake. It was the only time it could've been. "Shawn has enough sense to know how to handle himself, we have got to believe that." He tried to convince me, as well as everyone else standing in the opening between the living room and the dining room, probably even himself. "We're going to find him. We're not going to give up, okay?" He spoke as though we looked for a lost puppy.

"Okay?" He needed me to acknowledge him.

I nodded.

That night was horrible. I don't know when or how I fell asleep. When I awoke the next morning, it took a minute to realize it wasn't a normal day. The phone calls started all over, and the same people who'd left our house only a few hours earlier were back again. It was just as stressful as the night before.

Samson showed up on the doorstep mid-morning, but there was still no sign of Maxi. Dad was able to hold himself together better, and I stayed in my room through most of the chaos.

Nightfall approached once again, and there was still no sign of the missing five-foot, eleven-and-a-half-inch, blond-haired, blue-eyed boy who was now being searched for in ten states.

Chapter 52

The third day came to an end with still nothing.

I thought a lot about what Dad told us. If Shawn hadn't been found by now, to me, that meant there was a good chance he was still alive. I prayed Dad was right, that he was strong enough and resourceful enough to make it through whatever happened to him. Hopefully, he was as valuable to whoever had taken him as he was to his father. As sick of a thought as that was, at least maybe then, he stood a chance at survival.

Maxi came home on the fourth day with a strong limp and sad face. It was obvious she'd pushed herself as far as she could.

~

People eventually stopped gathering at our house. Nobody gave up looking. There wasn't a day that went by that something wasn't being done.

Daylight struggled more and more.

I was pulled out of school, but Bobby continued to go. He stopped hanging out with his friends and spent most of his time alone, getting high somewhere.

Josh stayed away from me as much as possible. It was for no other reason than that any time the two of us spent even a few minutes together, we would go back to that day and it would start all over again.

With each new day, the sun set and the darkness deepened.

It was so strange to think that the one person who brought our family back together—gave us our father back in a way we didn't think was possible and brought me closer to the brother I'd never had anything in common with—was now the missing link. Without him, it all fell apart again.

We all lived in the same house, but we didn't see each other anymore. There were no more Sunday afternoons spent with our cousins, and our house was no longer the center of social activity.

We once again lived under the heavy silence of loss.

~

Shawn's birthday came. I spent it alone in my room, unable to stop crying.

Susan made an ice cream cake. She brought it over and, with a sealed envelope with Shawn's name on it, put it in the freezer.

As evening approached, I snuck out and went to the quarry. I spent hours on the ledge reviewing every moment Shawn and I ever spent together.

Chapter 53

It was the second week in November. It was late in the afternoon. Josh and Bobby were upstairs, I on the couch in the living room escaping with a book when a car door slammed. And then another.

Dad and Uncle Vance headed for the house. Dad stopped and put his hand to his mouth. His body bent and the agony in his expression sent a chill through me.

He composed himself and started for the door again.

I shook my head as they came in. "Don't say it, Dad. Don't you dare say it."

He turned away. His emotions peaked and he wailed into his palms. Uncle Vance put his arms around him, and Josh and Bobby both appeared at the bottom of the stairs.

I stood from the couch and, through tear-filled eyes, pulled at Dad's arm. "Did you find him?"

He grasped me in a tight hug.

I pushed away. "Did you find him?" I asked louder.

"I can't do this." He looked to Uncle Vance.

"Dad?" Josh also waited for an answer as I stared steadfastly at the two men.

"C'mon, guys, let's sit down." Uncle Vance tried to defuse the moment.

"I'm not sitting down, just say it," I shouted.

"We didn't find Shawn," Uncle Vance said. "But we did find a crime scene."

My split second of relief resulted in a sharp kick to the gut. "What kind of crime scene?" Dad's reaction was alarming.

"His prints were there. There was blood."

Blood? "Shawn's?" *No.*

"We don't know yet."

"How much?"

"A bit."

I stopped him before he could go further. "He's not dead. I don't care what you say. I know he's not. I would feel it if he was." I truly did believe what I said.

"Meg."

"But you don't even know if it's his."

"They're testing it for DNA."

"It could be someone else's."

Uncle Vance's view dropped.

"It could be someone else's," I said again. "You didn't find *him*. No body, no case, right, Dad? Haven't I heard you say that before?"

407

Dad turned around to me and the despair in his eyes drew my tears again.

Josh tried to hold back, but for the first time since Mom's death, he broke down.

Bobby was wide-eyed and speechless.

I ran out the open front door.

I ran until I couldn't run anymore.

I couldn't accept it. I *wouldn't*. They didn't find *him*. They didn't even know if it was his blood yet. Even if it was, Shawn could withstand more than the average person. He was strong. He wouldn't let this happen. Not after all he'd been through. How far he'd come.

I couldn't let them accept it either and turned back.

I flung open the front door and, gasping for air, searched out Dad. He and Uncle Vance sat at the dining room table, heads hung.

"Where, Dad?"

"In a house about an hour and a half north."

"You need to keep looking. Bring Maxi with you. *Please.*"

"Megan, we already had dogs out there." Uncle Vance jumped to shut me down. "They didn't find anything."

"Not Maxi. If he's out there, she'll find him. *Please*, Dad. You know I'm right."

"It's a thickly wooded area," Uncle Vance said. "The brush is extremely dense."

"So?" Shawn practically lived in the woods.

Josh appeared in the wide door opening. "Dad, please just do it?" His eyes were red from crying. "It's worth a try."

408

"Max," Dad called as he stood. It didn't take much. Even if he didn't find what he wanted, there was the probability he would find something.

"Ed, it'll be pitch black by the time you get back there." Uncle Vance tried to talk sense into him.

"Max doesn't need to see, she just needs to smell."

"No, but you need to see," Uncle Vance said. "Never mind all the overgrowth."

"You coming or not?" Dad tried to hold onto whatever hope I grasped at. He grabbed both dogs' leashes off the doorknob, and Uncle Vance followed them out to the car.

I got my coat.

"Megan, you are not coming." I made it as far as the doorway.

I was desperate but didn't argue. Maxi jumped into the back seat with renewed excitement, and then Samson, and I watched them leave.

Josh leaned in the threshold between the living room and dining room, arms folded. I walked over to him and he extended an arm and pulled me to him in a solid grip. I hugged him, and his chest moved as if crying.

I couldn't handle the extra emotion, so I squeezed him, and then released myself and went into the kitchen. Bobby stood against the opposite threshold and wiped his tears when he saw me.

I didn't hesitate to acknowledge it was just as hard for him as it was anyone else. I went from one entryway to the other and curled my arms around his waist. He doubled his around my neck with a sniffle.

"Do you really believe he's not dead?" he asked.

I looked up from his chest to his tearing blue eyes. "With my whole heart. And you need to believe it too."

~

It was almost midnight when the headlights of Dad's car shone through the curtain of the picture window. We were all still awake, anxiously waiting to hear what they'd found—if anything. The front door opened and Maxi walked in panting, her tongue hung low.

Dad and Uncle Vance were weary and worn.

"Anything?" I asked.

Dad shook his head.

"Ed, I'm gonna go," Uncle Vance said.

"Alright. Thanks for your help." Dad was tired but grateful.

"Did she pick up a scent?"

"Yeah, she smelled him alright. They both did. If I hadn't leashed them before we got out of the car, they would've taken off."

"That's something, isn't it?" Bobby asked.

"I don't know."

"Of course, it's something," I said, frustrated.

"Megan, they could've smelled whoever took Shawn. They could've smelled Shawn on somebody else. I don't know *what* they smelled."

"They smelled *Shawn*. Why is that so hard for you to believe?"

"Megan, we see this shit all the time. The medical examiner was there. The scene was doused in blood. Beth was dead on the floor. I am trying. I don't know what else you want me to do."

I was stunned by the conviction in his voice. Everything in my

410

view blurred.

When my vision returned to normal, I turned for the stairs and went up to my room.

Chapter 54

Shawn was so widely searched for that the discovery of the crime scene made national news. The information about Beth shocked me. It was reported she was shot in the neck.

Including hers and Shawn's, there were six sets of fingerprints discovered. Some of the blood did belong to Shawn, as well as Beth and an unidentified male. There was too much cross-contamination to determine how much of it was Shawn's.

I didn't know what to think.

I prayed he'd gotten away and was on the run. At least I was pretty certain, now, after the dogs smelled him in the woods, he hadn't left in a trunk.

With each day that went by, the more everyone's hope he would be found alive decreased.

There was a memorial service held in his name. I didn't go. If I had, I would've, in some way, in my mind, been accepting that he was dead.

"Damian was there," Josh said.

He must've gotten out on a day pass.

"Did you hear me? Damian was there."

"I heard you."

The image of Shawn staring at me fazed that last day remained frozen in my mind. If only I knew then that it might be the last time I'd see him.

I thought a lot about the little things. Like the time he told me he would disappear. He may have been out of it when he said it, but he said it. And the money he told me he'd saved up for college. Maybe he'd wanted it to be for college, but it wasn't.

I thought mostly about when we were on the front step and he told me never to do what Romeo and Juliet did.

There were so many random things—comments he'd made—that when I thought about them as a whole, it made sense. He lived in a world of evil that was never able to truly capture his soul. He had a backpack with money in it and a gun, with a plan to leave. Maybe that plan changed when he came to live with us, but he kept his guard up and never let go of it. When he needed to, he put his plan into action. That's all I could hope for.

Dad agreed with Dana that it would now be even more emotionally difficult for me to return to school.

Weeks passed.

It snowed, covering any dwindling scents the dogs may have been able to follow.

Chapter 55

The pain came and went in waves. It didn't get any easier.

I lost count as to how many people told me what happened wasn't my fault. Also, that time healed.

There wasn't a lot about the following months I remembered. Winter was cold—the sky a perpetual color of bone.

All the mistakes I'd made. Maybe if I'd done even just one thing differently.

Chapter 56

My history now had yet another tragic chapter. One that seemed equally impossible to move past. I could've questioned why this stuff kept happening to me, but knowing all Shawn had been through, it didn't seem right.

Summer brought a flurry of hummingbirds. So many I could barely keep up with them.

Of course, knowing all they signified, I grasped at every possible meaning behind it.

The one-year anniversary of Shawn's disappearance approached and I planned to spend it at the quarry. Come the day, I was unable to pull myself out of bed.

The following morning, I made the trip.

The trees had just started to lose their leaves and the ground was slippery with pine needles. Fall knocked at the door and the air was cool.

I lowered to the ledge like I'd done so many times, the letters RM + JC chiseled into my spot.

A lover's etching.

Someone had sat there a long time carving it into the rock.

It was even harder than I thought it would be. The memories were as vivid as the day they were created.

Hours passed as if minutes, and I added at least an inch to the water.

~

It was a tough time for everyone.

Dad and I returned home from running errands, Josh solemn on the couch, the smell of marijuana strong in the air. Bobby made no effort to conceal his act as his fingers strummed gently along his guitar strings upstairs.

"I think he's writing a song," Josh said as Dad set his keys down. It was a delicate sound. He paused every so often as if trying to get it right.

I followed my ears up to Josh's room. Bobby sat on Shawn's bed, a thin ribbon of smoke ascending from a joint between his fingers gliding over the strings.

I leaned against the doorframe listening, unacknowledged, as he focused on the notes.

Dad's hand pushed over my shoulder from behind me as he, too, listened.

I didn't know the words, or what he attempted to achieve, but it was flawless.

He did a fine job ignoring us. And then his expression pinched and his eyes glistened.

Dad stepped past me. He eased the joint from between his fingers and, placing it in an ashtray on the bed next to him, sat down and curled his arm around him.

Bobby tried to nudge him off, but Dad was steadfast. He nodded at me, signaling for me to leave them alone.

Not once had I ever witnessed the two of them in such an exchange.

Bobby cried. And cried, and cried.

I nuzzled against Josh on the couch leaning his wet face into his palm, and for the first time, we gave in to our pain together.

~

Josh couldn't handle Shawn's stuff in his room anymore. It was too much to continue to bear.

It was hard for me to agree. Dad promised he would put it all in a safe place.

The more he brought it up, the more I prepared myself for the task of packing it all. I didn't want to get rid of any of it.

He didn't have much, so with a box in tow, I went into Josh's room one afternoon when no one was home and emptied the drawers of his bureau.

I'd been through them before, right after he disappeared. All were clothes, except for the bottom drawer, which was his personal belongings. There were magazines, his MP3 player, a notebook—mostly scribblings, a few jottings. You'd have to know hieroglyphics to read his writing. I'd been through every page.

The letters from Damian were in his backpack. Dad strongly advised me not to read them. Damian had written them to Shawn in confidence, and it would've been disrespectful. Whatever they said, Shawn valued them.

In the drawer beneath my two drawings that he'd rolled was also a copy of *Romeo and Juliet*. I didn't know if it was something Dad gave him, or if he had it all along, it was worn, used.

I took it out and rubbed my hand over the front cover.

I lay down on his bed in the mid-afternoon sunlight and opened to the first page. With his dresser drawers open and the contents of them scattered all over the floor, I forgot about packing and sunk myself into what Shawn thought was the greatest literature of all time.

I flipped from one page to another, putting in full effort to understand Shakespeare's epic writing style.

As I turned a page, a photograph slipped out. Shawn and me. The better of the two Susan took on the lounge chair on the deck when I snuck a kiss to the side of his head.

"Hey, Nutter Butter." Susan's smile was as soft and soothing as the sunlight as she and Josh came into the room.

"Hey." Mine, I'm pretty sure, matched as I held up the picture. "Did he ask you for this, or did you just give it to him?"

With a nod of recognition, she perked. "He asked me for it." She took it from me and gazed at it. "It's a great picture."

"Why did he like this book so much?"

"Ahh, either you love it, or you hate it," Josh said. "Romeo Montague and Juliet Capulet. I sure don't miss 'em."

418

His words stirred. *Romeo Montague and Juliet Capulet. Romeo Montague and Juliet Capulet. RM and JC.* It sounded right. I was pretty sure those were the letters carved into the ledge.

"I've gotta go." I left the book and the picture of the two of us and rushed out. I bolted down the stairs, shoved my shoes on, and Bobby's sweatshirt that was on the couch, and ran out the door.

My heart raced as I ran. I'd never seen that etching. I would've noticed it. I was sure of it.

Rain the day before kept the forest floor damp under the cooler cover of the trees.

I almost slipped off the edge of the quarry.

I slid down to the ledge and, with eager fingers, wiped the granite clean.

RM + JC

It couldn't have been a coincidence. I would've noticed it.

I would've noticed it.

Chapter 57

I saw the etching on the ledge a year and a day after Shawn disappeared. Before then, I hadn't been to the quarry since his seventeenth birthday, but was certain it wasn't there.

<I need you to come to the quarry>, I texted Bobby.

I didn't move. I stood staring down at the letters fearing they weren't real, not wanting to get too close, afraid they weren't real.

"Over here," I called to him when he appeared at the ravine's edge.

Bobby came over and peered down at me.

"What is that?" I pointed. I needed him to tell me I didn't see it wrong.

He got down on his knees from feet above me and squinted. "It looks like letters."

"What letters?"

"RM plus . . . J . . . C?"

I explained the significance.

He slid down and glided his fingers over. "You know it could be a coincidence, right?"

"Really?" I did but couldn't say it out loud. "How many people do you think would actually even notice this ledge was here?"

He sighed and continued to study them. "Are you *sure* it wasn't here last October? I mean, it'd only been a little over a month, I'm sure you were pretty distraught."

"The leaves hadn't started to fall yet, Bob. This ledge was clear. Don't you think I would've noticed it?" It wasn't just a small scratch on the rock, it was at least a foot in diameter.

The expression in his eyes turned grave. "You don't know when he did it, though." He implied he could've done it sometime after he disappeared but before the crime scene was found.

The hard edges of him diffused and he looked like a watercolor behind my tears. "He's not *dead*."

He heaved a breath, and stood and pulled me to him in a tight embrace.

Bobby floated on my hope. No matter how much people tried to talk me out of believing Shawn was alive, he never did.

I sobbed into his shoulder.

~

Neither Bobby nor I told anyone what I found. It would have a devastating impact if I was wrong, and I also didn't want to hear all the reasons I could be.

At home, on the way back up to Josh's room, I stopped at the small section of wall at the bottom of the stairs where I'd hung my drawing of

421

the willow tree with Mom's and my initials carved into it. The drawing that Shawn passed by nearly every day for three and half months. It was the only one of my drawings that hung anywhere in the house, so he knew I would know the significance.

All of his stuff not in the box yet went back into his drawers, and I took the copy of *Romeo and Juliet* and shut myself into my room.

I absorbed and dissected every word.

Standing out on a balcony, Juliet, thinking she was alone, professed her love for Romeo. Romeo, hiding below and unable to contain himself, leapt into view. They talked of love and vowed theirs to one another.

Between the pages was a torn piece of notebook paper with Shawn's writing in blue ink:

Red
Color of pain
Hurt, anger
HATE

Yellows
Oranges, pinks
All scrolled into one
Like the glow in the sky before sunrise

Warm

Peaceful, calming

Mesmerizing

Inviting me to stare

Yesterday, blackness was absolute.

Her light gives me hope.

I crave her. How she speaks, the things she

says.

Her subtle lullaby soothes the pain.

She makes me feel like a person. Like I

matter. Makes me feel things I didn't know I

could.

It's hard to be around her, to hide so many

parts of me. But I can't stand to be away

from her.

She's undoing me. Completely and utterly.

I wish I could tell her what she means to me. I have words, I just don't know how to make them sing.

It's stupid thinking it will all last. But, for now, how do I argue with the sun?

I asked for a miracle. I didn't expect her.

My own personal Juliet.

The words took my breath away. It was completely unexpected.

There was a knock on my door. It pushed open and Dad came in. I'd lost all track of time.

"Josh said you started packing Shawn's stuff today." He sat on my bed. "What's that?" he asked about the paper that shook in my hand.

My expression surely spoke volumes as I gave it to him.

A smile crossed his lips as he read. "I've seen this."

He had? "When?" *How?*

He looked up from Shawn's sloppy handwriting, his smile fading. "Do you remember when I told you about the gun Shawn had in his backpack? Along with other items?"

I nodded.

"Among those other items was a journal he kept."

A journal? There was more?

Sadness tugged at his eyes. "Most of the entries were about the things that happened to him." *Oh, dear God.* "It was how we knew some of the stuff we did . . . But there were also entries about you." He looked back down at the paper and a smile flickered. "Random things here and there."

Pure astonishment. "Why didn't you tell me?" It was pretty huge.

He lifted his gaze back up to me. "Because it wasn't for me to tell." He said it as if the answer was that simple. His expression became one of awe. "And from the looks of it, he just did."

The realization struck me.

A shine built on his eyes. "I'd say the words sang."

They did. It became too difficult to speak with the emotion that overwhelmed me.

"Megan, when I told you how much you'd already helped Shawn, that you played probably the biggest role, I wasn't just saying it. You meant so much to him. You did so much *for* him. His life was changed because of you."

If nothing else, I was fortunate enough to be able to go through the rest of mine knowing I'd made such a difference in his.

I was desperate to know what else he wrote. "Can I read the other entries?"

Dad rubbed his thumb over my cheek, his head tilting with sympathy. "They were his private thoughts, hon."

That was exactly why I needed them. "But you read them." I just wanted the ones about me.

425

"We had to, you know that. And he was very upset about it. He stopped writing after that." His hand rested on my cheek.

He gave me back the one entry. "Cherish this. It's a piece of him you didn't expect, and it sums up everything. You'll never have to doubt, now, what you meant to him."

I would cherish it. It was his thoughts, in his handwriting. The closest I could be to him without actually having him.

"He didn't know love, Nutty. You came along and he got to experience what he considered to be the ultimate form of it. He went from having nothing to having everything, in a breath."

It was a phenomenal thought. One that would help to carry me.

Chapter 58

Though home school was now my route to graduation, I decided I wanted to participate in the art show again, this time with a little more emphasis on "me."

"Megan." Miss Devereaux slowly turned the pages of my most cherished sketchbook. "These. Are . . ." She sat stupefied as she flipped through the drawings I'd done after Mom died.

She slowed more when she got to the ones that included Shawn.

It was evident the impact we had on one another.

Her mouth bent down in a chin-dimpling frown when she reached the one of our two hands.

The more she flipped through, the glassier her eyes got.

Pushing her fingers to her lower lids to gather the accruing water, she stood and stepped over to me and engulfed me in her arms.

"It is imperative, Megan." She took a step back, gripping my shoulders. "That you understand the gift that you have. Not only as an utterly caring and compassionate person, but—" She picked my pad up again and, with a deep inhale, started through again. "There's nakedness and vulnerability in your drawings that—" She seemed truly speechless, her head shaking as if in disbelief. "You possess the ability to capture the human experience in its rawest form."

As much as I hated to admit it, hardships really did develop my strengths. Had I not had the experiences I did, I never would've been able to create the depth and emotion I had.

"People can be good at putting on fronts, Megan." She nodded at me. "But we all hurt. *All* of us. In some form or another, for some reason or another." She let out another breath as she looked back to my pad in her hands. "The honesty and truth in these drawings . . . If they were in a gallery, people would come from all over to see them. Simply because of the ability to connect."

It was something I now knew to be true. It was the reason I showed Shawn—with hopes he would realize he wasn't alone. And the reason I stood in front of her now.

"So, you're saying you want to put these in the art show?"

"Not all of them." The ones of Shawn were off limits. At least the ones you could overtly tell were him. I didn't have his permission and didn't think he'd be all too thrilled with the idea.

She went through picking the ones she liked most.

It was scary because not even my family had seen any of them, now they'd be on display for all who wanted to look.

She chose abstracts, mostly, that depicted emotion more than anything.

"Are you okay with this one?" she asked about one that was obviously me. "It shows what you were going through even before becoming a new student here, which is a hard enough transition on its own."

"Sure." If I had to be. As long as I didn't actually have to attend the event to see everyone gawking at it.

"I absolutely *love* this one," she said about a drawing of a rose being weighted down by mud. I'd drawn it to go along with the poem I wrote about Shawn when he was at his most depressed.

"You can use that one." It was an easy decision.

"Megan, I can't wait," she said, shaking her head in awe again. "Thank you so much for this." She stood and hugged me again.

Before leaving, I gave her my idea for the new school logo, which they'd yet to come up with, along with some words to go with it.

~

After dinner, Dad sat in the dining room with me looking through my sketchbooks.

"I'm sorry I wasn't there for you, Megan." His eyes were glued to the colorless charcoal and graphite lines. "I did what I had to for me, but somehow forgot that the three of you also needed so much." He stopped on one of Mom, his skin shriveling beneath his hand as it pushed up his face, his eyes filling.

"It's okay, Dad." It was a devastating time for him. Besides, he was here now.

I told him what Miss Devereaux said.

"She sounds like a smart woman. Even more so, before you can

429

draw someone for who they really are, you must first be able to *see* them for who they truly are. A quality I've always known you had. One not many people possess."

His eyes crinkled with a smile when he got to a gleeful one of Shawn. "Before you drew him, Megan, the only pictures that probably existed of Shawn were ones no one should ever see. Had you not depicted him as you did in some of these, who knows if anyone ever would've seen this side of him."

He stopped on a particularly nice one of his smile, his own expression of joy enhancing. "How many people, besides us, do you think ever got to see that?" There was a sense of pride in his voice, and gratitude. "I truly do feel blessed that we were graced with his presence. Even if only for a few minutes."

I couldn't have agreed more. *It's not about the length of time spent, but the quality.*

"I think you should put this one in the show," he said. "I don't think he would mind. And I would take issue with it if he did. It's a very good one."

Maybe. I'd think about it.

"And I really think you should be there."

I had a feeling, now that I'd told him about it, he'd make me go.

~

The art show was open to the public. With so little to do in the area, even the town's most elderly made an effort to attend. People's projects, assignments mostly, arranged by lessons, decorated the walls of the cafeteria.

430

A display of the work I'd submitted hung at eye level where Shawn and I used to sit at lunch.

A cluster of people gathered, many with their eyes aimed down, admiring something beneath it. It took a bit of effort to even get close to see what it was.

On a small table adorned by cloth and flowers sat the one drawing of Shawn, framed, beside the one of the rose, with my poem scrolled across it—a last-minute addition I'd made. "Oh, God." My heart skipped through a moment of regret.

"Oh, God, what?" Dad said. "It's beautiful."

It was telling.

The chatter was as expected—sorrow-filled and distressed. The overall tone was that of disbelief, shock. Something that would surely linger for a while.

Seeing Shawn with an expression of such joy was, without a doubt, disquieting to some. There were a lot of comments of remorse.

It was troubling to think that I—so young and such a newbie to the town—was, more or less, the first person to take action in a place where people knew him pretty much his entire life. Especially of all those who certainly detected there was a problem but did nothing.

"I don't want to be here," I said to Dad. "If any one of these people made even a tiny effort to help him . . ." As far as I knew, his guidance counselor was the only one.

Dad sighed, and, with his hand rubbing over my back, he guided me to an uninhabited corner of the room. "I know it's hard to understand, hon." I could tell by his tone he felt the same way. "But we're all only

431

human." He looked around, appearing as if he deliberated. "I've reflected a lot on this, and I truly feel that our lives are mapped out for us from the get-go. It's just a matter of us choosing the right paths. With that, I'm pretty sure we're designed to make mistakes. It's how we learn." The cautiousness in his expression as he eyed the crowd made me leery that he actually believed what he said. "I'd like to think Shawn had a profound effect on this town. I'm pretty sure not one of these people would make the same mistake again. At least, I hope."

But why did it have to take some people so much longer to learn than others?

I stayed in the corner for most of the night, avoiding interaction. The crowds that gathered around my sketches were unremitting. Some viewed for longer than others, some for an amount of time I never would've expected.

It was weird to see a different side to certain people I thought I had pegged.

At one point, I looked over and saw Lucas D, the boy who'd written the letter to Shawn. He returned several times, the final time remaining.

Dad nudged me. "You should go say hi."

I wasn't sure I was mentally capable at that moment. It was the whole purpose of my display, though, so I mustered the energy and walked over.

"Hey," I said, standing next to him as he absorbed the emotion that poured off the wall.

He glanced at me. "I'm sorry, Megan." It couldn't have come off more sincere or heartfelt.

"Me too."

We silently stood there together inside of each other's hurt.

A man and woman eventually appeared next to him, the woman weaving her arm through his and resting her head against his. *His parents. Thank God.* He wouldn't be another one lost.

"Hello."

I turned to Dad's voice as he reached his hand out to the younger couple.

The woman clasped both of hers around his. "Hello, Chief Brennar." Her smile was thoroughly authentic. It was evident they'd met.

"This is my daughter, Megan."

My smile wasn't so much as Dad forced me to socialize in a moment I didn't feel like I could. She shook my hand as well. "Hello, Megan. It's nice to finally meet you. We've heard so much about you."

From who? Lucas?

"I have to say," she said, looking at my art on the wall, "I'm not sure Jessup will ever be the same." Her expression suggested it was a good thing. "I can only speak for my family, but we're immensely grateful for you and yours."

I wasn't sure what I'd missed—if Lucas knew I'd read his letter—had never given it to Shawn—but whatever the details were, it appeared all had turned out well. And that I was thankful for.

"You're obviously very gifted." She looked to the wall again. "It's easy to see why people are drawn to you."

"She's a lot like her mother." Dad winked at me.

I didn't know what Lucas's mom meant by it, but it was one of the nicest compliments Dad ever could've given me.

"I really hope drawing is something you keep up with," Mrs. D said. "And, for everyone's sake, that you continue to share your talent."

It became clearer and clearer it was something I was supposed to do.

Just before the end of the night, Miss Devereaux called everyone to attention. Standing at a podium near the back of the room, she announced that the student council had chosen the new logo for the school. She lifted her arm to the wall behind her as a student council member tugged on a rope, and a white sheet dropped, revealing my design.

My mighty little hummingbird in all of his fiery glory.

Attached was my "Hummingbird Hymn."

> Size does not equal strength. Be fierce
> and fly with courage.
> Be kind and work hard.
> Be graceful.
> Be passionate; be *com*passionate.
> Be positive, patient, and gracious.
> Be the light and shine from within.
> BE the fire.

"Thank you, Megan Brennar," Miss Devereaux said. "We feel this is a perfect fit."

The applause that started as clapping and cheering struck an un-expected level with hoots and hollers that created an electrifying sense

434

of unity.

Never, in my wildest imagination, did I think, when we first moved to town, that this would be the outcome.

Life-changing.

Chapter 59

The cut of his eyes, the curve of his lips, the bend of his jaw. I gazed, searching farther for pieces of Shawn I now knew existed more than just surface deep. Dark brown eyes that held a wealth of pain, murky but pleading.

"I never got a chance," Damian said, having a hard time holding himself together.

"Yes, you did. You had plenty of chances." It was just a matter of him waiting too long. He'd written to Shawn well after he disappeared, every letter still sealed atop Shawn's bureau waiting for his return. I didn't know if Shawn ever would've written him back, but I now understood the importance of the two of them having a relationship.

Damian's emotions plummeted.

I'd invited him to the quarry—the ledge—to show him the engraving. Just as Dad said, it was important not to judge someone not knowing their struggle or how much they were truly hurting.

436

Clutching a white envelope like the ones he'd sent, he choked on a breath. "He would've been eighteen."

Though they were brothers, I was still surprised he knew. "He is eighteen," I said, and swiped at a tear. I'd never accept him spoken of in past tense.

"Do you really think he's not dead?" Hope peeked from behind his pain.

I brushed my fingers along the letters, reminiscent of when I tickled Shawn's waist, so clearly able to see his smile. Warmth flooded me. "I wouldn't have shown you this if I thought he was." I didn't know his circumstances, but it would help to have something to believe in.

After seeing Damian react as he did, full of emotion, Bobby surely held a different view of him. "If I give Shawn nothing else, he's a clever mofo," he said from above us.

Damian looked up to him, Bobby's view of him confident, and I, too, benefited from it.

Damian set the envelope down over the engraving, holding his hand to it, seemingly unable to let go—his hand that was in every aspect identical to Shawn's. "Do you think he'll get this?"

If only I had the answer. "I don't think Jessup is someplace he'll ever come back to." Jessup, for Shawn, was a place of unbearable suffering. My bet was that he was somewhere in New England.

Damian's emotions took another plunge, and mine went with them.

In all there would've or may never have been, I reminded myself of what was. Shawn smiled. He laughed. He experienced deep, critical

437

emotions and touch like he never would have. In the short amount of time we spent together, he experienced life.

Whether I chose to accept the outcome or not, I was a different person than I would've been had I not known him. We all were. Even Damian.

I feared my family had fallen apart again, but it hadn't. We were stronger than we'd ever been. I thought we were the ones saving Shawn, but he was also saving us.

I worried I wouldn't know who I was without him. I knew who I was *because* of him.

Like the message behind *One Thousand Reasons*: When the image in the mirror shatters, it can either break you, or you can learn to see a thousand new possible pictures.

Shawn and I showed each other the possibilities, and with his help, I was able to find my true reflection.

It's not easy taking steps in the dark. We're all on a journey. I may never have all the answers, but my direction was clear, and I refused to believe my journey was over.

The season would change once more and the leaves would fall again. The birds would stop chirping, the smell of hope would dissipate as the trees shed their cloak of color, and the symphony of crunching leaves underfoot would be replaced by a dormant silence.

Here, the water would still fall.

Here, no matter what, was a place I could always return to, with an engraving that would never let me forget.

Just as Shawn gained strength from us, I, too, would be strong.

Snow, this year, would be but showers of confetti in celebration of a life I truly believed went on, touching others as it had already touched so many.

I could only pray that Shawn was somewhere he felt free.

Acknowledgments

There is an ocean of people to thank for getting *Touch* to where it is today, but a few specifically who played a major part in the process— those for whom this book wouldn't be possible without, the ones who deserve an extra special thank you.

First, to my husband Matt for building us a life that so easily allowed me to pursue this dream. For being my guiding light, the person who grounds me, the greatest partner in crime and father to our children that I could ever ask for. I couldn't do this life without you, and I shudder to think about if I had to.

To my children, for sharing me with imaginary people for so long. For inspiring me to be the best I can possibly be, for making all of my effort worthwhile. And to my son for giving me the swift kick in the butt I needed to finally release this book to the world after so many years of self-doubt.

To Julie Richardson for believing in this book from the beginning, oh so long ago. For being its biggest cheerleader and championing it wherever and whenever you could. Your patience and constructive advice set the bar high for those who followed. I have still yet to meet another person like you. You are truly one of a kind.

To Donna Godinmessier for being the random stranger who sought me out to let me know my little book had made it into a completely unexpected space and spread like wildfire. For dialing my phone number and putting young, vulnerable readers on to leave me messages of praise and gratitude, making me feel as though I may actually have something worth pursuing. I'm pretty sure this story would've stopped where it was, in all its sloppy, unperfected mess, if it wasn't for you.

To Kim Diffley. For showing up every time, no matter what else you had going on. For surpassing all human ability when you tackled all my struggles—writing *and* life—in addition to all of your own. I don't think there's a single person in their right mind who would volunteer to read as many drafts of this book as you did, especially with as much as you already had going on. Also, for being as critical as you were and having the guts to always tell me like it is—still. Not only did you help to grow this book, but also to grow me. I will forever be grateful for our friendship and all you have done and continue to do for me.

To Kristen Arruda for willfully exploring the deepest, darkest crevices of the mind with me, selfish and selfless personality traits, and all the other thought processes that helped to make this story believable. For staying awake all the late nights and prying your eyes open so many early mornings to help me through countless bouts of writer's block that made me a truly crazy person, and for talking me off the ledge all the times frustration took over.

To Robb Grindstaff, Katrina Kittle, and Kimberly Hunt for your professional guidance. This book has come a long way from where it began, and each one of you, with your individual talents and skills, raised it to a level I never would have been able to achieve on my own. An extra thank you to Kimberly Hunt for the final copyedit. Correct comma usage will forever elude me.

Finally, to Abigail Link for *crushing* the cover art. With less than two years experience drawing, at that! As fearful as I was to leave such a critical part of this project up to a complete stranger, you took the vision in my head and made it reality. AMAZING! I am in awe.

Mostly, thank you all for believing in me, even when I didn't. If not for all you very special people, this story would still live only in my computer.

Rebecca Miller lives on a farm in New England with her
husband, two children, and a variety of animals. She spent several
years in the human services field before stepping away to start her
family. She is a massive animal lover—dogs especially—and has a
hard time living without one at all times. She began writing in
her late twenties, shortly after her first child was born, when the
characters from *Touch* demanded to be written. She is also a
Realtor® and a professional photographer.

To connect with the author, find resources regarding the topics discussed in this book, or for group-centered guided questions, visit:

www.RebeccaMiller-Author.com

To discover how you can prevent, recognize, and react responsibly to child sexual abuse and trafficking, visit the Darkness to Light website at: www.D2L.org

If you enjoyed this book and feel it would be helpful to others, please review it on the website from which you purchased it, and then pass on the word.

Made in United States
Orlando, FL
17 December 2023

41278553R00274